VENGEANCE IS MINE . . .

saith Sarbat,

the evil tyrant who ruled Bergharra with fists of iron until an unlikely messiah, Jehan, rose from the ranks of the Empire's oppressed.

Day after day in the Emperor's dungeons the gigantic rebel Jehan was fed on human flesh and still he refused to beg for death. But with his own pubescent daughter naked before him, he faced a choice so maddening even Jehan the Man-Eater cringed!

Meanwhile, in the palace, elaborate intrigue was softening the Empire, and in the countryside revolt was seething on a monumental scale. But in the caverns beneath the palace, the gigantic rebel Jehan endured untold horror before he could wreak his unspeakable revenge . . .

CHILDREN OF THE DRAGON

FRANK S. ROBINSON

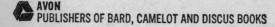

AVON
PUBLISHERS OF BARD, CAMELOT AND DISCUS BOOKS

CHILDREN OF THE DRAGON is an original publication of Avon Books. This work has never before appeared in book form.

AVON BOOKS
A division of
The Hearst Corporation
959 Eighth Avenue
New York, New York 10019

Copyright © 1978 by Frank S. Robinson
Published by arrangement with the author.
ISBN: 0-380-01819-5

First Avon Printing, January, 1978

AVON TRADEMARK REG. U.S. PAT. OFF. AND IN
OTHER COUNTRIES, MARCA REGISTRADA,
HECHO EN U.S.A.

Printed in the U.S.A.

To Virginia Kidd

NOTE ON PRONUNCIATION

TWO DIALECTS WERE SPOKEN by the Bergharran people who are the subject of this book: Tnemghadi and Urhemmedhin. The dialects are similar, and identical rules of pronunciation apply to both.

At the outset, it must be emphasized that the Bergharran language cannot be transliterated into the Roman alphabet with complete accuracy, since a few of the letters lack English equivalents. An example is the Bergharran letter *Qai*, which is pronounced somewhere between the sound of *q* and that of *g*.

Most problemsome is the frequently encountered *Hai* or *Chai,* which is uniformly transliterated in this book as *h,* even though its sound varies somewhat depending on the adjacent letters. Generally this letter is guttural, between *h* and *ch,* as in the Hebrew *Chanukah* or *Hanukkah.* The *Hai* is never silent, even when appearing between consonants, as in *Khrasanna,* or as a final letter, as in *Satanichadh,* where it adds what amounts to a partial syllable.

There is one compensation for the difficulty of pronouncing the *Hai:* it is often a useful guide for the accenting of syllables. In most cases, the *Hai* imposes the accent upon the syllable which it introduces. Examples: *Berg-HAR-ra, Tnem-GHA-di, De-vo-DHRI-sha, I-raj-DHAN.* (The *sh, ch* and *th* sounds are, of course, separate and should not be read as containing a *Hai.*) Occasionally, the *Hai* is weak and pronounced almost like an *h;* this usually happens when the *Hai* is an initial letter followed by a vowel, as in *Henghmani.*

The Bergharran vowel system is quite simple. Vowels should be pronounced uniformly as follows:

a	as	*ah*
e	as	*eh*
i	as	*ee*
o	as	*oh*
u	as	*oo*

Often encountered are Bergharran words beginning with double-consonant combinations difficult to pronounce, as in *Tnemghadi*. There, for example, the *T* and *n* should be pronounced almost as a single letter, as though one started out to say a *t* but midway switched to saying an *n.*

BOOK ONE

•

KSIRITSA

An entry from the *Public Auction Sale Catalog* of the Gustave Hauchschild Collection, Munzen-Gallerie, Zurich, August 15, 1976:

BERGHARRA—Tnemghadi Empire, gold hundred-tayel piece of Emperor Sarbat, Satanichadh Dynasty, circa 1160. *Obverse:* Crowned facing portrait of ruler (youthful effigy) with Tnemghadi inscription in exergue. *Reverse:* Imperial dragon, crown mintmark (Ksiritsa). This is plate coin 1338 of G. R. Breitenbach's *The Coinage of Bergharra*. 39 mm.; Extremely Fine, sharply struck and well centered, a beautiful coin and rare in such a splendid state of preservation.

·1·

Tnem Sarbat Satanichadh looked out upon the world with glittering eyes.

Everything was nothing.

That was because it all was his. The world was Sarbat Satanichadh's to exalt or curse, to fondle or lay waste. He shared the world with no god; Sarbat Satanichadh paid homage to no god at all.

For Tnem Sarbat Satanichadh himself was god.

He was the Emperor of Bergharra.

Sarbat Satanichadh beheld his world glittering in his eyes, and he glittered back at it. Sapphires, diamonds, emeralds and even rarer gems twinkled like stars, set in his dome-shaped crown and black velvet robe—so thickly bejewelled, it was more carapace than robe.

Long were the tines of Sarbat's waxen black moustache, and his beard and fingernails. His nails were curved and colored, ten scimitars dyed purple like the claws of a beast that's downed its prey.

Long too was Sarbat Satanichadh's reign. For half his forty years, this man had occupied Bergharra's throne.

That seat of power and magnificence, the ancient Tnemenghouri Throne, was wrought solidly in gold and sparkled too with gems. From a pedestal it dominated the cavernous throne room, and its high back was engraved in red gold with a fiery rising sun.

Red too was the velvet staircase leading to the throne. And it was whispered in the palace corridors that this carpet's crimson hue concealed the bloodstains of those who had incurred the Emperor's wrath.

Golden and jewel-emblazoned like the robe and throne was Sexrexatra, the dragon curled around the scepter

5

brandished by Sarbat Saṭanichadh. The eyes of the dragon Sexrexatra were bulging, burning rubies, and his horrible face was rent by a huge maw, jaws open wide, roaring to show his ivory teeth. His talons gripped and tore the scepter's golden flesh; the wounds bled shimmering precious stones.

The Sexrexatra Scepter was a very ancient relic, passed down from emperor to emperor through many ages. But the dragon himself, old Sexrexatra, was the most ancient being in all the world.

Before there were people in the world, there was Sexrexatra, the monstrous creature born together with the very earth itself, and retaining in his terrible jaws the fire of that creation. For eons Sexrexatra ruled the world all alone, snapping up into his jaws any other being who might dare to come there. Even his own children Sexrexatra would implacably devour.

But finally there was born to Sexrexatra a brood of children who were endowed with special cunning, and they managed to escape his fiery jaws. These children of the dragon were the first people in the world.

Sexrexatra was enraged by their escape, and for years he chased them across the mountains and deserts. Always these clever, resourceful children eluded him. But at last their monstrous father trapped them in a cave. They seemed surely doomed, and would indeed have been eaten were it not for the brave act of a girl named Pa-ma. This girl swallowed down a great quantity of poison, and before it could take effect, she ran from the cave and threw herself in Sexrexatra's path. The dragon ate her up in one bite, but quickly realized his mistake as the poison began to thread through his body.

"I will return some day," he thundered at the others huddled in the cave, "And I will devour all you misbegotten children, and your children too, and your children's children!"

And then the great dragon Sexrexatra was no more.

His children ventured forth from the cave. The whole country of Bergharra was their inheritance. Some of them journeyed north, and became the Tnemghadi people; the others went south, becoming the Urhemmedhins. But these people of Bergharra never forgot their cruel creator. They called themselves the children of the dragon, and awaited the fulfillment of his promise to return and destroy them.

The Sexrexatra Scepter was a ponderous, ungainly thing, and Sarbat's arm would ache when holding it aloft. This pain he deemed symbolic of his burden, a weight to counterpoise the glory of his power. No matter how it hurt his arm, Sarbat would hold the scepter high, for he knew that the image of the sun beneath which he sat could equally be a rising or a setting sun. To let the scepter fall from his hand would be an omen portending the fall of the Emperor himself.

For twenty years the scepter had been wielded without a falter by Tnem Sarbat Satanichadh. Before him, it was held by his father, Tnem Al-Khoum, and by his grandfather before that, and once by his ancestor Tnem Sharoun—Sharoun the Sword, the founder of the Satanichadh Dynasty. Almost two centuries before, in the year 986, Sharoun Satanichadh fought, clawed, murdered, and betrayed his way from a backwater Tnemurabad village to the Tnemenghouri Throne. Ever since, his descendants had ruled the Empire.

Today the people knelt before the idols of Tnem Sarbat as yesterday they had knelt before his father, Tnem Al-Khoum, and tomorrow they would do the same for his son, as Tnem Shayuq. The Satanichadh, and the great Empire of Bergharra, were eternal.

Eternal too was the City of Ksiritsa, and its grandiose Tnem-rab-Zhikh Palace, where the Satanichadh ruled. They were but the latest in a string of dynasties. Before there had been the Tsitpabana. The last of them, Tnem Riyadja Tsitpabana, had been a decayed and foolish autocrat who had let the crown fall like an overripe plum into the eager hands of Sharoun the Sword. Before the Tsitpabana there had been the Ozimhedi, the Yakrut, and Ibarouma, and before them other dynasties too, all emperors of Bergharra.

The first to rule the whole country—the first, that is, since the dragon Sexrexatra—was Tnem Khatto Trevendhani. He had led his armies forth from Ksiritsa on a grand crusade of conquest, and subjugated most of the Bergharran realms by the year 361.

But even before *that*, the Tnem-rab-Zhikh Palace had

housed Tnem Khatto's fathers, the Kings of Tnemurabad.
The origins of the Kingdom of Tnemurabad were lost in
the dust of history.

That ancient kingdom now formed the core of the Empire of Bergharra. Tnemurabad was the largest, richest
province; and the pearl of Tnemurabad was Ksiritsa, the
capital, the City of the Dragon. Legend had it that Ksiritsa was built upon the very cave where Sexrexatra died;
and that if the monster ever did return, he would return
here, at this city.

The wall of Ksiritsa was the longest and the highest and
the thickest in the world. It was built to withstand any attack, to insure that Ksiritsa would never be conquered.
Begun in the fifth century by Tnem Qinimir Ibarouma,
the wall consumed 300,000 Urhemmedhin slaves during
the eighty years it took to build.

Older than the wall was the incalculably ancient Palace
of the Heavens. A fortress city in itself, the Tnem-rab-
Zhikh Palace sprawled upon a hill in the center of
Ksiritsa. Through the centuries it had expanded steadily, gobbling up rude adjacent dwellings and replacing
them with towers of marble, copper-roofed and dazzling
in their opulence.

While the spires of the Palace snatched up at the
clouds, deep below in dank caverns lay the dungeons.
And while the rock-hewn cells overflowed with suffocating wretches, the Palace above was full of airy rooms that
only gathered dust. The chambers of the Palace numbered
well into the thousands, more rooms than Sarbat Satanichadh and his court could ever even visit, built with the
blood and sweat of slaves who were forbidden to set foot
there. And still the Emperor drove his slaves and taxed
his subjects to expand the Palace even further.

Tnem Sarbat Satanichadh sat upon the throne; his arm
ached in holding high the dragon scepter. But he thought
that was good, for it gave his face a fearsome grimace.

All Bergharra knew that face, gleaming from the coins
he struck. The Bergharran money showed on one side the
snarling Sexrexatra, and on the other, the Emperor.
Sarbat was portrayed full-faced with a scowl, his eyebrows formed into a sharp angle, meeting in the middle of
his forehead, hallmark of the Tnemghadi people. The eyes

were crescent slits, glinting out over puffy round cheeks. Tnem Sarbat's thick lips were parted to expose his yellow-stained teeth, framed by the drooping spikes of beard and moustache. And the great robe could not conceal the Emperor's obesity. His belly was protuberant, and his fingers so swollen that his rings could never be removed.

Tnem Sarbat Satanichadh was worshipped as the god of Bergharra. And he considered himself to be a very great ruler. His ego knew no bounds; he was cruel, tyrannical, opinionated, stubborn. He could decree the most ferocious and unjust punishments, and never be swayed from them. Never would he swerve from any path he had chosen, any design that became fixed in his head, any object for which he strove. Yet he did not surround himself with fawning sycophants, and took for his advisors men of independent mind and judgment, like the renowned old statesman Irajdhan.

Sarbat was a voluptuary, unstinting of indulgence in rich, exotic foods, spices, clothes, and women. His harem of concubines was thrice the size of his father's. But often the Emperor would leave the arms of his courtesans to indulge another love, the study of scrolls, for he was something of a scholar, and the author of innumerable poems and essays. If he tripled the harem, he also increased the imperial library many-fold, and added a collection of antiquities. The Emperor would always cast any other business aside to pore over some hoard of encrusted old coins and relics unearthed at a construction site. He was a devotee and patron of the arts, lavishly granting subsidies to poets, artists, and scholastics.

This was the man who scowled down upon his world, all at the foot of the red velvet staircase. In one corner, sitting regally on a cushion, was the Empress Denoi Devodhrisha. Not far from her there sat a concubine, a languorous Albaroda woman.

Sarbat allowed his eyes to dwell upon the Empress. She had once been Princess Denoi Vinga Gondwa, daughter of the Devodhrisha King of Laham Jat. Their marriage had been contracted by a treaty when Sarbat was a child of five. Denoi then was twelve; it was years before Sarbat ever saw her. By the time he was ready, she had grown into a grand beauty, soft and sensual. He had lain with her many nights. But now she was no longer soft, and it had been years since last they'd slept together. His consort was aging; besides, the Devodhrisha King of Laham Jat was dead, and his country had become a Bergharran client state of diminished importance.

So Sarbat looked down upon the Empress Denoi Vinga Gondwa Devodhrisha and she, like all, was nothing. Perhaps he'd have her summoned to his bed this night, only to mock her withered beauty. Perhaps he'd do away with her.

The Emperor remembered suddenly a girl whom he had fancied in his youth, an Urhemmedhin slave girl named Miretni. She was hardly more than a child, with large dewy eyes and creamy apricot skin. Willingly she had obeyed the summons to the then-prince's bedchamber.

Her lips and thin downy legs quivered when he entered her. With artful hands she drew him into her body. Prince Sarbat smiled and she tittered softly, birdlike, smiling back. In his hand he held her little budding breast, and he caressed her with the tips of his fingers.

Accidentally, Miretni's flesh was pierced by Sarbat's fingernail.

She raised the wound up to his lips; a pearl of blood appeared and the Prince tongued it off. For a long moment he rested with his cheek upon her breast while she stroked his hair.

"You are so unafraid of me," he said.

Prince Sarbat took her nipple between his fingertips and fondled it; and then his long nails suddenly closed upon it, and snipped it off.

The girl's whole body jerked and thin milky blood poured from the strange wound. She grimaced with pain; but did not cry out.

Sarbat looked at her and realized that he himself was trembling. This was odd; but pondering, the young prince began to glimpse the reason. He trembled not at what he had done to Miretni—but at the fact that she was within his power. Freely he could pinch off her nipple, freely he could pinch off her life itself. The quenching of a human life would mean nothing to him. After all, were there not countless millions in Bergharra? Wasn't every one of them doomed to die? A man might perish today, or in a hundred years, and in the end it wouldn't matter which. All the people of Bergharra were doomed ultimately to be devoured by the dragon. The death of this little Urhemmedhin girl would not diminish the world any more than would the squashing of a fly. In a thousand years, would the girl be remembered any better than the fly?

So Sarbat had trembled not because his hurting Miretni meant anything, but precisely because it meant nothing. Realizing this, Prince Sarbat ended his innocence.

He stroked Miretni's cheek with the backs of his fingers and kissed her forehead, and coaxed from her a wan smile. He kissed the wound he had made on her breast. He petted her face and hands, caressed her again and again, and then slowly drew his fingernail as a knife across her cheek.

She did not scream, but began to cry.

Again he pressed her down upon the bed and mounted her. And while he came, he gave her not his kiss nor his caress, but instead, his slashing fingernails. Over and over they cut her, on her arms and thighs and face and breast.

"Please," she whimpered, as a prayer.

Sarbat touched a silencing finger to her lips, and shook his head.

Now Miretni and the bed, and even the Prince, were glazed with blood. The girl's perfume had been turned rank, her deep eyes wild with terror, her freshness ravened forever by the Prince's fingernails. Yet he kept on, again and again, cutting her, until at last he grew tired and bored.

Then, with his nails sunk into her pudenda, Sarbat slept.

In the morning, the blood was crusted black all over him, and so he bathed in scented water. He fouled one bath and had to have a second. His bed and even the carpet were ruined, stained beyond repair.

The girl was also crusted with dark blood, and ruined. She was dead.

But Prince Sarbat did not tremble now. He shrugged. There were others; it was nothing.

BERGHARRA—Kingdom of Khrasanna, copper falu, first century or before. *Obverse:* Urhem, early god-king, facing left. *Reverse:* stylized figure of a goat. Breitenbach 26, 19 mm. Only good to very good or so, much worn and oxidized, but excessively rare, as are most pre-empire Bergharran coins. The only other recorded example is in the British Museum. (*Hauchschild Collection Catalog*)

· 2 ·

THE EMPIRE OF BERGHARRA was *not* the whole world; it only seemed to be.

But there were other kingdoms. To the south there was the jungle-bound Valpassu with its mysterious temple cities overgrown with vines and weeds; the spice island of Mohonghi; and the once-powerful Laham Jat, now reduced to playing the tail to the Bergharran dragon.

To the west there was the desert Empire of Kuloun, a poor and godforsaken land that never had enticed the conquering armies of Bergharra. Also to the west there was Ramhitta, an equally forbidding land, among whose mountain crags there dwelt a people ruled by priestesses. Ramhitta too the Bergharran armies never penetrated. And beyond Ramhitta and Kuloun were other kingdoms, practically unknown, with outlines barely sketched upon the maps.

To the north there roamed the Akfakh, the barbarian nomads of the steppes, fierce and strong, unruly tribesmen. Sometimes the Akfakh would swoop down and pillage through Bergharran northlands, stealing crops and cattle and Tnemghadi women, burning what they left behind. But always the Akfakh were driven back.

And finally, to the east of the Empire of Bergharra lay the Sea, another province that she never conquered. The ancient parchments said the Sea went on forever—and indeed, those ships that had been sent out to explore it never had returned.

Thus bounded, still Bergharra was a giant. There was no one living who had been in all the Empire's fourteen provinces, and the number populating them was said to be at least a hundred million. The Empire ranged from the cool and arid plains of Pramchadh in the north, through the grassy hills of Jaraghari, through deserts, forests, river valleys, through lands of red clay and of fertile loam, across half a dozen mountain ranges, finally to lose its boundaries in the lush steaming jungles and swamps of its southernmost extremity.

Bergharra was a vast, mighty nation that took in all of the people spawned by Sexrexatra, all of the Tnemghadi and Urhemmedhins. The two races were of nearly equal population, the Tnemghadi in the north and their Urhemmedhin cousins in the south, seven provinces of each.

The northern dominions were Tnemurabad, Rashid, Gharr, Kholandra, Muraven, Jammir, and Agabatur. Each of these had once been an independent kingdom before the conquest by Tnem Khatto Trevendhani. But in eight hundred years the Tnemghadi people had forgotten this, and these provinces had lost their separate identities. They were mere administrative units now, governed by viceroys sent from Ksiritsa.

It was said that the Tnemghadi eyebrows joined in the middle of their foreheads because they were still scowling over their choice of the northern path in leaving Sexrexatra's cave. It was true that the Bergharran North was much poorer than the South. The winds blew harder there, and the people had to wrench their crops from a dry, crusty earth, or else subsist by pasturing sheep, goats, and cattle on the yellow grasslands. The typical Tnemghadi house was walled with only cowhides and had a floor of beaten earth. Not only did they have to fight the cruelty of nature, but the barbarian Akfakh as well. Yet through all this, the Tnemghadi were a tough and hardy people. It had been, after all, the North that had conquered the South.

Thus were the Tnemghadi the people of the emperors; never had they suffered rule by any but their own race. From the Trevendhani up through the Satanichadh, the dynasties of Ksiritsa were all Tnemghadi.

And the Emperors were the gods of the Tnemghadi. Every city, town, or muddy village was centered upon a shrine to the Emperor, containing in its most sacred sanctum a golden idol representing him on his throne with the rising sun, brandishing the Sexrexatra Scepter. The people would come to pay their homage, chanting prayers and lighting candles at the idol's feet. Once each month they'd come, even if it meant journeying for days, in neglect of fields or flocks. And they would bring the priests an offering of their hard-earned produce, without which no one was admitted to the temples. That was the law.

The Emperor was the sole god; his dominion was absolute. There was no life admitted by this faith except the one on earth, and the only purpose of that life was the pleasure of the Emperor-god. Anyone alive was someone whom the Emperor wished to live; any death occurred because the Emperor desired it.

The people knew it wasn't justice that the Emperor dispensed, at least not any kind of justice they could fathom. There was no way of telling which deeds were right and pleasing to the Emperor, and which were repugnant to him. Their god was a perverse one who might kill or maim an infant for no reason anyone could see, and, equally without reason, allow a wicked man to prosper. All of this, while beyond mortal understanding, must be accepted. The people's lives were devoted to the pleasure of the Emperor-god, and yet they were unable— nay, *forbidden*—to understand the pleasure of a being so exalted.

They worshipped him on their knees, with faces ground into the dirt, chanting hymns of their subservience, not in veneration of his goodness or his justice, but because he was their god and had the power to destroy them.

That was all that counted. There was no salvation, only the wretched life on earth; and since even that belonged to the Emperor, they knew that they were nothing. They were flies, to whom the only thing that mattered was the fly-swatter. Regardless of their virtue or depravity, it would get them in the end.

And so the Tnemghadi worshipped their Emperor without qualm or question. They had once venerated other gods, before Tnem Khatto Trevendhani's armies had marched. In the eight centuries since, those old gods had been forgotten. Willingly the Tnemghadi people had embraced the Emperor-god of Ksiritsa.

But this was not true of the Urhemmedhins.

The name Urhem had originally belonged to a king of ancient times who had ruled at Naddeghomra. It was said that his domains covered all the seven southern provinces: Bhudabur, Khrasanna, Nitupsar, Ohreem, Taroloweh, Diorromeh, and Prewtna. It had been the great empire of its day, the center of civilization. Only centuries later did Naddeghomra yield to Ksiritsa as the premier city of the world.

Tradition held that King Urhem was a wise, just, and liberal ruler, of many great achievements. He had codified the kingdom's laws, and ensured that they were applied equally throughout the land. He was a skilled diplomat, and had expanded trade and commerce both within his realm and with foreign nations. At Naddeghomra, he built perhaps the greatest library of all time.

King Urhem was a virtuous man with but a single wife to whom he was enormously devoted. Her name was Osatsana. Contrary to what one might expect, she was far from the loveliest woman in the kingdom. In fact, she was harelipped and considered ugly. Yet Urhem had personally chosen her to be his queen. She was learned for a woman, accomplished in many fields, and beloved for her gentle wisdom. No one ever mocked her plainness of feature.

Throughout his reign, King Urhem ruled jointly with his queen. He bade the people bow to Osatsana just as they would bow to him. Under Urhem and Osatsana, the southern empire saw its zenith.

Then, Queen Osatsana fell gravely ill. All the men of science in the kingdom were summoned to Naddeghomra, but all of them failed to effect any cure. Daily her sickness worsened, and her death seemed imminent.

King Urhem was desperate to save her. On a moonless night, alone, he entered a temple, where he prostrated himself, invoking the name of every god he could think of, even the strange gods of foreign lands. To all of them he made an oath: If they would grant Osatsana's life, then he would want nothing evermore for himself. Should she recover, then in gratitude he would give up his throne and even make himself a beggar. So powerfully did he cherish her that he was willing to live in poverty without her, so long as she might survive.

When the King returned to the Palace, he was met at the gate with the news that his beloved queen had died. Her last breath was taken at the very moment that he'd made his oath before the gods.

King Urhem fell to his knees and wept. He was shattered by more than just grief, for he suddenly realized his foolish presumption. He had offered to trade worldly power and goods for human life—an offer which the gods had rightly spurned. His prayer had been a sin, in punishment for which Queen Osatsana's life was forfeit.

Crushed by the enormity of this, King Urhem threw down his crown and robes and fled the Palace. Just as he had sworn to do if she had lived, he became a beggar. He was never heard from again, and in poverty, unknown, somewhere, he died.

But King Urhem was not forgotten. Down through the ages his renunciation was venerated as a perfect act of piety and humility, the epitome of reverence. Urhem had sinned, but only once. His sin was a sin of love, and his punishment for it was great—a punishment administered not only by the gods but by himself as well. And in time the southern people came to worship not those old gods, but, instead, Urhem: the embodiment of wisdom and virtue, of selflessness and love.

And what King Urhem had learned that moonless night was at the center of their faith. Unlike the emperor-worshipping Tnemghadi, the Urhemmedhins believed above all in the sanctity of human life. To value human life materialistically was folly, even sacrilege, for the being of the drabbest peasant was yet the grandest thing in all creation. The Urhemmedhins believed that every person was unique, an enrichment of the world that would never be repeated.

And while the Tnemghadi would hold that life's only point was the service of the pleasure of the Emperor, the creed of Urhem held that love was life's fulfillment, the fullest bloom of the glory that was existence. And this too was derived from the legend of King Urhem, since his love for Osatsana made him everything he was.

The story of the great king, and the enunciation of the faith that story had inspired, were set down in the Book of Urhem. Books were copied by hand in those ancient days, and few could read or write; but the Book of Urhem was famed and treasured above all others, the only sacred book of the Urhemmedhin faith.

And then came Tnem Khatto Trevendhani.

By then the empire that Urhem had ruled had disintegrated into a dozen little fiefdoms, none of which could stand against the Tnemghadi horde. It did not take the ruthless Tnem Khatto long to add all the Urhemmedhin lands to his new Bergharran empire. Province after province in the south was pillaged by the invaders. The greatest battle was fought at Naddeghomra. There, King Urhem's old Palace was ransacked and destroyed, along with his famous library.

Tnem Khatto was especially vicious in stamping out the Urhemmedhin religion. Throughout the South the skies ran black and livid from the fires of the temples, the priests burned alive inside, nailed to the walls by their ears.

And in the place of the razed temples of Urhem rose taller, finer shrines, built by the Tnemghadi in the name of their emperor. The greatest of these temples was erected at Naddeghomra itself, upon the ruins of Urhem's Palace.

Those strict laws of worship that governed the North were now foisted on the South as well. Herded into the new temples, their faces pressed to the floor by Tnemghadi soldiers, the Urhemmedhin people paid their homage to the emperor.

For eight hundred years, the temples with their idols of the emperor were the only shrines permitted. In all those centuries there had not been an altar of Urhem, not a teacher of his creed, not a priest of his faith, nor a copy of his book. Yet no matter how the conquerors strove to eradicate his name, the Urhemmedhins clung dearly to their god. Through the centuries, Urhem was still worshipped; covertly in caves and cellars tiny groups would gather to venerate him and solemnly discuss his creed. The secret priests, by day disguised as merchants or beggars, spent the nights keeping alive the memory of Urhem and the faith of life and love.

These priests were skinned and burned alive when they were caught, but this only made their work easier. For the more brutally the Tnemghadi emperors pressed down, the deeper became the Urhemmedhins' hatred of them, and the more they clung to their old beliefs.

They would genuflect before the golden idols and recite the chants as they were ordered; but under their breaths, they would pray to Urhem, and pray the Tnemghadi would be devoured by their dragon Sexrexatra.

And sometimes they would actually rebel. Hardly a year would pass without some new disturbance, some half-crazed flare-up of hatred for the Tnemghadi. Many were the idols that were smashed, with the emperor's priests impaled upon them or incinerated on the altars that were meant for goats and sheep. Many were the soldiers set upon by savage mobs and hacked to pieces.

Grimly, the Urhemmedhins would rise up . . . but they knew it was hopeless. The Tnemghadi response was always swift and bloody; the southern farmers could not stand up against a wave of armored troops.

They knew they would never have the armed might to throw off the Tnemghadi yoke. So instead, they prayed for deliverance through the *Ur-Rasvadhi*.

This was the hero who would save them, a reincarnation of their Urhem, and like him a man of such wisdom, love, and virtue that the Urhemmedhins' weakness would no longer thwart their liberation. Not through force of arms, but through love and goodness, the *Ur-Rasvadhi* would deliver them to freedom, to *yarushkadharra*. This was their only hope.

But after eight hundred years of Urhemmedhin slavery, their savior still had not come.

· 3 ·

Tnem Sarbat Satanichadh looked with glittering eyes down the length of his throne-room: a colossal chamber brilliant with red silk and gold tapestries, illuminated by flaring lamps. Resplendent too were the intricate costumes of the councilors and ministers, the scribes, courtiers, priests and eunuchs, the guards and slaves and maids-in-waiting, down to the Emperor's clown, Halaf, in a preposterous feathered hat almost as big as he was.

The ruler's eyes lingered upon the Empress Denoi Devodhrisha, sitting so regally iron-haired. How everyone kowtowed to her! Yet, she was nothing, and he dismissed her finally from his glance.

Instead, he settled his gaze upon the Albaroda concubine, so much more lovely. But he had played with her many nights, and was growing bored with her. Other concubines Sarbat had put to death, but he was growing bored with death too. The only death that might relieve the tedium would be his own.

Other concubines had been beheaded, but Sarbat knew that that was wasteful. Beautiful women who had been favored by the Emperor were treasured above all others, and were valuable as gifts. He calculated that by bestowing them upon his underlings, they would not look up the velvet staircase enviously, but with gratitude and loyalty.

Thus it was that Sarbat made lavish gifts of women and gold to able men, and earned the sobriquet *Sarbat the Generous*. Yet he sometimes wondered whether, by giving ambitious men such tantalizing crumbs from his own overloaded table, he was sharpening their appetites rather than appeasing them.

Nevertheless, Sarbat decided, the Albaroda concubine would keep her lovely head. Besides, as Halaf the clown had been known to say, everyone must die, so death means nothing and killing is a pointless act.

Sarbat's reverie was interrupted by the resonant clang of a gong, reverberating through the gigantic chamber. At its far end could be seen a long-robed man with a wispy white beard, walking with the aid of a cane slowly toward the throne.

This venerable man was Lord Yasiruwam Irajdhan, the Grand Chamberlain of the Court, Viceroy of Tnemurabad and the foremost of the Emperor's councilors. The blue-blood Irajdhan had held this eminent rank since the days of Sarbat's father, Tnem Al-Khoum. Next to Sarbat himself, Irajdhan was the most important man in Bergharra.

Marching with slow dignity, the Grand Chamberlain finally reached Sarbat's pedestal, and he bowed with his forehead almost touching the velvet carpet.

"Rise, Lord," Sarbat commanded.

"May it please Your Majesty: there is news from Arayela, the town beset by the Akfakh. Our army is victorious; the Akfakh have been driven from our territory, back deep into their own lands. More than four hundred of them were killed; perhaps three thousand got away, but they've been rather chastened by the experience and I doubt this tribe will soon bother us again."

"Well, let us hope so."

"Indeed," said Irajdhan, "but I would point out that these raids by the barbarians have been on the increase, with ever-larger numbers of them involved. I believe the problem will get a lot worse before it gets better, and that we should strengthen the army on our northern borders."

Sarbat nodded. "Perhaps that would be prudent. Tell me, what were our casualties at Arayela?"

"Our own casualties were very light. Our army was most adroit."

"Who was in command?"

"General Qarafi."

"Ah, yes, Sureddin Qarafi, a most talented man. I will be sure to reward him. And to watch out for him. Tell me one thing more, though: How did Arayela weather the Akfakh attack?"

"I regret to say the town was burned, Your Majesty, and most of the inhabitants were slaughtered."

"Ah, well. At least we drove the villains back."

"There is one other piece of news, Your Majesty: from your dungeons."

Tnem Sarbat scowled. What news could come from that vile pest-hole to warrant his attention? Irajdhan was bidden to explain.

"Your Majesty, the executioner, Zakhar Wasfour, has been killed—by a prisoner."

Now Sarbat raised an intrigued eyebrow. Zakhar Wasfour was one of the burliest brutes in the province.

"Wasfour was preparing to execute the man," Irajdhan explained, "but although the prisoner's hands were bound, he somehow managed to wrench the ax right out of Wasfour's grasp. Before he could be subdued, the wretch did quite some damage. The executioner's skull was chopped open and two of the guards were gravely injured."

The Emperor leaned forward on his cushion, interest piqued. "Tell me, Lord Irajdhan, who was this prisoner who executed his own executioner?"

"Your Majesty, he was the ringleader of a gang of cutthroat bandits in Taroloweh Province."

"Ah, yes, another of these annoying Urhemmedhin risings."

"There was nothing political about them, Your Majesty; they were merely bandits. Indeed, they preyed upon their own people. It was Urhemmedhin villages they sacked, Urhemmedhins they robbed and killed."

Sarbat Satanichadh snorted. "Perhaps we should have left them alone."

Irajdhan did not smile. "I took the liberty of ordering that these bandits be wiped out, and the army has in fact decimated them. As for their leader, the one who killed Zakhar Wasfour, he was a pretty tough customer and it took nearly half the army to capture him."

"And what was his name?"

"His real name, Your Majesty, is unknown. But everyone in Taroloweh called him 'Jehan Henghmani.' "

"Jehan Henghmani," repeated the Emperor slowly. "In the Urhemmedhin dialect, that means *Man Eater*. He must have been quite a fellow. Tell me more about him."

Irajdhan shrugged. "I'm afraid there's not much to tell. He is about thirty-five years old; a native of Taroloweh; of sharecropper stock. He is an ignorant ox who can't even write his own name. He wasn't married, but had a woman and two daughters by her. An outlaw all his life, he led a band that terrorized the eastern part of Taroloweh, until we put them out of business. That's all there is to tell."

"Did this Jehan Henghmani finally die well?"

The old statesman hesitated briefly. "Oh, Your Majesty, he is not dead yet. It was thought Your Majesty might wish to prescribe some special punishment for this most special case."

"Very good, indeed; perhaps something special is called for. I would like to have a look at this Man Eater."

Irajdhan nodded crisply. "He will be brought up at once."

"No," said Sarbat. "I don't want him brought before me. We will go to the dungeon. Fetch my litter."

Irajdhan was not alone in feeling consternation at this odd whim of the ruler. But the Emperor could not, of course, be questioned. The Grand Chamberlain bowed low, and then whispered to a servant, who in turn bowed and struck the gong which summoned the litter bearers.

Came now the eight bald eunuchs, their smooth oiled heads glistening, all clothed as gloriously as the viceroy of a province, jewelry jingling as they stately pranced. Hoisted on their shoulders was the litter, gold- and jewel-encrusted with a canopy of vermilion silk. Behind the litter was assembled the entourage of criers, chamberlains, councilors, priests, pages, ministers, soldiers, concubines, and courtiers—and all their servants—into a ponderous caravan.

The Empress Denoi, Irajdhan, and the clown Halaf each climbed into the litter. Only then did the Emperor Tnem Sarbat Satanichadh decamp from his pedestal, walk down the velvet stairs, and take his seat.

Thereupon the boat of gold and silk was sent on its way by the braying of trumpets and the bong of cymbals, and the Emperor Sarbat was borne down from his mighty throne-room, the most awesome place in all the world, into his dungeon, the most godforsaken.

As the litter lurched its way down the corridors and stairs, the Empress Denoi Devodhrisha watched her husband. He had uttered no word since giving the command to fetch the litter.

"Your Majesty," the Empress said, "I wish to ask a question." All eyes turned to her. Would she give voice to what was puzzling everyone?

"Generous Emperor, why is it that we are going down to the prisoner, instead of hauling him up to grovel at our feet?"

Sarbat blinked, paused, and then spoke slowly. "I will answer you," he said. "In my studies of the ancient, sacred parchments of Bergharra, I once came upon a certain parable. It is the story of an emperor who dies in chains at the feet of a man whom he had first seen in chains at the emperor's own feet. And, as you know, the parables in the sacred parchments are considered to be prophetic."

"But Your Majesty," the Empress scoffed, "countless prisoners have come before you in chains."

"Yes, ordinary wretches. But a man who would rise out of his chains and destroy an emperor would not be ordinary. He would be the sort of man who would kill his own executioner; the sort of man Jehan Henghmani seems to be."

"But how do you know the parable applies to you specifically? It could be any emperor."

Sarbat narrowed his eyes and gave a queer, bitter smile. "The one in the parable was named Sahyid Sarvadakhush. He was the seventh of his dynasty.

"And I am the seventh Satanichadh."

· 4 ·

TNEM SARBAT SATANICHADH peeked out from his silken canopy upon a grimy, dingy tunnel.

Down ramps and narrow stairways the caravan had come, down into the bowels of the earth. Never before had the Emperor viewed this hidden part of the Palace. Repelled by the dank, pungent odor pouring from the labyrinth of cells and the vermin they contained, Sarbat covered his nose. The faces of the Empress and the clown paled; many others coughed and muttered curses as they breathed the foul air.

"I should condemn no one to death," the Emperor growled, "this stench is even worse than death."

"Indeed," chimed in the clown Halaf, "it would even make a dead man nauseated."

"It's hellish!"

"Not so, Your Majesty," returned the clown, "this is actually Hell itself. This is where the wicked go after they die."

"But the prisoners here are yet alive."

"Ah, no, they are dead, Majesty, dead to the world."

"Very clever, clown," the Emperor said. "You do amuse me. That's lucky for you; should you ever cease to be diverting, perhaps I'd send you down here to perish in torment."

"Oh, I've a better idea, Majesty. Should that day ever come, then crown me Emperor of Bergharra in your place. That would be a torment even worse than anything this dungeon could provide."

"How so, foolish clown?"

"Because if I were emperor, then everything would be nothing."

Sarbat considered this statement for a long moment. Then he concluded, "But clown, everything *is* nothing."

"Ah, to you, Majesty, to you alone! And that is because you have everything. To take a cup of water from the sea, or add a cup, is nothing; to shift a grain of sand upon the shore is nothing too. So it is with all your vast possessions: you have everything, and everything can be replaced, so everything is nothing. You are the only man in the world who has nothing. Even I, your silly clown, have something. You see, I have some things and lack some things. To me, everything is something and nothing is nothing."

"But if you added all the things that you say you lack to the things that you have, then you would have . . .?"

"Nothing, Your Majesty. I would then have absolutely nothing, just like you."

"I do not understand a word you're saying."

"That is why you are the mighty emperor, and I am just a pipsqueak clown."

"And if I did make you emperor, and I became the clown—"

"Excuse me, Lord, but if I became the emperor, I would not have you for my clown."

"What would you have me as?"

Halaf's eye openly appraised the iron-haired woman sitting opposite him. "I would make you consort to the Empress."

Sarbat smacked his belly with a shrill laugh. "Ha! In that case, clown, you are safe from ever being made emperor!"

The eyes of the Empress glinted stonily.

The dungeon guards had been lolling, gambling with their dice and picking their teeth. Little attention was paid to the prisoners, who were locked so tight in the cells that a lock would sometimes rust to seal the wretch inside forever. When such a prisoner would finally die, the guards found it easiest to seal up the door with mortar, to contain the stink. Sometimes they would not bother to wait until he was dead.

Now the cymbals were heard clanging through the tunnels, and so they hid away their dice and, donning full uniforms, smartly took up their posts. When the royal entourage arrived, the dungeon staff was all alert efficiency.

In the first vestibule, their chief, the warden, carefully smoothed his hair and cloak. This was a small, swarthy man named Nimajneb Grebzreh, who had spent his whole adult life in the dungeon. He was sick enough of it by now; but there was no place else for him to go. Hope for a promotion had long since died. Grumbling at the annoyance heralded by the cymbals, this Nimajneb Grebzreh cleared the orange rinds and other offal from his desk, and then settled into a meticulous pose, pretending to pore over an open document.

When the retinue arrived, Grebzreh and his underlings were dumbstruck to see that their visitor was the Emperor himself. This was absolutely beyond belief to them. They threw themselves down with their lips kissing the floor, cringing, pressing the dirt into their mouths and nostrils.

Wispy-bearded Irajdhan clambered down from the litter, and bade the men rise. Then he addressed Warden Grebzreh; "You are commanded to bring forward the prisoner Jehan Henghmani."

"No, no!" called Sarbat from inside the canopy. "I want to see him in his cell. Warden, lead the way."

Nimajneb Grebzreh's head spun. That the Emperor had come was incredible; that he would go to a prisoner was impossible. But the warden could only obey. Taking a ring of iron keys from its hook on the wall, he proceeded, trembling and with a bowed head, down the narrow corridor. His men and the cumbrous imperial parade followed.

The emperor Sarbat Satanichadh looked out from his silken canopy with eyes that glittered in the flickering torchlight of the dungeon's passageways. In this sputtering light he could see how rudely the stones were hewn, and how encrusted with age-old lichens, fungi, and nameless excrescences. How the oozing moisture glistened. How the tiny creatures darted about, fat cockroaches and lizards, eating the slime of the walls, and each other.

The Emperor heard, not the clopping sound of marching, but the squishing of feet upon muck. The tunnels were deep with a soupy, viscous mud that spattered all the courtiers, the gold of the litter, and even Sarbat's own jeweled robe.

But the sound that penetrated most was a steady wailing, shrieking, gibbering. Out of the narrow barred windows of their cells the prisoners could glimpse the dazzling entourage passing by, and they would cry out piteously, a frenzied chittering that rose to a shrill crescendo.

Some of them would call to the Emperor, pleading for his mercy; and when the caravan was past, they would whimper and fall silent, because it was useless to plead at empty air. These were the fortunate ones, because they could still understand, if only that.

The unfortunate ones could not. They moaned and keened without let-up, the unwavering screech of animal noise that was part of the very air itself here.

Those unfortunate ones had lost their minds and no longer even knew how unfortunate they were. The fortunate ones still knew. So it was the fortunate ones who were really the most unfortunate.

That was a stock joke of Warden Grebzreh and his guards.

Now Grebzreh stopped. Here was a door with no sound coming from behind it, the one the Emperor sought.

At the warden's command, one of the guards rapped a sword noisily on the bars of the opening in the door. "On your knees, scum!"

"No!" said Sarbat quickly. He must stand on his feet before I look at him. And his chains are to be removed."

Grebzreh took a deep breath; this order would be dangerous to execute. He motioned and gathered together his strongest guards, who drew their swords. "Do not waste yourself resisting," the warden said into the dark cell. "We do not come to harm you. His Imperial Majesty Tnem Sarbat Satanichadh wants to look at you."

Then Grebzreh put his key into the lock and pulled open the heavy wooden door; the guards entered the cell. There was a clanking of chains, and in another moment the guards hurried out, slamming the door shut behind them.

"Is he standing now?"

Grebzreh thrust a torch between the bars and looked inside. "Yes, the monster stands."

The eunuchs maneuvered the golden litter right before the door of the cell, and Grebzreh held up the torch so that the Emperor could see inside. He peered between the bars, squinting his eyes.

Inside there was a hulking shape, almost filling the cramped cell.

Eyes blinking and glittering in the harsh light of the torch, Jehan Henghmani looked out upon Sarbat Satani-chadh.

Jehan Henghmani was indeed a giant, approaching seven feet in height, and built like a thick stone pillar. The head upon this great body was itself ungainly huge, hairless, and peaked as a mountain, with a snow-cap of drying blood, which had dripped in rivulets down the man's face. His nose was that of a pig's snout, with wide splayed nostrils, and his mouth too was wide with rubbery lips like saddle flaps. Here was an extremely ugly brute —a monster, as Grebzreh had called him.

Standing with his hands freed from the manacles, Jehan Henghmani rubbed the dried blood off his cheeks, while glowering at his subduers with bitter steely eyes, spitting the fire of the torch back into their faces.

"So, this is the famous Man Eater!" exclaimed the Emperor Sarbat. "Why, he is truly big enough to be such!"

As he gaped at Jehan Henghmani from his litter, the monstrous prisoner dropped suddenly to his knees so that only the top of his head was visible through the bars.

Sarbat's face soured with anger. "Why do you kneel, Man Eater? Get up so I can look at you!"

"I kneel, Your Majesty," came the answer in a mocking voice, "because it was your pleasure that I stand."

"And what if I declare that it is death for you to kneel?"

"Am I not equally doomed to death, even if I stand?"

"Ha!" The Emperor spat a loud laugh and turned to his courtiers. "This creature is too magnificent to die. His audacious crime, and insolence, are too great to be punished with mere death. That would be lenient. He must never die, must never cease to suffer. That is my decree. Now harken: this Jehan Henghmani shall be tortured every day most horribly. But take care that he not die! The man who lets this monster die under torture will be put to the same death himself."

And, tauntingly, to Jehan Henghmani: "What do you say to that, Man Eater? Now, beg me for the mercy of death!"

"Death is nothingness. I do not beg for something that is nothing."

"What *do* you beg for, Man Eater?"

"I beg for nothing."

"Ah, he begs for nothing," interjected Halaf the clown. "But he also does not beg for nothing. This is a paradox, Majesty."

"Yes, this monster is amusing. How would you like to be my clown, Man Eater?"

"I would like to be nothing to you."

"Ha! But you *are* nothing to me. *Everything* is nothing to me. My clown tells me that because I am the Emperor, I have nothing. And I will tell you something else, Man Eater, to amuse you while you suffer. Do you know why I wished to see you standing? There was a parable in the ancient parchments about an emperor named Sahyid Sarvadakhush, the seventh of his dynasty, who came to his end at the feet of a man whom he first looked upon in chains at the Emperor's own feet. I am the seventh Satanichadh, and when I heard about your exploit, I thought you could be the man prophesied to destroy me. But now I have taken my first look at you standing up, not at my feet, and without chains. So you cannot be the man in the prophecy, and you can kneel all you like now; it does not displease me."

"It displeases me that it does not displease you."

"As you will, Man Eater." The Emperor's grin widened sardonically. He was enjoying the mutual baiting with the extraordinary prisoner in this stenchful place, and now he was pricked by an impish thought that gave him open amusement. "So, they call you Man Eater, eh? Well, Man Eater, I have an idea. We shall see that you become worthy of your name. And this is how:

"I now decree that the only food you shall ever eat will be human flesh—the flesh of the scum who die down here. And you *will* eat it, if it means stuffing it down your gullet with a ramrod. What do you say to that, Man Eater?"

"I shall eat human flesh, and you won't have to stuff it down my throat. I will eat it joyfully. And one fine day the flesh I eat will be your own!"

At this, Sarbat brayed laughter. "Aha, he gives us another prophecy! I like this; if only I could have you for my clown. But I will make this prophecy come true. When

I die, my entrails will be taken out and sent down here for you to eat. Yes, you will eat my guts—because when I die in my goosedown bed, you, Man Eater, will still be down in this hell-hole, still suffering dreadful torture and begging for a death that will be denied to you."

Tnem Sarbat laughed once more. "I have seen enough of this Man Eater. Let him sink now into the horror!" The Emperor turned to Warden Grebzreh. "You shall see that my decrees are carried out, Warden. Any deviation will mean that the same punishment will be your own. Lord Irajdhan will monitor you, to make certain my commands are followed.

"I have one more stipulation. Do not torture him nor feed him any flesh today. Let him sit and contemplate the nightmare that awaits him. Perhaps by tomorrow he will have gone mad."

"That would be merciful," whispered the Empress.

"Our generous Emperor is not without mercy!" said Halaf.

"Oh, merciful now too, not only generous?" said the Empress drily. "O, Sarbat the merciful; may Sexrexatra save us!"

To this, the clown ventured no reply. With the crash of the cymbals and horns, the caravan began its journey up out of the dungeons.

Tnem Sarbat watched the Empress Denoi Devodhrisha, saying nothing.

BERGHARRA—Tnemghadi Empire, cast brass temple token, circa 12th century. Used to gain admission to the temple and for placement on the altar as a substitute for the sacrificial offering; generally the offerings themselves were appropriated by the priests. *Obverse:* temple building flanked by palms. *Reverse:* dragon, similar to that on regular imperial coinage. Breitenbach 2833, attributed to Taroloweh Province, 37 mm., Very fine with pleasing greenish patina, but holed as is usual for these. Scarce. (*Hauchschild Collection Catalog*)

· 5 ·

THE SUN BEAT DOWN on the land of Samud Mussopo with glittering rays that shimmered through the heated air. As though seen through rippling water, the backs of the purple hills vibrated too. Half-visible streaks of heat wended their way across the landscape.

Samud Mussopo squinted at his land. Like an elephant's were Samud's eyes, small and black and framed with deep wrinkles from squinting into brilliant light like this. And the field was like his eyes, small and wrinkled. Its misshapen contours were heavy with growing rice.

Samud shielded his eyes with his hand and scanned the sky, as blue and endless as the sea. The sea was not far off, just sixty lim, a few days' journey eastward. Yet Samud had never seen it. Once, a neighbor who had been there told him of it, but Samud could not conceive of such a vast expanse of water. The farthest he had ever traveled was the forty lim to Anayatnas, to the nearest temple. He went there every month; it was coming time to go again.

Only a single puff of cloud marred the sky today. The man watched that cloud, hung on it, looking for darkness or movement. But it was white and motionless; the sky promised neither rain nor wind.

He dropped his hand, closed his eyes and stood quietly, baking in the sun. He gave himself over to the mallet of heat hammering down on him. Brilliant colors splashed inside his head. He felt close to sleep, unwilling to move.

In his mind's eye he saw the field: the spread of tall stalks, standing upright, unjostled by any wind, being enervated by the sun. Like Mussopo, the stalks of rice were close to sleep, unwilling to fend it off. Like him, they lacked the means to fight for their own lives; they could

37

accept only what the implacable elements might do to them, and if they begged the sky for mercy, it had no ears with which to hear them. It didn't care what happened to the rice, or to Samud Mussopo.

Samud could smell the sweat that oozed from his brown skin and caught the dust to make a gritty coating. He felt smothered by the dirt he carried on his clothes and body, and the River Qurwa was not far away. The man pictured himself being cleansed in the river, plunging in and dunking his head in the lukewarm but still refreshing water, taking strength from it. That water could give him new life, just as it could for his rice.

The river might not be far away, but it was unfortunately in the opposite direction from Anayatnas. Samud could not go to the river now, any more than could his rice go to it. Instead, he must go to Anayatnas.

"It's not going to rain soon, is it, Paban?"

The man turned sharply around. It was always a surprise to Samud when he looked at this son of his and saw how the boy was growing: his honey-colored limbs lean and well formed, his face and eyes clear, not yet crinkled from squinting at the sun.

"No, Gaffar. As you can see, there are no clouds or wind."

The boy felt a queasy foreboding. "The rice will be ruined," he said.

"Oh, don't worry. It's never happened."

This was untrue; there had been years in which the crop was wrecked by too much sun and too little water. Gaffar knew this as well did his father, but didn't contradict him. The boy also had some idea of what kind of year the Mussopo family would face if the crop failed. Already there was a knot in his stomach.

"We mustn't leave things to chance, though, Paban," he argued earnestly. "We could go to the river—make trips back and forth—bringing water in jugs. We should try to put some shades over the crop, to keep off the sun. With work, we could save some of it."

Samud slowly shook his head back and forth. "Surely you haven't forgotten what time of the month it is! I must go to Anayatnas."

Hot breath filled Gaffar's nostrils. He was infuriated

and struggled to rein it in. *"You would go—even now?"* the boy said, gesturing at the field of rice.

Samud looked harshly down at him. "It is time. There is nothing to discuss."

This enraged Gaffar even further, and his tone was no longer respectful. "Yes, there is something to discuss! This time, by Urhem, there is! Paban, you know what I've always thought of your going to Anayatnas to bow and scrape—"

"Hold your tongue!"

". . . to the Tnemghadi tyrant—"

"Take care what you say!"

"No! What have you got to be afraid of? The priests aren't here now, they can't hear us. Paban, surely you must hate them as much as I do—more."

"What I may think of the Tnemghadi and their priests doesn't matter. I must do what the law says. You foolish boy, you know well enough what happens to those who defy the Tnemghadi."

"But our crop is at stake. We'll lose it if you go!"

"Better to lose the crop than our heads."

"No, Paban. Better to lose our heads standing up for Urhem than to keep them bowing to the Emperor."

"Urhem!" Samud spat the name with contempt. "What has Urhem ever done for us? Will Urhem save our crop, will Urhem placate the Tnemghadi? Oh, yes, your Urhem is a pretty god. But the Tnemghadi rule this world, and it's them I bow before. The only thing a prayer to Urhem can bring you is death, if you're caught at it."

"Paban, don't you see? It's just that kind of thinking that keeps us all in slavery. If all the people of the South were united in defiance of the Emperor, there would not be enough Tnemghadi soldiers to keep them down. If everyone proclaimed his faith in Urhem, then we would be free."

"But that will never happen, Gaffar. You're dreaming."

"It will happen someday. It will!"

"When? When the *Ur-Rasvadhi* comes? Ha! I tell you, I'm not fool enough to wait holding my breath for the *Ur-Rasvadhi*. If all the millions in the South have not produced him after eight hundred years, he will never come. Such a man could never be."

"Paban, you just don't understand. It's not that there

haven't been men great enough. But our people weren't ready. When the time is right, there will be an *Ur-Rasvadhi*. When we are ready, we will find him among us."

"All right, Gaffar. When you find him, you will tell me. Then I'll stop going to Anayatnas, and I'll join you in celebration. But in the meantime I must go, whether I like it or not, even if it means neglecting the rice. Yes, I will go, and I will bow with my head in the dust to Sarbat the Generous, and I will offer up a goat."

"Oh, no, not a goat! We can't afford it—not with the rice in danger!"

"But it will be a goat all the same. A choice offering it will be; and maybe then, for once, Sarbat will grant our prayer for rain."

"Pah!"

"Besides," Samud said quietly, "the priests have been dissatisfied with our offerings. I have no choice now. Last month, old man Relleth bluntly warned me to do better."

"Damn them, thieving jackals! Aren't the priests rich enough from our sweat? Will they next want our blood?"

"It does no good to talk so rashly. There's not a thing we can do about it."

Gaffar wasn't even listening to his father. "Our sweat's not good enough," he cried, "they'll want our blood next!"

Samud seized the boy by the shoulders and shook him hard. "And if they ask for blood, Gaffar, I'll have to give them blood!"

"Are you so spineless, you'd give the monsters anything they demand? If they ask for your son, will you comply with that too? Will you take the knife yourself and cut out my heart on the altar to Sarbat?"

Samud gawked at his son, unnerved by the fire he saw in the boy's eyes and by his chilling words. He relaxed his grip on Gaffar's shoulders. "How can you ask such a question?"

Gaffar was looking straight through his father, as though transfixed by his own flight of rhetoric.

"Enough of this," said Samud with a quaver. "There's work to do."

The boy clenched his fists as his father walked away. His eyes stung with the tears he thought himself too big to let fall. It was incomprehensible that his father could endure such subservience to the Tnemghadi, even to the point of endangering the family's survival in order to pay homage to the Emperor. Gaffar vowed he would never suffer such humiliation. He would stand up to the oppressors!

But would he? Did he not love his life? Would he sacrifice it just to become yet another pointless Urhemmedhin martyr? Or, when the time arrived, would he, like countless other millions, swallow his pride and grit his teeth and bow before the idol of the Emperor?

Gaffar wished fervently that he might never have to confront such a choice. If only the *Ur-Rasvadhi* would come! Gaffar ached for the triumph of right, for the freedom of his people, and for the destruction of the Tnemghadi, avenging their degradation of his father.

But perhaps his father was right, that there would never be an *Ur-Rasvadhi*. How many like Gaffar had prayed for his coming, only to die disappointed? Why should Gaffar be blessed with a deliverance denied the millions before him?

For, in the end, the dream was too ridiculous: a man who would arise, not with a sword but with a book, who would triumph without force of arms but instead by force of love and wisdom. How could the invincible Tnemghadi, with their horses, spears, and steel armor, melt before such a preposterous challenge? This love and wisdom would not pierce the hearts of the cruel warriors; they would merely laugh at it, and trample its disciples.

That the Urhemmedhins had invented such a dream, and clung to it, was pathetic; it proved how weak and hopeless was their cause.

Gaffar Mussopo cried and beat his fists against his knees. He hated the Tnemghadi, hated them most of all for their invincibility. It was not love and virtue that he yearned to hurl against them. He dreamed instead of a vengeful savior who would visit fire and death upon them, who would make them suffer for the sufferings they had caused, who would annihilate them.

It was not the *Ur-Rasvadhi* for whose coming Gaffar prayed. It was Sexrexatra.

· 6 ·

THE EASTERNMOST PROVINCE in the Empire of Bergharra was Taroloweh. It pushed out into the sea as a timid bulge along the coastline, as though testing the waters without plunging into them.

Appropriately, Taroloweh's map had outlines resembling a boat, with its bow at the shore and its rudder five hundred lim inland. Once a part of Urhem's great southern empire, then an independent kingdom, this was the first Urhemmedhin province to be conquered by Tnem Khatto Trevendhani. It was also the most trouble-ridden and rebellious: Jehan Henghmani had been merely the latest Taroloweh outlaw quashed by the Tnemghadi.

Taroloweh was a place of rolling hills—gentle slopes, not mountains. Although this province was one of the Empire's breadbaskets, its agricultural endowments were not great. The soil was mediocre, the weather mercurial, and often the peasants had to wrench their grain and rice from an unwilling earth.

Almost all of those who worked this land were Urhemmedhin sharecroppers, tied to little plots sectioned off on great estates, sometimes hundreds of them all paying half their crops in rent to one great lord, to whom they half belonged. By law, although these tenant farmers were not free, they had certain meager rights. In practice, however, even those few legal rights were worthless. They were unenforceable against a nobleman who gouged on the rent, stole his tenant's goods, seized his tenant's daughter as a concubine or sold her into slavery. The only justice in the land was that meted out by the barons themselves. In the name of justice, they could punish and behead at will. A not untypical example of this justice was a case in which twenty men and twenty women had their eyes and tongues cut out in retribution for a theft of silver from the manor house.

The social and economic structure in Taroloweh (and indeed, throughout most of Bergharra) had not changed in centuries. There were actually many estates still owned by Urhemmedhin clans whose dominion dated back before the Tnemghadi conquest. But the great majority of these fiefdoms were in the hands of Tnemghadi, descendants of satrap officials, of officers in the occupation armies, or of priests who had enriched themselves upon the offerings in the temples.

In crushing any defiance by the peasants, the Tnemghadi land barons had always found ready allies in their less numerous Urhemmedhin counterparts. The survivors of Urhemmedhin nobility were allowed to prosper, securing their allegiance to the Emperor and their cooperation with the occupiers. These people formed a society unto themselves, despised by their peasant countrymen and the Tnemghadi alike. For while mutual self-interest bound all the barons together, the Tnemghadi held themselves to be superior. Intermarriage was unheard of. The proud people from the north kept their eyebrows meeting in the middle of their foreheads.

Such were the salient facts of life in Taroloweh.

Two cities dominated this province, perched at opposite ends of its boat-shaped map. In the east, by the sea, was the port of Zidneppa, home to fishing boats and trading ships that huddled up and down the coast. Toward the western end was the bigger city, Arbadakhar, the provincial capital.

There was also, in Taroloweh, a scattering of villages. One of these was known as Anayatnas.

Samud Mussopo rode to Anayatnas on his gaar. The Bergharran gaar is a large cow, dun-colored and of gentle disposition, valued for its milk, a staple of the peasants' diet. The beast has a long face topped with tiny eyes, a great expanse of nose between them and a small pursed mouth. This makes it look perpetually morose. But the gaar's most striking feature is its hump, a mountain topped with a thatch of strawlike hair; and it is a double hump, like the Bactrian camel's, easy for a man to ride.

Samud's gaar, Rassav, was the only big animal belonging to the Mussopo family. At this, they were considered quite well-off for peasants, and they had some goats and chickens too. One of the goats now was tied to the gaar, as a bundle on the side of the hump, her feet bound to restrain her kicking. Every so often she would bleat, and Samud Mussopo would give her a gentle pat to reassure her.

A slow, plodding creature is the Bergharran gaar, and so the forty-lim journey to Anayatnas took almost a full day. Samud had left in the morning, would arrive in the late afternoon, finish his business at the temple, and find a place to spend the night—probably in the open, by the road. Then, not until near evening of the next day would he reach home again. He made this journey once each month, as required by law.

This time the trip passed quickly; Samud was startled when he looked up and saw ahead the whitewashed town of Anayatnas, glowing from the sidelong rays of the waning sun. He had spent the day on the road wrapped deeply in thought. He had arrived at Anayatnas, but his mind was still back on his farm, and with his headstrong son, Gaffar.

For there was much to occupy the man's thoughts. Even here at Anayatnas, after journeying for a day, he found the sky blue and cloudless—no sign of the dearly needed rain. Along the way, Samud had passed fields where the crops were already withering in the heat and drought. He could see the ominous signs in the faces of the people and the boniness of their livestock. The desperation measures had begun: here and there Samud had noticed gaars dragging carts loaded with great water jugs, the peasants sloshing down parts of their fields, and erecting crude shades of palm leaves to blunt the relentless sun.

Tears came to his eyes as he thought of his rice fields, where he had sweated and labored so, and on which his very life and family depended. His absence at this critical time could mean their loss, and for this he cursed the priests of Anayatnas and the Tnemghadi law that required him to go to the temple once a month without fail.

Alone with his gaar, Samud Mussopo cursed the oppressors as darkly as might his son, Gaffar.

But he could never allow Gaffar to know how deeply ran his own hatred for the Tnemghadi—and for this, too, Samud Mussopo wanted to weep. He understood Gaffar's passion—only too well! But he was afraid for the boy. Hot-headed zealots could wind up hanging from a pole. Samud just had to make his son see the necessity of swallowing one's indignation in order to survive. He might burn with hatred against Tnemghadi injustice, curse the landlords, priests, and soldiers under his breath, but he must smile to their faces like a pet lap-dog. The cruelties were dreadful enough without provoking them to worse. Nothing was ever served by the deaths of Urhemmedhin fanatics.

This, Gaffar would have to learn. Active opposition was madness. It was well to adhere to the high-minded creed of Urhem, as Samud himself did; but it was foolish to persist in faith in the *Ur-Rasvadhi*. In younger days, Samud too had prayed for the savior, but by now he knew how hopeless that was. He had heard too many stories of rebellions smashed, too many would-be *Ur-Rasvadhi* martyred, and he had seen too many smug, armored Tnemghadi soldiers patrolling Anayatnas. Deliverance, yarushkadharra, would likely never come, and surely never through a messiah whose only weapons were piety and wisdom. Samud had learned what little they counted for in this world.

Gaffar was young and starry-eyed, his father thought, and hadn't learned this yet. Until that lesson was learned, Samud would have to play a role the boy despised.

And there was another reason behind the face Samud presented to Gaffar. It was humiliating enough to be held in contempt for subservience to the villains. But far worse it would be if Gaffar knew the depth of his father's compromise: that Samud hated the Tnemghadi bitterly, yet went to them on bended knee. Better that the boy should think his father too insensitive to hate his oppressors. It was better to be thought stupid than a coward.

So it wasn't only from the sun that Samud burned as he rode into the streets of Anayatnas. It was fear for his crops, his family, and especially his son; and he burned with shame for this trip, and with mortification over how Gaffar reviled him for it; and because of all this, he burned with venom for the Tnemghadi.

"Samud! Hello, Samud!"

There was a man waving to him as he rode through the bustling main street of Anayatnas.

"Ah, hello Muhamar!" Samud waved back at the old white-bearded man who sold fish from the port of Zidneppa, at a street-corner stand. Samud had sometimes bought his wares, to bring back to the farm as a special treat.

Samud reined his gaar to a stop and leaned down to the fish peddler. "How've you been, old fellow? Business good?"

"I'm quite well; fish, you know, is very healthy food. But as for my business, it's not so good. People are saving their money; there is great fear of famine. I hope I can sell you a little something, a prosperous man like you?"

"I've no money this month, Muhamar; frankly, I too fear famine."

"Well, I hope it rains quite soon. Anyhow, isn't that a fine little goat you've got there? Surely once you sell her, you can afford a bit of fish for your wife and children?"

Samud shook his head. "The goat's for the temple, I'm afraid."

The fish seller said, "Oh."

"So tell me, old man, what's the latest news? You know, out in those hills, we hear nothing of the world."

"Ah, Samud, there is news this month indeed, and good news at that. Those Tnemghadi are good for something at least. They've taken care of Jehan Henghmani."

"Really! That is truly good news. Nobody was safe while his scum were on the loose. The stories I've heard of his doings are enough to turn one's hair white. So, did they get the whole gang?"

"Practically; only a handful got away. And that monster giant, Jehan, wasn't one of them. They took him in a cart to Arbadakhar, and then they sent him all the way to Ksiritsa; and they chopped off his ugly head right in Sarbat's Palace."

"So, that's the end of that."

"I should say so. They'll catch the ones who got away, even the monster's women and children."

Samud chuckled grimly. "Yes, we can count on the Tnemghadi catching them. Not even the children will escape."

"Not even the little babies." Muhamar shrugged, and smiled. "Well, Samud, it's good seeing you again. I hope your offering of a goat brings an answer to your prayer. I will pray to Urhem that Sarbat answers your prayer!"

"I'm praying, actually, for some way to keep my goat!"

"Well, may that prayer be answered too. May you somehow wind up keeping your pretty goat, Samud."

"Thank you, Muhamar."

The old fish seller bowed his head crisply. "Good day to you, Samud."

"Good day to you too, Muhamer."

Samud Mussopo rode his gaar Rassav up to the outer entrance to the Anayatnas temple. It was a heavy, two-story structure built of marble, ringed by a low wall. Beside it, the rest of Anayatnas was a slum.

In the open courtyard, Samud dismounted from his lumbering beast and tethered her to a post. Then he undid the thongs binding the goat. She kicked her legs exuberantly in freedom, but Samud held her in his arms and carried her to a table where sat a pair of priests before large parchment ledgers.

These priests recorded the offerings before permitting worshippers to enter the temple. If an offering was accepted, the priests would exchange it for a small brass disk; which the worshipper would place upon the altar for Sarbat. The offering itself was kept by the priests. They had the right to turn away anyone whose offering they deemed insufficient; and of course, it was the law that every head of a household gain entry to the temple once each month.

A score or so of soldiers stood around the courtyard. Despite the sweltering weather, they wore heavy armor and carried long sharp pikes. These weapons were all embellished with an image of the dragon Sexrexatra.

Also in the temple's courtyard was a third priest, reclining in the shade on a divan. He wore long silk robes and jewelled rings sparkling on his fingers, and sat with his hands folded placidly on his belly, watching everything. This was Nimajneb Relleth.

Holding his goat, Samud stood before the table and bowed deeply. He recited his name, and where he was from, and the name of Adnan Khnotthros, his landlord. As he spoke, he was aware of old Relleth watching him from the divan.

One of the priests thumbed through his huge ledger and located the proper listing. "It is one month exactly, Mussopo."

"Yes, and may it please your holinesses, I've brought a goat this time."

"We can see perfectly well it's a goat," spoke up Relleth from his couch.

Samud flushed. "I'm sorry, I didn't mean to—"

"That's all right, son. We're glad you've brought a goat. That is, the Emperor will be more pleased with a goat than with a little rice."

Samud smiled wanly; even now he was being chastized.

"I understand it hasn't rained lately in your region," Relleth said, rising casually and walking toward Samud. "Is that so?"

"Yes, your holiness, that's very true."

"And it's a pity. I greatly fear a famine this year. How is your own crop doing, Mussopo?"

"Not too well, holiness." Samud was puzzled by this talk. Could Relleth really be concerned about the crop? Perhaps the old thief was worried that his takings would be reduced! And if there was a famine, would the priests do anything for the people?

"Well, I hope everything turns out all right for you, Mussopo." The senior priest strolled up now to Rassav the gaar, and stroked the beast's mountainous hump. "This is a fine gaar you have."

"Yes, thank you, holiness."

"She gives a lot of milk, I'd say."

"Yes, your holiness. I don't know what we'd do without her."

"Has she got a name?"

"Her name is Rassav, holiness."

"Well, I do hope everything turns out all right for you, Mussopo."

"Your concern, holiness, is a great blessing."

"Well, that's what we're here for. We will pray for you, for some rain to save your crop. Of course, you'll be praying for that yourself, when you go now before Tnem Sarbat the Generous."

"Yes, that's what I'll be praying for."

"And of course Sarbat is pleased at your offering a goat. That is not a bad offering; Sarbat may hear your prayer. But of course, there are so many millions always begging him for this or that, he can never grant them all. You must realize that, of course."

"Of course, your holiness."

"Of course, the better the offering, the better your chances with the Emperor. Some men, you know, needing rain so desperately, might offer even more than a little goat. Some in your place might even offer a gaar."

Samud Mussopo froze. Now he saw the reason for this peculiar conversation. And yet, the realization was so terrible it almost couldn't be true. He felt flung down a black hole, clutching wildly at empty air.

"Her name is Rassav, eh? A very fine animal she is. Of course, Sarbat would be so pleased to have this gaar instead of a measly goat. Now *that* would be an offering to get some rain! Don't you agree, Mussopo?"

"P-perhaps," Samud managed to answer hoarsely.

"Of course, that would be a very fine offering. Of course, we priests would be very pleased, and so impressed at your piety. We would all pray specially for you."

Samud plummeted down the pit, welling up tears of helpless wrath. The man wanted to fall down on the spot and weep.

Suddenly the goat kicked free of his arms with a triumphant bleat.

"Take her, take the gaar, take her," he said in a rush, his hands seizing his head. He would not be baited any longer. Relleth meant to have his gaar, and there was no avoiding it.

"Take her," he said broken-voiced, with a flinging gesture of renunciation. Then he whirled and ran up the stairs, scrambled up them, ran through the temple to its inmost sanctum, followed by the capering goat. Samud threw himself prostrate on his stomach before the golden idol of the Emperor.

He beat his clenched fists on the ground, coughing tears, while the bewildered goat bleated.

His prayer, he realized, had been granted after all:

He would keep the goat.

BERGHARRA—Tnemghadi Empire, copper double falu of Emperor Sarbat, Satanichadh Dynasty, middle period of reign, circa 1175. *Obverse:* facing portrait, Tnemghadi inscription in exergue. *Reverse:* dragon, fish mintmark (Arbadakhar). Breitenbach 1296, 31 mm. Basically fine–very fine, but unfortunately mutilated across portrait with heavy slash marks, probably as a gesture of hostility toward the Emperor. Interesting as such. (*Hauchschild Collection Catalog*)

·7·

WITH THE BRAYING OF TRUMPETS and cymbals the eunuchs marched, carrying away from the muddy dungeon the golden litter of Sarbat Satanichadh.

Nimajneb Grebzreh bowed as the grandiose procession left, and shook with thanksgiving. He knew the Emperor could have crushed a miserable dungeon warden between thumb and forefinger, like he did to insects; men were hardly different to him.

When Grebzreh recovered his composure, he turned back to Jehan Henghmani's cell. "Well, now, Man Eater, you should be grateful to His Majesty; we are not allowed to torture you today." The warden snorted. "But tomorrow's not far off. And I promise you, tomorrow you'll wish you'd let the executioner do his job. Sweet dreams, Man Eater."

"I'll sleep better than you, jackal," came the voice from the dark cell.

"Not if you knew what we have in store for you. You'll wish you were never born, you miserable beast."

"Your hatred for me is quite a thing to behold!"

"Yes! You're a filthy Urhemmedhin pig. All you people are a wretched, muling lot. How many of them, your own kind, did you kill? How many farms did you burn, how many girls did you rape? I don't care what you people do to each other; you're all no better than animals as far as I'm concerned. But you killed Zakhar the executioner too. He was my friend and you killed him."

"Yes, I killed him," Jehan said. "What would you have done in my place?"

"I would not be in your place. You're a criminal."

"You could be in my place tomorrow. What is a criminal? It's anyone whom someone else wants to punish— and has the power to punish. A criminal is anyone who

53

displeases the Emperor. Today he may be pleased with you, warden; tomorrow he may change his mind and your head will roll. And then, I suppose that I'll be fed your flesh."

"Then may you choke on it, you ugly monster. And let me tell you, you may be ugly now, but I'm going to make sure you get a lot uglier."

"You'll get uglier yourself, warden, growing old in this stinking dungeon."

"Yes, but I'll still be in one piece. I won't be all mutilated. I will still have my mind and I will still have my balls."

Nimajneb Grebzreh cackled like a hyena. *"I'll still have my balls."*

Jehan Henghmani, ferocious bandit chieftain, Man Eater of Taroloweh, sat huddled on the ground in his cell.

It was painfully cramped; Jehan had to sleep in the muck, and could not even stretch out doing so. There was no window save the small barred opening in the door, and the hinged flap through which food could be shoved. The stone walls were slimy, the air thick, rank with the stench of filth and vermin and the buzzing of the other wretched prisoners.

In this cell, Jehan was condemned to spend the rest of his life. It would probably not be long.

Huddled in the wet, cold mud, Jehan's huge body was speckled with wounds and bruises, some of them cherry red and festering. But he was rasped not by these injuries alone. He happened to be thinking of his woman, Jenefa, and their two daughters. Outlaw that he was, still there was tenderness in him for his girls.

He'd had many other women, and had doubtless sired many other children. But Jenefa, and his daughters by her, stood differently from all the rest.

He'd been little more than a boy when Jenefa had come upon him one night, a ragged fellow hiding on her father's farm, intent on stealing chickens. But she didn't know he was a thief. The girl herself was supposed to be in bed, but she liked to walk the fields alone at night. Jehan walked with her, and they spent the rest of the night lying in the grass, talking softly and looking at the stars. Jehan forgot about the chickens. When the sun came up, they ran away together.

She was not a pretty girl, just a coarse peasant. Jehan could not remember just why he had taken her with him away from that farm. He hadn't loved her, not then. And for some reason Jehan could never fathom, she stayed always faithful to him. No matter what other women he might take nor the atrocities he might commit, nor even if he beat her, Jenefa always stuck with him. She stayed nearby if he dallied with some other girl, and he always did come back to her. Unique among all the women he'd ever had, he'd no idea why she gave herself to him. There was nothing to make him worthy of it. And finally, it was this senseless, animal-like devotion of hers that won Jehan's affection.

She had borne him several children; some had died, but two survived. Maiya was now twelve years old, and Tsevni was eight. Jehan had hidden them in a cave when the imperial troops came hot after him. Now, his separation from them grieved Jehan, even while he found solace in their safety.

His physical pain was easier to take; he had suffered worse before. But the promise of torture was profoundly frightening, even to such a toughened bandit. Never before had he been the helpless victim of another's cruelty. This would be a terrible humiliation heaped upon the agony of the torture.

Jehan Henghmani brooded upon the ordeal facing him, and whether he would stand it. But he saw at once what a pointless question it was. He would stand it, because the sole alternative was death.

The Emperor had promised that Jehan would beg for death; but he knew he never would.

In his brutish brigand days, he had never thought much about death. But that changed once he was captured. Trundling along in the cart on the road to Ksiritsa, he had struggled to reconcile himself to death, trying to grasp the world going on without him. It never entered Jehan's mind that he might escape his fate. But when he was brought finally to the chopping block, and he looked at Zakhar Wasfour—bare-chested, black-hooded, muscled like a bullock, and hefting the blade to reduce Jehan's throat to pulp and his spine to gristle—something exploded inside his head. Some demon impulse hurled him at Wasfour, to wrench that awful ax away, even with his chained hands. And he killed his own executioner.

A more audacious crime could hardly be imagined. Yet what was his punishment?

The Emperor decreed that he would live—*must live!*

That was the important thing now. Not the torture, but life.

On the road to Ksiritsa, Jehan Henghmani had come to appreciate the essential of the life he was condemned to lose. His life had been squalid and violent, but it was not worthless. It was more than death, more than nothing, infinitely more. That was the value of his life.

Urhemmedhin by birth, Jehan Henghmani had never been an Urhem-worshipper. The religion held no interest for him. Jehan believed in no god, believed in no faith at all. And yet, he had nevertheless arrived at an understanding that life is priceless, without realizing that this was the nub of Urhemmedhin teaching.

Life: that was the gift Sarbat had given to Jehan Henghmani. He would be alive. No matter how he might suffer, no matter the horror, it would be life, incalculably precious. Jehan would never beg for death.

And he'd do more than live. In the hills of Taroloweh, he had existed as a wild beast—stealing, killing, and raping, to slake his hunger, cruelty, and lust. Even the primal nobility of jungle predators had been lacking in him. But that was over. Now that he knew what life was worth, he could no longer squander it like that.

Besides, it could not have been for justice's sake that Jehan was spared the ax. The miracle must have happened for a reason, and it could not be to allow the old Man Eater of Taroloweh to live. *That* Jehan was dead, as surely as though the executioner had done his work.

Tnem Sarbat Satanichadh returned to his palace thinking he had condemned a man to the life of an animal. But Jehan Henghmani knew that he had been transformed from an animal into a man, and more than a man.

Let them torture him: he would endure it.

Let them feed him human flesh: he would thrive on it.

And someday, he would come out of this dungeon and show them what they'd made of him.

· 8 ·

HE DID NOT KNOW how many hours might have passed before the guards came again.

Jehan had not slept. Squeezed inside the cagelike cell in blackness, Jehan Henghmani could see further than ever before. He had been reborn, just as a baby released from the womb is suddenly immersed in more new world than he'd ever dreamed could be. It was as though there'd been no life before at all: a butterfly forgetful of the caterpillar.

It wasn't the pain and hunger that had kept Jehan awake. He had slept through many storms before, but he couldn't sleep when the storm was inside his own head. Besides, Jehan had slept aplenty before; he had only just awakened!

The guards came again, and against his will, Jehan's heart hammered and he felt the stinging frost of fright.

In the intoxication of his metamorphosis, Jehan had forgotten his terror of the promised torture. But was the new Jehan immune to it? Would he not feel the pain? Or had he risen above pain as well as death?

The sound of feet slopping through the muck stopped outside Jehan Henghmani's cell. He heard the key grate in the rusty lock, the groan of the door pulled open; torchlight momentarily blinded him.

Jehan squinted up at the guards; they seemed to tower swaggeringly. Their swords and truncheons were poised in their hands.

While they unchained Jehan, he did not balk. Standing a cautious distance outside the cell was Nimajneb Grebzreh. "Well," he said, "you know what comes now, you Urhemmedhin pig." Then he turned to the guards and said, "Drag him. Drag him out like a pig."

This was a humiliating indignity, and Jehan seethed at

his impotence. But he fought to hold his temper. He would not squander his newfound energy gnashing his teeth; instead, he would channel it into bearing everything with stoic nobility. He might not escape their torture, but he would blunt their satisfaction in it.

Jehan had heard of holy men with such extraordinary self-control that they seemed oblivious to pain, and cheerfully thrust spikes through their palms and cheeks. This was what Jehan would work toward emulating.

Dragged through the mud, he swore that regardless of the torture, he would not allow himself to scream. He might groan and grimace, but he would not give them the satisfaction of hearing him scream. Gradually he might learn to overcome even the grimaces. He would strive toward a serene smile even under their most hideous tortures: an absurd nirvana.

This seemed an impossible goal. Yet only yesterday, it had seemed impossible that Jehan would be alive today. The possible is limited only by the imagination, nothing is impossible. It was not impossible that he could smile under torture. It was not impossible that he could become the Emperor of Bergharra.

They dragged him through the muddy tunnel and then into a chamber with a cold stone floor. The light was harsh. Jehan looked at the terrible display of torture implements all about, diabolical devices, and the deep redbrown stains they had squeezed out of those who'd gone before. He looked up at the men who had brought him to this place. Their eyes were tremulous with loathing, fear, and lust to see him suffer agony.

Chained tightly he was thrown on the floor, looking up at them, waiting, bracing himself. For a moment, nothing happened.

Then something, something infinitely more than nothing.

Back inside his cell, Jehan could not open his eyes.

He was being chewed up in razor jaws.

But through the fury of pain, he could remember what had happened. Despite all his resolve, he'd screamed. So quickly the jaws had snapped down upon him, with such ferocity, they wouldn't let go. Jehan bellowed; the fangs had only torn deeper through him. It was a terrible agony to defy imagination, and the teeth of it ripped ever deeper, chewing flesh and soul to shreds. Jehan bellowed.

And even while the horror ripped him to pieces, Jehan struggled to master himself. He was aware of the glee of Grebzreh and his cohorts, reveling in his screams, and he was as incensed at himself as at them.

With fitful, titanic effort, he fought through the agony to grit his teeth, to will the severance of body from mind.

Wrestling with the teeth that crushed him between steel jaws, Jehan gained a hold on himself. He knew that to stop his screams would only provoke worse tortures. But even stronger than the guards' lust to hear him scream was his will to deny them.

He clenched his teeth until they cracked, but he wouldn't scream. Blood spurted from his nose and ears, but he wouldn't scream.

Ground to pulp between the rending jaws, Jehan could taste sweet triumph. He had won, he would never cry out again. Let them invent phenomenally excruciating tortures, they might as well be tickling him with feathers.

Increase the torment they did. Jehan passed out—but he did not scream again.

Jehan lay now back in his cell, palpitating with the agony of what they'd done to him. The jaws had not spit him out, they were still tearing at him. There would be no respite—ever.

And yet, he knew that he had won, and they had lost.

At length, he managed to open his eyes and gather his wits into a semblance of order. He tried to force his thoughts upon Jenefa and his daughters, instead of the jaws that would never release him. But his mind went black with pain, and he had to struggle again to hold in a scream. Choking on it, he collapsed back into stupor.

A second time, he was restored to consciousness. The jaws had relaxed their grip, but not very much. He could at least, though, manage to think, and move.

He noticed in the weak light that something had been shoved through the flap in his door. Groping it with his hand, he found a rude wooden platter, and on it was food—the food of the gods.

Jehan's warders were complying with the Emperor's decree that he be fed human flesh.

It was a severed hand and forearm. Jehan took it into his hands and stared at it in the dim light. It did not repel him; he had seen dismembered bodies before, not a few of which he had dismembered himself. Yet this thing had a strange impersonality to it. Jehan found it difficult to imagine the arm as part of a whole being.

He held it in the light, manipulating its fingers and wondering about its former owner. The man's age was difficult to guess. His skin was browned by the sun, the hand calloused, the fingernails cracked and black with dirt. The arm had been amputated neatly at the elbow. Yet it appeared to be a healthy limb, so presumably had been cut off a corpse. Had this fellow been executed, perhaps with the same ax Jehan had used to kill Zakhar Wasfour? He was obviously just a peasant. Possibly his crime was refusal to pay crop-rent, or maybe he had balked at a daughter being sold into concubinage. But then, only special criminals were brought here, to the dungeons of Ksiritsa. Maybe this man had been an Urhemmedhin zealot.

Jehan's warders were making no effort yet to force this food down his throat. Perhaps they thought him a monster who wouldn't blanch at eating human flesh. But at any rate, this was meat, and all he'd get to eat. It would nourish him. He could even count himself lucky; other prisoners had their food rations embezzled by the guards.

Jehan sniffed at the arm; it seemed fairly fresh. He wondered how it would taste. Some might even regard this a delicacy; there were land barons who enjoyed human milk squeezed from the breasts of sharecropper mothers whose babies were killed for that purpose.

Experimentally, Jehan sank his teeth into the soft underside of the arm. The meat was tough and stringy, hard to pull off the bone. After his devastating ordeal, Jehan almost lacked the strength. When he did manage to gnaw loose a mouthful, the taste was flat.

Nevertheless, the Man Eater of Taroloweh stripped the forearm clean down to the bone.

The rest of that peasant man was fed to him piecemeal, and he ate everything—arms and legs, torso, lungs, heart, liver, intestines, stomach. He ate the bowels with feces still in them. He even ate the genitals.

When, at the end of many weeks, he was given the head, he could at last see the face of the man whose flesh had nourished him. Jehan had envisioned the courageous face of an Urhemmedhin martyr. But to his surprise, it turned out to be a Tnemghadi. With broad nose and drooping mouth, the converging eyebrows accentuated its moronic look.

Jehan chewed the skull white, and then he cracked it open against the wall to get at the brains.

And while the Emperor's edict was carried out respecting Jehan's diet, so too was the daily regimen of torture unstintingly inflicted. Jehan was the prisoner in the dungeon upon whom all attention was focused. The Warden Grebzreh took personal delight in setting the program and watching it implemented, continually inventing ingenious new torments for Jehan.

They froze him and baked him until the blood oozed from his pores. They set scorpions upon him, cracked his bones with rack and chains, tormented him with thirst, they beat him blue with lead pipes, scalded, branded, and lacerated him, rasped off his skin with files, and they salted all his wounds. They stuck needles in his flesh and eyes, hot burning needles; they cut off his ears and nose, sliced slowly away, whittled down to stumps.

Jehan had been an ugly man before, but now they truly made a hideous monster of him.

Let them, Jehan said, *in the end this monster will rise up to devour them.*

They burned him, cut him, beat him, slashed him, pulled out his fingernails and toenails, they peeled off his skin in sheets and hacked off his toes, one by one, bit by bit and smashed his fingers with hammers. But he fought against them, fought especially to save his fingers, balling his hands into tight fists they couldn't open no matter how they beat him. And once they'd put out an eye with a red-hot poker, he wouldn't let them take the other, wouldn't let them make him blind. And he wouldn't stand for being made a eunuch, either.

They did abominable things to him, but when they tried to cripple him like that, he would fight back. Despite the unending ordeal, his power did not wane; he seemed to absorb the strength of the men whose flesh he ate. And he would dole out almost as many scars and mutilations as were visited upon him.

He would throw the fire back at them; and they would scream as he would not.

BERGHARRA—Tnemghadi Empire, silver pastari or five-tayel piece of Emperor Sarbat, Satanichadh Dynasty, middle period of reign, circa 1175. *Obverse:* facing portrait of Sarbat, Tnemghadi inscription in exergue. *Reverse:* facing portrait of a woman, thought to be one of the Emperor's favorites, or possibly the Empress. Crown mintmark (Ksiritsa). A most unusual special issue, since almost all Tnemghadi coinage bears the imperial dragon on the reverse. Breitenbach 1356, 33 mm., struck slightly off center and with a small planchet crack at 7 o'clock, mentioned only for the sake of accuracy. Virtually uncirculated with deep bluish toning, undoubtedly the finest extant specimen of this great rarity. (*Hauchschild Collection Catalog*)

· 9 ·

TNEM SARBAT SATANICHADH sat like the god he was upon
the Tnemenghouri Throne beneath the rising sun engraved
in fiery gold. From the scepter perch, the dragon Sexrexatra overlooked the throne room with his glittering
ruby eyes.

The vast chamber was filled, with every member of
the Court in the spot assigned according to rank, to attend upon the ceremonies of state. The most eminent
were close to the throne; the lesser creatures were relegated to the rear.

Nearest of all to Sarbat was Yasiruwam Irajdhan. The
venerable Grand Chamberlain was making the ritual
presentation to Sarbat of the new envoy plenipotentiary
from Valpassu, the jungle kingdom to the south. Irajdhan
stood in dignified silence while the envoy and the Emperor exchanged pleasantries, formalistic and substance-
less. The ambassador conveyed the salutations of the
ruler of Valpassu, along with various gifts: carved ivory
figurines, bejeweled candlesticks, and bolts of fine-weave
colored silk. Sarbat in turn voiced gratitude and respect
to the ruler of Valpassu.

Then Irajdhan took the envoy by the arm and escorted
him down the crimson carpet. Nothing was said; later,
Irajdhan would ply him with wine and girls. Then the
Grand Chamberlain would demand an increase in
Valpassu's tribute payment to Bergharra, soldiers from
Valpassu for the Bergharran army, and the appointment
of Tnemghadi officials to key posts at the Valpassu court.
This would, once and for all, reduce the jungle kingdom
to vassal status. Failing capitulation, Bergharra would in-
vade Valpassu.

The Chamberlain and the envoy exchanged ceremonial
bows, and parted. A page boy took this opportune mo-

ment to hand Irajdhan a dainty little silver tray, carrying a leather pouch and a folded parchment, upon which was embossed the seal of the Imperial Mint of Ksiritsa.

Irajdhan marched back across the chamber to the throne; all business was held in respectful abeyance until he got there. Then he handed the tray up to Sarbat. Nestling it in his lap, the Emperor broke the seal on the document and read it. He at once brightened with pleasure.

"Aha," he announced, "the Master Coiner sends us samples of the new pastari."

Sarbat opened the pouch with a flourish and up-ended it; a dozen shining silver coins clinked out onto the tray. Taking one of them, the Emperor studied it carefully on both sides, tilting it at various angles to catch the light. Then he displayed it to the Court between thumb and forefinger.

"There it is: a magnificent coin, this new pastari piece, the finest artistry in the history of coinage anywhere. It shows the portrait of our dearest Lady Sirimava. Did ever a lovelier face adorn a coin?"

"Why don't you put my face on a coin?" asked Halaf the clown.

"I would, were you as beautiful as Sirimava," said the Emperor as he kissed the coin with smacking lips and a lewd grin. The courtiers all laughed amiably.

"Well, Majesty," said Halaf, "I can put my face on a coin anyway." And the clown took a copper out of his pocket, held it flat in his palm, and slowly lowered his face onto it. This coaxed a mild titter from the assemblage.

"Here, good Irajdhan," Sarbat said, holding out the coin he'd kissed, "this one is for the beautiful lady herself."

The Chamberlain brought the piece to Sirimava, who was seated on a cushion nearby. She gazed at it with her head cocked prettily.

Halaf had meanwhile scampered up the arm of the throne, and he patted the head of the dragon on the scepter. "Poor old Sexrexatra," the clown lamented, "you've been replaced on the pastari by a better-looking dragon. Or, I should say, *dragoness*."

This time his joke brought gales of laughter. Even Sirimava laughed.

Sarbat was fingering the remaining coins, and suddenly frowned. "Oh, look, here's one that's got a crack, and it's not even properly centered. Those swine at the Mint! We can't have the lovely face of Sirimava marred like that. How dare they give me such shoddy work? Friend Irajdhan, find the workman responsible; he must be punished."

"He will lose his hand, Your Majesty."

"No, not his hand," objected Halaf the clown. "The culprit is obviously insensitive to womanly charms. Let the punishment fit the crime, then; it's not his *hand* to be chopped off!"

This once more scored with laughter.

"My royal fool is right; he'd make a wise judge. We will carry out his sentence, good Irajdhan."

Irajdhan bowed deeply to hide his flushing, infuriated that his own counsel was superseded by the clown's. "It will be done, Your Majesty."

"And here, let the members of our Court have a look at these coins. Distribute them."

"Give the cracked one to the Empress!" cried Halaf, and yet again there was a peal of general laughter.

"Yes," Sarbat agreed, "I don't think the Empress appreciates the Lady Sirimava's beauty either." He handed the tray down to Irajdhan; his eyes, smiling wrily, were on the Empress Denoi Devodhrisha. And she was looking straight at him, her face betraying no clue of her thoughts.

When Irajdhan handed her the coin, she didn't give it a glance. She reached inside her robe and withdrew a folded square of parchment. With her gaze still fixed upon the Emperor, she motioned to a page, who took the note and, resting it upon a silver tray, waited until Irajdhan finished distributing the coins. Then the boy handed him the tray.

Irajdhan looked at it gravely. This was a message from the Empress to Sarbat.

When it was handed to the Emperor, she still had her eyes coldly locked on him. He tore the message open; a silver coin tumbled into his lap. It was the cracked Sirimava coin, returned to him.

The written note was brief; Sarbat took its contents at

a glance. "Her Majesty, the serene and honored Empress Denoi Devodhrisha," he announced in solemn tones, "informs us that she wishes a private audience with the Emperor."

He paused; they stared at each other. Everyone held his breath.

"The Empress' request shall, of course, be granted with pleasure. We will be delighted to receive the Empress in our private chambers this evening, directly after dinner."

The Empress, leaving her maidservants outside, entered her husband's chamber unattended.

She had not set foot in his private rooms in fifteen years. In fifteen years, they hadn't been alone together; never before had she requested a private audience.

Sarbat was in readiness for it, as he would prepare for a state conference. She found him sitting in his high great-chair, a reduced version of the Tnemenghouri Throne, and he was dressed in full regalia, postured ceremoniously.

Striking a pose too was Sirimava. She lay stretched out on a divan, naked but for jewels, facing Sarbat. Her head, enswathed in its remarkable yellow hair, rested on one elbow; her other hand caressed her own rump. Her nipples were pierced with delicate gold hangings, like earrings. Sirimava was a very tall and more than very handsome woman. Not only was her hair an exotic contrast to the dark tresses so common to Bergharra, but her skin was fairer too, a milky pink. Her name meant "fair woman" in the language of Kuloun, whose king had given her to Sarbat as a gift, having acquired her from a land even further west.

"Good evening, honored Empress Denoi," Sarbat said.

She bowed and bade him a good evening, as perfunctory an obeisance to form as she could make it. Sirimava meanwhile said nothing; she ignored the Empress.

"I have something most fascinating to show you," said Sarbat, holding out a glass cube. Inside it was a broken little statuette. "This specimen has just been unearthed on the banks of the Gnanad, near Sajnithaddhani. Come and look at it."

"Your Majesty, I did not come here to discuss your antiquities," said the Empress curtly.

"Very well." Sarbat placed the glass box aside.

"Nor will I speak to you with this woman present."

"You will speak if I command you."

"Or suffer the consequences—which I am willing to do. But I will not speak for her ears, especially not with her lying naked as a plum. It is an offense to me. Perhaps it pleases you to give such offense; that is precisely what I've come to talk about." The graying woman spoke quietly and slowly, and her eyes held Sarbat like fish-hooks. "I will no longer tolerate such offenses, starting right now, with her presence. If she does not leave this room, I will—I will leave for Laham Jat."

"You shall not threaten me."

"And you shall not bully me; you cannot, because I only care for one thing now, and it isn't my life."

"What is it?"

"My honor, and the honor of the House of Devodhrisha. Now, you send this woman away. Remember that you have the honor of the House of Satanichadh to think of, too."

Sarbat deliberated briefly, then snapped his fingers at Sirimava. The yellow-haired woman rose snakily from the couch and bowed to the Emperor. Then, with one hand postured at the back of her neck and the other on her hip, she pranced out of the room.

"There, I've respected your wishes. Now you may speak freely."

"And speak I shall. No longer will I countenance offenses to my honor, nor tolerate being made a mockery, not by you nor anyone else. I will not suffer to be made a joke in your court, as I was this afternoon."

"But it was Halaf—"

"Yes, and is he not *your* clown? And did you not join in the joke? But this matter of Sirimava is no joke.

"I have never protested your concubines. I have never been jealous, not even when we were younger and I did share your bed. It was not my place to be jealous nor to object to your amusements. Now I'm old and dried up, and I don't expect preferment over women like your *dragoness*. Not in your private quarters, not in your bed. But out there in the throne-room, I am still the Empress of Bergharra. Halaf is your clown, not me, and I won't permit you to make me your clown.

"I don't begrudge you your concubines; you can fornicate with them day and night and lavish gifts upon them. But not when it makes a mockery of me. You can give your *dragoness* a golden chariot, a palace, but you shall not give her my place. You shall not mint coins portraying her.

"Those coins are an insult to yourself as well as to me, and you must stop their minting at once. The palace is laughing at you for putting a slave-girl on our money. The whole world will laugh at you if these coins ever circulate."

"And why do you care if they laugh?"

"Because I am your empress. You know by now my opinion of you—that I hold you a poor sovereign, in fact, that I despise you. I make no secret of it. I remain your empress only because that is my duty. And while it is my duty to be the empress to a cruel, irresponsible emperor, it is not my duty to stand by an emperor who is ridiculed as a fool. Were I not the Empress, I would not care who laughed at you. I would laugh with them.

"You have done many vile things, Sarbat Satanichadh. My duty was silence. But if you continue like this, humiliating me and humiliating yourself, then my duty is at an end."

Sarbat hadn't interrupted her save once, and sat as though impassive through her speech, staring down at the ancient statuette in the glass box. When she was finished, he remained stiff, unblinking. Then he quietly leaned forward.

"I should behead you for such insolence."

"That is the response I expected," the Empress said in a flat voice.

"You are fortunate that I value your head more than you yourself do."

"Why *don't* you cut my head off, once and for all?"

"Because it would bring me contempt."

"Contempt? How so?"

"Because it would be so pointless, so unnecessary."

"Are you sure of that? And what if I speak out at Court, as I have spoken here tonight?"

Sarbat chuckled thinly. "It almost seems as if you *want* to be killed. And you're not alone in wanting that gray head of yours cut off. My little chicken Sirimava has asked me to do it, in fact, to torture you to death, as a personal boon to her. Imagine that, the bloodthirsty little wench! Halaf didn't know how right he was in calling her a dragoness. Sirimava knows she can't be empress, so she wants the next best thing: the power of death over the Empress.

"And do you know what I've told her? I promised my dragoness that, just to please her, I would indeed have you murdered."

Sarbat paused to let this sink in. The Empress did not flinch.

"But even so, it is still unnecessary, even pointless. You will not lose your head—nor will you speak out at Court. You are going away."

The Empress Denoi was astonished. "I think that would be ideal, if it happens with your assent. But I never expected you—"

"To sanction it? But why not? As you said, it would be best, and shouldn't a wise ruler do what is best? But then, you don't think me a wise ruler. That's why you're so surprised. Well, if I'm not wise, at least I am surprising."

"Is that a creditable quality?"

"Yes, it is good if one's enemies never know what to expect. At any rate, you will say your farewells at Court tomorrow and depart for Laham Jat the following morning."

"And what of your promise to your dragoness?"

"She will consider it fulfilled. You see, I've already told her that the announcement of your trip will be my subterfuge for secretly having you killed."

"Will it?"

"You think my capacity for betrayal is limitless!"

"You will have to break your promise to one of us."

"Perhaps I will find a way to break neither promise— or even better, to break both. But for now, this audience is concluded. Good night, serene and honored Empress Denoi Vinga Gondwa Devodhrisha."

· 10 ·

THE EMPEROR kept his promise that Jehan Henghmani would live. And Jehan's promise to himself was kept too —he would bear his torment, even thrive upon it.

While the subterranean tunnels hummed with keening and gibbering, Jehan was quiet. He did not go mad like the others. Surrounded by madness, cruelty, and horror, with human flesh for food, Jehan did not go mad. He fought against the crippling of his body, and wouldn't let his spirit be crippled either. He convinced himself that someday the ordeal would end—and then it would be like waking up from a bad dream.

So he smiled in the faces of his torturers, the figments of his nightmare.

The cell door opened as it had a hundred times before. Grebzreh and a squad entered. They unlocked Jehan's chains, leaving only his hands bound behind his back.

"There'll be no dragging you in the muck this time," Grebzreh said. "Today is a special day. You have visitors."

Jehan snickered. "The last time I had a visitor, it was Emperor Sarbat."

"Well, it's not the Emperor this time. It happens to be your woman and two little girls."

Jehan's insides went cold and sour. "No," he said, "you're lying!"

"Why, you stupid ox, you don't think *family visits* are permitted here?" Grebzreh cackled. "Not only is this visit permitted, but in fact, the three of them have been transported all the way from Taroloweh, at no little expense to the Bergharran treasury."

"Damned liar, you're just baiting me!"

"Ah, Man Eater, you didn't think they could be found, is that it? But you see, the government makes special efforts to provide family visits for prisoners, and you should be grateful. It wasn't easy locating your girls. But one of your former comrades, I'm told, was kind enough to put the authorities in touch with them. You want to know who that comrade was? I'm afraid he asked that his name not be mentioned. He's a very modest fellow."

Jehan grit his teeth; he was sweating and sick with anxiety. One of his own men had betrayed Jenefa and the girls! The cur had probably sold them out to save his own skin. Most likely, once he'd revealed the hiding place, the Tnemghadi would have killed him anyway.

They herded Jehan into the largest of the dungeon's vaults, a spacious salon cut right out of the rock, carpeted and furnished with chairs, couches, and tables. Incongruous in the dreary dungeon surroundings, this gay-looking room was used for the entertainments of Grebzreh and his guards; wine jugs and goblets were cluttered on the tables.

There were a score of men lounging about, some resting their feet up on the chairs, a few already slurping wine. When Jehan was shoved in, they jeered at him with their eyes. Plainly, some sort of bacchanal was in prospect.

Nimajneb Grebzreh took a chair at the head of the room, leaned back, gulped a swallow of wine, and said, "All right, bring them in."

A door opened and a pair of guards pushed Jenefa and the two girls into the salon. They were thin and dirty, still dressed in the same coarse peasant smocks they'd been wearing when Jehan had left them hidden in the cave, months before.

The woman saw Jehan and bit her hand to stifle a gasp of horror at his mutilations. The two girls clutched at her. Guards held all three from rushing toward Jehan.

She stretched out her hand to him, straining against the guards' grip, her eyes bulged and mouth twisted into an anguished mask.

"Well, Man Eater, don't you even say hello to them? Aren't you glad to see them? Aren't you going to thank us for bringing them here?"

Jehan said nothing; he felt tears hot behind his eyes, and struggled against them.

Grebzreh guffawed to Jenefa. "Look at that, woman, he doesn't even bid you hello."

Now the warden rose and padded slowly toward her. He took his time. "It seems the pig doesn't even want you any more, woman. Imagine that!" Grebzreh ran his finger lightly down her bare arm.

Meanwhile, his men chained Jehan into a heavy steel chair that was bolted to the floor; he strained but was completely helpless.

Grebzreh patted Jenefa's hair and then tried to stroke her cheek; but she squirmed her head away.

Then he drew a dagger from his belt.

Nimajneb Grebzreh fingered the blade and his eyes glittered at Jenefa.

He slipped the blade under her smock at the shoulder and sawed through the fabric. Then the other shoulder, and the torn garment hung loosely on the woman. Grebzreh gave it a sharp tug, baring her breasts. Then he ripped the rest of the smock from her body.

Jenefa stood naked in full view of everyone. She did not try to cover herself or to resist; she had not flinched at being stripped, she had expected it. Her nostrils flared, but she was otherwise expressionless.

Grebzreh sheathed the dagger, and motioned to his men. Two of them seized Jenefa by the waist and, with a rough laugh, hoisted her up onto a table.

"Let's see you give us an Urhemmedhin dance!" the warden said. One of the men picked up a zindala, a crescent-shaped stringed instrument, and began strumming it. The others started clapping their hands in time with the music.

"Dance!" Grebzreh shouted; "I said *dance!*"

But she stood still on the table, rigid. Someone reached up and slapped her thigh, leaving a livid hand print. The clapping died down, and the zindala was cast aside.

"Oh, pretty woman, won't you please dance for us," Grebzreh satirically implored.

A wine jug stood on Jenefa's table at her feet, and she suddenly lashed out with a kick that sent it flying, spurting wine, to smash on the carpet.

"Now there's a clumsy dancer," Grebzreh said. "We'll

teach you to be more graceful. Come down from there."

When Jenefa didn't move, a man clambered up behind her and kicked her very hard on the small of her back. She was knocked off the table and across the floor, landing with a loud thump. The woman grimaced, but did not cry out.

"Maban!" screamed the girl Tsevni, and she began to whimper.

Two guardsmen wrenched Jenefa up off the floor and held her pinioned with her arms twisted behind her back. Grebzreh swaggered over to her, grinning. He stared at her with his hands on his hips.

"Let's see what an Urhemmedhin bitch tastes like."

He squeezed her face between his hands and pressed his lips against her mouth. When she managed to pull away, he laughed, and the men tightened their lock on her arms. Grebzreh ran his hands slowly down the front of her body, hard, his fingers leaving deep red trails. He squeezed her breasts until she gasped and tears came to her eyes, but she chewed her lip and wouldn't cry out.

Then they pushed her to the floor and held her down while Grebzreh methodically raped her.

Jehan, bound tight in the chair, shut his eyes and hoped the men would not see the throbbing at his throat and temples.

Grebzreh finished with Jenefa and stood over her spread-eagled body; the marks of his fingers still striped her flesh. Now he pulled her up by the arm. "So, the Man Eater apparently no longer wants this woman? Ha! Maybe he prefers boys!"

The warden shoved Jenefa to one of his men, who flung her down on the floor again like a rag doll, and raped her. The others hooted and guffawed, and when he was done, they applauded.

Grebzreh removed his shoe. "She's not enjoying it enough," he said; "let's see if we can make it better." He thrust his bare foot between her legs and massaged her. Then he giggled, and stomped down on her, again and again, while she writhed to avert the blows, and bright blood began to flow.

"Let's see if that helps."

Another of the men mounted the prostrate woman. When he forced himself into her, she shrieked.

"I thought that would do it," Grebzreh chortled.

One by one, each of the twenty guards took his turn.

Meanwhile, the warden seized eight-year-old Tsevni, tore her clothing asunder and, pressing her small body against the seat of a chair, violated her. The child screamed, as much from a vivid sense of something awful happening as from the pain.

All this Maiya Henghmani watched, with a guard's grip heavy on her shoulder. She was twelve, and understood what they were doing to her mother and sister. Her eyes were bound to the scene in terror-stricken fascination, knowing that momentarily she would join it.

Maiya wondered how it would feel: to be naked before all these strange, crude men, grabbing at her, beating her, invading her body in its most secret places. Her little sister, being passed from one to another, was howling in bewilderment, and her mother's cries were agony. On and on it went, yet Maiya remained untouched. Were they reserving her for some special abomination?

After what seemed like endless hours, all the men had taken their turns on Tsevni and Jenefa. The two lay on the floor, naked, dirty, bruised, hurt, with blood dripping down their thighs, breathing in gasps and not moving.

Jenefa knew the natural aftermath of rape. It is not only satisfaction of the flesh the rapist seeks, but the subjugation of his victim and of the males who would protect her. Jenefa knew what must come now.

Nimajneb Grebzreh lolled back on the couch, guzzling from a wine jug and splashing it red on his chin. He stared openly at his naked victims. Neither was attractive. Jenefa had never been pretty, and now she was past thirty with wrinkles, blue veins, and sagging breasts. Tsevni was too young to be anything at all, no more than an orifice to be used. Grebzreh deemed them both worthless now—except to give Jehan Henghmani pain.

The warden drew the dagger once more from his belt.

· 11 ·

GREBZREH tossed his dagger at Tsevni.

The girl flinched; the weapon clattered to a harmless stop at her feet.

"Pick it up," the warden commanded. Tsevni took the dagger by the blade and looked queerly at it.

"See that tall fellow with the moustache?" He pointed out a man whose name was Jephos Kirdahi. "I want you to kill him."

All of the men, including Kirdahi, laughed in merriment. But Tsevni didn't budge. What strange game were they playing now?

"Go ahead, little girl. I want to see you duel with him."

Jenefa screamed and covered her face with her hands. Quaveringly, as though in a trance, Tsevni walked toward the moustachioed Kirdahi. The man towered ridiculously over the little naked child clumsily brandishing a dagger. There was a tittering of amusement as Kirdahi drew his own long knife.

Jenefa was convulsed with sobs of shock.

Kirdahi's blade flashed; there was no pretence of a contest. In one deft thrust he opened Tsevni's belly. Her cry was dry and throttled; she stumbled backward, with a stunned look. Blood poured from the slash across her abdomen.

Kirdahi cut again. The girl's viscera tumbled out of the gaping wound, bloody and steaming. She stared down at herself in utter shock, and this time wailed horribly out loud. Finally the guardsman thrust his knife straight into her throat. Blood spurted and her cry was cut off.

Unable to watch any more, Jenefa leaped up and folded her child into an embrace, weeping and kissing her. But Tsevni was already dead.

Jehan, bound to his chair, held silent. He knew Jenefa

and his children were doomed. Whatever sadistic pleasure Grebzreh and his henchmen derived from this was secondary; their purpose was to torment Jehan.

He was as torn apart inside as poor Tsevni: he wanted to flood the room with his tears. But he couldn't let his torturers see the grief they were inflicting on him. These contradictory imperatives wrestled in him, and the hatred forced back the tears of love. He had come to hate these cruel men more powerfully than he had loved his children. He hated them all the more bitterly for having made him hate so deeply that he could let his children die without his tears.

Jenefa lifted her daughter's torn body into her arms. The blood poured over her, but she ignored it, and walked to Grebzreh sitting on his couch. They stared at each other.

She opened her mouth and bared her teeth.

Then she struck like a cobra and sank her teeth into his face.

The warden yelped, writhed, and grappled Jenefa around the neck, frantic to get free, to strangle her. But she hung on, still carrying her dead child, she hung on with just her teeth, tightening upon the man's nose and chewing on him like a jungle beast.

Grebzreh was blinded and unmanned by the agony, he couldn't get her off. His men stood still, for fear that he'd regard a rush to his aid as insulting.

Jenefa dropped the child, but hung onto Grebzreh, clawing at him with her stubby fingers. She got her hand under his tunic and savagely grabbed his testicles. The man stiffened, half paralyzed.

Then abruptly Jenefa's head jerked backward. She had his nose in her mouth, she had chewed it off. He hit her with his fist and she fell on top of Tsevni's body, the mangled nose flung from her mouth. He jumped down on her.

"Urhem bitch!" he shouted, beating her head with loud cracks against the hard floor. "Sow, bitch!"

He was beating her into a pool of blood; the back of her head was pulp, she was dead.

Agonizingly, Grebzreh stood up, the middle of his face a shapeless smear. He was tottering, and sank back upon the couch with a heavy breath, spreading his legs apart and moaning. A man put a wet towel over his face.

"Not a wet one, moron—damn, stop the bleeding." Dry rags were brought; these rapidly soaked through with blood.

The warden lay back very still, trembling with labored breath, and chafing that he could not tear Jehan Henghmani limb from limb for what his woman had done. But the Emperor's decree forbade it. Only torture was permitted—which seemed to have less effect the more severe it became.

But he would show this monster! There was still Maiya, and before Jehan's eyes, he would commit unspeakable atrocities upon her, chop her hands and feet off, flay the skin from her, slowly roast her black!

But no, he knew Jehan would take it all impassively, a demon sent from Hell, who endured all horrors in silence, tormenting his torturer.

Grebzreh opened his eyes and took the measure of this girl, Maiya. She'd been spared her parents' ugliness. In fact, she was uncommonly pretty, having a well-formed oval face with a tiny nose, high cheekbones, and blue eyes. Her skin was smooth and coffee-colored. Under her smock could be seen the bumps of a precocious bosom. Though still a child, she was already a woman, a most entrancing duality.

Grebzreh didn't lust for her now, though. What he yearned for was to break Jehan Henghmani; and his raping Maiya, or killing her, wouldn't break him.

But the girl *would* be violated, and it would bring Jehan down. There was only one man whose copulation with her could accomplish it.

"Bring the girl forward," Grebzreh said in a voice hoarsened by his wound.

Maiya was shoved into the middle of the room.

The warden gestured, and one of the men took her by the neck and with a few harsh tugs tore off her smock. Then he stepped back.

She stood alone, naked, with her hands clasped at her heart.

When Jehan had last seen her, she'd been nothing but a child. Now the girl seemed an angel, with her hands folded as in prayer, her big round eyes accentuated by terror. She had slim, shapely legs; a small, taut belly; high, pink nipples.

Jehan felt a strange excitement at having begotten such a lovely creature. But it was unbearable that she would, very shortly, be despoiled.

"Take a good look at her, Man Eater," the warden said. "She's a little virgin, eh?"

Jehan turned his eyes away and didn't answer.

"Do you like them young like that, Man Eater? Fruit picked fresh and juicy off the tree?" Grebzreh smacked his lips lecherously. "Ah, look at her breasts, such charming little breasts. Tell me, did you ever cuddle her and feel them bump up against you? Ever sneak your hand on them? Did you ever think of bedding her?

"No, of course not, she's your daughter. It would be vile, depraved.

"But, tell me, Man Eater: how long since you've had a woman? A long time, eh, for a stud like you. You must've had them left and right while you were rampaging through Taroloweh. Now I'll bet you're horny as a dog in heat, just burning to grab someone and stick it in her. Think about it. Think how much you want it."

Jehan snickered with disdain.

"Oh, you think I'm teasing you, Man Eater? But that's not so at all. I *am* going to let you have a woman today —*that* one," Grebzreh said, and his finger darted toward Maiya. He gave a sniggering laugh.

Jehan was startled by the calculated, savage baseness of it. Maiya was his daughter, but she was also very nubile, and in Jehan's straits, bedding her was not completely unthinkable. Grebzreh was tantalizing him, and what made it excruciating was the certainty of Maiya being raped and killed *anyway*. In this pit of horrors, would it matter that she be violated by her father as well?

Somehow, here, the incest taboo seemed singularly irrelevant. What difference did it make that she was his daughter? Even while he loved her as a daughter, he could want her too as a woman. If he loved her, why abjure making love to her?

He felt himself melting toward it.

But then his back stiffened. He remembered his vow— to be stoic in the face of everything, to show transcendant fortitude, and to gain power even from his ordeal. That would be his glorification, his apotheosis. The longing for it was a lust of the mind, hence a strength; and he was fighting now the lust of the body, a weakness. He knew the triumph of the body would mean the subjugation of the mind, and all his suffering would go for nought.

Jehan the man ached for Maiya's flesh; Jehan the superman forbade it.

He flashed his teeth wrily at Grebzreh. "If I say I want her, then surely you'd withhold her from me. This is all a perfectly transparent game. You're going to kill her sooner or later, so you might as well get it over with."

Grebzreh chuckled. "You're right that if I thought you really wanted her, then I'd use her only to tantalize you. But you are the one who is transparent. You hold yourself as some kind of exalted being; you wouldn't lower yourself to such a vulgar act. You'd hate yourself if you fornicated with your daughter.

"You do see it now, don't you, Man Eater? I want to watch you defile your daughter, defiling yourself in the process. I can't force you. But I can bribe you. *With her life.*"

Jehan answered in contempt. "You take me for a fool. You would entice me into this infamous act, and then you'd mock me by killing her anyway. I won't play your game."

"Very well, don't. Then she dies, at once, and very unpleasantly." Grebzreh gestured toward the mangled bodies on the floor before his couch. "But if you agree to my terms . . . then who knows? It may just be my whim today to fulfill my bargain. So make your choice: Will you commit incest upon her, or watch her raped and tortured to death?"

"You ask me to trust you that she won't suffer both. How can I?"

"How can you not? Between trust and certain death, is there anything to choose? At least, will you not give your daughter a *chance* to live?"

"And give you the pleasure of an obscene joke at her expense? Better that you are the first to defile her, not me. You would never keep your promise, you hate me too much. Once you'd gotten the performance you want, then you'd surely kill her."

Grebzreh clucked his tongue in feigned sadness, and

spoke softly to Maiya. "Girl, do you understand my proposal?"

Maiya nodded.

"Would you rather die, than have your father do what I ask?"

The girl looked at the bodies of her mother and sister. "No," she said with a shudder, "Paban, no!"

Jehan shut his eyes and clenched his teeth and fists. "I'd never know if you fulfilled your bargain," he protested to Grebzreh. "You could lead her out of here, only to cut her throat in the next room."

"That's true," the warden admitted readily. Then he slapped his knee in mirth. "Come now! You are trying to rationalize condemning your daughter to a certain and horrible death!"

Jehan's face suddenly purpled. "You filthy cur, why don't you just give me a sword so I can kill her myself and be done with it."

"You would rather stick a knife into her than your prick?"

Jehan refused to answer.

"This I should like to see."

Grebzreh ordered his men to place themselves in a wide circle around Jehan's chair, arming themselves with their longest pikes. Then, ignoring their warnings of its dangerousness, he had the prisoner unchained. Maiya was shoved into his arms.

They embraced, and wept. He stroked her hair, and she did not shrink from putting her hand up to his grotesque face.

Now Grebzreh tossed a small dagger to Jehan. "It's up to you, Man Eater. If you do nothing, I guarantee that she will be raped and tortured to death. You can slit her throat to spare her that. Or you can deflower her yourself. If you do, then I'll let her go free and unharmed."

Maiya whispered urgently, "Please, Paban, do what he asks. Please, I don't want to die."

Jehan had taken up Grebzreh's dagger, his knuckles were wrapped white around its hilt. Abruptly she pushed away. "Look at me," she said, touching her breasts and pubic fuzz. "Am I not a woman? Am I not pretty? Look at me, don't you want me?"

The onlookers sizzled with intense amusement.

"Stop, Maiya," Jehan said, "it's indecent!" His face was pinched with anguish. But now she threw herself back upon him, in the chair, seized his face in her hands and kissed him full on the lips. She took his free hand and pressed it against her breast and then to her groin, moving his hand to stroke her body, rubbing up against him. Jehan begged her to stop.

"We must, it's the only hope," she said.

And after months of cruelty and torture, he could not fend off the girl's caresses. She was warm and soft; she pulled open his tattered clothing and took his genitals in her hand. Jehan felt the blood gorge, his organ swelled; he couldn't fight it. He could hear the merriment of the guardsmen. His mind still protested, but he was smothered in a fog of lassitude by Maiya. His body didn't know she was his daughter.

Maiya impaled herself upon him with a gasp. Jehan tried to push her off, but as the act reached the consummation he could not prevent, he was frozen, drained of will.

Finally he did push her free, but it was over. All around him, Grebzreh and his men were reveling, hooting, capering.

Jehan shut his eyes. He could not bear to look at them, or at Maiya.

Then he remembered the knife still in his hand. He opened his eyes; Maiya was flushed, even triumphant.

Jehan Henghmani raised the knife.

Grebzreh shouted, and the guards rushed at him. The tip of a pike hit his knuckles and the knife went flying. Before he knew what happened, he was chained once more. The girl was led away.

Jehan drooped in the steel chair. Grebzreh was looking hard at him. Despite the bloody bandages covering half the warden's face, he was smug with victory.

He had promised to set Maiya free; but Jehan knew there was no reason for that promise to be kept.

Warden Grebzreh stood smirking at Jehan with his arms folded on his chest. He stood that way a long time, and Jehan knew he was laughing.

Then the warden turned, without a word, and walked away.

· 12 ·

THE EMPRESS DENOI DEVODHRISHA looked up at Tnem Sarbat Satanichadh, sitting inscrutable on his throne.

Sarbat had promised to send her home to Laham Jat. But he had also promised her death to Sirimava, and the Empress wondered which promise he would keep.

The answer was not revealed in his face, as he announced in the solemn tones of state business that the Empress would be granted leave to make a journey to her native land, of indefinite duration, to commence the next morning. She would convey Bergharra's salutations to the Court of Laham Jat and bear gifts for its leading officials.

Now the Empress approached the throne and bowed low. In the flowery formal Court language, she affected gratitude at the granting of her request. Then the other nobles, one at a time and in strict order of precedence, came up to her and bowed. Some brought small gifts. They all bade her farewell and wished her a pleasant journey. The first was her son, Prince Shayuq, and then came old Yasiruwam Irajdhan.

"You shall be missed," said Irajdhan. He was the only one to say this.

"I shall miss you too, Yasir," she told him.

One of those who said farewell was Sirimava; the yellow-haired concubine bowed deeply and kissed the Empress' hand. Her lips formed a queer smile.

The Empress deliberated whether to tell this woman how Sarbat was deceiving her. That would scotch her little smile, but it might be dangerous. So the Empress smiled back at Sirimava and said nothing.

Regardless of Sarbat's promises, the Empress and everyone else present knew that this farewell was a final one. If she were truly permitted to leave, she would not return; she would never see Irajdhan again, nor her husband, nor her son. At this, she felt a great calm, even relief. She did not lament her departure from this Court, whether by exile or by death. She was liberated, and it was exhilaration that she felt: should death come, then this would be the proper time to die.

The Empress Denoi Devodhrisha, accompanied by her maids-in-waiting, retired from the throne-room to her private quarters. She would quickly complete the preparations for her journey, and would go at dawn. By both necessity and choice, her entourage would be a small one; there was little she wished to take with her.

At the antechamber of her suite in the palace, three guardsmen were posted.

"There are a few heavy packages I'd like taken out to the wagons," the Empress said.

"Your Majesty," the captain answered, "that isn't what we're here for."

"Then won't you do me the favor of helping anyway?"

The captain did not respond, except to place his hand gently on the Empress' shoulder, directing her toward her inner room. With a quizzical look, she crossed its threshold. It was empty.

"Yes, what is it?" she asked impatiently. "Speak up."

"By order of His Majesty, the Emperor, you are to remain in this room."

"What? For how long?"

"Forever," the captain said, shutting the door upon the Empress Denoi Vinga Gondwa Devodhrisha.

Jehan Henghmani was locked back into his cell, all strength sucked out of him as though by a thousand leeches.

This day he had been spared the red-hot irons, the knotted whip, the razor knives—but of all the days of his torment, this was far the worst. He'd been forced to sit helpless watching his woman and child raped and cold-bloodedly killed. He'd been seduced by his own daughter, to the vast amusement of his torturers. His stoic exterior had been stripped away to reveal pulpy weakness, a weakness that could not stave off the spears of grief, and that had stayed his hand from cutting Maiya's throat.

That, at least, would have aborted her suffering. Now Jehan's mind was enflamed with visions of what those cruel men were doing to his little girl.

They would never let her go. They had raped Tsevni and Jenefa, but Maiya was the choicest of the three. Jehan's flesh still tingled from the soft warmth of her touch. . . .

He beat his fists against his head to expel these illicit pictures, to escape the mire of wickedness into which she had seduced him. He huddled, trembling, quaking, trying not to think at all.

Shock still numbed him. The full horror hadn't yet penetrated, and he knew it. Only gradually would he come to grips with its enormity. So much comfort had he taken in Jenefa's devotion, and in his daughters, but that was snuffed out now.

Nothing remained but Jehan alone. Tormented daily, mauled in body and soul, still he clung to life. It was life only in the barest sense that it wasn't death, it was merely somethingness against the black void of nothingness. But it was life.

Jehan thought back to the resolve he had taken at the start of his ordeal, and began to sense how the destruction of his loved ones fitted—indeed, had been necessary. It placed their destruction, the most rending torture of all, behind him. If he survived it, he would survive all else.

He had learned this day that he was no superman. Today they had humbled him, had brought tears to his eyes. Yet, they had failed to break him. So now, superman or not, he would never be broken. In defeat, he was given knowledge of his ultimate victory.

On this most horror-swept of days, Jehan Henghmani felt himself reach a new plateau of purification. On this day of death, he achieved a new consciousness of life.

Locked back in his cell, alone, he had been freed, at last and forever.

Soon afterward, he was fed the first small pieces of what appeared to be a woman. Not until he was given an intact hand did Jehan realize it was his own Jenefa.

He stared at the hand, on its wooden platter, and hesitantly reached out to touch it. What had been so familiar was now so grimly altered; the hand that had caressed him warmly was now cold.

He lifted it to his heart, just as he had warmed Jenefa's hand when she'd been chilly, that first night in her father's grain field, gazing up at the stars. He closed his eyes and tried to conjure her alive and with him. He kissed the hand, held it against his cheek, its fingers entwined with his own.

"Give me strength," he whispered. "Give me nourishment, Jenefa, your final act of devotion. And with the strength you give me, let me transcend."

For the last time, he kissed her hand.

They gave him, piece by piece on those rude wooden platters, the rest of her. And praying for strength, he consumed her.

Then, Tsevni.

"You came from my flesh, and there you return. May you build my flesh that I shall transcend."

His daughter Tsevni too he kissed, and like the dragon Sexrexatra who devoured its children, he ate all of her. When there was nothing more of Tsevni, he was certain what was coming next: his lovely Maiya. He cringed at this, afraid to see from her remains what tortures she endured before dying.

But Maiya was not delivered to him; instead, it was next another nameless peasant corpse. And when he saw this, he reflected: could this mean Maiya had escaped? After all, Grebzreh had promised her freedom. Could that strange, demented little man have inexplicably held true to his word?

But Jehan banished such thoughts from his mind; there was no use in them. If Grebzreh withheld Maiya's body, this was obviously to engender in Jehan a vain hope that she lived. Never would Grebzreh reveal the truth; at most, he might bait Jehan by hinting at it.

She was dead, Jehan decided. He would not permit himself to imagine otherwise, even if he was never given her remains to eat.

Perhaps Grebzreh had eaten her himself.

The warden was a driven man now. On his face he wore a pointed little pyramid of silver, tied on with thongs, to replace the nose Jenefa had bitten off. It made his face an inhuman mask like a harlequin's, but perpetually cold and hard; he seemed almost a golem assembled by some wizard.

From underneath that silver nose-piece, his breath would come strained and hissing, a noise that echoed constantly through the dungeon's passageways, for Grebzreh never left them now. He slept little and never went out to the surface. He prowled the muddy tunnels hour after hour, hissing through his silver nose, racking his fevered mind to think up new tortures for Jehan Henghmani.

In the warden's twisted thinking, it galled him that Jehan's own nose had been cut off at the start of his imprisonment. Grebzreh itched fiercely to bite Jehan's nose off, just as Jenefa had done to him; but this was not possible, and moreover, Jehan's loss of his nose seemed so much less than did Grebzreh's loss. Jehan had even, somehow, escaped the curse of hissing breath. The warden was obsessed by his silver nose. It was a constant reminder of what Jehan had caused him, a constant goad to torture Jehan ever more savagely.

And the glint of that silver nose was a goad to Jehan as well, reminding him how Grebzreh had murdered his woman and children. It goaded him to withstand the tortures ever more stoically.

Jehan Henghmani seemed made of a steel even tougher than their torture implements. Grebzreh would watch his prisoner smile under torture, and he would stammer with fury, beating his own guardsmen with a stick to make them work harder on Jehan. But the prisoner would only laugh, and even taunt him, call him "Silver Nose" and mimic his hissing breath. And Jehan would remind him of the Emperor's decree that he must never die.

"Yes, that's right," Grebzreh would say, "you'll never be allowed to die, you hellish monster. I'll make you suffer till the end of time!"

BERGHARRA—Tnemghadi Empire, cast brass "tvah-dik," or rent token, circa 12th Century. Given to sharecroppers as proof of rent payment, i.e., a receipt. Uniface with a sheaf of rice above a monogram, "A.K." in Tnemghadi script. Breitenbach 3106, 41 mm., fine–very fine. (*Hauchschild Collection Catalog*)

· 13 ·

THE TWENTIETH YEAR of the reign of Tnem Sarbat Satanichadh was not a good year in Taroloweh.

The only encouraging event in this year 1176 was the demise of Jehan Henghmani's brigand troop. But nature treated Taroloweh more harshly than a score of bandit armies.

This year's crop was small. Afflicted by too much sun and too little water, much of it was withered and puny. Poverty and hunger were the result. Few sharecroppers had much left after paying their rents, taxes, and temple tribute. Many of them defaulted, and so were forced off their land, sometimes sold into slavery to make up the rent due. Even where a family was only a little bit short, the rent collectors—the Tvahoud—would take everything, expropriating the land and seizing the people as slaves. Some peasants sold their own children in order to at least keep their land.

And many abandoned their farms to save at least their freedom. They took little else but freedom with them, for they had nothing left. Dispossessed, they had no place to go. On the open roads they traveled in despair, searching without knowing for what.

Sometimes they would form gypsy-like encampments, living in make-shift tents, hovels, or the open air, scrounging for the dregs of food they could cadge or steal from farms and other travelers. There wasn't much of it; the marks were just as poor as the thieves.

These victims of the hard times found the Tnemghadi authorities callous toward their plight. But the Tnemghadi did not ignore the problem; their aim was to restore order. The army moved in to disperse the gypsy camps. It would not suffice to break up a camp, only to have its members resume wandering the countryside; and so the army would sweep down and wipe them out, trampling through the camps on horseback, setting fires and slashing at everything that moved. There was no compassion; if allowed to escape, these wretches would only starve to death, or cause more trouble. So all—old men, women, babies— were cut down. They fought back with bare hands and teeth, and those who would survive the massacres would flee into the hills, to scratch out an almost animal existence, or starve.

The Viceroy of Taroloweh, Assaf Drzhub, viewed the situation with mounting alarm. The Viceroy loathed what he considered wanton bloodshed. From the Vraddagoon, the government palace at Arbadakhar, he sent letters to the army commanders, begging them to stop the massacres lest they provoke a general uprising. But the generals answered bluntly that there were too many people and not enough food.

Yet the public granaries were stuffed with produce collected as taxes. Drzhub wanted to open up the granaries to feed the peasants, but he knew this would drive down prices and the powerful barons wouldn't stand for it. The Viceroy wrote directly to Ksiritsa painting a bleak picture of conditions in the province, begging for a decree opening the granaries.

But the Emperor replied that he would not deplete tax collections to feed Urhemmedhins; instead, he promised to send more troops.

Soon, the streets and roads were clogged with homeless, hopeless people, the victims of disease and hunger, with wandering children, bellies bloated and their arms and legs like sticks. Many were the fallen corpses in the streets and roads, left for days before they could be burned. Many of those who survived did so eating cats and dogs and cowhide and the bark off trees.

Outbreaks of violence were on the rise, even in the towns. Tnemghadi citizens would be set upon by hungry mobs; some, in fear, would shave off their telltale eyebrows. Sometimes the mobs would even attack Tnemghadi homes; news of gypsy massacres would often spark such retaliation.

One day in the town of Dorlexa, an old Urhemmedhin had the folly to shout a curse at some Tnemghadi horsemen as they paraded by. They ran him down and trampled him to death. This murder committed in full public view instigated a barrage of stones thrown from all sides, and the frightened soldiers reacted by running other people down, slashing at them with their swords. But the townspeople weren't scared off by the bloody ruckus. They came running toward the scene like lemmings, almost throwing themselves beneath the horses' hooves. Soon the men were dragged down from their mounts and hacked to pieces with their own swords. Even the horses were slaughtered, and the hungry people cut steaming chunks of meat out of their carcasses.

Then the mob, gathered now to several hundred strong, ran amuck. They stormed the temple, smashing through its gates with the press of their bodies. None of the priests within escaped; some were trampled, kicked and beaten to death, some thrown from the temple's tower, and at least one was hung upside down from the ceiling and burned. Meanwhile, the stores of offerings hoarded up by the priests were ransacked, along with all the gold and bejeweled temple ornamentation. Furniture was piled up for bonfires, and the smoke suffused the temple. But the great marble structure itself resisted the flames, and so the mob tore the temple apart block by block, with ropes and levers, sending the huge blocks smashing down and crushing some of their own number in their frenzy.

This orgy of destruction at Dorlexa was quickly ended by a Tnemghadi army battalion. The rioters—and many innocent citizens—were butchered. Afterward, additional taxes were imposed on Dorlexa to finance restoration of the wrecked temple.

Samud Mussopo and his family survived this grim year 1176. They had lost their gaar, but there had been a little rain upon their lands, saving much of their crop, and their lives. They'd scraped together enough to pay their rents and taxes, but there wasn't much left over for food, and through the winter, they had no choice but to eat their goats and chickens. This got them past the bad year, but left them completely dependent on the rice crop. Unless it was good, they were finished.

The next year's crop was indeed a little better. Yet, because they had no more livestock—and no milk or eggs—the year was harder than the one before. The story was the same for many in Taroloweh, and even with its improved crop, 1177 produced more misery, swelled the ranks of the dispossessed and continued the attrition of starvation.

That fall, too, Samud Mussopo's eleven-year-old daughter, Zina, fell sick. They did not know why, for there was no doctor, and there was nothing they could do for her but pray. But prayers proved unavailing, and the girl was buried by Samud himself in the rice field.

Samud grieved deeply for his daughter. Still, had it not been for the loss of that one mouth to feed, the Mussopos might not have endured through that winter at all. It was a close thing. Spring greeted them with their skins tight on their bones, their cheeks hollow.

These years were bad for their landlord, too. Lord Adnan Khnotthros' sharecroppers had done poorly; many couldn't pay their rent and some had even left the land. A year later, acres of it were still lying fallow; there was no one to buy it. Lord Khnotthros was not starving, but it was impossible to keep up with the expense of running the Syad-Rekked, his manor.

Consequently, in the year 1178, Lord Khnotthros raised his rents. It seemed to him a logical step. No one would tell the Lord that a higher rent would mean more defaults, and more land fallow next year. And even if he realized that, he had little alternative. He was already in debt for 1178; he would have to worry about the next year when it arrived.

Gaffar Mussopo sprinted across the field toward his father. "They're coming," he called out, "The Tvahoud!"

The rent collectors came in an enormous wooden wagon, with wheels wider than a man is tall, pulled by a team of gaars, two men driving them, two more riding their backs, and a third pair in the wagon itself. One of these was the Ram-Tvahoud, the Chief Collector; each estate had one. The Khnotthros Ram-Tvahoud was Uthsharamon Yarif, a short, ferret-faced Tnemghadi, finely dressed and greatly loathed.

This Yarif was the final arbiter of the rents. If he was peeved at a farmer for withholding a daughter who'd caught the Chief Collector's eye, that man could be marked down as delinquent in the rent. It wouldn't matter whether it was true or not. The man, and his family, would be ruined.

Lord Khnotthros was feared and hated, but remotely—the peasants never saw him. When they thought of Khnotthros, they would picture his delegate, Yarif. Uthsharamon Yarif they saw and knew, and it was Yarif who was the focus of their fear and hatred.

"The Tvahoud are coming, Paban!"

Samud Mussopo squinted into the distance. He could see the great wagon approaching, raising a plume of yellow dust high into the sky.

"So let them come. We're ready; we have the rent. They increased it, but we made it somehow. We may starve, *but we have their damned rent for them.*" He didn't try to conceal his bitterness from Gaffar. There could be no pretense after their gaar was stolen, and certainly none now, with food taken from their hungry mouths.

"If only there were some way we could cheat them," the boy said.

"It would be death for sure if they caught us in a game like that."

"It may be death, if we *don't* save some of that rice. And there's nothing we can do when *they* cheat. Those damned Tvahoud jackals, they always have to skim off a little extra before they'll give you that precious little tvahdik piece."

"Well, everybody knows they do it. Khnotthros knows it; it's really part of the rent."

"Like an extra little tax," Gaffar said with tight-lipped irony.

"There's nothing we can do."

"We can pay them the proper rent and not one ounce more!"

"And what if Yarif marks us down short and holds back the tvahdik? Will you contradict him?"

"No. I'll cut his throat."

"Gaffar! Don't talk that way. Sometimes I think you mean it, and I worry for you."

"You *should* worry. For all of us. For everyone."

The colossal wagon, creaking loudly under the heavy load of produce already collected, lumbered gradually to a stop in front of the Mussopo hut. Yarif climbed down a ladder, carrying his leather-bound record book, and he dusted off his cloak. The family was standing outside, waiting for him.

"Let me see," Yarif grumbled, thumbing through his book. "Samud Mussopo, is that you?"

Samud bowed his head. "Yes, Ram-Tvahoud."

"And wife Yaveta, son Gaffar, daughter Zina. Where's the girl?"

"She died last fall, Ram-Tvahoud."

The Chief Collector wrote a notation on the page. "All right, Mussopo, your rent is twelve and a half shokh."

"Yes, it's all measured out. Everything's in order, in fact, the baskets are brimming over." Samud waved his hand with a toothy smile at the shokh-baskets, lined up in a row. He hoped the Tvahoud would be satisfied with the extra amounts he had added to make them more than the minimum necessary to appease their greed.

Yarif picked up a handful of rice from one of the baskets and gave it a cursory look. "Good, Mussopo. But let's just make sure your shokh-baskets are accurate measures."

"Oh, they're accurate all right, Ram-Tvahoud. They're the same baskets as we've always used; they've been checked before. I wouldn't cheat!"

"Then what are you worrying about?" Yarif smiled amiably. "It can't hurt to make absolutely sure."

Samud shrugged his shoulders quizzically. He knew his baskets were accurate, Yarif himself had tested them before. But now the other man atop the wagon handed down to Yarif an empty basket to make a new test, and Samud was suddenly struck with a drowning feeling. All at once, he understood.

It was the same as when he first grasped that the priest Relleth meant to have his gaar. His head swam, boiling with rage; but he held his tongue.

Gaffar did not. "That basket's too big!" he blurted out.

Yarif's eyes flashed. "Just what are you suggesting, boy?"

"He meant nothing," Samud rushed to say.

"Let him speak for himself. What did you say, boy?"

"My name's not 'boy,' it's Gaffar Mussopo."

Yarif struck Gaffar across the mouth, sending him stumbling, almost knocked off his feet. His lip was split and his mouth filled with blood.

"Watch your insolence, you puny Urhem swine. You're lucky I don't have you flogged, or worse."

Gaffar, tottering and red with fury and hurt, said nothing.

"Empty one of your baskets into ours," the Chief Collector snapped at Samud, and the man quickly obeyed, with his hands shaking, spilling a little rice. The rice that had been overflowing in Samud's shokh-basket did not even fill Yarif's.

The Ram-Tvahoud's face was stern. "This is quite serious, Mussopo. It looks like you're at least two shokh short in all. But that's not the half of it: you obviously tried to cheat us. It will go pretty hard on you if Lord Khnotthros finds out. What have you got to say, Mussopo?"

Samud swallowed in discomfort. "I will make up the difference," he murmured.

"Well, of course. But I would still have to report your cheating to the Lord. On the other hand, since you tried to cheat by two shokh, if you make amends now by paying two shokh extra, possibly we could let you off with that."

"Four shokh more then? I'm . . . I think . . . yes, Ram-Tvahoud, I guess I can manage that. Barely."

Samud said the last word inaudibly. He ducked inside the hut and dragged out the extra baskets, feeling as though in a trance. He couldn't think straight, couldn't gauge how much he'd have left after paying these extra four shokh—more than four, by Yarif's dishonest basket! But clearly there wouldn't be much left—not enough to see the family through the winter. In handing over this rice, he was giving up survival itself. Would it be better to refuse? But Samud couldn't think straight.

Numbly, he filled Yarif's basket four times.

"Very well," the Ram-Tvahoud said, handing over the brass tvahdik piece that meant the rent was paid. "You'll watch your step in the future. And you'd better teach that loutish son of yours some manners."

"Yes, Ram-Tvahoud."

"You can be grateful I'm letting you off this easy."

"Yes, Ram-Tvahoud."

Uthsharamon Yarif climbed back up into the wagon, bulging with rice, a lot of it rice that Lord Khnotthros would never see. Yarif looked down and raised his hand.

"Until next year," he said, but he knew it wasn't true. Yarif could see what was happening to Khnotthros' lands, exacerbated by the Lord's stupid act of raising the rent, and he foresaw ever thinner pickings from his chief collectorship. This year would be his last, then; Yarif would take as much as possible, and leave wealthy. In the process, he would destroy the peasants, thereby destroying Khnotthros. But before the Lord would realize this, Uthsharamon Yarif would be far away.

Mussopo bowed once more as the gaars were whipped and the huge wagon began to rumble away. Like Yarif, he did not believe this scene would ever be reenacted. Yaveta and Gaffar, watching the dust balloon as the wagon disappeared, did not have to be told.

"Well, we're lucky for one thing at least," Samud said. "I thought he'd kill you, Gaffar. It was a good thing you didn't say anything more."

Gaffar did not take his eyes off the yellow dust cloud. "Words are good for nothing anyway."

He realized this fully now. Words could not bring back Rassav, the gaar. They could not restore his dead sister, or the rice Yarif had stolen. Words could not bring back the blessed days of Urhem.

So Gaffar had nothing more to say; instead, he had things to do. In his enflamed mind, it was all unclear just what he must do, except for one thing.

If he stayed here, the Mussopos would all starve. He would have to run away to have a chance of saving himself, and his parents. And he would run away to fight the Tnemghadi. This fight would start close to home:

He would kill Uthsharamon Yarif.

· 14 ·

GAFFAR MUSSOPO LAY ABED with his open eyes glittering in the dark.

He tingled; his lip was swollen and still hurt dully from Yarif's blow, but more than that, he tingled with a passion. There was so much injustice! So much oppression! The Tnemghadi would not let them live; it was defiance to even think one's own way. Only in hiding could the southern people venerate their god Urhem. To speak his creed of life and love in public would mean swift death, and even underground it wasn't safe; half the Urhem worshippers could turn out to be Tnemghadi spies. Forbidden their own religion, the Urhemmedhins were instead forced to bow before the Emperor's idol and to swallow the tenet that life was meaningless, a human being worthless, existing only at the whim of a reasonless tyrant. This bankrupt morality filled not just the Tnemghadi prayers, but seemed to underlay their every deed.

Gaffar seethed with his outrage and tingled with fright: not only at the prospect of striking forth alone, but at the thing he knew he had to do.

In the morning, as soon as his parents rose, he told them brusquely of his decision to leave. His mother embraced and kissed him. She did not try to dissuade him. Neither did Samud, who understood and nodded with solemnity.

"Don't worry," the boy said, "I'm sixteen; I'll be all right." He did not mention his determination to kill Uthsharamon Yarif.

"Where will you go? Will you go far away?"

"I don't know."

"Take some rice to eat on the road," said Yaveta.

"No, keep it for yourself. I'll find what to eat, I won't starve."

"Will we never see you again? How will we know if you're all right?"

"Perhaps I'll come back some day—when things are better. Or else I'll send word. This isn't goodbye forever."

The couple kissed their son on both cheeks, and hugged him tightly, patting his back. "We'll be praying for you, Gaffar," his father said.

"Pray for all of our people. And I will pray too," Gaffar said, "to Urhem."

"Pray for the *Ur-Rasvadhi!*"

Gaffar grinned. "Just for you, Paban, I'll pray for the *Ur-Rasvadhi.*"

Samud grinned back, his browned skin crinkling deeply. Gaffar put his few belongings into a little rucksack, and headed for the road.

Many times he turned around to wave back. Samud and Yaveta, standing outside the hut, kept waving too, following the boy toward the horizon with their eyes, until not even the dust of his wake could be seen against the ochre landscape.

Gaffar was heading for the Syad-Rekked, the centuries-old manor house of the Khnotthros estate, where he would find Uthsharamon Yarif. He knew in what direction it lay, but had never been there before.

As he walked barefoot on the shoulder of the dirt road, Yarif obsessed his thoughts to the exclusion of all else. To Gaffar the Ram-Tvahoud was the incarnation of everything Tnemghadi; every villainy ever perpetrated upon Urhemmedhins was behind Yarif's smug face. Clenching his fists, the boy burned with his murderous resolve. And yet, he hadn't the least idea of how to carry it out.

That didn't deter him, though. Once he reached Yarif, Gaffar was sure his ingenuity and courage wouldn't fail him.

The Syad-Rekked was less than thirty lim from the Mussopo farm. Walking briskly, Gaffar reached it in the afternoon. He had imagined it a dark gloomy fortress, towering with walls of stone. But instead the Syad-Rekked was a complex of buildings upon a low hill, many of them wooden, and only one of them imposing. This structure, three-storied, well built, and crisply clean with red and white trim, was obviously Lord Khnotthros' lair. The subsidiary buildings circled around a wide courtyard, deeply scored with wheel-furrows and mud puddles. Chickens and pigs ran about loose, and horses and gaars were tethered to posts. The whole complex was surrounded by a wooden fence.

Choosing a direct approach, Gaffar walked up the road and addressed himself to the gatesman, a burly Urhemmedhin seated on a stool: "I wish to see Ram-Tvahoud Yarif."

The gatesman sneered down at Gaffar. "And just what does the likes of you have to do with the Ram-Tvahoud?"

The boy feigned humility, lowering his eyes. "Please, sir, tell the good Ram-Tvahoud that a young worm wishes to make his honor an apology for having spoken foolishly yesterday."

"An apology?" the gatesman said with contempt. "You think a man like that's got time to listen to sniveling apologies?"

"Please sir, at least tell him. I've come a very long way."

"Well, the Ram-Tvahoud's not here, anyway. He's out collecting rents and won't be back till late tonight."

"I'd like to wait for him. Could you tell me, please, where he lives?" This was the information Gaffar needed.

"He lives over in that house," said the gatesman, pointing. "But of course, I can't let you in. On the other hand, I suppose there's no harm in your waiting here outside the gate."

Having learned where Yarif lived, Gaffar would just as soon have been turned away. But, to maintain his pose, he thanked the gatesman profusely for allowing him to wait, and then sat down in the shadow of the fence. He tried to be as inconspicuous as possible, keeping his face hidden as carts and horses clattered in and out through the gate.

Hours passed and the sky darkened. The dusk had brought rainclouds. It began to drizzle, for the first time in many weeks. Gaffar huddled against the fence, cursing the gatesman and cursing what was ordinarily considered a godsend: the rain.

After it had fallen dark, and been pouring for some

time, the gatesman called out from his little covered booth. "Hey, boy, you still there?"

Gaffar answered that he was. He hadn't dared arouse suspicion by slinking away.

"You must be soaked, boy. You may as well come in here under the gate, before you get washed away."

"You're very kind, sir," Gaffar said as he accepted the invitation, brushing the water off his hair.

When the moon was well up, the great wagon of the Tvahoud lumbered up toward the gate. Canvas had been spread over the rice-laden baskets to protect them from the downpour, and Yarif was holding a sheet of canvas over his head.

"Ram-Tvahoud," the gatesman shouted, pulling the gate open wide, "there's some boy here, wants to apologize to you."

"What?" Yarif said sharply. "You idiot, can't you see it's raining? Get out of the way!"

The wagon rolled past, into the muddy courtyard. Yarif had not even seen Gaffar.

"Well, you heard the Ram-Tvahoud," the gatesman said. "I guess you've waited for nothing."

Gaffar faked a forlorn pout. "Perhaps I'll try again tomorrow. Thanks, anyway; I'll be going now."

"Where can you go in this rain?"

The boy shrugged. It was coming down in heavy iridescent waves, sizzling loud against the ground, and Gaffar again cursed his ill-luck to be caught in it.

"Look, boy, I shouldn't do this—but do you see that barn there? I won't say anything if you sneak in there and sleep, if you leave by dawn."

Gaffar grabbed the gatesman's hand and loudly thanked him. "You don't know what you're doing for me!"

"Never mind that, just make sure no one sees you."

Gaffar had spoken the truth—the gatesman didn't realize what he was doing for the boy. And the rain, which he had cursed, had become his murder weapon.

· 15 ·

THOSE PRECIOUS DROPS OF WATER! Millions welcomed the rain because it fed their crops. For Gaffar, it was the rain that had gotten him inside the Syad-Rekked, past the gatesman. Moreover, the rain had kept all the inhabitants indoors, snug in their beds. No one saw Gaffar skulking about, breaking into Yarif's house. The steady noise of the rain covered his footsteps; the rain was a lullaby that kept Uthsharamon Yarif asleep while Gaffar slipped through the house and found the bedroom.

The noise of the rain crackling upon the ground had also covered Yarif's gasps when Gaffar pinned him on his bed and choked him to death.

Finally, the rain even covered the boy's escape, up to the roof of the barn, then a wild leap over the fence and to the ground outside. But for the soggy ground, Gaffar might have broken a bone in that jump. Right to the end, it was the rain that was his weapon.

Away from the Syad-Rekked he ran, splashing through the puddles, heedless of the downpour, exulting in it, holding up his hands and letting it wash over him in cascades. In the dark he stumbled upon a road, and knew only that it wasn't the road by which he'd come. He followed it, not knowing where it would take him, except that it led away from the Syad-Rekked.

Despite having neither slept nor eaten in almost two days, the boy skipped and ran with exhilarated vigor. He was thrilled by his adventure. He had killed Uthsharamon Yarif! He had murdered a Tnemghadi Ram-Tvahoud! The villain had been roused from sleep to find Gaffar Mussopo's hands around his neck; and while his life was being choked out, Yarif had recognized the boy and understood the reason he was dying. That made Gaffar's triumph all the more delicious.

103

He ran the rest of the night. The rain had stopped and the morning sun had dried him off before Gaffar could think about anything except his glorious deed. Not until then did he realize how tired and hungry he was. And then, too, it hit him suddenly: fixed so single-mindedly on the assassination, he had wasted a grand opportunity to steal food or even money from Yarif's house!

Gaffar slumped down by the road and smacked his head, castigating himself for his stupidity. Yarif was a rich man. How much gold might have been taken from him! Gold that Yarif had stolen in the first place from Urhemmedhins—including Gaffar's own father! Gold with which he could have fed himself, saved his family, even used to fight the Tnemghadi!

But in his blind lust to kill Yarif, he had never thought of gold. Now the opportunity was gone, and he was hungry.

"Well, there's nothing to be done about it now," Gaffar lamented; and he consoled himself with the likelihood that he would never be apprehended. No one had seen him but the gatesman, and Gaffar had never mentioned his name. The boy had now become just one more poor peasant wandering down the roads, indistinguishable from countless others. It would be pointless for the Tnemghadi to even hunt for him.

Just the same, prudence dictated that he flee Khnotthros' territory. Indeed, he had left it before dawn; this terrain was wholly unfamiliar. Gaffar felt only a small lump of homesickness. He sensed a certain rightness in that he had taken from this land, and from his family, all they had to offer; it had been good to him, but now it was time to move on. The world was wider than the Khnotthros lands, and would hold much for him.

It was many months later, in a gypsy camp, that Gaffar learned of the aftermath of Yarif's murder. Gaffar had changed his name and concealed his deed. When the story was related at a campfire, he sat rigid and quivering, desperate against giving himself away.

According to the story, when the Ram-Tvahoud was found strangled in his bed, Lord Khnotthros was both infuriated and frightened. If a mere boy could murder a Ram-Tvahoud, why not the Lord himself? So the gatesman was replaced by a squad of guards, and the fence strengthened. Meanwhile, the hunt was on for the killer. Gaffar's absence from the Mussopo hut was noticed although, of course, people were running off constantly during those troubled times. On the other hand, some of Yarif's men recalled how their master had struck Gaffar the day before the murder. Since the boy also roughly matched the gatesman's description, the mystery was deemed solved.

Samud and Yaveta Mussopo were tortured, to make them reveal their son's whereabouts, but they insisted they didn't know. Then Khnotthros decreed that even though the murderer had escaped, the highest punishment would nevertheless be meted out, as a lesson to anyone else who might contemplate such a fantastic crime. Administered upon the innocent, the punishment would appear all the more terrible! Accordingly, Gaffar's mother and father were dragged behind horses to the Syad-Rekked, and there publicly put out of their misery: burned at the stake.

That was the story Gaffar heard at the campfire, and he was compelled to listen in silence.

He had become a vagabond. At the start, he had vaguely dedicated himself to fighting for the freedom of his people; but after his one great act, he had his hands full just staying alive.

There were many like him, the dispossessed, the starving poor, all wandering aimlessly along the roads, and Gaffar fell easily among them. It was a scrabbling life; his clothes wore out and he was reduced to scarcely more than a loincloth. Always there was the search for food, it was the universal focus. Sometimes a little rice could be picked off a field; sometimes Gaffar would rob travelers. But itinerants were cautious now and rarely carried much. If Gaffar risked his life in a daring hold-up and came away with a loaf of black bread, he would count himself lucky.

The unlucky surrounded him: the roadsides were littered with them, bones jutting out under stretched skin. He would see mothers carrying wasted babies, flies crawling on their faces.

Hunger preyed upon him, shadowed him. If he could assuage it today, he knew it would afflict him tomorrow. Often for days on end the land was barren, dry, gray.

Gaffar would feel light-headed, stiff with torpor, unwilling even to lift himself. Somehow, he would do it, and keep on. His own body became to him an accursed, alien encumbrance. The bones bulged, ribs and spine standing out in bold relief along his torso, his knees and elbows were knobs. Bruises wouldn't heal, sores stayed with him; he collected them like tattoos.

He was only one of faceless thousands. Occasionally he would travel with some kindred fellow, but these partnerships were fleeting, and the boys would lose each other before long. Sometimes they would never even learn each other's names.

The road was the way of life, but once, out of inertia more than anything, Gaffar settled in with a gypsy camp. He would sleep in a ditch dug into the sloping ground; there was not even a piece of cowhide to cover it. Sometimes, though, the others in the camp would manage to get a fire going, and he would spend the night huddled in its woozy warmth.

This was a camp of drifters, none of them with an identity. Although they kept glumly to themselves, their collective namelessness was in some strange way a leavening, even unifying factor. They spoke nothing, shared nothing, yet there was a tacit jointure among these people stripped to their barest skin of humanness.

One of them was a girl of seventeen. She looked much older, with a worn, washed-out face. She was small and slender, narrow-boned, with large eyes and dark hair down to her waist that somehow, despite her hunger, retained its sheen. She was alone, her family destroyed in some convulsion of which she refused to ever speak. The girl spoke very little at all, but that was true of most people in the camp. Gaffar did manage to learn her name, which was Geyl. With very little ado, she joined Gaffar in his ditch-home.

Geyl had, of course, been raped several times. Among these bedraggled people living in the open, it could scarcely be avoided. But at any rate, for Gaffar, she happened to be the first lover. They exchanged few words, but that didn't matter; there was little to be said. Even to himself, Gaffar remarked little about her. Instead, he numbly accepted her coming into his life. He was too enervated to be excited about it.

What she provided was a quiet comfort to him, a safe harbor. There were in truth only a few times that they made love, but it was sweet to hold her small body close to his while he slept. He liked her most when they snuggled together in the warmth of a fire, and she would press her head to his shoulder, with her soft hair cascading over him. In that warmth, Geyl would smile, and that was such a rare thing.

But the warmth was always too brief. The story was the same for all the camps like this: the surrounding lands were soon stripped clean. Ever larger distances had to be searched for food. A few people would move on; many would stay, rooted to the ground by some hypnotic force, long after all food was gone. If the Tnemghadi didn't strike the camp, its people would starve, one by one, until the last dessicated one of them was dead.

The exodus had begun from Gaffar's camp, and he was worried. Yet he was afraid to go, an inarticulate fear. He knew that he and Geyl would have to leave eventually, he even told her so, but they kept putting it off. She did not want to go either, and he feared losing her unless they stayed. As the food ran ever thinner, leaving was the only thing they ever talked about; but inertia held sway, and they could not summon up the resolution to go.

Finally, one night, Gaffar found himself returning home empty-handed; his foray had not turned up a scrap to eat. This decided him once and for all: He would take Geyl by the hand and they would leave the doomed camp. They would make a life for themselves on the open road.

With that decision hot in his mind, he reached the camp and found it destroyed by the Tnemghadi.

Everything had been trampled under their horses' hooves. The hovels made of hide or branches had been torched; some of them were still smoking quietly. The campsite was strewn with mangled bodies, left right where they'd fallen. No one would bury them; they would rot in the sun.

Gaffar stood frozen for an endless moment. What he had so carefully decided was shattered, but he could not make the effort to reassemble anything in his mind. His eyes dumbly scanned across the scene of carnage. He could hear moans, and in the moonlight, here and there, a limb would weakly move.

He simply could neither absorb it nor do anything about it. He did not shake or weep. He did not scream out Geyl's name, he did not search for her among the dying injured. She might have been whimpering for help at his feet, but all he could do was look on with blank eyes, and then he turned away and kept on walking down the road.

Gaffar would someday come to understand what he had done that night, in walking away from the wrecked encampment and from the people, including his own Geyl, who might have been salvaged from it. That night all faith, all love, all sense of humanity, were cauterized out of him by bitter fire.

That dark night was long, but not endless. Gaffar grew away from it, but he did not forget the night he had left those people, and his Geyl, and left his own faith among their mangled bodies.

Those poor souls of the camp could never be redeemed. But the same was not true of Gaffar's spirit.

· 16 ·

"KIRDAHI!"

The tall, moustachioed dungeon guard heard his name called out as he plodded through the corridors. As a rule, the guards ignored the howlings of the prisoners. But the one who had called out was Jehan Henghmani; and Kirdahi stopped.

"Kirdahi—I want to talk to you."

"You do, eh?" The guardsman attempted condescending sarcasm, but it was half-hearted. Despite the bolted door separating him from the prisoner, Kirdahi, like everyone, feared Jehan Henghmani.

"What's your first name, Kirdahi?"

"What do you need to know that for?"

"Is it a secret? Just tell me your name, that's all."

"It's Jephos," the guardsman answered grudgingly.

"*Jephos Kirdahi . . .*" Jehan pronounced the name slowly, exaggerating the stress on the final syllable. "So now I know the full name of the man who murdered my daughter Tsevni."

"What are you talking about?"

"Surely you remember. It was only a couple of years ago when you cut her down with your knife. When you killed my little daughter."

"It was really Grebzreh," Kirdahi argued, chilled by this sudden mention of the nearly forgotten detail. "I did only what he ordered. She was going to die one way or another; what did it matter which one of us held the sword?"

"But it was you, Jephos Kirdahi. And for that, I'm going to kill you."

Kirdahi sucked in his breath.

"I killed your executioner, and a couple more of you dogs since then. I haven't gotten you yet, Jephos Kirdahi, but you've just been lucky up to now. Next to Silver Nose, you're the one I most want to get my hands on. Silver Nose always keeps his distance, but you can't do that, and one of these days, I'm going to get you. However, you do have an alternative."

"What are you talking about?"

"Look, Kirdahi—I want vengeance, but what I want much more than that is freedom. You can give me freedom, and if you do, your crime will be expiated. My hatred for you will be replaced by gratitude. What does it benefit either of us to remain enemies? Let us in fact become allies. In here I may be nothing, but on the outside, I can be everything. So join me—for your own sake."

Kirdahi pondered this. "If I help you to escape, what's to stop you from turning around and taking your revenge on me anyway?"

"You are shrewd, but think on this: I want more than just freedom. I want everything, do you understand? *Everything!* I will need an army—literally. I will need tough men like you. But if you fear me that much, then you needn't come with me. Surely if you fear my vengeance, you are better off if I am gone from here; so just give me the key.

"You see, Kirdahi, your choice is pretty simple. You will either help me, or you will die. I swear it."

The guard snickered. "You swear to kill me, yet you expect me to set you free. No thanks. I'll take my chances with you locked up."

Kirdahi had heard enough. He walked swiftly away, glad to put some distance between Jehan and himself. The cell door, and Jehan's chains, provided Kirdahi with little sense of safety; the man trembled.

Afterward, Kirdahi sweat cold buttons every time he passed that cell, and Jehan Henghmani even haunted his dreams. The worst of it came whenever it was Kirdahi's task to work the torture on Jehan. Yet somehow, the guardsman couldn't think of running away. He was bound into Jehan's nightmare as tightly as Jehan himself.

They all were prisoners: Jehan, the silver-nosed Grebzreh, the guards. Kirdahi sometimes thought it was an insane dance-macabre being performed by the warden and Jehan, the warden tearing up Jehan's flesh, but tearing up his own soul. Grebzreh became so maniacal in his obsession that the guards began to fear him almost as much as they feared Jehan. The nightmare seemed endless and all-consuming.

Jehan's threat to Kirdahi was no idle one. The day came when the guardsman clumsily approached too close. Quick as a beast of prey, Jehan seized Kirdahi's throat in his teeth. The man screamed and flailed. Others rushed to rain blows upon the prisoner, but he ground his teeth around his victim's larynx. Finally, one of the guards pulled Kirdahi away by the shoulders; Jehan was left with part of Kirdahi's torn neck in his mouth. The guardsman was lucky to escape with his life.

He was the guard, and Jehan was the prisoner—but Kirdahi knew that it was he himself who was the condemned man.

Soon afterward he came in the dead of night to Jehan's cell with a key.

It was not quite dawn; the grass was wet and the sky streaked pink and gray. Along part of the horizon there was still blue darkness, and a few stars glimmered.

Silhouetted against that sky were the great blockish walls, bulking purple-black, the walls of Ksiritsa, the City of the Dragon. Built by three hundred thousand Urhemmedhin slaves, those walls had endured for seven centuries. Unconquerable, they loomed as a cliff against the early morning sky.

Behind the walls, its tallest buildings peeping up, was the city itself. It was barely stirring at this hour, a slumbering behemoth.

The sun was coming up, splashing white and crimson on the city, showing up its angularities of planes of light and stark black shadows. The hill behind the walls was coming into view, and rising from it were the spires and towers of the Palace of the Heavens. They seemed so far away that they were not within the realm of Man. On those marble palace walls and copper roofs, the beginning sunlight burned with fiery incandescence.

Jehan Henghmani looked back upon this dazzling scene. Here, he had spent three years that seemed forever. He had seen this vista only once before, when he was carried up the road tied like a bundle in an open cart; and he hadn't imagined that he'd ever see it, or any other sight, again.

But now he was looking on it once more, leaving it. He was still alive; alive again, and more than ever.

He kept his gaze on the glowing city. The vision was arresting, and for more than just its beauty.

"*Ksiritsa*," he pronounced solemnly. He held his arm out toward the city, saluting it, and taking leave of it.

And then, wondering if he would ever look upon its walls again, Jehan Henghmani turned from gloried Ksiritsa.

BOOK TWO

•

ZIDNEPPA

· 1 ·

JEHAN HENGHMANI looked with a glittering eye upon the green hills of Taroloweh.

Only one eye was left to him after his thousand days of horror in the dungeon. Looking upon these hills, a landscape once so comfortably familiar, it was difficult to imagine that the last three years had really happened.

But there were plenty of souvenirs attesting to those years' reality. He had literally left part of himself at Ksiritsa, and Ksiritsa had left itself with him. The pain was not left behind; it lashed him with every step he took, burned him every waking moment and assailed his nights. There was no help for it; he would suffer as long as he might live.

And if he'd left part of his very flesh at the Dragon City, so too was there part of him buried in these soft hills. "Three years ago," he said, "I was a man to reckon with in these hills. I had an army of a hundred, and the fear of the entire province."

"And now," said Jephos Kirdahi, "you have nothing."

"No. It was then that I had nothing. Now, I have everything."

"I don't see what you mean."

"Not even with your two eyes? But when I had two eyes, I didn't see either."

Kirdahi shrugged and squatted in the grass, to watch Jehan stand like a monument with his eye fixed on the horizon.

Strangely, its magnetism for Jehan was heightened by the way he'd once raped this land. Throughout the years in the dungeon, these hills had pulled at him. He had dreamed of this day, and it had sustained him through the torment. And yet, to be once more in the hills of

Taroloweh seemed very much a miracle, something he should never have dared hope for.

His hand encircled the purple landscape, and then he pointed. "In that direction lies Arbadakhar. And over there, Zidneppa, and the sea. We aren't ready for them yet; but there is a village a few lim from here, named Sratamzar. It will do for now."

Kirdahi nodded, and hefted up their sack of belongings. He had decided to follow Jehan with grave misgivings. This was to save his neck, lest his complicity in the escape be discovered. Out of fear, he had fled Ksiritsa, and he was likewise afraid to flee Jehan. Kirdahi was now an outlaw, and there was at least some safety in Jehan's experience at outlawry. And he was afraid to run away, too, lest Jehan come after him.

Since the escape, Jehan had never mentioned Tsevni. While he had promised to absolve Kirdahi in return for setting him free, Jehan had never uttered the words of absolution. Kirdahi still feared the monster would kill him.

It was night when the pair arrived at Sratamzar, in the northeast corner of the province. The town was nestled along a dirt road between two hills, like a locket hung between a woman's breasts. It had no street but the dirt road; Sratamzar was scattered desultorily on either side of it. The town had very little, but it did have a run-down inn.

They knocked at its door, and it was opened by a white-haired old cripple. What he saw was a pair of road-worn men, matted with yellow dust. Their clothes were threadbare and faded, patched in places, their faces burnt dark by the sun and grown with rough beards. Their only possessions were in a small sack slung over Kirdahi's shoulder.

But even so, Jehan was a sight to behold. Enormous in size, his face a labyrinth of mutilations, he was an apparition that would have stricken the innkeeper speechless, even had there never been a Jehan Henghmani. And of course, Jehan Henghmani had not been forgotten in Sratamzar. The old innkeeper's eyes bulged.

"What are you gawking at, old fool?" snapped Jehan.

"N-nothing, sir. I'm sorry."

"My name," Jehan said, "is Brashir Atokhad, and my companion is Sahyid Rama. Do you have lodging for the night, or perhaps a few days?"

The innkeeper peered hard at "Brashir Atokhad," studying the scarred features. Then he prostrated himself in a deep bow. "Yes, honored guests, it will be a privilege to give you the finest accommodations in our humble town, and without charge."

"What are you babbling, old man? Honored guests? What an idea! You must be mistaken. We haven't much money, but we will pay for our lodging."

"Just as you wish, good sir, whatever you say. A room for each of you. And please tell me if there's anything else you need?"

"A woman," said Jehan.

"Yes, that can be arranged, certainly."

"How much?"

"The youngest and the prettiest, only two tayel apiece."

"Good," said Jehan.

Upstairs, Kirdahi came to Jehan's room and grabbed him urgently by the arm. "What folly; you're known here! The innkeeper recognized you. Some of the others in the inn have recognized you too, I'll wager!"

"I hope so," Jehan replied evenly.

"Then what's the point of using false names?"

"I want these people to know who I really am; but my purposes must remain concealed. So, let them believe I want to hide my true identity. Whatever falsehoods people believe about me are to my advantage."

"But word of your being here will reach the authorities!"

"Yes. But it should reach certain others first; criminals are always smarter than the authorities."

"Who is it that you hope to meet?"

"We will know when they come. We'll give it two days; if nothing happens, then we'll move on."

"But the Tnemghadi are sure to come after us, once they've got this lead."

"I hope so. It mustn't be suspected that I'm in the Emperor's pay. I must convince people that I wasn't set free to spy for the Tnemghadi."

"Then what about me?" protested Kirdahi. "I *am* a Tnemghadi."

"Yes," said Jehan, with an enigmatic smile.

Later that night, there was a knock on Jehan's door. "I am Araxa," came a female voice. "I was sent for."

Jehan pulled her by the arm into his room. "I am Brashir Atokhad," he said, but the girl made no reply; she was petrified to look at him in the candle-light. Never in her life had she seen anyone so huge, or so horrible a face. Her impulse was to turn and run, but she steeled herself, remembering what she'd been told about this special customer. While she thought the ogre might strangle her in his bed for sport, she was too afraid of him to run away.

So, stiff with fright and revulsion, Araxa sat down on Jehan's bed and removed her clothes. Then she lay back and closed her eyes, hiding her clenched hands beneath her. She lay rigid as Jehan came to her.

And he came at once, and in a moment took his great body off her. He'd had no contact with any woman since unwillingly defiling his daughter Maiya. All he could think about, suddenly, was Maiya.

He shoved Araxa's clothes into her hands, together with a silver coin.

"Is that all?" she asked, perplexed.

"Don't ask me questions. Just go."

The girl hastily donned her clothes, and then looked at the coin Jehan had given her. It was a pastari piece, which he'd robbed from some traveler.

"But this is too much money," she argued.

"Just go!" Jehan said with barely contained fury.

Araxa hurried out.

· 2 ·

IN THE MORNING, Jehan and Kirdahi came from their rooms into the modest main hall of the inn. A few of the wooden tables were occupied by people eating breakfast; a pair was playing cards and another man was stretched out asleep. Jehan took a table and motioned Kirdahi into a seat.

The moustachioed man leaned forward and whispered, "Well, what now?"

"We are going to have some food, and then we are going to play dominoes." And indeed, after a meal of rice cereal with gaar's milk, the innkeeper was asked to provide the dominoes. A well-used set was brought out, with cracked, stained, faded tiles.

The pair spent the day playing dominoes, breaking only for another meal late in the afternoon. Hardly a word was exchanged between them. Only whenever someone new entered the room would their eyes flicker up briefly.

Travelers came in and out, through the door and down the stairs, asking directions or seeking other information. A few came in to buy a meal; or to deliver stores of food, wine, candles, and other necessaries; or just to pass the time of day with the old innkeeper. Jehan glanced at all of them, only to return his attention to the dominoes. But all of them looked long and hard at the huge, disfigured guest. They stared at him, stopped cold with boggled eyes, but no one dared speak to him.

"Don't turn around," Kirdahi whispered once. "That man who just came in is talking to the innkeeper in a low voice, and he pointed at you."

"Good," Jehan said, and put another domino down on the table.

So went their first day in Sratamzar.

*   *   *
119

On the morning of the second, they came down once more into the main room. The card-playing pair and a few others of the previous day had left. But there were four new arrivals: one who sat alone, and a trio sitting at a table with two conspicuously vacant chairs.

These three were the men for whom Jehan was waiting.

One of them, a swarthy fellow with unkempt hair, was a stranger. But the second, Jehan knew well: he was Hnayim Yahu, a heavyset thug who had been a member of Jehan's old bandit army. This Yahu was a violence-prone bully with a crude personal magnetism, whose loyalty to Jehan had been nevertheless deep-seated.

The third man Jehan knew better still: his name was Nattahnam Ubuvasakh, but he was generally called "Leopard," a nickname earned by his slinky fleetness and savage cunning. The Leopard, a handsome, long-legged man with curly black hair, had been close to Jehan since the very start of his brigand career. Indeed, it was Jehan who first joined Ubuvasakh's gang, not the other way around. He was the Leopard's protégé, but it wasn't long before the pupil usurped the master's place. As the gang grew, it was Jehan who emerged as its leader.

In the end though, living up to his name, the Leopard was one of the few to slip through the Emperor's clutches. *I should have known that fellow'd get away,* Jehan murmured to himself. And then a bitter thought struck him. Maiya, Tsevni, and Jenefa—and probably Jehan himself—had obviously been betrayed by one of the gang. Was the Leopard that betrayer?

Through all the years, the man had never openly voiced resentment at being displaced as gang leader. Yet Jehan had always sensed the resentment must be there. Cast into the shadow by Jehan, had the Leopard bided his time, waiting for the chance to square accounts?

Jehan wondered. If Ubuvasakh had been the betrayer, why did he come here now? Might he still be working for the Tnemghadi? But Jehan realized that just as he had reason to suspect the trio, so must they reciprocate that suspicion.

Jehan and Kirdahi came down the stairs to the table where Yahu, Ubuvasakh, and the stranger sat. Without a word they took the vacant chairs. There followed a long, awkward silence, which Jehan did not see fit to break.

Then the Leopard suddenly leaned forward. "Well, it's really you," he said.

Jehan took private amusement at this self-conscious, noncommittal opening gambit. "Of course," he responded in a fatherly tone. Then he asked a blunt question: "Who is the stranger?"

"His name is Kamil Kawaras; he's been a comrade of Yahu and me."

"Now tell me how you managed to get away, three years ago."

"They do not call me *Leopard* for nothing. It's you, Jehan Henghmani, who has some explaining to do. I point out to you that we three are not here alone. So you will explain how it is that you are still alive. You will explain how *you've* managed to get away, and you will explain this Tnemghadi friend you have."

Jehan leveled his one good eye at his inquisitor. "All right; now listen to what I say. You suspect that I'm in the Emperor's pay, sent back here to smoke out the remnants of the old gang. You are amply entitled to suspect that. But the answer is simple: Just look at me." He held up his hands, displaying their missing fingers, and pointed to his grotesque face. "I am alive because death was considered too lenient. I was condemned to live, tortured every day; it went on for three years. I saw my woman and daughters raped and murdered. Do you suppose I'd agree to work for the men who did all that to me?" Jehan shook his head.

"This man with me is Jephos Kirdahi, a dungeon guard who helped me escape. It took a little persuading—that scar you see on his neck. He can be trusted now. After all, for setting me free, he must be one of the most wanted criminals in Bergharra."

Hnayim Yahu, of such past loyalty, was skeptical. "Then why did you come near this place, where you were sure to be recognized? It must be that you have nothing to worry about; they won't come after you because you're in league with them."

"Obviously I came here expecting to be recognized. But if I had come to betray you, wouldn't I have done so under cover, not by opening up this sort of confrontation?

I deliberately put myself in danger by coming here—danger both from the Tnemghadi and from men like you who would distrust me. But the Tnemghadi would pick up my trail sooner or later—I can scarcely disguise myself —and my only chance is to get help. I simply gambled that some of my old friends would find me sooner than the Tnemghadi."

"Then why did you use a false name?"

"If I had come here brazenly calling myself Jehan Henghmani, then you'd surely have thought I was without fear of the Tnemghadi, and must be in cahoots with them."

"You take us for fools, Jehan, explaining your trickery to our faces!"

"On the contrary, I take you for shrewd men who understand that sometimes even the truth needs a little help to make it convincing."

"So—are you asking us to hide you?"

"No! I refuse to spend my life hiding in holes. I've already spent three years out of the sunlight. The kind of man I once was, I shall be again."

This was a lie.

"I shall be that kind of man with your help or without. But know that if you turn your backs on me today, we will be enemies. There will not be room for all of us in Taroloweh."

"You have overlooked one of our alternatives," said Leopard Ubuvasakh. He spread his cloak a few inches, revealing a hefty blade. Yahu and Kamil Kawaras were likewise armed; and of course, they had boasted of hidden confederates.

"Indeed," said Jehan calmly, his one eye boring into the Leopard. He went on to say that many had lifted arms against Jehan Henghmani, and had died for it; that three years of torture hadn't brought him down; and that their threat of violence was ridiculous. All of these things he said with his one eye, because they did not require words. The Leopard understood.

"I gambled in coming here," Jehan said. "Now you gamble by trusting me."

The Leopard nodded, and extended his open hand.

· 3 ·

SITTING IN A GAARHIDE TENT beneath the trees, Jehan surveyed his growing army.

First there had been just Kirdahi, who belonged to him like a slave, cowed by fear into obedience. And then there came three more into Jehan's nucleus: Nattahnam Ubuvasakh, Kamil Kawaras, and Hnayim Yahu, who followed him from Sratamzar into the forested hills, bringing their cronies with them.

In these gentle green hills Jehan had been born, and now he turned to them for his rebirth. Hidden away in these soft hills like an embryo emplanted in a uterus wall, Jehan's new army grew. Like an embryo it quietly took form, the mother scarcely aware of its presence.

Ostensibly, it duplicated the bandit troop he'd led before: highwaymen, murderers, desperadoes, outcasts, tinhorn adventurers some of them, all throwing in with Jehan because his enterprise seemed promising. Times had been rough, and many would jump at this opportunity. Some had even once been peasant farmers who had lost their land through drought or the cheating of the Tvahoud. Some had been among the roving gypsy bands, until the Tnemghadi had caught up with them. But most in Jehan's new army were simply toughened criminals, some of them the worst scum in Taroloweh.

Jehan did not scruple against taking in these vicious brutes. He needed them, for the present.

He was openly using his old name again. So the rumors started filtering through the countryside: once more there was a "Man Eater" lurking in the hills. They said he was a horrible, disfigured monster, a titan of inhuman strength. No wonder he had named himself after the legendary Jehan Henghmani! And there were even some who swore this was the same Jehan Henghmani who supposedly had been killed three years before. It was said he had miraculously survived, or was such a demon that he'd returned from the country of the dead.

But such talk was scoffed at. Few could believe Jehan had escaped the ax, and Urhemmedhins did not accept that anyone could come back out of the grave. All the same, though, the advent of this new Man Eater made the people of the province shudder. They remembered vividly the swath of fire and death cut by the old Jehan. Would this new one copy him in more than name alone?

And while the peasants shivered at the rumors of this new Jehan, there were those who sought him out: the dispossessed, with nothing more to lose; guerrilla bandits who had prowled the hills and roads. They were attracted by the tumultuous history attached to Jehan Henghmani's name, even if they didn't believe it was the same man as the one of old. They sought him in the hills, but he wasn't easy to find; he kept his men in tents and always on the move, because the Tnemghadi were on the lookout for him too.

Every new recruit was handled gingerly, lest he be a Tnemghadi agent; but there was no way to be sure of anyone. So Jehan kept looking over his shoulder, and kept his men to a nomadic life.

And indeed, it wasn't just betrayal by some new recruit that he feared; he looked uneasily at everyone around him. Not the least of his qualms were focused upon the handsome Leopard Ubuvasakh. If there was any resentment lingering from the old days, the man was adeptly hiding it. But was he the one who had betrayed Jehan before? Would he do it again?

Meanwhile, the Leopard was a cunning veteran of the hills, and a useful man to have around.

Then there was this swarthy stranger, Kamil Kawaras. Here was a quiet, enigmatic man, totally unconcerned about personal comfort. He was slovenly about his clothes and meals, never grumbled about anything, yet he did become exercised upon a single topic. Detestation of everything Tnemghadi seemed to be the man's consuming passion. So violent were Kawaras' imprecations that Jehan would wonder at his sanity. But Kamil Kawaras possessed a cold intelligence, and the Leopard kept him always close.

And then, Jephos Kirdahi. The murderer of Tsevni had

to live in constant terror that Jehan might one day exact vengeance after all. Would he act to preclude that—perhaps by dispatching Jehan while he lay sleeping in his tent?

But Kirdahi was outwardly unwavering in his loyalty, and like the Leopard, he was useful to have around, attending to the little details of running the encampments. And whenever anyone complained about there being a Tnemghadi in their midst, Jehan defended Kirdahi.

Hidden in the wooded hills they lived from hand to mouth, in rude tents or even in the open air. Unlike the old days, there were no raids of plunder and rapine upon farms and villages. Instead, there were only roadside hold-ups, and occasional modest forays at night to steal some bread or chickens.

That was how Jehan insisted it must be, in the face of demands that he organize a major expedition. The men did not lust for blood so much as they chafed with inactivity. And while they'd joined Jehan with dreams of gaining riches, they were still as poor and hungry as ever.

But Jehan held them. He urged patience upon them: patience would bring strength, and the strength would ultimately bring success. Not forever would they slink among the hills, he told them. He had great plans; riches and glory awaited them.

He hypnotized his men with grand visions of the future, and yet, he did not dare reveal to them the full breadth of his visions. It was fortunate for Jehan that he was speaking to the garbage of Taroloweh—for smarter men, with more to lose, would have snickered at his words and walked away. It was the fortune of these men that they were not that smart. Jehan had all the brains his army needed, as long as it was stupid enough to follow him blindly.

And it was not just a vision of the future with which he held them. More important was the vision of Jehan Henghmani himself. They gaped in wonder at this man, this towering hulk, a beast of mangled flesh with the strength of steel. They knew their leader was no ordinary man.

He never asserted that he was the original Jehan Henghmani. But he never told them that he wasn't, either.

· 4 ·

Standing on a hilltop, Jehan Henghmani looked out upon the City of Zidneppa.

There was little to be seen, for it was past midnight on a moonless evening. Jehan had waited for this darkest night, and now, although the city was spread out at his feet, only a few stray lights marked its presence. Out beyond, other lights bobbed slowly up and down, the lights of the boats moored in Zidneppa's harbor. Farther out, there was a blackness deeper than the night, unbroken by lights or stars. That was the sea.

Zidneppa was far from a great metropolis on the scale of Ksiritsa; but it was the second city of Taroloweh, supporting a considerable fishing industry, and a major link in the chain of trading ports along Bergharra's coastline. It was a city with a permanent Tnemghadi garrison, an opulent temple, and was the site of one of the two largest granaries in the province.

In the old days, Jehan would never have dared to attack a city like this. He'd had no wish to bring down all the wrath of Ksiritsa upon his head. But now, Jehan's objectives were quite different. And so he stood at the threshold of Zidneppa.

It was the fifteenth day of the month of Nrava, early in the year 1181.

Zidneppa had gone to bed the night before as it had for a thousand years. Fishermen had pulled in their boats and nets, merchants boarded up their shops, laborers went to their hammocks.

In the early hours of the fifteenth of Nrava, few heard the gentle thumping footfalls of Jehan's army slinking through the portals of Zidneppa. There were no walls to keep it out. It moved swiftly, softly, and as one being, like a snake, wending its way through the deserted streets, beneath the closed windows. It did not waver, intent upon its prey.

The imperial garrison was bedded for the night in its stonewalled compound, adjacent to the marble temple. A few sentries were in position, and a scattering of other soldiers patrolled or caroused through the streets. The few encountered by the snake on its way were easily swallowed.

Outside the compound, the sentries heard the hissing of the snake.

"Who goes there?" they called out, but the snake gave no answer, and in this moonless night, could not be seen. Jittery at this invisible threat, the guards stood poised with their hands on their sword hilts.

"Who goes there?" they called out again.

And then the snake was all at once upon them, no longer a snake but an army of men jumping out of the darkness. There were brief cries of surprise, terror, pain; it lasted only seconds. The handful of guards, who could offer scant resistance to the sudden onslaught of armed guerrillas, were cut down like reeds. In seconds, the compound was rendered unguarded, left like a fat helpless rabbit within the coils of the snake.

Inside, the soldiers were groggy and disoriented by the commotion shattering the night without warning. They rubbed their eyes, groping to light their candles and find their clothes. They never had a chance. The furtive invaders streamed through the compound before their victims could bring sword to hand. All were slaughtered, cut to pieces in the darkness by invisible hands.

Swept away with the soldiers' lives was Tnemghadi rule at Zidneppa, eight hundred years abruptly brought to an end in the early hours of the fifteenth day of Nrava, 1181.

After the fall of the garrison, the rest was merely mopping up.

"Now let's slit the throat of every damned Tnemghadi we can find!" urged Kamil Kawaras in the flush of triumph.

"No!" Jehan answered instantly. "Follow my orders. Kirdahi and Leopard, take some men with you to round up the soldiers. Look through all the taverns and brothels. But don't kill them; take them prisoner."

Kirdahi and Ubuvasakh left at once.

"Now, Yahu, you find the Mayor. Remember, I've told you where he lives. Tell him nothing; just bring him here.

"And you, Kawaras—you make sure this garrison is searched and every soldier accounted for. Anyone alive must be taken prisoner; any wounded will be patched up."

"But they're the worst Tnemghadi swine!"

"Never mind that, just do as I say."

There was no point in arguing with Jehan, nor could he be disobeyed. Kawaras saluted and briskly set off on the appointed task. Meanwhile, torches were set up to light the courtyard of the compound, making it the impromptu headquarters of the operation. The courtyard bustled with activity as Jehan issued orders right and left and men rushed in and out, all details proceeding according to plan.

Soon Hnayim Yahu returned with his important captive. The Mayor of Zidneppa, appointed long before by the Emperor Tnem Al-Khoum Satanichadh, was a shriveled old man, his hair a brittle white brush. He was dressed only in a nightshirt.

"Just what do you think you're doing?" the Mayor blustered. He did not know the breadth of what was happening. "What are you ruffians doing in the compound?"

"I am Jehan Henghmani," was the answer.

"Oh," said the Mayor, a quavering syllable. He sank into a nearby chair, suddenly perceiving the enormity of the situation.

Jehan handed the old man a wooden board with a sheet of parchment tacked to it, and placed an inkstand on the arm of the chair. "Now, you are going to inscribe a decree. Write it exactly as I tell you."

The Mayor complied with a resigned sigh. He dipped the pen into the ink and wrote what he was told.

"First: in your capacity as Mayor, you appoint Jehan Henghmani to be Chief of the Municipal Constabulary of Zidneppa, with all of the powers of that office. You appoint Jephos Kirdahi the Deputy Chief. And you appoint Nattahnam Ubuvasakh to be the Magistrate.

"Next: write that you, the Mayor, are an enemy of the people of Zidneppa. As a Tnemghadi, you had no right to rule an Urhemmedhin city. That you have been guilty of great crimes against the people."

"Excuse me, what crimes are you talking about?" The Mayor looked up with a crooked, slightly defiant smile.

"You have oppressed the people, you have robbed them, you have starved them when your granaries were full of rice."

"I had no authority to open the granaries."

"You don't seem to understand what is happening here. Just write down what I tell you; its literal truth is irrelevant. The only thing that matters is that you are a Tnemghadi mayor. Now write down that you personally expropriated tax money for your private use; that you failed to observe even the Tnemghadi law; that you ignored the rights of the people you ruled; that you profited from the sale of Urhemmedhins into slavery, and that you took their children as concubines."

The old man's pen scratched many lines.

"Is that all?"

"Not quite. Last of all, write that you are resigning as mayor on account of your crimes, and that you regard yourself fit only for an ignominious death."

The old man hesitated; then, with his hand shaking, he wrote the final lines.

"Sign it."

The Mayor obeyed, affixing his name in crabbed letters to the foot of the document. Then Jehan seized it out of the man's hands and pretended to read it carefully.

"Good. Now, Mayor, you may have the honor of cutting your own throat. I will give you that as a boon."

Jehan placed a dagger in the old man's lap. He reached out a gnarled finger to touch the blade, but recoiled from it almost instantly. "I can't," he whispered hoarsely.

"You poor old relic," Jehan said to him, "you're hardly worth killing."

The sun was coming up to begin a new day in Zidneppa.

A large wooden table had been dragged out into the main public square, fronting upon the temple and the military compound. At this table stood Jehan Henghmani and his junto: Yahu, Kawaras, Kirdahi, and Ubuvasakh. All around was their ragtag army of bandits, and lined up against the wall were the scores of bound Tnemghadi prisoners. Quite a few of them bore bloody bandages. Out of sight, in the courtyard, a squad of Jehan's men was already at work digging a mass grave for the dead.

And in the streets, in the corners and shadows, the people were gathering to see what was afoot. As the sun rose, wild rumors spread quickly through the city. No one knew exactly what had happened.

And then, in terror-hushed whispers, the name sizzled through Zidneppa: *Jehan Henghmani.* The people cringed to think this monstrous, bloodthirsty killer had taken over their town! In the early hours of that morning, they frantically hid away their silver and their money, buried it in clay jugs, and locked their womenfolk in closets. Many even grabbed up a few belongings and fled the city.

But many too, drawn by curiosity in spite of fear, came to the public square.

For an hour they watched and waited, all eyes upon the legendary monster, who stood conferring in low tones with his associates, while the bandits came in and out of the army compound. He was waiting for Zidneppa to come fully awake. Soon, the sun was fairly up in the sky, and the streets around the square, the windows facing it, and even the rooftops were dark with clusters of onlookers.

Then, abruptly, everything quieted down. Yahu, Kawaras, Kirdahi, and Ubuvasakh all took seats flanking Jehan. He remained standing, towering taller than ever. His ghastly ruin of a face confronted the crowd; some felt nausea and turned away, but others stared at him, compelled by the fascination of the grotesque.

Jehan let them gawk at him for a long time; he turned slowly so that all of them could get a good look. Then, without preliminary, he picked up the parchment written by the Mayor, and called the old man forward. The giant stood with his arms folded on his chest while the ancient man read aloud his self-indictment, exactly as Jehan had dictated it.

When the public reading was completed, Jehan took a chair. In turn, Ubuvasakh stood. "As the duly appointed magistrate of this city," he announced, "I pronounce the sentence of death upon the Mayor."

Two men marched out from the ranks on cue, took

the Mayor by his arms and escorted him into the very center of the square. They pushed him down to his knees, and stepped to the side. The shriveled old man knelt alone in the sand, casting a long shadow in the early morning sunlight. He neither moved nor spoke; he looked so fragile that the slightest breeze would blow him away.

Now came the executioner dragging a heavy sword. The Mayor did not flinch as the man set his footing and aimed. There was a seemingly endless pause. Then the sword came down upon the old man's bared neck. But the blow was not heavy enough, and instead of severing the head, it opened a huge gash. The Mayor twisted and croaked an agonized cry, his hands seizing his broken neck. The swordsman swung again, splitting the old man's hand before hitting the neck. This blow killed him, but a third blow was required before the head bounced on the ground. Then the body sagged and toppled over on its side.

Jehan watched the blood spurting, staining the whitish sand. He would permit himself no pity for the old man. Coldly he stood letting some minutes tick by, so that the onlookers could absorb the gory execution they had witnessed.

The next victim was General Mazrouk Nem, the commander of the Zidneppa garrison, who had been arrested in his bed.

His name announced, the commander too was ushered to the middle of the square, right beside the Mayor's headless body, his feet wetted by the blood puddle. General Nem was a squat, snaggle-toothed man with a full black beard. He turned around to face his captors, stuck out his bearded chin and shouted a curseword.

In response, the Magistrate Ubuvasakh enunciated a single syllable: *"Nyert."*

It meant death.

The contumacious commander was shoved to his knees. This time, the executioner's job was neatly done. There was not even a cry—only a brief thunking, crunching sound. No second blow was needed.

There remained a host of ordinary prisoners. The time had come to deal with them.

"You," Jehan called out, pointing to one of the bound men. "Come forward."

The gangly young soldier so addressed, uninjured and

with his hands trussed behind his back, walked awkwardly with his head bowed. He was looking at the bloody bodies, not at Jehan.

"What is your name, boy?"

"It is Nemir Mattaq . . . your honor."

"Where are you from?"

"Sajnithaddhani City, in the Province of Muraven."

"What are you doing here, so far away from home?"

"This is where the army sent me."

"Why did you become a Tnemghadi soldier?"

"I don't know. It seemed a good life."

"Do you still think it's good to be a soldier?"

"No, your honor."

"And why not, Nemir Mattaq?"

"Because you are going to cut my head off." The youth choked forth a cough that was a whimper.

"Tell me, why should I cut your head off?"

Nemir Mattaq shrugged.

"Is there any good reason why I *shouldn't* cut your head off?"

The young soldier said nothing. He did not know what to say.

"Nemir Mattaq, you are free to go home. The same for all you soldiers: You don't belong here. Go home, up north where you came from, and don't ever come back."

·5·

THE CITIZENS OF ZIDNEPPA had stood rapt to watch the executions of the Mayor and of their Tnemghadi general. These men had surely been unloved; and yet, Zidneppa was terrified to see their heads roll. It saw the murder of these men as a harbinger of what lay in store for the whole city at the hands of a demon usurper. The people cringed at the bloodstains in the sand, believing them to be the beginnings of a river.

Then they had turned to look at the captured soldiers. These men too were quite unloved. But where would the river of blood trickle out? Whom would it fail to sweep away?

And then, beyond comprehension, Jehan released the soldiers. Some of them thought they were being toyed with prior to execution. But Nemir Mattaq's bonds were actually undone, and all the others were freed too. A few edged warily away from the wall where they had been lined up; and then in the blink of an eye, they all broke loose, making haste to disappear lest this crazy monster change his mind.

Indeed, consistency did not appear to be his hallmark. He had peremptorily slain the Mayor and the commander, but had let the soldiers go—while making it clear that he might just as well have butchered them, too. His dialog with the soldier Mattaq showed that it didn't matter whether he killed them or not. And this was something he had deliberately chosen to make clear.

Jehan Henghmani looked at the people of Zidneppa with an appraising eye. They were small people, most of them: small of stature from meager diet, and small in circumstance. There were old men and women, many prematurely so, white-haired and wrinkled at forty, dying; there were younger people, ill-clad little waifs, ordinary,

133

anonymous people. There were millions of them in the
southlands.

These people had been lorded over by rich gouging
merchants, land barons, thieving rent collectors, Tnemghadi noblemen and even nobles of their own race, by
the Mayor, by the constabulary, by the greedy priests,
and by the ever-present army. Now, this crisp morning,
they found themselves lorded over by someone new, a
marauding bandit whose name was Man Eater. On their
faces he could see a resigned understanding that in the
end, much as things may change, yet they remain the
same. Whatever Jehan's hellions might do to them, it
would be nothing new; if it wasn't these bandits, then it
would be the Tnemghadi.

All this Jehan appreciated, and so did Zidneppa. It
might have been the only true thing understood this morning. There is a difference between liberalism and generosity, and when Jehan released the soldiers, it was an act
of generosity, not liberalism. He had shown that the soldiers deserved neither freedom nor death, except as Jehan
saw fit. A liberal ruler might have freed them for justice's
sake. A generous ruler would free them regardless. That
was what Jehan did, and no one in Zidneppa missed the
point.

The city was being offered a choice by Jehan. It was
not a choice between absolutism and liberalism, not a
choice between tyranny and democracy, but an even
more elemental choice than that: it was the choice between beneficence and malevolence. It was good versus
evil.

That was what this gruesome monster offered.

That was why he freed his prisoners.

Once the soldiers were dispersed, all eyes converged
upon the massive marble temple, which dwarfed all the
rest of Zidneppa and brooded over the square. There
was not a man in the crowd who hadn't been forced into
that temple, forced to kneel before the image of Tnem
Sarbat Satanichadh, forced to hand over some of his abject possessions.

Originally Jehan had planned to seize the temple together with the adjacent garrison, but that plan had been
thwarted: the temple's great oaken doors were shut up

tightly for the night. The temple was in fact more a fortress than the army compound.

Inside were the priests, hiding with all their gold, all their hoarded tribute payments, stolen from the people as ritual offerings. It wouldn't do to try to starve them out, since their store of foodstuffs was presumably colossal. Besides, now that the Tnemghadi had been overthrown, the lust to get the priests was universal in Zidneppa. If stares could have pierced the temple's oaken doors, they would have shattered into splinters.

Jehan Henghmani announced for all to hear that he would now proceed to bring down this priestly bastion. And its occupants, he gave assurance, would not get off as easily as did the soldiers.

A score of men had already been dispatched to fetch one of a group of huge fallen logs that lay just outside the city; and just as Jehan was speaking, the squad returned. On their shoulders they hefted an enormous wooden pillar, thicker than a barrel and long as a ship. A loud buzz of excitement swept the crowd.

A few bold young men and even women from the crowd joined those carrying the log. They positioned it as far back as they could, in a straight path to the door; and after a brief pause to renew their grip on it, they started the forward run, rapidly gaining speed.

It hit with a peal of thunder, with the screech of wood straining and breaking. The ground heaved, and the recoil flung the log off the men's shoulders. But the temple door had withstood the blow.

"Again!" shouted Jehan, undaunted, and the crowd took up the cry. More people joined the effort, and Jehan himself took up the rear of the battering ram. They shot it against the door a second time.

For a brief instant of jarring sound, the log hesitated in midair as it smacked into the barrier; then the bolt gave way and the doors swung open. Unbalanced by the blow, the men tumbled against each other like toys, and the log came crashing down to the ground.

The men regained their footing; a few were limping, bloodied, leaning on their fellows' shoulders. Now they could peer through the open doors into the temple's black innards; it was an oddly chilling maw.

"It's the mouth of Sexrexatra," someone muttered.

Quiet settled over the crowd, staring into the dark sanctum. Such was the mystique of the temple that no one rushed to cross its theshold. Many were the times they had entered that temple when they hated to do so. Yet it was unsettling now to find the obnoxious temple opened to them like a cracked walnut in their palms.

"We will drag out the jackal priests!" Jehan declaimed to the crowd, and with a sword in his hand, he led a troop through the dark jaws of the temple. The cyclopean building seemed to swallow them up.

The onlookers fidgeted while Jehan was inside. No sound issued from between the broken doors.

The minutes mounted up. Nervous whispers were exchanged, but no one made a move to follow Jehan into the temple; it seemed as though that dark maw was ready to devour all who dared trespass. With every passing minute, the black entrance and indeed the whole huge structure loomed more and more sinister, a silent, giant gremlin, grinning through its jagged wooden teeth.

Had the priests been armed and ready; had they ambushed Jehan in the temple's black interior?

At last, Jehan Henghmani and his troop reemerged, unscathed but with slumped shoulders. The bandit leader seemed dwarfed by the splintered portals.

"The priests," he announced, "are gone. There must have been some secret passageway, leading underground out of the city. Perhaps they closed it up behind them. And they took with them all the gold and jewels. But one piece of gold they did leave behind: the idol of Sarbat Satanichadh.

"We can be thankful to the Emperor Sarbat. He was too big and fat for the priests to carry off."

· 6 ·

JEHAN HENGHMANI awaited his distinguished visitor on a plush couch that had once served the High Priest of Zidneppa.

Shunning the more modest structures that had accommodated the Tnemghadi officials, he had made his headquarters in the temple. Not only was it the most magnificent building in Zidneppa, but it epitomized the overthrow of the old order here. The broken temple doors were not repaired; they were instead torn down completely. And no longer would this temple serve the worship of a golden idol; the statue of the Emperor, left behind by the fleeing priests, was being dismantled for its gold and jewels.

Jhay Parmar Harkout was coming to the Zidneppa temple, borne on a litter by eight slaves. The Jhay was one of the great barons, overlord of Kalanhi, a vast estate not far south of Zidneppa. Jehan had been expecting his visit.

For five years now, Taroloweh had suffered thin times. Rice, the chief staple, was particularly scarce, and hence its price was high. That meant big profits for those landholders who were able to keep all their lands intensively cultivated.

Throughout the five years, the Tnemghadi had continued to exact their taxes, paid mostly in grain and rice. Huge amounts of these foodstuffs had been hoarded up in the governmental granaries, but despite the widespread hunger, these supplies were withheld from the market. Ironically, it was only in times of plenty, when prices were low, that public grain and rice would be sold off. Obviously the Tnemghadi officials were in collusion with the big land barons, and sharing the profits from the tight market.

137

This corruption was a fairly open secret, but there was nothing to be done about it. Not even Tnem Sarbat Satanichadh, whose treasury was victimized by the scandal, would take action. He had plenty of funds; it didn't matter to him if his satraps fattened themselves on graft. Nor did it matter if Urhemmedhins starved.

So starve they did, while the municipal granaries bulged.

Jehan Henghmani rubbed his hands in satisfaction. The visit of Jhay Parmar Harkout fell in precisely with his plans.

Harkout arrived on a litter that was wrought of silver, inlaid with agates, turquoises, and lapis lazuli. The Jhay was a pinkish-skinned old man with a misshapen body, narrow at the chest and spindly-legged, but bulging broadly at the hips, more so on the left than on the right. His hair was thin, white, close-cropped; on his upper lip a tiny, dirty-looking moustache bristled. His chin receded in a mass of wrinkles, and his earlobes dangled as bulbous fleshy growths. Amid this ugliness, his eyes seemed out of place: they were bright, blue, cool.

"Greetings, Jehan Henghmani," said the baron, not leaving his silver litter. "May I congratulate you upon your bold and courageous stroke?"

Jehan smirked and folded his arms. "No; please let's skip this nonsense."

The Jhay was taken aback by the deliberate rudeness, but he did not let it ruffle him. "Very well," he said, "may I then speak to you of, ah, business?"

"Some may not speak to me at all; others may speak to me of anything but business. And you, Jhay, may speak to me of nothing but business.

Harkout nodded genially. "Just so. Perhaps we can get along after all. I do believe our interests coincide."

"Perhaps."

"You are no doubt aware, sir, of the large amounts of grain and rice being held in the Zidneppa granaries."

Jehan told the baron precisely how many shokh of rice and of grain were in storage. And he pointedly mentioned the prevailing prices those commodities were enjoying in Taroloweh.

The Jhay nodded. "Perfectly correct. I compliment your knowledge."

"Those are very high prices," Jehan emphasized, showing his teeth.

"Yes, that is quite true. Prices have never been higher. It would seem to be an auspicious time for someone with control of a large store of these commodities. But I'm sure a shrewd man like you must know that your grain could not realize such a fancy price on the market."

"Of course. Dumping so much onto the market would depress the price disastrously."

"Yes, disastrously." The Jhay's blue eyes glittered.

"Such a fall in the price would be perilous for the stability of the economy of the region."

Jhay Parmar Harkout's smile broadened. "You are most perceptive, sir. Most perceptive indeed. And might I be so bold as to point out that if for some reason you should find it necessary to sell out in a hurry, the effect upon the market would be quite aggravated. In such circumstances, your hoard would fetch hardly any price at all."

Jehan agreed. "So much simply can't be sold all at once. These miserable peasants have no money for lump-purchases. They live from hand to mouth, from day to day. If I had to sell all the rice in a hurry, there would be no one to buy it all."

These references to a quick sale could not be more plain: They were really talking about the presumed brevity of Jehan's domination of Zidneppa. Bandits had captured towns before, taken from them what they could, and fled at the first Tnemghadi onslaught. The story was expected to be repeated at Zidneppa. It was taken for granted that a leisurely sale of the commodities was not one of Jehan's options.

"Naturally then," said the Jhay, "you agree that the release of the city's stores would be most undesirable and foolish."

"Naturally. And naturally, you realize that if I don't sell the grain, I would need other sources of revenue."

"Of course. Certain exactions, certain taxes, would have to be collected."

"And collected, certainly, from those who are profiting so greatly from the high prices."

"That is only fair," the Jhay admitted readily.

Jehan fixed him, stabbed deep into him with his one eye, and the rich lord stiffened. The formalistic niceties, the mincing of words, were put aside now.

The ultimatum was blunt: unless the landowners paid a large sum in gold, the grain and rice would be released at once, dumped onto the market.

Harkout protested at the fabulous amount Jehan was demanding. His face a picture of reasonableness, he made a counteroffer. This Jehan brushed aside with a contemptuous gesture. There would be no haggling.

Harkout thoughtfully fingered the silver fretwork on his litter. If Jehan opened the granaries, the barons would be snowed right out of the market; buried in the outpouring of produce, they would sustain mammoth losses. The Jhay did some quick mental arithmetic, and determined that the bandit had quite shrewdly set his blackmail price: It was only a little less than the barons stood to lose if the market was ruined. Although Jehan was not budging from his exorbitant figure, he had still left the barons an advantage if they met his terms.

Jhay Parmar Harkout nodded gravely. Then, bowing to each other, the nobleman and the bandit sealed their deal.

Carried on his silver litter, the Jhay returned to his fellow barons to report the outcome, and to raise the stipulated sum. Each landlord in the region would contribute according to the size of his holdings; the largest assessment was upon Harkout himself. Moreover, he grumbled, *that vile bandit* had set the price so high as to leave Harkout no room to rake off a little for himself from what the others would contribute.

BERGHARRA—City of Zidneppa, counterstamp of Jehan Henghmani on a silver two-tayel piece of Emperor Sarbat, Satanichadh Dynasty, middle period of reign, circa 1180. Fish mintmark (Zidneppa). The counterstamp is a square with the initials J H in Urhemmedhin script above, Z below. Probably done at the Zidneppa mint during Jehan's occupation of the city in 1181. Breitenbach 1627, 25 mm. Host coin very fine, the counterstamp is extremely fine. Fewer than half a dozen known. (*Hauchschild Collection Catalog*)

·7·

WITH A DEEP BREATH OF RELIEF—nay, of deliverance—
the girl flung herself down into the coarse gray-green
grass by the road.

Although she had almost collapsed, now she sprawled
out comfortably on her back upon a cloudless blue sky.
She closed her eyes; in exhaustion from her journey, sleep
drew powerfully upon her. But she wrenched herself from
its cloying arms and sat upright, to gaze down the road,
down the hill whose crest she had just rounded.

As she had reached the top of this hill, the City of
Zidneppa at last had risen into view. Now it was spread
neatly before her, like a meal on a plate, and beyond
shone the great flat blue expanse of sea. The sun was
brilliant in the eastern sky. This was the morning of the
third day of her journey. She had trekked, walking almost without respite, as though on a forced march. Each
night she had allowed herself but little sleep, and somehow she would rouse herself to push on before the sky
lightened.

By now her feet and legs burned with every step, her
neck and hips ached, her shoulders stung with pain from
the burden she carried, her child. She had ported him on
her back most of the way. He was the only thing she
carried; everything else had been left behind. In her
haste, she had taken neither food nor money, and had
eaten almost nothing since starting out. Her stomach
groaned with hunger. And her clothes were filthy with
sweat and the dun-hued dust of the road. The dust was
matted all over her, caked in her hair and on her legs
and face. She could feel it like a gritty bandage, stifling
her. It made her pretty face seem ugly, and made her
appear much older than her not quite seventeen years.

All in all, at the threshold of Zidneppa, the girl was in a rather sorry state.

The child she had brought all this way on her back was a little less than four years of age. He too hadn't eaten since the start of the journey, and by now he was crying more or less continuously, from tiredness, hunger, and discomfort. As the girl lay down in the grass, he ran away from her.

Wearily she jumped up to catch the little boy, chasing him a few yards and then grabbing him up in her arms. "We're almost there," she chirped to him. "Look, there it is!"

She hoisted him up to look down the road at the city below them, and at the sea. The child had never seen a city, or the sea. The girl took it in with wide eyes herself; she had never seen the great ocean either.

"It's Zidneppa! You'll be treated like a little prince there. Don't you remember all I've told you?"

The child bawled, uninterested in what she was talking about.

The girl sighed and, renewing her grip around his middle, started trotting down the hill.

In the temple building of Zidneppa, the Chief Constable was nervously pacing back and forth. It was the twenty-fourth day of Nrava, the tenth day of his occupation of the city, and he was waiting now with growing impatience. Despite several reassuring messages, Jhay Parmar Harkout had yet to deliver a single gold tayel, and was requesting more time to gather the money together. But Jehan suspected that the old baron was playing for time to see if the army might quickly recapture Zidneppa, together with its grain and rice hoard. That was, of course, the other thing for which Jehan was waiting: the army. Ten days had passed, and no attack had come.

The waiting made him edgy. He kept to himself in a chamber of the temple, pacing. He jumped at every knock on the door, expecting momentous news.

The knock came. It was Kamil Kawaras.

"Yes, what is it?" Jehan snapped in a rush.

"Not important," Kawaras advised so that Jehan could relax. "In fact, I must apologize to bother you with it, only . . . I thought I'd better make sure. There's some young girl who insists that she must see you. She says her name is Maiya. Didn't you have a daughter by that name?"

"Yes. But she is dead."

"Oh, I'm sorry. I will send the girl away." Kawaras bowed his tousled head and turned to leave.

"Wait a moment," said Jehan. "Did this girl actually claim to be my daughter?"

"Not in so many words. But what's the difference, if your Maiya is dead?"

"I never actually saw her body. I had every reason to assume she was killed, but I must confess, from time to time, I have had a little grain of hope. I might just as well grant this girl a brief audience, at least to set my mind at rest. If I see that she isn't the one, then it won't come back to haunt me, and nothing will have been lost."

"I understand."

"She came here all alone?"

"Not exactly. There's a little boy with her." Kawaras smiled wrily. "Perhaps you are a grandfather!"

"Never mind the quips. Just fetch her."

Kawaras exited with a salute. Jehan plumped down on a couch and purposefully surrendered himself to the sweet pleasure of hope. But it quickly soured, for he knew it was false. It was indeed foolhardy to rise on a cloud of hope, since he would only be dashed to disappointment in the end.

This little affair should have been expected, he grumbled to himself. It was inevitable that some addle-headed peasant maid, carried away by the stories of Jehan Henghmani and his exploits, would take to fancying herself his daughter. Perhaps, in her innocent dream-world, she really believed it.

He was suddenly sorry that he'd mentioned to Kawaras his sometime hope for Maiya. That had been an invitation to trouble. If word of it spread, half the young girls of Taroloweh would plague him with their claims. Jehan would have to innure himself against vain hope. This girl would merely be the first of many; there would be no end to it. And the only thing it would accomplish would be to make him constantly relive that anguished day at Ksiritsa.

Jehan eschewed the couch and resumed pacing. He chided himself for his anxiety, tried not to dwell on the fact of his waiting, tried to deny sustenance to his hope, so that his unavoidable disappointment would be minimized. But in spite of himself, he hoped.

The door opened.

There stood slovenly Kawaras, and the girl, far more filthy. She was leading her child by the hand. Jehan peered dumbly at this bedraggled stick figure, not knowing what to say.

But she bolted toward him, threw herself upon him.

"Paban!" she screamed, exploding into tears.

She was Maiya, Jehan's Maiya.

They embraced tightly, Jehan restraining himself from crushing her in his brawny arms. She buried her face in his chest, his face was in her dusty hair; it was as though they were afraid to look at each other too closely, lest an illusion be dispelled. Their tears of joy sluiced together.

Maiya pulled forward the little boy, as comically dirty as she. He wailed in terror at huge Jehan with his monster-face, and redoubled his cries when Jehan picked him up and bounced him playfully on his shoulder. Maiya laughed and patted the boy on the head, trying to calm him.

"He's very tired and hungry. His name is Jehan," she said. "I named him for you."

"Jehandai—*little Jehan*—my grandson! This is too much —a daughter and a grandson, all at once!"

"Not exactly," Maiya said in a suddenly changed voice, quiet and precise. "Not a daughter and a grandson. A daughter and a son."

Jehan tweaked the boy's cheek. "I don't understand your riddle, but never mind now. You must have had a rough trip! I'm sure you want a bath and a meal."

"Oh, yes!"

"You shall have that, and much more. Nothing will be too good for my lost daughter, so miraculously returned to me."

"Did you give me up for lost?"

Jehan smiled. "Hope never died."

Later, after she had been well scrubbed, clothed in

crisp fresh linen, and treated to a lavish feast, Maiya sat with her father and told him the story of her years since they had seen each other last, in the dungeon of Ksiritsa. But the tale she recited was not the complete one.

· 8 ·

OUT OF THE SIDES of his glittering eyes, Nimajneb
Grebzreh peered at Maiya.

He was pulling her by the hand, a naked twelve-year-
old child. Ironically, she had been rescued by Grebzreh
from her father's murderous intention, but that was no
comfort to her. Jehan had wanted to kill her only to
spare her from even worse horrors.

The girl understood that. Having seen her mother
and sister raped and killed, and the hideous scars of torture on her father, she was frightened to the bottom of her
soul.

There was no point in trying to resist. It could only
aggravate her captor. So she followed meekly as the
warden led her alone down a dark corridor and stopped
in front of a locked door. Then he unsheathed his dagger
and touched its point to the underside of her breast.
"Is there any reason," he asked in a soft vibrato, "why
I should not cut you open to have a look at what's inside this pretty body?"

The picture of her sister, disemboweled alive, was still
vivid in Maiya's mind. But the cold touch of steel against
her body was strangely galvanizing. "I've done nothing to
deserve it," she heard a firm voice say. "And you promised my freedom!"

Grebzreh snickered. "Foolish little chicken; what
does all that mean here? My promise means nothing. The
only thing that matters is what I feel like doing."

"And what do you feel like doing?"

Beneath the bloody bandage covering his nose, the warden grinned, flashing his yellow-green teeth. "You will find
out in due course."

He pulled back the dagger with a jerky motion,
deliberately pricking her. Then he drew a key from his

belt and unlocked the door. Grabbing Maiya by the back of her neck, he shoved her inside and quickly slammed the door on her, locking it again.

The room was absolutely dark. Maiya stood petrified, waiting for something to happen. Had she been thrown into a den of tigers? Poisonous serpents? Would knives come at her, or would the walls close upon her?

But nothing happened. She could tell that this was not a dungeon cell; it was much larger and lacked the dankness. Maiya stretched her hands out and began to explore gropingly, touching everything in the darkness. It soon dawned upon her that she must be in Grebzreh's private quarters. Realizing this, Maiya gained an inkling of the warden's plans for her. And she did not forget his toothy grin.

Later, the sound of the key in the lock was heard again.

Nimajneb Grebzreh entered carrying a lamp. His face was expressionless at first, bandaged more neatly now where Jenefa had bitten off his nose. But then he flushed with satisfaction. He stopped and looked long and hard at Maiya.

She was stretched out on her back upon his bed. Her pose was wantonly naked in a way that seemed to exude concupiscence. When she looked up at Grebzreh, her eyes were far from hostile.

Perhaps she liked her first taste of a man! Grebzreh said to himself. Without taking his eyes off her, he placed the lamp on a bed-stand, and then stripped off his armored uniform, and then his underclothing. Not a word was said. When he sidled into the bed the girl did not shrink away, nor did she resist when he began rubbing her breast and thighs. He pressed himself down on her, and she spread her legs.

He didn't rush to take her. Flabbergasted at her willingness, he made love slowly, and wished he hadn't spent himself earlier in raping the girl's mother and sister.

Afterward, he lay back, panting, eyes glazed. He closed them, thoroughly exhausted. But she wouldn't let him sleep! She stroked his privates, rubbing her breasts against his arms. Although drugged torpid by the day's exertions, sexual and otherwise, light-headed from his loss of blood and the dulling pain where his nose used to be, Nimajneb Grebzreh roused himself once more and mounted her.

Afterward, spent down to his last embers, the warden dropped off to sleep almost immediately. His snore through the bandage was a grating hiss. He had fallen asleep without even bothering to blow out the candle.

Maiya lay seemingly inert at his side; but her eyes were open wide. *Sleep,* she said to herself, *sleep, you vicious man!* She had drugged him well with the only potion she had.

Grebzreh's rasping snore was steady, and he didn't even twitch. With belabored caution, Maiya slid away from him. Aided by the light of the candle, she padded catlike to the closet and appropriated one of Grebzreh's cloaks. Since he was a small man, the fit was not unreasonable. Then she moved to a bureau and opened one drawer just enough to slip her hand inside. She extracted a small leather pouch, holding it firmly about the bottom so that the coins it contained would not jingle. From the same drawer she drew a long, narrow dagger.

All this was accomplished quickly and deftly. Maiya did not have to search for what she sought, since all the searching had been done in Grebzreh's absence, in the dark. She gloated: The man had been a fool to leave her alone in his own room. Foolishly, too, he had let her drug him to debility with sex, and then gone to sleep confident that she was too afraid to take advantage. He hadn't even locked the door.

And his worst mistake had been his grin.

Maiya looked back at him in the candle-light. He looked tiny and pathetic, lying naked, his face bandaged, snoring hoarsely. The girl fingered the dagger she had taken.

But she hesitated. She wanted to avenge her mother and sister, and her father's ordeal, and to repay this villain for the indignities to which he had subjected Maiya herself. On the other hand, if she plunged the dagger into him, he might scream, and thereby thwart her escape. Reluctantly, she decided against it.

Opening the door a crack, she made a quick reconnaissance of the corridor. It was empty. Then she turned back to blow out the candle, supposing that Grebzreh would sleep more soundly in the dark.

That was *her* mistake.

As the room was swallowed abruptly by darkness, the man on the bed jerked and coughed. Maiya froze.

"What are you doing?" he asked groggily. She had left the door slightly ajar, and in the dim light from the corridor, he could see her standing up and wrapped in the cloak.

Maiya brandished the dagger violently in the air. "Shhh!"

Grebzreh gawked at her for a moment, not moving. *She's afraid I might cry out,* he thought, and that was silly: Nothing was more commonplace in this dungeon than a human scream. No one would come running to his aid. But he did not tell this to Maiya.

He struggled to pull himself awake. "You damned little fool," he said to her. "I thought you were smarter. Don't you realize that without me, your life's not worth a falu?"

Maiya tossed this aside with a wave of her head; she had not forgotten Grebzreh's reckless grin. "You would have killed me. My father was right; you never had the slightest intention of letting me go free. I have nothing to lose in killing you. So tell me," she mimicked, *"why I should not cut you open to have a look at what's inside this ugly body."*

Grebzreh gulped uncomfortably. There was a sudden slash of pain from his facial wound. "Yes, there is a reason," he said. "I will let you go free now. I swear it."

"I've heard that before. Ha! And I was just on my way out anyway."

"You know the way out, do you now?"

"I'll find my way."

"Possibly. But what if you run into a guard?"

Maiya thought for a moment, and then shook the dagger at him. "Are you proposing to lead me out of here yourself?"

The warden nodded.

"I'll be right behind you, pointing this at you. Lead me false, or to where your men are, and I'll kill you at once. The minute I see a guard, I'll kill you. Is that clear?"

Grebzreh nodded again, and rose from the bed. "Can I put on some clothes?"

"No. You'll stay naked as you are. That will teach you to"—she blushed—"to be careful about little girls."

Maiya prodded Grebzreh, naked but for his bandaged face, at knifepoint through the corridors. Only hours before, she had been prodded naked by Grebzreh through the same passageways.

It was a few hours before sunrise. The only sounds were the chitterings and moanings of the prisoners; most of the guards had gone to bed after their "entertainment." A skeleton crew patrolled, but Grebzreh knew their rounds and was able to avoid them.

The route, through narrow tunnels lit by foul-smelling torches and up steep stairwells, was a tortuous one. From shadow to shadow the pair slinked. Maiya never relaxed her guard, keeping the dagger always poised to strike. Keyed up by terror and excitement, she was almost giddy with alertness. And underneath the steely exterior with which she intimidated Grebzreh, she was a very frightened little girl. Maiya still did not know if she would come out of this alive.

After what seemed an unending labyrinth of passageways, Maiya was led to a small door in an alcove. Nimajneb Grebzreh pulled back its heavy bolt.

"This leads into a little alleyway. That alley runs underneath the wall of the palace itself. If you follow it, you'll soon find yourself outside, in the slums of the city."

Maiya motioned him aside. Still covering him with her weapon, she pulled the door open a few inches. She could smell the crisp blue air of night outside, could feel its coolness, its outsideness.

Grebzreh, naked, shivered in the draft. "Well, I've done as I promised. You see, I'm not such a scoundrel."

"Humph! You kept your promise only because I kept the dagger. And you deserve to feel this dagger now."

Grebzreh was afraid of a struggle; his reflexes were dulled by pain and satiation. His gaping wound was sending jagged shards of agony through his head, till he could hardly see straight. "You agreed not to kill me if I set you free," he pleaded.

"Promises mean nothing in this. godforsaken place, you said that yourself. And you proved it." Maiya hesitated, considering. She had almost made good her escape. Why jeopardize it by getting into a tussle with a man who might yet overpower her? "You deserve to die. But I will not kill you. Go!"

Grebzreh wiped his sweating forehead. With a nod of acknowledgment, he turned and ran, vanishing quickly down the stairs.

Maiya stared after him, almost disbelieving that she was alone. She stared down the sloping passageway. Down there was a place of unspeakable horror, and she had escaped from it, possibly the first ever to have done so. She had escaped—but her father was still burning in that hell. Suddenly she wondered: When she'd had Grebzreh at her mercy, might she have contrived freedom for her father as well as herself?

A lance of guilt shuddered through her. With her own life at stake, she hadn't thought of her father at all. Now it was too late.

Maiya flung the dagger away, and disappeared through the door into the night.

· 9 ·

THE SKY WAS LIT by a silver semicircle, a fishscale hanging in the heavens. Morning was still hours away.

Even at this hour, the City of the Dragon was wakeful. A great cosmopolis never really sleeps; parts may dim and nod off, only for others to brighten in their stead. Each hour has its own special fauna, the creatures of the night bearing scant resemblance to those who live by day. The denizens of the dark hours, like grubs squirming in the moonlight, possess a vileness felt in the marrow of one's bones.

Maiya felt it keenly. Even free of the dungeon, the stifling air of evil hadn't left her; malignant, it screeched along the backs of her teeth.

She felt a violent urge to get away from this city, but did not know her way. Aimlessly she wandered, walking jerkily, almost at a run, down streets and alleys, often in circles, dragging the hem of the over-sized cloak, doped with exhaustion, jumping at every shadow.

All that night she coursed the streets of gloried Ksiritsa; sprawling, menacing Ksiritsa. She was no longer really thinking. Her mind was a jumble of terror and wonder, winding down from its pitch of excitement into weariness. Her cool determination was dissolving into a sticky pool and tears trickled down her cheeks.

Once she blundered into a wall that towered halfway to the stars, a smooth stone cliff. Bending her neck far back, she ogled up at its rim. Suddenly she realized this was the Tnem-rab-Zhikh Palace. With a scream, and lifting the cloak to bare her legs, she fled.

At last the sky began to grow light. Here and there shops showed activity. Maiya squatted down in the gutter and rubbed her face. No one, apparently, had come out of the dungeons searching for her. There had been some disreputable-looking people about in the streets, but no one had paid her any mind.

For the first time she examined the cloak she had taken. It was not especially fine, but it was obviously a man's garment and too big for her. Dressed in it, she might attract attention, so she resolved to procure more commonplace garb at the first opportunity. To this end, she drew out the money pouch which she had also stolen from the warden.

Maiya poured some of the coins into her cupped hand, and her eyes became saucers. There were coins of all sizes, some smaller than a fingernail, some covering half her palm. All of them bore the portrait of an emperor, either Sarbat or Al-Khoum; on the other side, was snarling Sexrexatra.

A few were silver; but most were gold!

This bonanza took her breath away. She had never handled a gold piece in her life, and this certainly seemed a vast fortune. Maiya sighed deeply. The discovery that she was wealthy had a calming effect. She had much against her—she was a fugitive, a child, an Urhemmedhin, uneducated, alone, lost—but she had money. She kissed the pouch. Without it, she would have been helpless.

Maiya selected a silver piece to buy a new tunic, and hid away the rest of the money. She soon found an open shop, a stall in the bazaar area, with bright-colored clothes displayed on long poles. Pointing to a plain blue smock, she warily handed the vendor her coin. "One tayel, six falu," the man said. Maiya didn't know the value of the coin she had given him. But she held out her hand and the man returned to her a smaller silver piece and a few coppers.

In a shadowed alley, Maiya changed clothes. Crumpling Grebzreh's discarded cloak into a ball, she pressed it into the mud with her foot, and quickly returned to the market area. With her coppers she now bought a loaf of dark bread, and ate it while she walked.

Daytime Ksiritsa emerged as a different, and far less unpleasant city than it had been at night, noisy and bustling, reassuring in its crowded streets. Although this was a Tnemghadi city, there were many Urhemmedhins about, and Maiya could feel safely anonymous in her plain blue smock. The bread tasted good, and it felt good to fill her empty belly. Before she knew it, she had eaten the entire loaf.

Never had she seen such an exciting city. Maiya gawked at everything: the big buildings, the hectic bazaars with their fascinating displays of varied wares, and the people, hordes of people, many of them in exotic dress. Up on its hill, the Heaven Palace was perpetually visible; and with the yellow sunlight shimmering on its copper roofs and tall white spires, it was a beautiful sight.

Maiya strolled, enthralled, for hours. She bought another loaf of bread and some little sugared cakes and then some fruits, and continued eating while she walked. With another silver piece, she bought a pair of sandals and then a bracelet, and a ring, and then an extra smock to wear, this one with a striking red and orange pattern. She walked jauntily, enjoying her purchases and the feel of the heavy pouch thumping against her, inside her pocket. She hadn't even touched any of the gold yet!

The girl was mesmerized by Ksiritsa, whose grandeur surpassed anything she had ever imagined. No wonder the Dragon City was often spoken of as *gloried Ksiritsa!* She reveled in it, drank it in like heady wine. Buoyed by exhilaration, it was late in the afternoon before she realized how long she'd been walking. Her feet and legs were suddenly aching. She felt scarcely able to walk another step.

Part of the city's traffic consisted of rickshaws pulled by bent peasant men. Considering herself now a girl of wealth, Maiya treated herself to the luxury of a ride. For a few coppers, she was transported in style to a nearby lodging house.

In the room she rented, she paused only long enough to hide her pouch of money under the mattress; then, still wearing her blue smock, she threw herself on the bed and plunged at once into a deep slumber.

Maiya awoke to a room full of light; it was midday. Her body was sticky with sweat; the bedclothes and her blue smock were crumpled and damp. During her prolonged sleep she had been tormented by nightmares, unable to escape by waking up.

The full enormity of everything that had happened

in the dungeon hit her. The horrors had been eclipsed by her romp through Ksiritsa, but now they crackled at her vividly: her sister disemboweled, her mother stomped by Grebzreh, her father's awful scars, and Grebzreh's grin at Maiya herself promising death. Finally, thinking only of herself, Maiya had wasted a chance at procuring freedom for her father.

In a great clear rush, Maiya saw it all, and she screamed. It was too much. Her mind clouded, burying the pain so that it wouldn't crush her.

Maiya got up off the bed. Meticulously, she washed her face in a basin, and put on her fresh smock. The wrinkled blue one was smoothed out and folded with care. She retrieved her money pouch from under the mattress, and left the room, moving like an automaton.

Outside, she bought some more bread and a little wine. Inquiries revealed that a coach was soon due to leave for the old southern city of Naddeghomra. On its way, it would pass through the hill country of Taroloweh. That was where she wanted to go. No other possible course was given consideration.

These coaches were an opulent way to travel, and the fare required Maiya to part with one of her gold coins. But she was ignorant of any other way to go, and perfectly settled upon her intended destination.

She was joined by three other passengers, all of them men and all Tnemghadi. One was an officer en route to his station at the Naddeghomra garrison, and the other two were merchants. Throughout the journey of many days, these men tried often to engage the girl in conversation, but without success. She never said a word.

She viewed the men with caution, especially when they whispered among themselves and she thought they were discussing her. She imagined them to be plotting rape, robbery, or worse. Under the smock, her hand never relaxed its grip upon her money pouch. At the first night's stop, in addition to her dinner, Maiya purchased a new dagger.

It was at the town called Anayatnas that Maiya disembarked. Although she had heard of this town, she had never seen it before. Nevertheless, she supposed that it was as close as she would get to home.

There was an inn at Anayatnas where she took lodging.

She refused to give her name or advise how long she planned to stay. She would simply pay by the day, and leave when she chose.

In this dingy, tiny room at the inn, Maiya passed her days alone. She ventured out very little; compared to Ksiritsa, Anayatnas was devoid of attractions. Moreover, she did not want to be recognized as the daughter of Jehan Henghmani; she still feared the Tnemghadi. But in truth, she did not wish to be recognized as anyone at all. She did not know what identity, if any, she wanted. She was herself and herself only, unto herself but not unto the world—a goldfish in a bowl of opaque glass.

Sometimes when she did go out, she would watch the people whispering with their hands concealing their mouths, and she knew whom they were whispering about. The girl had fast become the town's leading gossip topic, a tantalizing mystery: a beautiful young girl who stepped off a coach from Ksiritsa, who spoke to no one and concealed her name, whose face was an expressionless mask.

She was especially intriguing because she had money, and was an Urhemmedhin. Some theorized her to be a slave who had absconded with part of her master's fortune; others believed she was a spurned concubine, possibly even one of the Emperor's. No one guessed the truth.

Maiya ignored the whirls of speculation that surrounded her. While the townsfolk gave a great deal of thought to Maiya's past, she herself did not. She spent her hours like a prisoner in her little room, lying on the bed and gazing absently at the ceiling, or out the window. Her slim body took on fat. The days passed by; she didn't count them. She seemed to be waiting for some unknown event.

Something *was* happening, in fact, without her knowing it. Her increasing plumpness covered up a swelling in her belly that was not due to overeating. Oblivious to it, Maiya waited in darkness.

And then one day, catastrophe befell her. She went out on a brief shopping trip for food. When she returned to her room she reached into her pocket to restore the money pouch to its place of hiding. It was gone. An adroit thief with a razor had neatly sliced open her pocket and made off with her fortune.

That pouch of golden coins had been a womb to Maiya, dark and warm, in which she'd floated as though unborn, insulated from the world and even from her own life. Now, abruptly, she was wrenched out and expelled into the harsh daylight. Maiya stood there, staring at the empty place where her gold had been, and she saw her scarred father, and the ill-lit dungeon, and the grinning Grebzreh, her raped mother, the smirking guards, her bloodied sister, all the beastliness, degradation, and horror. What in her waking sleep she had concealed in mist was now seen clear, and she felt its sting as a fiery lesion upon herself.

Never again would she be able to run away and hide from it.

· 10 ·

MAIYA WAS COMPLETELY ALONE and penniless, unable to pay even for her night's lodging. Worse, the black devil of the dungeon had risen up and seized her by the throat. She beat her fists upon her head and cried hysterically, but nothing could exorcise that devil.

It was perhaps an elemental will to survive that propelled Maiya now. She hastily gathered up her few belongings and decamped out into the streets of Anayatnas. The sight of her stirred whispers, which intensified when she was actually seen walking up to people, talking at them half incoherently. And oddest of all, when she made any sense, the girl appeared to be looking for work!

None of the flabbergasted villagers could provide her with employment, but one woman did observe that a nearby farmer, named Gadour Pasny, had recently been widowed and had talked of hiring a woman to do chores and look after his children. Maiya set out at once for the Pasny farm.

It was not far from Anayatnas, and she reached it while the sun was still up. In the field, she found Gadour Pasny mounted atop a gaar and dragging a plow.

"I've heard you need a woman to do chores," she called to him.

Pasny smiled cheerfully. Although plumper than she had once been, and somewhat unkempt, Maiya's charms were obvious.

"Yes, that's right. And to mind my children. I've got three of the little beggars."

"I can do it," Maiya affirmed.

"How old are you?"

"Seventeen," she lied.

Pasny knew she must be younger, but ignored this. He peered down at her from atop the gaar. "Say now," he

said, "I wager I know who you are. You're that girl
that's come from Ksiritsa, aren't you?"

"No. I'm from Anayatnas."

Pasny was sure she was lying. "What's your name?"

"Maiya."

"What's your family name?"

"Er, it's Draviyana."

"All right, 'Maiya Draviyana,' you can stay. I've
got a pretty good little house," he said, pointing. "You
can sleep there and you'll get your meals too. You'll
cook, take care of the house, watch the children, do
the washing and mending, and farm work when I need
you. Does that suit you, 'Maiya Draviyana'?"

"Well, what will you pay me for all that work?"

Gadour Pasny lauged. "Pay you? This isn't Ksiritsa,
little chicken. Don't you know it's been a bad year, that
people are homeless and starving? You should count
yourself lucky to be getting a roof over your head and
food in your belly."

Maiya nodded glumly. She would miss having money.
But she accepted Gadour Pasny's offer and went to work.

There was much for her to learn, but Pasny was
a patient master. Her cooking progressed by trial and
error, and it was some time before the unruly children
would submit to her discipline. But eventually, the Pasny
household was running smoothly.

Pasny was a sharecropper on the great estate of
Kalanhi, which stretched from Anayatnas halfway to
Zidneppa, the proud domain of Jhay Parmar Harkout.
For an Urhemmedhin tenant farmer, Pasny was well off,
working almost a double-sized plot, and a very fertile one
at that. With good crops even in the hard past year,
Pasny had been able to put some money aside. They lived
simply, but not in poverty.

The farmer treated Maiya not as a servant, but
almost as though she were his daughter. He was an
indulgent master who sometimes, after trips into town,
would bring her hair ribbons or other little presents.
Nevertheless, Maiya held Gadour at arm's-length. She
never answered his questions about her past, never told
him who she really was or how she had become pregnant.

Several months after her arrival at the farm, Maiya

gave birth. Gadour had brought in a midwife from Anayatnas to assure a safe delivery—a wild extravagance, especially since the child was not his own.

"It's a boy," he told her enthusiastically when she awoke. "What are you going to name him?"

Maiya thought for a moment. "Jehan," she said.

Pasny nodded approvingly. "Jehan; that's a fine name. It means *man*. I'm sure your little one will grow to be quite a *man* one day."

The farmer clucked the infant under the chin. "He ought to have a proper family name, though."

"He has a family name," Maiya murmured.

"Oh, well, he could have your name, Draviyana, that's true. But he should have a father's name. Let his name be *Jehan Pasny*."

Maiya did not want to marry Gadour Pasny, but had no strong feelings against it. He was a decent enough man, who had been good to her. If it made him happy, and preserved her place on his farm, Maiya was willing to marry him. She could not face being cast out into poverty.

She gave her husband two more children, both of them daughters; she insisted upon naming them Jenefa and Tsevni. The entire brood was thus expanded to six, and became a wearying occupation. Filled with children, cooking, washing, and working in the fields, years passed.

Maiya settled stolidly into this life, harder than she'd have wished but pacific in its drab security. Conditions throughout the province continued to be poor, but Pasny's rich earth still yielded good crops, and the growing family was well fed. There was no reason to think she would not end her days here, an old matriarch with grandchildren, Mother Maiya Draviyana Pasny.

And yet, there was a shallowness about her role here that told Maiya this was nothing but an interlude. Everything—the farm, her husband, even her daughters—smacked of unreality. This was not really her life. Only Jehan, her firstborn, was real to her, a concrete enclave of Maiya's true realm. In her son, she saw the dungeon, her father, and the nightmare of her life that could never really be escaped.

Secretly she would call the boy not Jehan Pasny, but

Jehan Henghmani. Her husband was never told who the father was, although Maiya herself never doubted who it was.

Sometimes Gadour Pasny would be chilled to see her staring, with half-crazed eyes, at nothing. Often at night she would writhe convulsively, choked by vivid and terrible dreams. Pasny was terrified to watch her, but he never guessed that her torment was no dream-world at all.

Gossip drifted from the town of Anayatnas: A man had been seen at Sratamzar, calling himself Brashir Atokhad. It was said that he was a monstrous giant, that he really was Jehan Henghmani, risen from the dead. Many people scoffed, but Maiya listened carefully to the gossip.

And then, more: Up in the hills, hidden in the forests, a bandit army was coalescing, harking back to the days when the notorious Man Eater rode roughshod over the province. The new brigand leader was in fact spoken of as Jehan himself, with awe and skepticism in equal portions. And so potent was the mystique of the Jehan Henghmani legend that despite skepticism, the outlaws of Taroloweh were flocking to this new Jehan.

Maiya contrived frequent errands to take her into Anayatnas, so that she could ferret out the latest rumors. Of course, it wasn't *really* the old Jehan resurrected, the people said; and even had Maiya wished to seek him out, she would not have known where to look. So she held her tongue and waited.

At last, one day, it was her husband who brought the electrifying news.

"Maiya, I've heard the most remarkable thing! This new Jehan Henghmani's finally struck, and in a big way! He's taken Zidneppa, *taken* it—killed the Mayor and wiped out the Tnemghadi garrison! Only the priests got away. Those accursed jackals wormed their way out through an underground tunnel! How do you like that?"

"And what do they say about Jehan?"

"Oh, he's a pretty grim customer, an ugly giant like the old Jehan. But this one's even worse, they say. He's a regular monster with his face all chopped up. You wouldn't want to cross paths with him, Maiya, eh?"

Gadour Pasny's wife stared back at him, stared right through him.

"What's the matter, Maiya, have I frightened you?"

"No," she said. "You haven't frightened me." Her voice was cold and distant, as were her eyes. She took off her apron, and then separated her son, Jehan, from the other children playing in a corner of the room.

"Where are you going?"

"Just for a little walk," said Maiya, taking her son by the hand. "I'll be back soon."

Gadour Pasny never saw them again.

She had left for good, left her husband and even her own two daughters. They were part of the unreality that was now over. Maiya left everything behind her, except for the young Jehan.

Her new life, her real life, was her father. She lived with him in the Zidneppa temple, and stayed perpetually close by him. Daughter, maidservant, valet—so completely did she devote herself to him. She cooked his meals, washed his clothes and mended them, prepared his bed. No chore was beneath her. She was a slave, a worshipper, a penitent.

The other axis about which she orbited was the boy. Jehandai, *little Jehan*, she insisted, was not her father's grandson. The boy, she swore, could only have been sired by his namesake. She was convinced that her father would come to rule an empire, and his son, her son, would be the heir. Maiya, through her flesh, would rule.

Jehan loved playing with the little boy, making him funny hats out of parchment sheets, bouncing him on his knee. "My little grandson, Jehandai," he would say fondly.

"No. He is your son," Maiya always answered. She pressed this claim persistently, and with equal persistence Jehan refused to entertain it.

"How can you deny your son his rightful place?" she would argue.

"And you would brand him illegitimate, or even worse, conceived in incest. It is unspeakable, better wiped from memory than harped upon. Take care, Maiya, that people don't hear you talk this way."

"But it is the truth. You deny the truth."

"Whose truth?"

"There can be only one truth!"

"For a man who rules," said Jehan quietly, "there can be many truths. I have learned this much already in my brief career. The truth is merely what the ruler deems true."

"Or what is manifest," argued Maiya doggedly. "Not even an emperor can turn black to white!"

"Manifest truth? What is manifest is only that Jehandai is the son of my daughter. Nothing else."

"O, Paban, have you no place in your heart for your son?" she wailed, the last word torn out of her.

Jehan shook his head wearily. Ever since Maiya's arrival at Zidneppa, she had been possessed of this dual obsession: her father and her son. She seemed to glory in the idea that her child was the product of carnal relations with her father! Jehan Henghmani didn't understand.

Maiya closed her eyes and submitted to a kiss of affection. They would cease arguing, for the time being. It made no difference, Jehan had no male descendants but Jehandai. The little boy, whether son or grandson, was equally the heir.

Maiya composed herself and vouchsafed a smile, for the time being.

· 11 ·

AND STILL Jehan Henghmani paced and fretted, waiting for Jhay Parmar Harkout to deliver the agreed-upon sum.

To stop the baron's stalling, Jehan put a sharp deadline on his demand. He gave Harkout just four more days to pay the bribe. Unless Harkout complied, the Zidneppa grain and rice bins would be promptly opened. But this was not a threat for whose execution Jehan had any zest. What he wanted was the money.

Meanwhile, inevitably, rumors spread of his bargain with the Lord of Kalanhi. And the people merely shrugged in resignation. In eight hundred years, nothing had changed. Jehan seemed to behave just like the Tnemghadi, keeping the food-stores locked up to enrich himself while the people starved. Why expect otherwise? It was a fact of life that the interests of the rich must conjoin with the interests of those holding power.

Yet it was precisely because of this that Jehan alone understood how fundamentally the great barons were his enemies. No one realized better than Jehan that he was not a power holder at all. No matter that he strutted in Zidneppa, the Emperor at Ksiritsa was where the real power lay. The land barons—both Tnemghadi and Urhemmedhin—were still wedded to their alliance with the Emperor and his satraps and military muscle.

Those barons would never reconcile themselves to a bandit in place of the Emperor. Only necessity had driven them to deal with Jehan now, and even so, they would expect him to abscond into the hills with their money, or else be crushed by the Imperium.

Jehan could not make these barons his enemies, regardless of what he might do, simply because they were his enemies already. Since he could never win them over, it cost him nothing to betray them.

So, when at last they met his deadline and paid the bribe—carts laden with gold, enough to feed and arm a great horde—Jehan Henghmani opened the granaries anyway, and sold every bit of grain and rice at the lowest price in history.

He gave it away, free.

Of course, once he had decided to double-cross the barons, he could have made even more money by selling the grain and rice for whatever it would bring. But while he did need money to equip an army, there was a prior need, and that was to *raise* an army.

This he aimed to do through political appeal. He was not merely double-crossing the barons, he was doing it for the sole benefit of the peasantry, and he hoped this would attract them to his banner by the thousands. No longer would Jehan Henghmani be the bandit marauder who plundered villages. Henceforward he would be the white knight of populism, the tribune of the people, re-deemer of the downtrodden.

It was all carefully calculated. Even before they swooped down on Zidneppa, Jehan's men had been in-structed in detail, given an inkling of what he had in mind. Restraint now, they were told, would pay ample dividends later. There would be no looting at Zidneppa, there would be no burning, no rape. They were not in Zidneppa to abuse the inhabitants, but, quite the con-trary, to curry their favor. Once the people had trembled at the mention of Jehan Henghmani's name. Now they would cheer it. Once they had hated his ragtag army; now they would join it.

Jehan's men were a motley assortment of thieves, cut-throats, and outlaws, the poor, the wretched, and the depraved. But all of them were bound by the power of Jehan's magnetism, and they obeyed him fully and without cavil. They not only behaved themselves in Zidneppa with complete decorum, but they actually became the city's police force.

They replaced the old constabulary, mostly Tnemghadi, which was disbanded. Like the Mayor and the garrison, the old police were unloved in Zidneppa. They had functioned to protect the property of the city's Tnemghadi upper class. When ordinary citizens were victimized by crimes, the police typically did nothing. They were seen not as guardians of public order, but as one cog in the machinery of oppression.

Nevertheless, the citizens at first viewed the replacements with alarm. Bad as the old police had been, would the new force, made up of outlaws, be any better? These people had been weaned on hair-raising tales of outlaw mayhem. But it did not take long for them to gain confidence in Jehan's new police force.

Its members might be thieves, but they did not steal. Indeed, in Zidneppa now, the apocryphal brotherhood among thieves did not obtain, at least not between Jehan's thieves and the indigenous variety. The former proved to be the scourge of the latter, rooting them out and bringing them to justice. The new magistrate, the handsome Leopard Ubuvasakh, commenced holding court sessions in the main square, and the trials became an almost daily public spectacle. Almost no one was acquitted in that court. The mere fact that one of Jehan's men had collared the miscreant was deemed sufficient evidence of guilt. And Ubuvasakh's justice was as rigorous as it was certain. For thieves, the traditional penalty—severing a hand—was administered without mercy, and then the villains would be kicked out of town.

Few tried to come back.

An army of criminals had given Zidneppa to Jehan, but he knew that more could be gained from stamping out the criminal element than by absorbing it. So, just out of the dungeon, this chieftain of a cutthroat band became the most relentless persecutor of public enemies that Zidneppa ever saw.

Even before the free grain distribution, this clean-up won the townspeople to his support. Many of them, in fact, including citizens of substance, volunteered to join his new constabulary. One of these was a stocky, pugnacious fish dealer named Revi Ontondra, who had often loudly protested about the derelictions of the Tnemghadi police. Ontondra's outspokenness had caused him to be regarded as a troublemaker, and the response of the old police to his criticism was to harass him. He was even once jailed on a trumped-up charge, but so great was the public outcry that the Mayor was compelled to set him free. Revi Ontondra welcomed the change brought by Jehan, and was quick to lend a hand, becoming in fact an officer in the new police force. This fish dealer played a major role in molding Jehan's force into a citizen militia.

Most of those prosecuted by the new regime at Zidneppa were petty thieves, hoodlums, and gangsters, but they were not the only ones. Jehan knew, just as did the commonfolk, who the real victimizers were. The minor criminals were a public nuisance, but the major force keeping the people in poverty was the systematic exploitation practiced upon them by a handful of commercial princelings.

Nemir Alatassi Qapuriah was a very wealthy man who operated several lucrative businesses. Most of his fortune was made as a wholesale purveyor of foodstuffs. He lived in a large mansion near the edge of town, attended by many servants. This Qapuriah had been considerably irritated by Jehan Henghmani's seizure of Zidneppa, and by the murder of his friends, the Mayor and General Nem. Closeted in his big house, the rich man waited for the storm to pass, waited for Jehan Henghmani and his bandits to head back into the hills.

The brutal executions had been shocking to Qapuriah; the great grain holiday was an even bigger shock. Although Qapuriah could understand a bandit who would butcher an old official, he could not make head nor tail of a bandit who gave away valuable produce for free. The rich man became increasingly apprehensive.

Two days after the grain holiday, there was a knock on the door of his big house. A servant opened it; standing outside was Jephos Kirdahi with a squad of rough-looking men. Despite his intimidating appearance, Kirdahi was scrupulously polite in inquiring if the master was at home.

With equal politeness, the servant explained that Qapuriah was not to be disturbed.

Shoving the servant aside, Kirdahi and his men invaded the house. The other servants, and the Qapuriah family, were aghast, and cowered in corners while the intruders combed through the mansion. It did not take them long to find Nemir Qapuriah, relaxing in his study.

"You are under arrest," said Kirdahi bluntly.

"Pah!" said the rich man dressed in fine robes, and he glowered haughtily at Kirdahi. "Where is your warrant? For what offense do you purport to make this arrest? By what law? What is your authority?"

Kirdahi was unperturbed by Qapuriah's spouting. "These armed men are my authority," he said.

"So might makes right, is that it?" Qapuriah was more indignant than afraid. "Well, let me tell you, this is completely improper, it's an outrage. You can't break into homes like this and seize people. What law have I violated, I ask you again?"

"You will find out at your trial."

"Oh, so I am to have a mock trial, eh? But don't tell me the charges, that would not suit you. I am to be given a trial, but no opportunity to defend myself."

"There will be no need for you to mount a defense," said Kirdahi, "since the outcome of the trial has already been decided."

"Your candor is remarkable," Qapuriah said wrily.

But this was as much of a discussion as Kirdahi would countenance. He ordered his men to seize the merchant by the arms.

"Get your hands off me, you swine. I'll not be dragged like a carcass."

"Save your breath, old fellow. You can't tell us what to do."

The men took Qapuriah by the arms. He did not squirm or resist, but held his arms stiffly in the air, as though he were leading his captors, rather than the other way around. They hustled him through the house, before the horrified eyes of his family and servants, and out the front door. Down through the City of Zidneppa they took him on foot. People stopped in astonishment to see so eminent a personage being shoved through the streets. Many dropped what they were doing and followed, to see what would unfold.

At the central square, the court had already been set up. The commencement of the trial awaited only the defendant's arrival. A crowd had gathered thickly around, and now it swelled even further with those who had followed Qapuriah through the streets. Word had spread quickly of this event, and it seemed as though the entire city was turning out to witness it.

The Leopard, Nattahnam Ubuvasakh, was once again

presiding, but he was not alone at the dais. This trial was attended by Jehan Henghmani in person. Sitting nearby was his daughter, with her son in her lap. All the other leaders were present too: Yahu, Kawaras, Ontondra.

Kirdahi brought the prisoner before the bar of the court. At once, Qapuriah raised his voice in protest against the trial's illegality. But he was silenced by an explosion of hoots from the crowd as well as by the judge's gavel. Unable to make himself heard, Qapuriah closed his mouth and stood with his arms folded, a defiant lour on his face.

Ubuvasakh recited the charges; there was no written indictment. Nemir Alatassi Qapuriah was accused of perpetrating the sale of watered milk and wine, of stale meats colored with dyes to make them appear wholesome, as well as further unscrupulous adulterations of his wares; of lending money at exorbitant rates of interest; of bribing Tnemghadi officials; of participating in the slave trade; and a few other crimes of similar nature.

"Does the prisoner wish to enter a plea?"

"You are only play-acting at conducting a court. No one is fooled by this charade. I will not dignify this illegal proceeding by entering a plea. I will not allow you to imagine that you are doing anything other than committing murder."

Ubuvasakh rapped his gavel sharply. "You will be silent," he admonished.

"That's right, silence me! That's easier than to hear the truth."

"We will indeed hear the truth, but not from a lying scoundrel like you. We will hear it from the witnesses. Let the first witness come forward."

A grubby-looking laborer wearing greasy clothes and a disheveled beard came, on unsteady feet, to the dais.

"What is your name?" asked the Magistrate.

"I am Sahyid Neskalo."

"Do you know the defendant?" Ubuvasakh continued, assuming the role of prosecutor as well as judge.

Clearly nervous before the large crowd, Sahyid Neskalo spoke haltingly and in a low voice. Prompted by questions from the bench, he told of how, at the illness of his wife, he had wanted to borrow some money, and had been referred to Nemir Qapuriah. After inquiring about the ages of

Neskalo's children, Qapuriah had lent him fifteen tayel, and made him sign a document.

"What repayment was called for?" Ubuvasakh asked.

"I was to pay thirty tayel in two months."

"That would mean an interest rate of six hundred percent a year?"

"I don't know; I guess so."

"Did you pay the money back?"

"No, I couldn't pay it. My woman didn't get well; in fact, she died."

"What happened when the two months were up?"

"Some policemen came to where I lived. They had the paper I'd signed," Neskalo said. "When I told them I didn't have the money, they pointed out some writing in the paper. They said it gave them the right to take away my little girl. So they took her."

"What did the writing say?"

"I don't know. I can't read."

"How old was your child?"

"Six, your honor."

"And what became of her?"

"I don't know. I never saw her again."

"Thank you for your testimony, Sahyid Neskalo. You may go."

At that point, Nemir Qapuriah thrust himself forward, fist smacking palm. "What is this, don't I have the right to question him? This man is lying! I insist upon my right to question him."

"You have no rights here, you stinking swine!" shot back the Leopard, and the crowd snarled at Qapuriah. They had listened in rapt silence to the testimony of Sahyid Neskalo, and were incensed by it. Often before they had heard such grim stories, and they'd been powerless to do anything about it. Now they were thirsty for the blood of the villain.

There were more witnesses; each of them tersely recited his story of Qapuriah's venality, touching upon all of the points in the indictment. The defendant made no further attempt to inject himself into the proceedings; instead he stood with his nose in the air, looking down contemptuously at his prosecutors. He was surrounded now by a cordon of Kirdahi's men. This was not to restrain Qapuriah, but rather to protect him from the crowd, whose outrage was being whipped to a higher pitch by each successive witness.

Finally, all of the witnesses against Qapuriah had been heard; there were none in his defense. The time for pronouncing judgment had arrived, and Leopard Ubuvasakh rose behind the dais, cocking his handsome head with all the air of judicial dignity he could muster. Jehan looked on approvingly, as the Leopard delivered his rehearsed speech.

"The testimony we have heard today has aroused our deepest feelings, has outraged us—but it hasn't shocked us. We are not shocked because we have become used to these crimes; they are drearily familiar throughout the land. Always there have been rich men like this who have exploited and oppressed the poor, perpetrating countless crimes against the Urhemmedhin people."

"You sanctimonious fraud!" cried Qapuriah suddenly. "You hypocrite! What crimes have *you* committed against your own people?"

"Be silent!"

"How many have you robbed and raped and killed? And you dare to judge me!"

"Silence him!" shouted Ubuvasakh. The squad surrounding Qapuriah grabbed him and jostled him roughly, but it did not squelch his tirade.

"You're not friends of the people, you're murderers, and you're proving it by murdering me! You're the ones who should be on trial!"

The prisoner's words were drowned out by the savage roar of the crowd. Fists were shaking in the air, curses were shouted, and many were scrabbling to get at Qapuriah. The guards had to struggle to hold them back.

"Let them through," he cried, "let them at me! No more charades—let them tear me to pieces!"

Pounding his gavel furiously, the Leopard begged for order, screaming himself hoarse. But it was futile. Overwhelmed by the push of the howling crowd, the cordon surrounding Qapuriah suddenly dissolved. The merchant was swept up by the human wave that closed in upon him. In seconds, he was covered with blood. There was one last defiant gesture, an upraised clenched fist. Then the mangled body of Nemir Qapuriah sank from view like a piece of flotsam in a roiling sea. His screams went unheard in the shrieking din of the mob.

The blood of Qapuriah did not assuage their thirst, but only sharpened it. While the merchant was being torn limb from limb, part of the mob was already swarming out of the square, waving broomhandles and pitchforks. They were headed toward an obvious target: the edge of town where stood the mansions of the rich.

Jehan watched this, stricken with a queasy sense that the mob was an elemental force beyond control. This was unreasoning, total havoc.

What must happen now was clear. The mob, a thousand humans transformed into a single savage beast, would destroy the houses of Qapuriah and the other wealthy men. Everyone caught inside those houses would be slaughtered, be they Tnemghadi noblemen or Urhemmedhin slaves. The mob would make no distinctions; some of the rioters themselves would be torn apart in the tumult. The houses would be put to the torch, and not even the dogs and cats would escape the conflagration.

All this Jehan could see as the mob surged up the street. He was jolted by the power of the forces he had unleashed and felt like a little wizard who had summoned up a great demon. It took his breath away.

He watched and remarked, "What is happening now is that which must happen. Zidneppa has waited eight hundred years."

And Zidneppa, he knew, had not waited alone. Millions of Urhemmedhins had suffered grievously in those eight centuries. The retribution was at hand, and it would be terrible to behold.

Already, the black smoke was billowing up.

Assaf Drzhub scanned the latest dispatch with angry eyes. His lips were bloodless, his nostrils flared.

With a curse, he crumpled the message and flung it to the floor.

For some time, Assaf Drzhub, the Imperial Viceroy of Taroloweh, had been aware of a bandit gang coalescing in the eastern forests of his province. At first this was a minor matter eclipsed by the enormous headaches with which Drzhub was struggling to cope. In a time of famine and unrest, a bandit troop could almost be ignored; and this one kept hidden in the hills and made no nuisance of itself.

Nevertheless, the gang had intrigued the Viceroy. He thought its leader showed an impressive flair by naming himself after Jehan Henghmani, and wondered idly what the fellow was like. He was rumored to resemble the old Jehan, except for being uglier, but Viceroy Drzhub was skeptical. He doubted anyone could surpass the old Jehan in ugliness. At any rate, there was no doubt this new Jehan would ultimately share the same fate as his predecessor.

This casual attitude toward the new Jehan Henghmani was abruptly shattered on the fifteenth day of Nrava, in the year 1181.

Even then, there still had seemed no point in sending out an expedition to recapture Zidneppa. It was presumed that, running true to form, the rascals would simply sate themselves on whatever loot and women they could get their hands on, and then would scamper back into the hills. They would probably have run off even before an expedition could reach Zidneppa, or so the official thinking went.

But according to this latest intelligence, the bandits were not fleeing at all. Instead, they were actually entrenching themselves at Zidneppa, with Jehan posturing in charge of the city as its chief constable, soliciting bribes

from the barons while currying the cheers of the Urhemmedhin canaille with inflaming rhetoric and high-handed
assaults upon the gentry.

The dispatches being slow, Viceroy Drzhub was as yet
unaware of Jehan's free grain distribution, and of the trial
of Nemir Qapuriah and the burning of the wealthy part of
town. But it did not require this further news for the Viceroy to be convinced of the situation's gravity.

His lips still thin and bloodless, Assaf Drzhub rang a bell
to summon a scribe.

"I want to send an urgent dispatch to Ksiritsa."

"To whom shall I address it, Lord?"

"Tnem Sarbat Satanichadh."

At Ksiritsa, in the dungeons deep below the Heaven
Palace, Nimajneb Grebzreh still tromped ceaselessly
through the muddy passageways.

His hissing breath, through the silver pyramid that sub-
stituted for a nose, was heard now as a most sinister sound.
The little dungeon warden had with the passage of years
grown into a depraved fiend, and no one was safe from his
violent temper, not the prisoners nor even his own corps of
guards. The vehemence that had once been channeled into
the torture of Jehan Henghmani now ran unchecked
against everyone who crossed Grebzreh's path.

The warden's disfigurement by Jenefa, and then his humiliation by Maiya, had enflamed his hatred of Jehan into
a mania. And of course, when Jehan escaped, Grebzreh
was thrown into a paroxysm of helpless fury. He did manage to hold his wits together sufficiently to conceal the escape, but aside from that, the warden was left a madman,
a raving madman.

And now there came to him a pageboy from the Court,
bearing a summons. The boy shivered in the dank, foul
dungeon air, and stammered his message: Nimajneb
Grebzreh was summoned to appear before the Emperor
of Bergharra.

When the boy blurted out this news, Grebzreh gave a
wild shriek, and banged on a table with his hands. Only
once before in his life had Grebzreh come into the presence of his ruler-god. Now he brushed and donned his best
uniform, washed his face and shaved and carefully combed
his hair, singing and shrieking all the time. Grebzreh was

giddy with his belief that the Emperor was summoning him to fill some important and lucrative post. Perhaps he would be made viceroy of some province, or perhaps one of the Emperor's own ministers of state. As he pranced and capered up the stairs toward the throne-room, he composed in his head a speech of humble gratitude.

Nimajneb Grebzreh marched exuberantly, down the red carpet toward the Tnemenghouri Throne, and then, with extravagant gestures, he prostrated himself in a bow before the Emperor. Through pink, blotched, thick-lidded eyes, Tnem Sarbat Satanichadh scowled down at him.

"Are you the warden of the dungeon?"

"Yes, I am indeed, Your Majesty," Grebzreh answered, grinning and bowing his head repeatedly.

"Stop that bouncing up and down. And why do you wear that silver nose?"

Grebzreh purpled with embarrassment, but he managed to puff out his chest and say proudly, "I lost my nose in the service of Your Majesty."

"Tell me your name."

All at once, Grebzreh realized that his high hopes were blasted. He mumbled his name, but even his addled mind could appreciate that if his name were unknown, he could hardly have been summoned for a promotion. Why, then, had he been summoned? A chill of apprehension sliced through him.

"How long have you been the warden down there?"

"Thirteen years, Your Majesty."

The Emperor spread his lips, displaying an expanse of teeth. Grebzreh suddenly felt himself falling into that mouth. The ruler's grin completely unnerved the man.

"I have summoned you here so that I may ascertain the status of a certain matter."

"Yes, Your Majesty."

"Some five years ago or so, I believe, you received a certain prisoner. His name was Jehan Henghmani. Is that correct?"

Grebzreh nodded jerkily. Nothing could have unhinged him more than this mention of Jehan. Could it be that somehow the great monster had returned to dog him again? In confusion, Grebzreh struggled to think of something to say, some lie that might satisfy the Emperor.

"Well, tell me, Warden: What became of the prisoner Jehan Henghmani?"

"Oh, Your Majesty, your orders were carried out. I swear they were carried out to the letter. But Jehan—well, he—that is, he died, yes, that's right, he died two years ago. Not from the tortures, mind you! No, he died from a disease, from a cancerous disease. You see, there was nothing we could do; he had a cancer in his belly the size of a melon."

The Emperor's grin mellowed into an enigmatic smile. "A cancer the size of a melon? Tell me, what kind of melon?"

"Oh, it was like a big melon, Your Majesty. Like a Lahamese melon."

"A Lahamese melon, eh? That sounds like quite a cancer. How pathetic!"

"Yes, Your Majesty, quite pathetic and ironic."

"Ironies abound. Now tell me something, Warden: Do you remember the day I came down into your dungeon to have a look at this Jehan Henghmani?"

Grebzreh was not breathing, he was tingling. Was it just possible, after all, that his outlandish lie would pass muster? "Of course I remember," he said. "I remember most clearly, Your Majesty. It isn't every day that we are honored by your exalted presence."

"I should say not—what a stinking place down there! But tell me, Warden, do you remember my exact decree about this prisoner?"

"Of course, Your—"

"Did I not decree that this Jehan Henghmani never be allowed to die?"

Grebzreh's face went white. "But Your Majesty, he died of a cancer—"

"Can you prove that?"

"Yes!" the little man said emphatically, but he knew this desperate lie would not save him.

"But you should not even have permitted him to die of a cancer. You should have notified the Throne, or summoned doctors. You knew my will." The Emperor was thundering now, the thunder of a god from atop a mountain.

"But Your Majesty, we tried—"

"And failed! You worthless, incompetent idiot. I don't know how you have the gall to tell me that. For deliberate disobedience there might be some reason, but you are guilty of the worse sin of just plain bungling. What do you suppose should be done with you now?"

"Your Majesty, this abject worm begs your mercy. I have served faithfully and long—"

"And now you're finished. You, Warden Nimajneb Grebzreh, are guilty of having violated a decree of the Emperor, by permitting the prisoner Jehan Henghmani to die. And according to that decree, you are condemned to death yourself."

"Wait, Your Majesty," Grebzreh cried out, throwing all caution to the winds. "It isn't true! He didn't die—"

"Hold your insolent tongue! You've had your say and heard your sentence. Be thankful for my mercy in sparing you a death by torture." The Emperor clapped his pudgy hands together twice. "Take him away."

A pair of soldiers collared Grebzreh. He squirmed helplessly, and they dragged the little man away, his heels leaving dark trails upon the red velvet carpet. But while still within sight of the throne, he screamed out a few words:

"Jehan is alive, Emperor Sahyid Sarvadakhush!"

They stifled him and removed him from the throneroom. The Emperor sat coldly as he watched the poor madman dragged away.

"Your Majesty," whispered Hassim Baraka-Hatu, the new Grand Chamberlain. "What did he mean, calling you Sahyid Sarvadakhush?"

"There is a parable in the sacred parchments about an emperor of that name. He dies in chains at the feet of a man whom he first saw in chains and at his own feet."

"And this Jehan Henghmani . . . ?"

"No, he cannot be the one prophesied. I made sure that I did not first see him in chains at my feet."

"But what about this cancer story?" asked Baraka-Hatu.

"That fool was lying," said Sarbat, handing his chief minister the letter from Viceroy Drzhub. And the Emperor was wondering whether, despite his precautions, by some unfathomed secret in the parable, he ought to fear Jehan Henghmani.

In the depths of his own foul-aired dungeon, Nimajneb Grebzreh's head was shoved against the wooden block, black with the blood of countless other victims.

The axman had torn off Grebzreh's silver nose-piece, stealing it for himself, and the warden's scarred face was pressed bare upon the block. Even now he felt a twinge of pain, and for the millionth and last time, he cursed Jehan Henghmani. It had always been Jehan who tormented Grebzreh, not the other way around.

And now, the ultimate irony: Grebzreh was to lose his head in punishment for the death of Jehan—when all the while Jehan lived, still laughing at him!

The ax came down.

Everything was nothing.

· 13 ·

WITH HOPEFUL EYES, the youth fixed upon the City of Zidneppa.

In the early morning sun, he could see the city more clearly than he saw himself. Indeed, his own self-image was poorly focused. While he still vaguely regarded himself as a boy, he was in reality quite tall, fully grown. He was an awkward figure though, very lean, with narrow slats for arms and legs. These limbs, and his face and torso, were toned a deep dark brown. He was naked save for a dirty little rag around his pelvis. The rest of him was dirty too, the dust caked white at his feet and knees and elbows. For years, only the rain had ever washed him.

This young tramp, barefoot and without a possession in the world, quivered as he loped down toward the gate of Zidneppa. He was sick with apprehension, knowing this might be the place where he would die. And yet he was flushed with excitement too. What lay at his feet was nothing less than a new world.

He was at the dizzying brink of another great change in a life that had been changed so radically already. The boy he had once been seemed unconnected to the man he had become. And still, he was only at the threshold of his life. What lay beyond that threshold was impossible to know. He could sense only that his years of wandering had been just that: a wandering in the wilderness, waiting for the right time to emerge.

And so at last, after years in the hills and forests and on the roads, he had come to Zidneppa. It lay just ahead, at the edge of the blue expanse of sea. The sight took his breath away.

As he neared the entrance to the city, he shaded his eyes to peer at the soldiers standing guard—and his heart leaped. They were not wearing Tnemghadi armor, nor did

their eyebrows converge. They were indeed Urhemmedhins, a simple but staggering fact.

The gaunt youth stopped and his eyes went heaven-
ward. The sight of those men filled him with rapture,
pride, and reverence; it was something he had hardly ever
dared to dream. "Praises unto Urhem," he murmured,
"thy day shall truly come!"

Tingling and flushed, he resumed his walk, quickening
it, throwing one thin leg exuberantly ahead and then the
other. The final distance he swiftly closed with a vigorous
sprint.

"Hello!" he shouted, breathless, waving his arms.

The guardsmen were taken aback by this apparition
coming toward them at a run. But one of them laughed
and returned the greeting. Then the youth reached them,
panting.

"You're free to enter," said one of the men.

"Then it's true, isn't it—this city has been taken by
Urhemmedhins?"

The guards nodded.

"And the army and the priests have run away, and the
big Tnemghadi here are being put on trial? And that
you're giving away free all the grain and rice?"

The youth asked these things with a rising excitement,
and each time the guards nodded.

He had come to join them, to join the Urhemmedhin
army of Jehan Henghmani. It had grown far beyond the
bandit troop that had taken Zidneppa on the fifteenth of
Nrava. Its ranks swelled at first with sympathetic towns-
men, the army was now enjoying a steady stream of new
recruits from all over the surrounding countryside.

"I want to fight the Tnemghadi!" declared the youth.

"Well, we expect they'll attack us pretty soon. But are
you sure you're up to it?" The guardsman pointed at the
young man's emaciated body.

"Up to it? Listen, *my name is Gaffar Mussopo!*" It almost stunned him to speak his own name. He hadn't done
so since he had become a fugitive, and it seemed fantastic
bravado to finally reveal himself. But he did so fully: "I
am Gaffar Mussopo. I am the assassin of a Tnemghadi
Ram-Tvahoud!"

The soldier raised his eyebrows. "*You* killed a Ram-
Tvahoud?"

"That's right. A couple of years ago. I killed the Ram-Tvahoud Uthsharamon Yarif of the Khnotthros lands. And I got away. So what do you say to that?"

Gravely, the soldier nodded. "Come with me."

The General's eyes were cool and haughty as he sat erect in his saddle, reviewing the neat rows of his troops.

There were six thousand of them, an even more powerful force than the Viceroy had requested. And they were commanded by General Ezir Zoitthakis.

It was a name calculated to make the defenders of Zidneppa tremble. Ezir Zoitthakis was only twenty-nine years old, but he was already famous, one of the glamorous stars of the Tnemghadi military. He was an impressive figure of a man, tall with the leanness of energy, his sharp black eyes aristocratic and urbane. Zoitthakis traced his lineage back to the Ibarouma Dynasty; his father was the Viceroy of Agabatur, and his mother's father had been a leading palace official in the reign of Tnem Al-Khoum Satanichadh.

But it was not to his distinguished birth that Ezir Zoitthakis owed his reputation. He had made the army his career, and had early covered himself with glory as a junior officer by rallying his troops to victory against a savage attack by the Akfakh, the northern wildmen.

Now Zoitthakis was the youngest general in the Bergharran army. He was known as a fierce, ruthless leader, who never took prisoners. His watchword was complete destruction of the enemy. He was unloved by his men, who often cursed him for his tough discipline. But no one ever crossed Ezir Zoitthakis, who was looked upon as some demonic force.

Many were those who feared this General Zoitthakis, and one of them was Tnem Sarbat Satanichadh. The Emperor had bestowed high rank on the young man, but knew Zoitthakis wasn't satisfied. The ambition of such a man would know no bounds. He would surely covet the Tnemenghouri Throne itself.

Indeed, Zoitthakis had closely studied history, and his hero was Sharoun the Sword, the founder of the Satanichadh Dynasty—a man who had come up through the army, and used it to overthrow the decadent Tnem Riyadja Tsitpabana. Sharoun's descendant Sarbat was regarded as an unworthy heir by Ezir Zoitthakis. He believed the time ripe for history to repeat itself, and he was already casting about for sharp young officers to join his cause.

Sarbat knew nothing of this, but suspected all of it and more. In time, he would have to deal with Ezir Zoitthakis; but for the nonce, he needed a tough, skilled general. If he feared Zoitthakis, he feared Jehan Henghmani too. So he would pit them against each other, and whoever won, the Emperor would have one fewer man to fear.

So late in the month of Endrashah in the year 1181, Ezir Zoitthakis led his army of six thousand into Taroloweh.

On the night of the twenty-fifth, they arrived at the hills outside of Zidneppa.

According to custom, the attack would wait until dawn. Zoitthakis took advantage of the night to array his soldiers on the hilltops, in carefully deployed rows. The horsemen formed the first rank; the footmen would follow them. The bowmen would stand in the rear, to augment the attack with their arrows as the others charged. All was arranged to deliver one terrible, devastating, and conclusive blow upon Zidneppa.

As the night waned, these six thousand crack troops perfected their formations, readying themselves for battle, peering down through the darkness at the rebellious city they had come to crush.

Thus dawned the twenty-sixth of Endrashah.

Through the night, too, the Urhemmedhins were alive with preparations. Long expecting this attack, they now added the final touches to their defense.

Revi Ontondra, the former fish dealer well familiar with the city's layout, was the mastermind of the elaborate barricades. They were made of dug-up earth, logs, the hulls of old boats, overturned wagons, bales of hay, and whatever else had come to hand. A few yards in front of this barrier, a narrow little trench had been dug. Behind it stood almost every able-bodied person in Zidneppa, women not excluded.

One of them was Gaffar Mussopo. The youth harbored no illusions about his newfound leader. He knew Jehan Henghmani was not the good and selfless *Ur-Rasvadhi*, whose battle cries would be love and virtue, but Gaffar didn't care. It was not some mystical ascetic that his people needed, he believed, but a tough fighter.

Jehan postured as the champion of the people, but Gaffar saw through this. Three years of torture could not have reformed the old bandit, it could only have made him harder and more cynical, using the peasants for his own ends. But Jehan's sincerity, or lack of it, was beside the point. For once the unscrubbed masses had a strong leader whose own interests were inextricably bound up with their own. Only through the power of their arms and numbers could Jehan realize his aims, and so he was compelled to give them what they wanted. They had food in their bellies and it didn't matter that the giver wanted something for himself as well as for them.

So they would flock to join his army, to fight to keep what he had given them. And as for the people of Zidneppa itself, they knew what Tnemghadi soldiers did in towns they occupied, they knew the fate of Dorlexa and others that had dared rebel. The people of Zidneppa would resist the Emperor's onslaught, not only to support Jehan, but to save their city and their lives.

As the sun rose on the twenty-sixth of Endrashah, they looked out from behind their barricades, and they saw the Tnemghadi army poised to strike. Six thousand strong they saw, in close formation on the hilltops, all ready to swoop down upon the city. The horsemen formed the first rank, bristling in full armor, with spike-topped steel helmets and broad shields emblazoned with the dragon Sexrexatra. They were brandishing aloft their long, curved, tempered swords, which caught the first rays of the sun and gleamed like fire. And behind the horsemen could be seen the tips of the foot-soldiers' pikes, a forest of lethal points.

This great army stood almost motionless in the still morning air. Equally motionless, the defenders watched them and waited. They felt very small. They knew that in eight hundred years countless rebels had been crushed by armies far less powerful than the one now facing them. They knew that never once in eight centuries had Urhemmedhins managed to stand against the mighty Tnemghadi army.

Thus dawned the twenty-sixth of Endrashah.

The still air was suddenly shattered as the Tnemghadi line exploded into its ferocious charge, hurling itself down the slopes with war whoops shredding the air, gaudy banners flying, and blades flashing in the sun.

All at once they came down upon Zidneppa, smashing down upon the city like the breaking of a sudden tempest. The storm's lightning was the brilliance of their swords, and the thunder was the rumble of their horses' hooves, shaking the ground. And the rain was the rain of their arrows, coming down out of the sky with the noise of hail.

But Revi Ontondra had foreseen how the bluffs could be used to pepper the city with arrows, and the defenses included roofed bunkers. So while some arrows did strike home, most bit harmlessly into wood or cowhide.

The defenders' homemade bows did not have the great range of the longbows wielded by the Tnemghadi archers; they'd been given strict orders to hold their fire until the attackers were sufficiently close. Despite the terrorizing impact of the Tnemghadi charge screaming down upon them, not an arrow was let fly.

The shaking of the ground rose as the onslaught neared. The air was thick with dust and noise and the shrieking whoops of the galloping horsemen. The nearer they came, the faster they seemed to move. Only seconds separated them from the barricades.

Suddenly, every Zidneppan arrow was launched at the same instant. And with the attackers charging directly into their faces, hardly an arrow in that fussilade failed to find a mark. If a man was not struck, a horse would be. Dozens went down into the dust, faltering and skidding. Horses reared and stumbled and lost their riders. Others behind them crashed upon the fallen and went down too.

The charge wavered. The wounded, thrashing horses formed a barrier that stopped the others; the obstacles could not be seen in the dust. Horses were backing up and cantering in all directions. More arrows whizzed at them. In seconds, Zoitthakis' carefully arranged formations were in complete disarray.

Nevertheless, they were not stopped. Hundreds were trampling straight into the city's defenses. But in the dust and confusion, Ontondra's little ditch was treacherously inconspicuous. Many were its victims, their horses crashing down with broken legs, throwing their riders over their heads.

Some did get past the arrows and the ditch, and these the Zidneppans attacked with their pikes. Although made only of wood, they could rip open the belly of a horse as it jumped the barricade; and when a horse came down, so did the horseman, often crushed beneath the injured animal.

Hundreds of the Tnemghadi did get through, coming down on the defenders with killing hooves as well as swords. Upon and behind the barricades, a pitched battle developed. But only a fraction of the six thousand attackers arrived, and in the end, they were easy prey for the more numerous defenders. They were slaughtered on pikes and pitchforks.

Meanwhile, the advance continued. Zoitthakis' archers were useless now. They had stopped their barrage, to avoid killing their own men. The footmen were still edging their way forward, crouching behind their shields to dodge the Urhemmedhin arrows, unnerved by all the death around them. Some of them were falling back. Riderless horses were trotting aimlessly. Many who had gotten a taste of fighting at the barricades began to run away.

General Zoitthakis looked on from the bluffs, infuriated as his army—and his glorious career—were cut to pieces by unwashed Urhemmedhins. As he watched the backward movement of his troops take hold, the enraged General spurred his horse, so violently that he bloodied its flanks.

Zoitthakis plunged among his fleeing men, cursing at them. His sword hacked away at his own troops as they ran past him. But he could not stop them. His face was a flaming purple, his lips almost frothing as he screamed in vain. The General slashed at a fleeing soldier, and the man parried with a blow of his own pike, opening a wound in Zoitthakis' forehead that covered his face with blood and almost toppled him from his mount.

Zoitthakis' screams were unintelligible, and with his eyes clouded by his own blood, he was slashing at empty air. Then an arrow struck his horse, and it went out of control, galloping off in the direction of the retreat.

The dust was beginning to settle, and the Bergharran army was gone. Half of Zoitthakis' men lay dead or wounded, and the rest were in disorderly flight. But the battle was not over: Jehan Henghmani leaped to capitalize upon his victory. Bellowing orders, pushing the Zidneppans over their barricades and into the field, he led an attack upon the fleeing army, pursuing its stragglers and cutting them down.

The operation consumed the next two days, as Jehan's men fanned out sixty lim into the hinterlands, tracking down and decimating scattered bands of Tnemghadi soldiers. Along the way, the Urhemmedhins they met cheered them on, and often joined them. In the end, few of the six thousand Tnemghadi soldiers survived, while Jehan's army was even larger than at the start.

General Ezir Zoitthakis was never captured, nor ever heard from again. He was listed among the missing.

The Emperor no longer had to fear Zoitthakis.

He had to fear Jehan Henghmani.

BERGHARRA—Taroloweh Province, silver pastari or five-tayel piece of Jehan Henghmani as warlord, 1181–82. *Obverse:* portrait of Jehan on horseback, with Urhemmedhin inscription. *Reverse:* two cornucopiae. Breitenbach 1982, 32 mm., crudely designed and struck, weak in the obverse lower left quarter and correspondingly on the reverse. Otherwise fine and free of defects. A very scarce insurgent issue. (*Hauchschild Collection Catalog*)

·14·

WITH A GLITTERING EYE, Jehan Henghmani looked out across the Province of Taroloweh.

This was truly his land now. Much of Taroloweh belonged to him, stretches of territory where his followers had penetrated, welcomed by the people, distributing among them Jehan's grain and rice. And the people looked with awe upon this heroic Jehan Henghmani, who had defeated the great Tnemghadi Army.

The Tnemghadi still regarded him as an upstart bandit. But they did not know how to deal with him. They pulled back into their manor houses and marble temples, praying that somehow the monster would vanish from the earth. At Arbadakhar, the Viceroy Assaf Drzhub was trembling, for he knew Jehan was not about to vanish. The monster was even boasting that he'd soon be sitting in the Vraddagoon in the Viceroy's own chair.

Already, Jehan Henghmani had seized power greater than any Urhemmedhin had wielded in eight centuries. Already, he was the most successful rebel in the Empire's history. But this was not enough for him: He was not content to lord over a corner chewed from Sarbat's empire, nor would he limit himself to buying adherents with the grain and rice he had stolen. The Tnemghadi were too entrenched to be rooted out that way. Jehan would not only have to gain the allegiance of the peasants, but put it to work in a concrete way. He needed men for his army, yes, but that was only part of it. The whole populace would have to be mobilized to uproot the Tnemghadi, to uproot them from the land itself.

Thus came the Land Decree of the First Day of the Month of Ksavra, in the year 1181.

The thrust of this decree, promulgated by Jehan Henghmani, was brief and simple: All owners of land worked by sharecroppers would turn over to their tenants free and clear title to all such lands. The land would be forfeited without compensation. The entire institution of landholding and tenant farming was abolished.

Scribes working at Zidneppa prepared hundreds of copies of this decree in big, clear lettering, and the proclamations were taken by the soldiers out into the countryside, and nailed up on trees and walls. Few of the peasants who saw the actual posters could read, but that was immaterial. The gist of the decree was spread by word of mouth.

As Jehan had calculated, the Land Decree of the First of Ksavra had an electrifying impact. Suddenly all of the peasants in the province became aware that a true revolution was being attempted, and that they were part of it.

The decree was issued upon no authority but Jehan's own military power, which was still actually quite limited. It was one thing to declare the land free, and quite another to make it so. But the point was to plant the idea in peasants' heads; that alone was an apocalyptic step. The sharecropper system had always prevailed and, however oppressive it was to the peasants, it had always been taken for granted. The peasants had seen their struggle as one of meeting the rent payments and persevering. Never had they considered a struggle to change the system and end the payment of rent altogether. But Jehan Henghmani did not blanch from so revolutionary a concept. He blankly told the peasants that *the land was theirs*. They must destroy the land barons once and for all, and they'd be free forever.

It was an idea so bold that no one had dared to whisper it before. Now, shouted from Zidneppa, it set the province on fire.

Over the area they effectively controlled, Jehan's legions went from estate to estate and manor house to manor house to enforce the great Land Decree, to bludgeon the recalcitrant landlords into submission. Usually the arrival of Jehan's army would incite the local sharecroppers to join in the overthrow of their own lord. The barons' private armies—some Tnemghadi, some Urhemmedhin—would defend to the death. Sometimes there were lengthy sieges, but always the insurgents would win. In the end the landlords and their forces would be defeated, their manor houses sacked, and the earth taken over by the peasants.

The greatest of the estates in the Zidneppa region was Kalanhi. Its lord, Jhay Parmar Harkout, possessed a considerable retinue of personal mercenaries and servants. His fortified manor house walled with stone was also the headquarters of a regular Tnemghadi army garrison, and hence was doubly defended. The assault upon Kalanhi was the premier battle in the land war.

A major detachment of Jehan's army led the first attack, and was thrown back with heavy casualties. But meanwhile the peasants from all across the Harkout lands were gathering around the manor house, thousands of them, even old men, children, and women, gaunt and impoverished. Though most of them had never set eyes upon the Jhay and his sumptuous residence, their hatred was ample. They had feared the Jhay, his power had been a mystic force upon them; but now they saw the manor house besieged, the Jhay at bay, vulnerable. They needed no prodding to attack; it was sudden and spontaneous. All at once the thousands threw themselves helter-skelter against the fortifications, flying like moths into a flame. Even Jehan's hardened soldiers stood in awe of the mindless savagery of their assault, fueled by eight centuries of pent-up resentment. These peasants didn't seem to care if they were killed; they felt already dead.

And so, emaciated, half-naked, dirty, goggle-eyed, they threw themselves straight into Harkout's defenders. They were unarmed save for rocks and sticks, but this didn't faze them. Mowed down by spears and arrows, they kept coming, undeterred by the carnage surrounding them. They kept coming, as though there were no end to them. Old crones with flaccid breasts, swollen-bellied children, the hopeless and the helpless, they charged straight into death.

Like worms after a rainstorm, their pathetic bodies littered the approaches to the Harkout manor house. But there were just too many of them; they could not be fended off indefinitely. The defenders exhausted their supply of arrows, and started throwing stones and even pieces of their own armor at the unstoppable horde. But with the force of a locust plague, it swarmed over the fortifications.

The slaughter inside was as complete as it was inevitable. Not a single soul escaped the vengeance of the aroused peasants. Old Harkout himself limped to hide in a closet, but to no avail. The invaders dragged him out. Never had the Jhay seen people like this, bony, unclean, so mad they slavered. They would not listen to his screams. He was overcome by their stink as they closed in on him, pummeling him with punches and kicks and tearing at his flesh with their nails. Finally they dangled him out of a window by his crippled feet, and from below, they vented their fury on Harkout by hacking at him with knives and pikes.

They kept slashing at his corpse, mutilating it beyond recognition, heedless of the flames that rose around them. And in those flames, some of Harkout's defilers perished with him.

Aware of the sanguinary consequences of resisting, many barons yielded to the Land Decree. At the approach of the insurgent troops they would open their gates and hand over elaborate documents of title to their lands. But they were praying that they could ride out this storm, and that the Emperor would soon act forcefully to restore order.

With the deeds delivered into the hands of the illiterate peasants, Jehan's soldiers would move on, wondering whether these ostensibly compliant landlords would renege.

Many of them did repudiate the deeds. But even if the peasants could not read the parchment documents, they understood what was happening, and for the first time they would fight back. They refused to pay their rents and rose up fiercely against the Tvahoud. And of course, the bloodletting was felt on both sides. Thousands of tenant farmers who dared claim the land as their own were burned out of their homes, their crops were seized, and their families were chased off by the barons' thugs. Violence reigned throughout eastern Taroloweh.

The story was different, however, on the estate of Adnan Khnotthros. He was an old and tired man, ground down by the years of troubles, sick at heart at the poor state of his lands and the impoverishment of his tenants. He was smothered by debts, and it was beyond his ability to remedy the situation.

And so, when the legions of Jehan reached the Syad-Rekked, Lord Khnotthros meekly surrendered everything to them. For centuries his Tnemghadi family had lived and ruled in this Urhemmedhin land, but the time had come to go home. Nothing was left here for the once-proud Khnotthros line. Packing his family and his most faithful servants into wagons, he abandoned the estate and set off northward.

Two days later, on the road, the Khnotthros caravan was stopped by a roving band of dispossesed, many of them former sharecroppers of Lord Adnan. The old lord and his people were forced to watch while their women were raped and their breasts cut off. A pregnant servant girl had her belly slashed open, the foetus pulled out and chopped to pieces. They tried to stuff its remains down her throat before they killed her. Then they killed them all.

This butchery was not an isolated incident. While Jehan's troops roved through eastern Taroloweh, catalyzing the class war provoked by the Land Decree, that was often superfluous. The peasants frequently took matters into their own hands without waiting for the army. The rising was not even confined to the rural areas; even the towns and cities seethed.

Years past had seen scattered outbreaks like Dorlexa's, but now the province was ablaze with them. Dorlexa itself was the scene of yet another bloody riot. The Urhemmedhins were lashing out in all directions, but especially did they vent their wrath upon the priests. Everywhere, temples were falling to Urhemmedhin mobs. At Anayatnas the priests, including old Nimajneb Relleth, were stripped naked and paraded at knifepoint, to be jeered and pelted with stones and rotten eggs. Then, one at a time, the priests were tethered behind horses and dragged at a gallop across the hard ground, the pieces torn from them leaving rust-red trails in the dirt.

This was the summer and fall of 1181: a time of blood and fire in Taroloweh.

The Decree of Ksavra frequently brought disaster to the peasants, but this only redoubled their hatred of the privileged classes and their loyalty to Jehan Henghmani. That was what he wanted. He didn't care if those wretches had food or not, whether they owned land or not, nor did he care how many perished in the holocaust. The death of millions didn't matter; they were like insects.

Jehan Henghmani, the benefactor of the peasantry,

would beam with satisfaction every time a baron burned his tenants' homes and ran them off the land. He beamed at the carnage of their wives and children at the hands of murderous thugs. For every man who survived this nightmare would wind up in Jehan's army, with a lust for vengeance.

Taroloweh and its people were in flames, and Jehan Henghmani, their champion, was on the rise.

·15·

HOWEVER VITAL IT WAS to Jehan's plans, he knew the land reform crusade was actually not the main event. The Emperor would not long countenance a limb of his domain being severed. While the war against the barons proceeded from victory to victory, putting great stretches of farmland into peasant hands, Jehan was uncertain whether he could withstand the inevitable Tnemghadi retaliation.

With that impending confrontation firmly in view, the ever-growing peasant army was reorganized. It had to be whipped into shape, finally, as a disciplined military machine. Four divisions were created: one of cavalry, the remainder foot-soldiers, comprising in turn two divisions of infantrymen and one of archers. Each of these divisions was commanded by a general: Leopard Ubuvasakh led the cavalry, while Revi Ontondra took charge of the archers; Kamil Kawaras and Hnayim Yahu each commanded an infantry division.

Each of the divisions was further subdivided into a trio of battalions, with the generals left free to appoint their own battalion leaders. One of those so appointed by General Kawaras was the tall, thin young man from the hills who had distinguished himself in the defense of Zidneppa, and who shared Kawaras' pathological venom against everything Tnemghadi. This was Gaffar Mussopo.

Jephos Kirdahi was given no division to command, but he was appointed a general nevertheless, as Deputy Commander to Jehan. Kirdahi acquiesced in this arrangement; the leader's purposes were, as ever, obscure to him. Did Jehan fear his troops would not obey a Tnemghadi? Yet, if anything happened to Jehan, Kirdahi ostensibly stood to inherit command over the entire army. How could an Urhemmedhin rebellion be led by a Tnemghadi from Ksiritsa? Did Jehan assume that Kirdahi would simply be shoved aside by the other Generals? And the man was sure that his crimes against Jehan, in the dungeon, were not forgotten. Why did he continue to be suffered here at all?

Kirdahi could not answer these questions, but he knew he must follow Jehan. He could never return to the North; in fact, to leave the encampment at all would be suicidal for a Tnemghadi in this province. The other officers barely tolerated him. Thus did Kirdahi grasp how closely his own fate was entwined with Jehan's. And he wondered whether that very fact might underlie Jehan's apparent trust.

It was late in the fall—nine months after the seizure of Zidneppa—that a second imperial army came down upon Taroloweh.

This time, the commander chosen was no young glamor-boy, but instead, as tough a veteran as Sarbat could find: Sureddin Qarafi, victor of the famous battles of Arayela, Hanaleh, and Bouka Lawiy. Qarafi had spent all of his long career fighting the Akfakh; he was no plotter of place intrigues.

The white-haired General closely studied the situation in Taroloweh, and he knew just what he was in for. Unlike Ezir Zoitthakis, Qarafi vowed that he would not be taken by surprise.

Indeed, he was preparing a surprise of his own for Jehan.

Qarafi took closed-mouthed satisfaction as he bent over his maps, his finger circling the port of Zidneppa with its crescent harbor. Then his finger traced slowly up the coastline.

Nevertheless, the battle would open with a surprise for Sureddin Qarafi.

The Zidneppans had not relaxed their attention to the city's defenses, and Revi Ontondra continued to supervise their strengthening, since the forthcoming attack was expected to be much more powerful than the previous one. Although there wasn't sufficient time to wall the city, Zidneppa was fortified as much as possible. Its defenders were to be protected by an elaborate series of ditches, obstacles, and breastworks, with roofs overhead to ward off arrows. For the Urhemmedhin archers, the defenses were laced with small apertures, and erected behind them were huge catapults to hurl destruction at the attackers. These catapults would reverse any advantage to be gained from the bluffs overlooking the city.

Sureddin Qarafi's intelligence corps had gathered all the facts concerning this sophisticated array of defenseworks, and the Tnemghadi commander had carefully coached his officers on how they must prosecute the assault to overcome them. So it was not the Urhemmedhins' bristling defenses that took Qarafi by surprise. The surprise was that they did not rely on those defense-works at all. Instead, they attacked.

Qarafi had arrived at the northern twist of the River Qurwa, about two days' march from Zidneppa. His army was estimated to number between twenty and twenty-five thousand, perhaps four times the size of Zoitthakis'. This great force camped for the night on the western bank of the Qurwa, while their commander pondered the best way of crossing the river.

It would have been possible to ford the river where it narrowed, a few lim to the south. This would have been a quick crossing, but Qarafi feared losing his wagons in the river, and he was in no hurry. Curiously, the Urhemmedhins had left standing a bridge not far north of the encampment. During the night, Qarafi sent scouts ahead to examine the bridge, and when they reported it sturdy, his decision was made.

The next morning, the Tnemghadi army marched northward along the river, to mass at the western end of the bridge. Of course, the crossing of that narrow bridge was a slow undertaking; the army was able to filter across only three abreast. This did not concern Qarafi, since he had plenty of time.

The sun had reached its zenith in the sky, and approximately half of the Tnemghadi army had crossed. These men waited on the east bank while their comrades continued to march across the bridge. It was a relaxing way to spend the day.

That was when the Urhemmedhins struck.

All at once the forests near the east bank were alive with them as they broke cover and charged, from all directions, into the lounging Tnemghadi. Jehan's army was outnumbered heavily by Qarafi's, but the rebels had waited for just the right moment, when the Tnemghadi were divided in half by the river.

On horseback, Jehan Henghmani and Jephos Kirdahi personally led the onslaught. The seven-foot Jehan was alone enough to terrorize the enemy, his face a mangled mass of scars with one burning eye. Screaming, his sword whirling in the air, Jehan galloped directly into the Tnemghadi.

So better to hide, the Urhemmedhins had left most of their horses behind, and most of them now attacked on foot. There were no orderly formations in this battle, no punctilio governing the ensuing close-rank combat. The Tnemghadi quickly recovered their wits, and many managed to mount their horses as the melee got under way. The horsemen took a terrible toll of the rebel foot-soldiers, but the bloodshed was terrific on both sides. They cut each other down, and the dead quickly blanketed the ground.

Meanwhile, all was confusion on the bridge. Scores of soldiers tried to flee back across it, while the officers on the west bank were struggling to move the rest of the army quickly across and into the battle. The result was a squirming mass of humanity going nowhere; many were crushed, trampled, or thrown into the river. At the same time, some of the agitated Tnemghadi commanders were herding their men into the water to swim across; weighed down by their armor, hundreds drowned. The battle itself, too, was splashing along the east bank, and the river was soon running red with blood.

The carnage went on for hours. The Urhemmedhins had started out sweeping the field against only half of the Tnemghadi army on the east bank. But as the fighting was prolonged, there was a constant stream of reinforcements from the west bank.

Finally, the much-abused bridge collapsed with such a roar that it momentarily stopped the battle. More than two hundred soldiers were on the bridge at the time, and almost all of them perished in the crimson waters. The debris of the old bridge was swiftly washed away by the current.

A thousand or more Tnemghadi remained on the east bank. It was pointless now to try to get across, so they fell back and left the scene. Their comrades, equally stranded on the west side, were heavily outnumbered by the

Urhemmedhins at that point. Their massacre brought the battle to a rapid conclusion.

The survivors were somewhat dazed. They could begin to appreciate the cost in lives with which their victory had been purchased; much of their army had been wiped out. Jehan was cantering around, still on horseback, virtually unscathed. The men cheered him, and he saluted them, but he would not give himself over to rejoicing. He had sustained devastating losses, but that was not the only thing troubling him.

"Back to Zidneppa," he ordered, "we must return at once." He was uncertain why it seemed so imperative to march quickly homeward, save for a vague premonition that the battle was not yet over.

After a breakneck march, Jehan brought his army back to Zidneppa, and his inarticulate suspicion was proven right.

He found Sureddin Qarafi's surprise.

Smoke hung in blotchy streamers above the city, and flames were shooting up all over. At first there was no sign of the Tnemghadi; then, the flashing trails of fireballs could be seen, arcing gracefully from the middle of the harbor, to fall within the city.

There were four of them, the largest ships in the Emperor's navy—quite probably, the largest battlecraft in the world. Like smug bloated behemoths, they sat in the middle of Zidneppa's harbor. There was no telling how many more Tnemghadi soldiers were waiting hidden in the bowels of the enormous vessels.

This sea attack was a master stroke, rendering useless the city's whole elaborate defense system. Not only were the Tnemghadi catapults, three to a ship, far more sophisticated in design than the crude Urhemmedhin weapons, but the defense catapults had been installed to face a land assault. Even if these could be turned around to face the harbor, the city's clumsy artillery was neither strong enough nor accurate enough to hit the ships. The citizens had tried to attack the ships by sea, setting out in their fishing boats, but this likewise proved futile. The open boats were sitting targets for the marksmen on the ships. Indeed, the whole city stood helpless while the Tnemghadi were lobbing a continuous barrage of deadly fire bombs into its midst.

These projectiles were made of loosely joined shards of naphtha-soaked wood which were set ablaze. They would burst into pieces when they struck, scattering fragments of fire in all directions. The rude dwellings of Zidneppa, walled with wood, hide, or cloth, went up quickly in flames.

Jehan stood on the rise overlooking the city spread out at his feet. Everywhere were flames; no section had been spared by the diabolic fire balls. Clearly, no defense was possible against the ships. Zidneppa, Jehan's first glorious conquest, was lost, being pounded into a graveyard of ashes before his eyes.

For a long minute he stared, contemplating the disaster in silence. Then he summoned Kirdahi and Kawaras, and dispatched them down into the city, directing them to immediately organize a complete evacuation. There was nothing else to be done.

Pelted by the hail of fire, the people of Zidneppa left their homes forever, while Jehan's army—their own army of liberation—looked on, impotent. The only thing the Urhemmedhin soldiers could do was to coax the people along. Those not already burned out had quickly thrown together their possessions into sacks and carts; many fled with little more than the clothes on their backs.

Jehan remained on the bluff, standing to watch the refugees stream out of their city. He knew what they must be thinking.

These people had persevered through centuries of poverty and oppression. Then, for a few brief months, they had glimpsed the promise of a better life, a moment in the sun. Now they were paying dearly for that one precious moment. The night would descend on them again, and forever.

How they must wonder at their shaken faith—and at the power of the Emperor-god, to punish them so swiftly for their impudence! And the punishment was as harsh as it was speedy. Zidneppa would be razed, never to be rebuilt, nor could these people ever rebuild their shattered lives. They were going forth now into a wilderness where terror, bloodshed, and starvation reigned.

They snorted grimly, some of them, thinking that only fools had expected the moment in the sun to last. Life isn't like that, they knew. Did anyone really imagine that their savior had come? Fools! Did they suppose this mutilated cutthroat was the *Ur-Rasvadhi?* There would never be one; there would never be a promised land. Life promised nothing except misery.

All day it continued, the stream of people out of Zidneppa, trudging with their belongings and slatternly children, tears streaking their sooty faces. As night fell, the refugees huddled on the windy bluffs above the city to watch the spectacle of its burning. By now, Zidneppa was in the throes of a single all-consuming fire. They watched it lighting up the sky, and they mourned the loss of everything, of all their hopes, all they'd held dear. And there were many, many lives to mourn as well: their sons and husbands slaughtered on the battlefield, their people cut down by fire bombs. Horrible pictures were seared into their memories, of friends or brothers staggering enswathed with flames, screaming as they died in agony.

They mourned too for the thousands left behind, who had refused to quit their homes. Mostly aged people, poor and ignorant, they had lived in one spot all their lives, and would not budge. Despite the hopelessness of their situation, the fire falling from the sky, they refused to be dragged out. There was nothing to be done for them. Clinging bitterly to their homes or hovels, they were swallowed by the flames.

At sunrise, the bombardment stopped. Coming in close to shore, the Tnemghadi ships disgorged their cargoes of fresh imperial troops.

They spent the early morning in cumbrous disembarcation. Since Zidneppa was still a fire pit, they were forced to circle the long way around it, in order to launch their attack upon the people who had escaped from the city. This gave the Urhemmedhins ample warning, and time to develop a strategy. The refugees remained camped on the hilltops, giving every appearance of being a helpless civilian target. But meanwhile, Jehan's soldiers hid out of sight behind the hills.

The Tnemghadi never reached the refugee bait. In a well-executed maneuver, the insurgent troops swooped down from the crests of the hills. The imperial forces had the burning city at their backs, and their lines of retreat around it had been cut off by Jehan's men. Thusly trapped, none escaped; they were massacred. It was Jehan's second victory in as many days, and this time, he knew the victory would stick.

There was nothing now for the battleships to do, save pull up their anchors and return back up the coast.

Swelled with triumph, Jehan Henghmani watched the four ships sail away. Then, he looked one last time at the smoking ruins of Zidneppa.

He would not forget this city. Nevertheless, he was bigger than Zidneppa now, and much remained ahead of him. And so, the victor of the Battle of Zidneppa did not waste time in mourning for the city that had given him that victory.

He turned and marched his army westward.

BOOK THREE

•

ARBADAKHAR

·1·

IN THE SIXTEENTH YEAR of the reign of Tnem Al-Khoum Satanichadh, there was born a child at Arbadakhar, to a man named Giradi Resseh.

This Giradi Resseh had come there years before, from the Province of Rashid, as a foot-soldier in the Bergharran army. Unsatisfied with the mean life of a common infantryman, he had managed to learn reading and writing, and became a scribe at the Vraddagoon, the viceregal palace. In time, through perspicacity and prudence, Giradi Resseh had risen to a position of some small authority: he was deputy to the Provincial Tax Assessor, with a private office in the Vraddagoon.

Resseh married a young woman named Zeni, the daughter of a fellow government functionary; and when, in the sixteenth year of Tnem Al-Khoum, his wife grew large with child, he prayed that his firstborn would be a son.

Day after day he went into the temple, prostrating himself before the idol of the Emperor, begging to receive the blessing of a son, who might grow into a man of eminence. Resseh dreamed of spending his later years basking in the glow of a successful son, perhaps a viceroy or a minister of state. The boy's name had already been settled: he would be called Golan, which meant "wise ruler."

But the Emperor-god ignored Resseh's prayers, and the child was a girl. Resseh was bitterly disappointed, even indignant, after all the veneration he had lavished upon the ruler! And despite the seeming absurdity of a female being a "wise ruler," Resseh nevertheless bestowed the selected name upon his daughter: Golana.

In due course, Zeni Resseh again became pregnant, and her husband felt confident that this time his prayers would finally be rewarded. In a grand flourish of piety, Resseh visited the temple every morning and every evening, and half impoverished himself with offerings. Yet this time, his disappointment was even more bitter: Not only was his wife delivered of another girl, but she herself did not survive the rigors of childbirth.

Giradi Resseh reeled from this dual blow. He cried aloud that the Emperor was mocking him, and that his life was cursed.

Saddled with two small daughters and no wife, he was forced to hire a nursemaid, and his finances were severely pinched. Moreover, he could not spare away from his home as many hours as his post at the Vraddagoon demanded. Giradi found his work deteriorating, his position slipping. Life was all sour.

Its only bright spot was Golana, fortunately a robust, clever child who quickly grew tall. When she was eight, there were no more nursemaids, and the entire management of the household fell upon the girl. She had to do all the chores herself, all the shopping, mending, sewing, cleaning, and cooking, and minding her little sister, Tama. But she did all this without visible strain.

Golana was a handsome girl. Her hair was abundant and black, a pure blue-black made all the more striking by her complexion, which was peach-pink instead of the familiar brown. Presumably there was some foreign blood in her mother's lineage. Perhaps the only flaw in her looks was the single Tnemghadi eyebrow line bisecting her face. It made her appear humorless and stern.

She grew tall, outstripping her father while still a child. Her long body was slender and supple like a racing hound's, even as she passed into the beginnings of womanhood. Her limbs were finely hewn, and one always noticed her fingers, deft and delicate.

Much as Giradi Resseh loved this fine daughter, the lack of a son still rankled. Such great things he had envisioned for that son! But he realized that he might have them yet, albeit once removed. When Golana commenced to flower, her father began to think of marriage for her.

It was not unusual for a Tnemghadi girl to be married off at an early age, and often such marriages would be contracted while the bride and groom were still in their cribs. In seeking a husband for Golana, Resseh hoped that her exceptional attributes would offset his lack of station.

He was determined to arrange a match that would enhance his status at the Vraddagoon, and his little wealth. Perhaps he could then afford servants and slaves, perhaps even a pretty young girl or two, whom he could take to bed.

It came to Giradi Resseh's ears that a certain Eshom Mutsukh was interested in marriage. Now this was a man of substance: Of good family, owning rich lands, Mutsukh was a poet, scholar, and historian. Most important, Eshom Mutsukh had recently been appointed Magistrate of Arbadakhar, the chief judicial officer of the province. A stout, slightly hunchbacked man of forty, he had lost his wife to cholera some years before.

It took considerable courage on Resseh's part to approach such a man, but he did go to Mutsukh's house. There he bluntly broached his proposal. Although the Magistrate was hardly impressed with Resseh, he did recall hearing somewhere that the man's daughter was quite a girl. Accordingly, he agreed to come to Resseh's home for dinner several evenings hence.

Her father did not tell Golana why the Magistrate was coming, only that she must prepare the finest meal she had ever cooked. Then, before the distingushed guest arrived, the girl was bathed and perfumed, her hair carefully arranged; and she was decked out in a sparkling new white gown, low-necked and armless to display her radiant pink skin, and tight-fitting to manifest her sleek figure.

The Magistrate was instantly captivated by this tall young girl, especially by the firm intelligence of her eyes. Immediately after dinner, taken aside by Resseh, Mutsukh agreed to marry Golana, and agreed to Resseh's marriage-price as well. Resseh had the contract already prepared, and it was signed that very night, with Mutsukh's personal seal impressed in red wax by his ring.

Golana had already gone off to bed; her father roused her to explain everything. The girl was aghast. At fourteen years of age, she had never thought of marriage, and had only a vague conception of what it would entail. But she understood enough to know it would be a radical change in her life. Up to now she had been confident and secure, taking quiet joy in running the house. Now that was all swept away, and she faced a great unknown.

The girl remonstrated with her father for an hour to

revoke the marriage contract, but he refused. It couldn't be done. At last he said that he would hear no more, that she must obey her father. Left alone, Golana sobbed until dawn.

In the next few weeks, she was the bewildered center of a whirlwind of preparations. All at Mutsukh's expense, dressmakers besieged her with measurements and fittings, hairdressers fussed over her head, and manicurists pounced upon her fingers. A woman-servant was sent to instruct her on how to be a lady. She was taught the proper table etiquette, how to walk and how to speak in refined company, and a hundred other things she'd never thought about.

Not until the morning of her wedding day was Golana first brought to her bridegroom's house. It was one of the grand houses of Arbadakhar, a two-storied structure with an open central courtyard, ornamented with trees and flower beds and stately live peacocks. It was all so beautiful that it flooded over the banks of her imagination.

A servant gave her a rapid tour through all the rooms, and then she was told to wait in the garden the final hour before the wedding. But she disobeyed, and returned to the room in the house which she had found to be the most curious. It was the library, in fact the finest in Taroloweh, but Golana had no idea of that. She didn't know what a book was, had never seen one before. It was their strangeness that had drawn her back to the library. Now, alone there, she handled Mutsukh's books and scrolls, passing her hands over them in reverent awe. She knew only that their writing contained mysteries far beyond her; and the illustrated texts were maddeningly tantalizing.

Then came the marriage ceremony, a brief one performed by one of the chief priests of the temple. It was dull and sober, and Golana went through it feeling like an object manipulated by her elders. But the feast that followed was more pleasant. It lasted from early in the afternoon through well into the night, and Golana tasted many unfamiliar delicacies. Festooned with Mutsukh's jewels in her elaborate marriage dress, she was a center of fond attention, with all the guests generous in their compliments. Between such flattery and the delicious food, the young girl's aversion to the marriage softened.

At the wedding, too, Golana met her husband's children, a fifteen-year-old boy named Eshom after his father, and a girl of twelve named Mara. They exchanged shy smiles with her, and she hoped these children could become her friends in the big house. Golana didn't grasp that she was to be their mother; and she didn't yet comprehend what it would mean for her to be the wife of the old and ugly man who was their father.

But her initiation was not to be delayed. When the feast was finally over, and the last sodden guest had departed, Eshom Mutsukh took his bride by the hand and led her to the bedchamber. Entranced by all the glitter, all the food and wine she'd had, Golana was aglow, and avowed that she would be happy here.

"I'm very glad," her husband answered. "I want you to be happy."

In the bedchamber, Mutsukh lit a dim yellow lamp. He drew slowly close to Golana, and taking her face in his hands, he gently kissed her on the forehead and then on the lips. The touch of his hands was hot, and she did not like his face so close to hers, but she tried to smile and please him.

Then his fingers went to the front of her marriage gown, and he began undoing its buttons. Golana's eyes suddenly enlarged with distress—this old man was trying to unclothe her!

She pushed Mutsukh away; she was taller and stronger than her squat, hunchbacked husband. But he only laughed lightly at this rebuff, and looked at her with bovine eyes.

"Don't be shy," he whispered. "Don't you understand? You are my wife now."

Golana stared blankly at him.

"Don't worry, I'll be gentle. But you must take off your dress, Golana."

Her heart gripped with ice, the girl's mind spun. Her father had given her no instructions save one: that she must obey her husband in all things. And so, her eyes stinging with silent tears, Golana undid her wedding dress, and then the shift beneath it.

Quivering with shame, she stood naked.

Mutsukh came forward and took her in his arms. She felt dizzy with loathing at the touch of this ugly creature, yet she was stricken stiff by her father's firm instruction.

Her muscles were locked rigid as Mutsukh kissed her face and neck.

The Magistrate was gentle, as promised, when he laid her down upon the bed, caressing her hair and face and body lightly, whispering again that she need not be afraid. But she was startled by the liberty with which his hands explored her body, stroking her breasts and private parts, and her horror was not alleviated by the pleasurable tingles it gave her. They were grossly incongruous with what she was feeling, and thus made her ordeal all the more frightening. For all Mutsukh's gentle whispers, it might just as soon have been some enormous slimy worm that was pressing down upon her. Eyes pinched shut, Golana forced herself to submit.

When he spread her legs and squeezed his organ into her, she did not even realize what it was, only that it hurt her. After everything that had already happened, this ripping pain scalded her with its awful prospect. Where would this end, how far would he torment her?

At last his fat misshapen body rolled off. He lay panting for a moment, and then blew out the light. Golana did not move, she couldn't. She waited with a pounding heart for what travesty might happen next, in the dark.

But there were only some more soft words from her husband, and then his snoring, and she surmised her ordeal was over for the nonce. Still shivering with misery, she crawled under the covers, pulled them over her head and drew her knees up into a foetal ball. She was in pain and her legs were damp with blood, but it was the repulsive vision that assaulted her, and she spit forth coughing sobs. How could such monstrosities have happened to her? She wished furiously that she were back in her own bed in her father's house.

When Golana awoke, late the next morning, Mutsukh was gone. She felt stiff, her joints were aching. Worse, though, she was still full of the night's horror, and she huddled a long time beneath the covers. At last, wrapping herself in a blanket, she went to the door and opened it a crack.

"Good morning, Madame," came the voice of a servant woman. She had been waiting dutifully outside the door, probably for hours.

Golana, saying nothing, opened the door and surrendered into the custody of this woman. The servant led her to a bath in perfumed water, scrubbed off the blood from her thighs, and then dressed her in a fresh silk robe. Finally, Golana was served a breakfast on a tray, but she ate very little.

She was informed that Eshom Mutsukh had gone to the Vraddagoon to conduct the affairs of his high office. As for Eshomdai and Mara, they were locked away with their tutors and governess respectively. Thus, except for servants, Golana found herself alone in the big house.

She made her way down into the kitchen, and tried to engage the serving-maids in conversation on various household topics. But she was the mistress of the house, and so they only spoke respectfully and circumspectly to her, agreeing with everything she said. Despite the women's outward obeisance, the attempt at conversation made Golana feel herself a fool.

Out into the courtyard she went next, to walk dreamily among the trees, admiring their sinuous beauty. It was cool and pleasant here. She stooped to inhale the fragrance of the flowers and to chase the shimmering peacocks. But not even these gaudy birds would let her touch them, and she soon grew bored, and returned to the house, idly exploring its rooms. She encountered servants here and there, at work, but they let her wander wherever she wished without scolding her. She felt invisible. Finally, in the afternoon, she wound up in the library, nestled in a chair and slowly turning the pages of a book she couldn't read.

Thus did Madame Golana Resseh Mutsukh pass the day, which she was not anxious to end, because she feared the torments of the night. But finally it was time to dress in her evening clothes. Soon the Magistrate returned home, and she was escorted to meet him in the dining hall for dinner.

Eshom Mutsukh smiled broadly at her, and gently squeezed her hand as they were seated. The children had come to dinner too, but Mutsukh placed his bride close beside him, and insisted on making her the sole subject of conversation. Through dinner, the Magistrate and his children spoke with animation of all the details of the previous day's wedding, and of all the eminent guests who had attended. But Golana said almost nothing, and only nibbled her dinner.

At last he drew up close to her and whispered in her ear. "I can see that you're unhappy. It is quite understandable right now. Your life has met with a great and sudden change. You miss your father and your sister and your little house; you don't feel at home here yet; everything must seem so strange."

"Yes," the girl admitted, "that's part of it."

"I understand completely. Last night, I frightened and upset you. And it hurt. I'm sorry."

Hesitantly, Golana nodded.

Mutsukh smiled warmly and patted her hand. "Please don't fret over it. Only the first time hurts so much. I wouldn't willfully hurt you."

Golana closed her eyes, not knowing how to look at him. Speaking softly like this, in the glow of the dinner candles, he seemed such a gentle soul. She did not dislike him now, he was not a bad man. How could she speak to his face of the terrible loathing that had come over her when he had pressed his body on her—and which would recur when he repeated the act?

"I want you to be happy," Mutsukh affirmed forcefully. "I want you to respect me, and more, to love me."

Golana nodded dully. She did not see how it could ever be that way at all. She would never regain happiness. She felt very small and helpless, a child with prison walls closing upon her.

·2·

IN TIME, Golana's pain at being trapped in the house of Eshom Mutsukh ceased to burn; it settled down into a nagging, irritating sort of pain. She spent her days in languid boredom, her only goal being to somehow consume the hours, wandering aimlessly through the house or sitting in the cool garden, staring after the movements of the peacocks. For hours on end she watched them. With these peacocks she felt a closer kinship than with anyone else in the house. Prized only for their beauty, they too were imprisoned here.

Most of the hours, though, she spent in what became her private sanctuary, where rarely did a servant intrude. This was the library, with its shelves and shelves of books and scrolls she didn't fathom. In a deep chair she would curl up with a heavy tome in her lap and slowly turn its pages, drifting, mesmerized by line on line of script, all unreadable to her. Golana would admire the fluid beauty of the writing, copied out by the hands of faceless scribes. She would trace the lines with her fingers, wondering at their significance. Sometimes Mutsukh would leave a few scraps of parchment on the desk, on which he had been working; and taking his pen and ink, the girl would try to copy from the books onto the blank scraps. Drawing with care, she could faithfully reproduce the writing, but this brought her no closer to its meaning. Sometimes too she would find pictures in the books, painted by hand in glittering colors, even gold and silver; and she would long gaze at these illustrations, looking back and forth between them and the writing, struggling in vain to penetrate the riddle of their relationship.

Often at night, Mutsukh himself would spend hours alone in the library, and having a sense of its sacredness, she never dared disturb him there. Instead, she would wait for him in their bedchamber.

He had been truthful in promising that their intercourse would stop hurting and making her bleed. It seemed to give her husband so much pleasure that she tolerated it without complaint. She would shut her eyes and try to think of pretty things—the peacocks, or more often the pictures of tall, dark-haired princes she had seen in the books. If she could keep her mind off the ugly hunchbacked Mutsukh, suffusing it instead with pleasant visions and especially with those strange jolts of sweetness rising within her from her loins, the act was not so terrible. Indeed, the anxiety preceding it was much worse now than the thing itself.

"You still don't like it," Mutsukh whispered one night afterward.

"I don't mind," Golana replied almost automatically. But she realized this was gradually coming to be the truth.

"I know that I'm an ugly beast."

"Oh, no!"

"Don't say no, it's true. I am not a man who shuns the truth. It doesn't bother me very much. I can't do anything about the looks I was born with, and I'm not resentful, since I was given other blessings to offset them. If I were an evil man instead of ugly, that would be different; I would be responsible for my evil. It is by being a good man that I try to compensate for my ugliness. But I'm sorry if my ugliness makes you unhappy, because I so dearly want to see you happy."

Golana was at a loss to respond.

"So you don't deny it: you are still unhappy. I had hoped you would grow to like it here and feel at home, but I've failed, and you're still miserable. You must tell me what it is that I can do to make you happy. I stand ready to do anything you ask . . . even . . . letting you alone at night."

The girl could hear the lump in Mutsukh's throat as he said this, and her heart went out to him. For the first time she felt a surge of affection, and a deep bond with this man. Before he had seemed so distant, but now she realized they were both unhappy in their awkward situation. And it was equally her fault as his.

In the dark, Golana leaned over and kissed her husband's face, and she pressed her arms around him. She could feel his cheeks damp.

"No," she said, "that wouldn't make me happy. In truth, not at all!"

"Golana, you are such an angel," he whispered hoarsely. "I knew it the first moment I met you, in your father's house. I knew somehow that you are very, very special. For a time, I feared this marriage was nevertheless a terrible error, but now I see that my first impression was right after all. You are a wonderful wife. I would do anything for you. Please help me to make you happy."

After a long silence, Golana spoke. "There is one thing that I wish."

"Yes?"

"Is it possible—or am I presumptuous for a girl?—is it possible that I could learn the magic of your books?"

Mutsukh chuckled softly. "Why, it isn't magic at all. Just ordinary books. Why do you wish this learning? It's nothing for a woman."

"Woman or not, I want to learn. The books are a mystery that torments me. If I learn, perhaps I'll find that I'm not interested in them after all. But I must find out for myself."

"Very well. If that's your wish, you'll have it. The children's tutor shall teach you to read."

"Teach me yourself! Please!"

The darkness covered Mutsukh's flushing. "All right; yes, I will teach you myself," he said. "I would love to."

Now each evening Golana eagerly counted the hours to her husband's coming home. Her ears were peeled for the sound of his arrival, and she would rush down to greet him. They would polish off dinner in some haste, and afterward Mutsukh would take his young wife by the hand, up into his library, to teach her the secret of language.

It was not easy at first. The Magistrate took his own reading skill quite for granted, and his attempt to convey the knowledge was a stumbling one. But Golana was an apt and avid pupil, and soon, by teaching her the sounds of all the letters, he had her reading fluently. She was learning the rudiments of grammar too, and writing; her first letter was to her father, and it naturally took him quite by surprise. Few were the women who could read, let alone write a cogent letter.

Once she had gained these basics, Golana spent every possible hour in the library, poring over the books and scrolls, puzzling out difficult words and expressions. Many of them were in an old, archaic style, but she soon mastered these as well. She was immeasurably excited not just at her ability to decipher the long-mysterious scripts, but at the feast of wonders that the books contained. At the beginning she'd had no idea whether their contents would be worth the trouble of digging out, but she quickly found herself reading in complete absorption. Golana was thirstily soaking up an ocean of knowledge that she'd never known existed. All at once, the world was infinitely greater than the narrow confines that had theretofore bounded her vision.

Her reading was indiscriminate but diligent, so as not to miss the tiniest morsel, even in abstruse texts she could hardly understand. She read history, poetry, science, geography, mathematics, and the sacred books of theology, all precious realms completely new to her. Forgotten was her boredom; her life now, in Mutsukh's library, was an ecstatic romp.

"What does the tutor teach Eshomdai?" she asked one day, referring to her stepson.

Mutsukh replied that he was taught everything a boy should know: literature, religion, history, every conceivable subject.

"Oh, just like in your books!"

"Yes, that's right."

"I would so much enjoy listening to his lessons."

"But such lessons are for boys, not girls."

"You said the same of your books—but I love to read! Oh, please let me listen to Eshomdai's lessons!"

The Magistrate waggled his head in consternation at the remarkable wife he had acquired. But in fact, he was pleased by her hunger for knowledge; it set her quite apart from the ordinary run of pampered women whom he might have married. "Very well," he said, "you may certainly attend the lessons."

At first Golana exercised this privilege sheepishly, hiding herself in a corner while the tutor lectured Eshomdai and engaged him in dialogues. She sat quiet as a cat, as an interloper who knew she didn't belong there. Sometimes, though, the master and the boy touched upon topics that she had encountered herself in the library, and her breath was taken away when she knew the answers to questions propounded by the tutor. But she kept her silence.

One day Eshomdai was studying geography, and he was asked to identify the capital of Diorromeh Province.

The boy casually answered, "It's Ganda Saingam."

And Golana knew that was wrong! She had just been reading about Diorromeh, and while Ganda Saingam was, true enough, its largest city, the capital was actually at Anda Lusis. This time, she could not restrain herself. "No, Eshomdai," she called out from her corner, "the capital is Anda Lusis!"

Both master and pupil looked up, startled. "That's right," the tutor said, "you should be ashamed of yourself, Eshomdai. Even this girl knows that Anda Lusis is the capital of Diorromeh. Even this ignorant girl!"

"I am *not* ignorant!"

"Oh, a hundred pardons, I did not mean to offend you, dear Madame Mutsukh," the red-faced tutor hastily apologized. "I only meant that, obviously, women have no knowledge of these things."

This only aggravated Golana's indignation. "No knowledge? Indeed! Do you suppose it was 'intuition' that told me about Anda Lusis? I know some geography, and I know a great deal more!"

"Then tell me, what is the capital of Kholandra?"

"Vertetis!" Golana answered proudly.

"And of Muraven?"

"Sajnithaddhani!"

"Who was the author of the *Principles of Mathematic Inquiry?*"

"Avdoulzakhar Benna!"

The tutor gasped.

And nevermore would Golana sit in a corner through her stepson's lessons.

As Golana's studies progressed, she began to discuss the things she read with the tutor and Eshom Mutsukh. In the sessions with the tutor, Eshomdai began taking a back seat to his quick-witted but younger stepmother. And the Magistrate took a growing pleasure in his exchanges with Golana. Who ever imagined that a wife could be a stimulating intellectual companion? More and more, Eshom Mutsukh reserved time to spend alone with her.

She read many books about the history of the Bergharran Empire, from the legend of Sexrexatra down through all the dynasties and rulers. She delved too into the related sacred texts, so steeped in their veneration of the emperor-deity. It had previously been her habit to ignore religious matters; that was exclusively the province of men. As a woman, Golana was not expected to make appearances at temple. No one had ever tried to inculcate her with reverence or even belief. Now, her sharpening analytical mind began to ponder.

Her wonderings were propelled by events at Ksiritsa. There, at the Dragon City, in the Palace of the Heavens, the old Tnem Al-Khoum Satanichadh had died. He had sat three decades upon the Tnemenghouri Throne. A new emperor was taking up the Scepter, the twenty-year-old Prince Sarbat, crowned in a fabulous ceremony. Thus too passed the godship; and accordingly, at the temple of Arbadakhar, there was performed a glorious pageant to inaugurate worship of this new god.

But was not this Sarbat a man, had he not been born of woman? What then distinguished between a god and a mere mortal? That one was *called* a god and worshipped by credulous people?

Sarbat received that worship now because he was the son of a god; and so too, Tnem Al-Khoum had inherited the godship from his father. But the line was not unbroken. Golana had read in books of how Sharoun the Sword had risen from the army to overthrow Riyadja Tsitpabana. How could a peasant unseat a god, and deify himself instead, through very earthly cleverness and bloodshed? How could this make gods of the usurper's descendants? And what if some general came along now and knocked Sarbat off the throne?

But the sacred books solemnly and simply held that the throne was the seat of godhood. They also decreed that every human event was according to the god's whim, and his whim followed no logic any mortal could understand. "The Emperor works mysteriously," the parchments said; "do not attempt to comprehend his justice, for to mortals, there is none." Golana wondered if this nihilistic mumbo-jumbo was just a mask to conceal the truth: that the Emperor was powerless, neither hearing nor responding to prayers. In fact, no god at all.

The world, she observed, was indeed devoid of justice. There was no rightness in her being rich and pampered while millions starved. There was no reason for the good to suffer while evil men thrived. The world was fraught with inequity, Golana concluded, not because the Emperor's whim was beyond comprehension, but because the Emperor was no god. People clung to their belief in a god only to impose a façade of order upon a world which, in their hearts, they knew was orderless if not insane.

Such a faith was fundamentally repellent to Golana. She could not believe the scriptures were true, but more than that, she would reject them *even if true!* The perverse god they depicted was hateful to Golana. It was bad enough for the world to be unjust and insane—but it would be far worse to believe there was a conscious agency making it so. If such a tyrant god existed, she would not worship him, but fight him.

Skillful a reader as Golana became, Mutsukh's library contained many books that baffled her. Their scripts resembled the one she knew, but with different letters and words she couldn't understand. She could never puzzle out any of these texts, could not even scratch their surfaces. And there were even books with writing that was wholly alien.

When she inquired about this problem, Eshom Mutsukh patiently explained that he had taught her to read only Tnemghadi. Some of his books, however, were Urhemmedhin, and he also owned some rare volumes from foreign lands like Kuloun, Mohonghi, Laham Jat, and Valpassu.

"Can you read those languages?" she asked.

"Some of them, yes."

"Would you teach me Urhemmedhin?"

Eshom Mutsukh was nonplussed by this request. It was extraordinary enough that his wife could read Tnemghadi. While he was pleased by her zest for learning, to read Urhemmedhin was another matter. It was true that Mutsukh and other high officials learned the language, in order to govern the province. But for anyone else, a knowledge of Urhemmedhin would be regarded as subversive and heretical.

Mutsukh pondered long before speaking. Then he said, "You can't possibly have read all the Tnemghadi books I have."

"No, I haven't."

"Then why do you want to read the Urhemmedhin ones?"

"Because there *are* Urhemmedhin books."

The man pursed his lips and thought some more. "Very well," he whispered slowly, "I will teach you, but on one condition. You must never reveal to anyone that you can read Urhemmedhin."

Golana nodded, and her lessons began.

The southern tongue was not difficult to learn. As she had suspected, it was closely related to Tnemghadi in its script, vocabulary, and grammar, and Golana tackled it enthusiastically. Her progress was speeded by her impatience to plunge into this whole new realm, too. Mutsukh's proviso that her knowledge remain a secret enhanced her pleasure in it. Within weeks, Golana had mastered the Urhemmedhin language.

At first her readings in it were pedestrian: ancient poems and parables, and dusty histories of long-forgotten dynasties. This history, predating the conquest by Khatto Trevendhani, had been ignored in all Tnemghadi texts. It was with curiosity, but little more, that Golana read this old southern history.

After some weeks of such books, she happened to remember a certain scroll that had intrigued her long before. It had a relatively modern casing, and embossed on the outside was the name of an insignificant Tnemghadi poet of Ozimhedi times. However, on opening that scroll, she found the parchment crisp and brown with age, and written in a script that was unreadable to her. Golana had shrugged and put the scroll away, assuming that it had accidentally been stored inside the wrong casing. But now she thought of it again, and decided to have another look.

With her new knowledge, it took but a moment to discern the identity of this moth-eaten scroll, and the reason for its concealment in an innocuous Tnemghadi casing.

This was the Book of Urhem.

Golana's heart thrilled when she realized what she was holding in her hands. This was the great forbidden book, the one book the Tnemghadi dynasties had tried for centuries to suppress. This was the most important book ever written, yet no one dared speak its name, and countless people had been burned to death for possession of it.

It was no accident that this book was hidden in Eshom Mutsukh's library. Golana's respect for her husband waxed, to know that despite the danger and proscriptions upon the Book of Urhem, his wide-ranging intellect had led him to procure and preserve a copy.

With infinite care, Golana spread the precious scroll upon the desk. Plainly it was centuries old. Probably some wretched fugitive in a hidden cellar had copied it onto this fragile parchment. Hungrily, she drank in the words.

Written in a simple, clear, almost poetic prose, here was the story of King Urhem. From his palace at Naddeghomra, he and his Queen Osatsana had reigned over seven provinces. Detailed were the virtuous deeds and wise teachings of King Urhem, and his love for Osatsana.

Riveted to the scroll, Golana read of how the Queen fell ill, and all the wise men despaired of saving her. But the girl smiled at this. Her reading of countless fables gave her confidence that soon, some miracle would be described, saving the heroine.

King Urhem, according to the book, invoked the names of all the gods, and swore that if Osatsana were spared, he would forsake everything he had—including her! But the result was not at all what Golana had so blithely expected. The King was rebuked by the gods, for trying to exchange power and wealth for human life. Osatsana perished, and shattered by grief and guilt, poor Urhem fled the palace to become a beggar.

Golana was stunned by the tragedy of this story. And for the first time in her life, she became aware of an alternative to the Tnemghadi emperor-worship which she so despised. Whereas the Tnemghadi held human life worthless, the lesson of King Urhem was that life was priceless. Queen Osatsana, for whose life Urhem had sinfully tried to bargain, was a great and good woman, but that was irrelevant. If every life is infinite in value, then all are equal, peasants as precious as queens. And finally, just as

Urhem's love for Osatsana had been the glory of his life, his scroll decreed that if human life is sacred, then love, the nexus of two lives, is their apotheosis.

Golana devoted days in the library to studying this forbidden scroll, savoring every line and committing many passages to memory. But only obliquely did she ever dare to discuss it with Mutsukh. When years passed, they came to share an unspoken understanding that she must have stumbled upon it one time or another; but never did she confirm the fact, or speak openly of the profound impression the book had made on her.

By now, she had studied enough books to read with vigilant skepticism. She knew there were discrepancies from book to book on points of history or science. Surely the truth about such subjects as life and gods and love would be an elusive thing, that no one book could ever monopolize. As for the Book of Urhem, despite her reverence for it, she could not be sure the story had happened quite that way.

Thus, while she had spurned the Tnemghadi faith, she did not become a secret acolyte of Urhem. Much as it venerated human life, the Urhemmedhin creed was an abject failure at protecting life. The Urhemmedhins' own lives had been treated as worthless, subhuman. They were demeaned, tormented, wantonly destroyed. The worst of all fell on those who actually worshipped Urhem. Their lives were not blessed with love at all, but dogged by the hatred and contempt harbored by the Tnemghadi against them, and by the hatred they bore for the Tnemghadi in return. The southern people were no better pupils of Urhem than were the Tnemghadi, when their mobs would riot and commit unspeakable atrocities.

And yet, Golana kept the Book of Urhem in her heart. Its ideas had a power and a majesty. She understood why the Tnemghadi had so vehemently striven to stamp out that creed, so inconsistent with their own. And she understood the strength in that uplifting creed that had sustained it through eight centuries of suppression.

·3·

Like an irresistible tide was Jehan Henghmani's westward march across Taroloweh.

Eight hundred years before, the conquerors had marched through this land, spreading terror and destruction, pressing the Tnemghadi yoke upon the people's necks. Now came the liberator, lifting off that yoke.

From town to town he marched: Sratamzar, Dorlexa, Anayatnas, and systematically on westward, on through Ravdasbur, Deb Rabotch, Yeruthsheri and Lahjama. It was a triumphant march, for the Tnemghadi army didn't oppose him. At his approach the garrisons would close down, the officers hurrying their troops westward to Arbadakhar, there to make their stand.

But the towns were left to Jehan, and in all of them the people came out to celebrate the arrival of the hero. Through their main streets he would march his army, and thousands would come, from miles around, to see the spectacle. They would gasp at Jehan's gigantic frame and his gruesome face. They knew he was an illiterate brigand of raw ambition, but he was nonetheless their liberator.

And so they danced and flailed the air with their salutes, and clapped their hands and waved their banners, and they screamed out their ecstatic cheers: *Vahiy Jehan!—Victory to Jehan!*

Yet this triumphant march, this jubilant euphoria, did not mean a cessation of the fire and bloodshed. As Jehan moved through new territory in the central and western portions of the province, the war against the barons followed him, like a fearful plague sweeping across the land. Word of the Ksavra decree had spread into these parts, stimulating no little unrest. Now, the coming of the peasant army was the matchstick that ignited the conflagration. It was war between the sharecroppers and their landlords, and by force of their overwhelming numbers, the peasants everywhere prevailed. The manor houses were sacked, the lands seized, the baronial class exterminated; but the peasants paid for their liberation with lakes of blood.

It was desperation that made them throw away their lives so readily. They were squeezed white with hunger, and Jehan had exhausted his store of free food. But the rising, and seizure of baronial food hoards, was only a temporary solution. Jehan had to provision his army, too, and there simply was not enough to go around. If anything, the disorder would even further disrupt sources of food.

But it was not full bellies Jehan was aiming at, it was revolution; and revolution is fed by empty bellies.

And indeed, despite all of the suffering and death that Jehan brought down upon them, still the people cheered him on. They put all blame on the eternal villains, the Tnemghadi, and their hatred for the northern race was sent into a vicious pitch by the burning of Zidneppa. The news of it shuddered through the province like a black cloud. Never before had any rebellious town been dealt so harsh a retribution. The city's destruction was a chilling warning, and frightened as they were by it, the Urhemmedhins were not intimidated. Zidneppa had to be avenged, and the city's name became a battle cry.

And so, as he marched across Taroloweh, Jehan's army swelled with thousands of inspired recruits. The heavy losses incurred to defeat the Tnemghadi at Zidneppa were more than replaced. And the more powerful his army grew, the more quickly he drove it westward, to administer the final blow—at Arbadakhar.

At Arbadakhar, Assaf Drzhub was waiting for Jehan Henghmani.

To wait was all the harried Viceroy could do. He paced the floors of the Vraddagoon, feeling himself at the mercy of events, maddeningly impotent. He had begged Ksiritsa for another army, but knew it would never come in time. Two proud armies had already been chewed up by this rebel, a feral opponent who abided by no civilized conventions. Hadn't they burned his home base, Zidneppa? And what had Jehan done? He turned his back on the flames and marched. Monster! How could you fight a man like that? In time, of course, the rising would be crushed.

But that was scant comfort to Assaf Drzhub, with the rebel army breathing down upon Arbadakhar.

The Viceroy had already abandoned the rest of the province to Jehan. He had made an early decision that to fight it out in the hills and towns would be self-defeating. Instead, Drzhub pulled all his forces back to defend the capital. This way, perhaps he could at least save Arbadakhar—and himself.

The entire city shared the tension of its Viceroy. Never had so many soldiers been seen in the streets, which itself was a provocative situation. And the Tnemghadi here were not alone in their fright. The Urhemmedhins also understood what the battle might be like. They were praying for Jehan's victory, but praying too that they'd survive it.

The rebel army, so much feared, came softly.

There it was without fanfare one morning, arraying itself into an encampment surrounding Arbadakhar's walls. There was no panoply, no martial noise, no attack. It had the air of a harmless gypsy band squatting unobtrusively.

And so they remained for several days, the two sides seemingly ignoring each other. The city's gates were locked, and no one ventured out. But from the ramparts the Tnemghadi sentries kept an anxious vigil, not knowing when the unnatural calm might explode. The waiting ground upon their nerves.

Then one night Jehan's force rose up all at once, gathering itself from all around the city into one dark beast that flung itself snarling at the gates of Arbadakhar.

The Tnemghadi were surprised but not unready. Reinforced, the gates withstood Jehan's battering rams. Meanwhile the Urhemmedhins were swarming up the walls on wooden scaling ladders, but this too the Tnemghadi had anticipated. Grappling the ladder-tops on big iron hooks, they shoved them back from the walls, toppling them over, and the Urhemmedhins clinging to the ladders like flies were plunged to their deaths. And the attackers were pelted savagely too with arrows, heavy stones, fireballs, and even flaming, boiling oil. Many trapped on burning ladders were roasted as on spits.

Great numbers were mangled, burned, and killed, but they persisted almost until dawn. Then, at Jehan's sudden order, they pulled back as quickly as they'd attacked, leaving the dead and dying alike piled up at the foot of the walls.

Even the casualties were made instruments of the siege now. Strewn about beneath the walls, some of them were still alive, but there they would stay. When the gates opened and a Tnemghadi corps emerged to attend to these unfortunates, they were driven back inside by a barrage of arrows.

A few of the wounded did manage to crawl back to Jehan's camp, but the rest were left to die slowly in the sun. They could not be buried, and their stench rose and permeated half of Arbadakhar, a pungent miasma that nauseated those inside the walls.

The night attack had caused the Tnemghadi comparatively light casualties. Still, the assault had been unmanningly ferocious, and they were not spoiling for another. The dead and wounded left so horribly outside the gates seemed proof that the Urhemmedhins were inhuman, barbarous. Furthermore, supplies within the walls were dwindling. What would happen when they ran out?

The Urhemmedhin population of the city asked this question too. No one had slept the night of the attack, listening to the din of screams and crashes, watching the display of deadly fire. Jehan Henghmani was their champion, and yet, such a holocaust was hammering at their gates that they found themselves praying those gates would hold.

They were caught between the two opposing forces, and their deliverance could come only if the city were peaceably surrendered to Jehan. Some of the leading Urhemmedhin citizens had begged the Viceroy to do just that, and save the city from destruction. Now, after the attack, with the stench of death polluting their nostrils, even many Tnemghadi were beseeching the Viceroy to relent. They argued that Jehan might, after all, be merciful. But Assaf Drzhub would hear none of this; he knew what his own fate would be, in the event of surrender.

Nevertheless, despite the Viceroy's resolve, the situation inside the city was crumbling rapidly. Bitter enmity between citizens and troops was a corrosive in the air; it crackled with violence. They fought over food. Hoarding became rampant; storekeepers were beaten and robbed when they withheld their wares. With nerves grated raw, order was disintegrating. Riots erupted on streetcorners, and suddenly the city was alive with pitched battles between maddened soldiers and bloodthirsty peasant mobs.

The Tnemghadi troops were abandoning their patrols, and barricading themselves in their garrisons. Mutinous sentiment swelled. At night, one of the principal barracks was put to the torch by unknown incendiaries. Also anonymous were the assassins of Falor Jemiry and Yasiruwam Iohanidis, two of the top-ranking Tnemghadi officers. Apparently, some younger officers seized the Vraddagoon and arrested Viceroy Drzhub, but all was shrouded in tumult.

Sensing this upheaval among the Tnemghadi, the mobs ran wild. In frenzy they attacked the garrisons and temple. The whole city was convulsed by rioting and looting. Fire and blood were everywhere. It was a night of terror in Arbadakhar.

As the night waned, Jehan Henghmani watched the plumes of thick gray smoke snake into the dark sky above the city and guessed at the collapse within. He would wait while the mobs spent their fury upon the Tnemghadi, rather than waste his own army doing the same job.

Let them die in droves to liberate their city, he told himself. Thus will they treasure its liberation all the more.

At last, as morning broke, the huge gates swung open; and Arbadakhar was delivered to Jehan Henghmani, the deliverer.

· 4 ·

THE WOMAN SQUINTED and sniffed distastefully at the foul air.

She covered her face with her hands; the air stank so, she felt smothered. For days, there had been the rising putrid stench of the bodies left to rot outside the city's walls. Now there was the acrid tang of smoke and fire close at hand, stinging her eyes. The early morning sky was blackened with smoke. And there was, too, the filthy smell of the mob, a pungent animal stink.

The mob was, at this very moment, raging through her house.

She knelt down, coughing, in the ruin of her garden. They had been here only seconds ago. They had torn up the garden, and with it the beautiful peacocks that she had adored so many years. Shrieking, the poor birds had been dismembered alive, their blood and feathers scattered all over.

The woman lifted one long, delicate feather off the ground. She held it to her face, and turned it slowly, watching its iridescent colors change, from indigo to cool blue-green, and then to gold.

She was alone; all her servants had fled. For a quarter of a century they had served her faithfully, no less devoted to Golana than to her late husband, Eshom Mutsukh. There had seemed a family relationship among them, between the Tnemghadi aristocrats and their Urhemmedhin servants. But when the city fell into the throes of chaos, they scattered, leaving her alone in the house, probably to share the fate of her peacocks. Golana sadly shook her head. At least her servants hadn't joined the mob in ransacking the house.

All night she had been up, stalking through the house. When she found herself abandoned and alone, she did not know whether she would stand defiantly against the storm, or lie down and die. Her whole world was being extinguished. Some moments she was wracked with gales of grotesque laughter; some moments she wept piteously. And she remained within the empty house, strangely calm as morning broke. She was no longer laughing or weeping, but instead was gripped by a lassitude of dumbweight sadness.

She could hear the wild cries of the mob, but stood quietly still. Only at the last possible moment, as they struck the house, did she rouse herself to hide under a stairway. They smashed down the doors, and in their frenzy swept out into the open courtyard, where they ravaged the garden, uprooting all the plants and shrubs and tearing the live peacocks limb from limb. Golana pressed her hands over her ears to shut out the birds' terrified shrieks, but forced herself to stay hidden until the mob had passed from the courtyard to sack the house itself.

Now, heavy with a syrupy inertia, she knelt in the wrecked garden, slowly twirling the feather. She sat quite still, listening to the screaming mob smash everything inside her house. Already flames were spurting. She listened with an eerie detachment, feeling no impetus even to save her own life. Completely unrooted by the holocaust, she would sit here in the garden, awaiting its conclusion.

But then with a sudden gasp she leaped up. Dropping the feather, Golana burst into the house, dashing upstairs two steps at a time.

The scene at the library struck her like a blow on the face. Half a dozen rioters were tearing the shelves off the walls, ripping apart the books and scrolls, stomping on them. The floor was littered with heaps of shredded parchment.

In the tumult they didn't see her, and for an instant she was stung dumb by what she was looking at.

Then she screamed, *"Stop it!"*

The men froze and gawked at her, this brazen Tnemghadi woman. One of them was holding a leather-cased scroll, about to rip it apart. Golana's finger jabbed at him. "Do you know what that book is?" she demanded.

"Do you know what it is? *That is the Book of Urhem!*"

The man looked stupidly at the thing he held in his hands.

"Don't you know how many of your people died for that book? You will not destroy it. Give it to me!" Golana held her hand out, it was a command. The man shoved the book into her arms and then fled past her.

"Now get out, all of you. Destroy whatever else you wish, but you will not touch these books!"

And indeed, the intruders broke and bolted from the library, leaving Golana behind.

She dropped to her knees, as though awakening from a trance. Cold sweat glazed her body. It was a miracle they hadn't torn her to pieces like the peacocks. The noise of devastation through the rest of the house still pounded at her ears, and the smoky air bit at her, but she realized she was a survivor.

Golana hugged the book in her arms, pressed it to her breast and kissed it reverently. It was, in fact, an almost worthless old geography.

Then she scrabbled among the parchment scraps littering the floor like sawdust. Here were the remains of the Book of Urhem, the fragile ancient scroll shredded beyond reclamation. Golana threw herself down upon the torn pieces and burst into tears.

Sitting in his makeshift throne-room, Jehan Henghmani was an imposing figure. This was the holy sanctum of the Arbadakhar temple. Jehan had appropriated one of the Chief Priest's great stone chairs, and set it up on the platform that had previously held the golden idol of Tnem Sarbat Satanichadh. Now he sat there flanked by his aides, towering over them as godlike as the Emperor.

A woman stood before him, her eyes glittering.

She was not a young woman, almost forty, but her skin was taut and of an extraordinarily fair hue. Her facial contours retained the imprint of high-cheekboned beauty, and, although streaked with gray, her black hair was still striking. Tall and slim, she bore herself regally.

She had come here on foot, from the burned-out shell of her once-grand home. Two Urhemmedhin servants had accompanied her, having sheepishly returned after the riots quieted down. But they waited outside. She came before Jehan alone.

Jehan looked coldly at her. He surmised she was after some special treatment, perhaps even restitution of her losses. Many from the old privileged classes had come like that to grovel before Jehan. All had been spurned, and he resolved this woman would fare no differently.

Perhaps she would offer herself to him, but it would not help her. It was a familiar sequence by now: Jehan would take these women to his bed, use them, and then cast them out. Their pleas would be refused.

The woman stepped forward and bowed before the warlord, but not too low. Her homage was proper, not lavish. Jehan noted her graceful bearing in this brief ritual. Here was a woman of true refinement, which was disappointing: While it enhanced her desirability, it also made her unlikely to submit to him.

"Salutations, General," she said, dipping her head a second time. "With your leave, I wish to introduce myself. I am Madame Golana Resseh Mutsukh, widow of the late Magistrate of Arbadakhar, Eshom Mutsukh."

"I see," said Jehan, deliberately brusque.

"Perhaps you will remember who my late husband was?"

"Should I?"

Golana smiled tightly. "Six years ago, when you were captured by the army, you were brought here to Arbadakhar. You were arraigned before the Magistrate—my husband, Eshom Mutsukh."

"Only six years? It seems longer. At any rate, perhaps I should be grateful to your husband. His sending me to Ksiritsa saved my life."

"It was my idea that you be sent there."

"Then what kind of man was your husband, to take the advice of a woman?"

"He was a very wise man. He was wise enough to take the advice of a woman when it was sound advice. I wish you the good fortune of such an adviser, as well as the wisdom to heed her."

Jehan gave Golana a penetrating look, then chuckled. "That was well said, Madame."

She merely nodded.

"So speak equally well your business here."

"That, I have already done," she replied.

Jehan squinted his one eye at her. "Don't play games with me," he warned.

"Begging your pardon, General, I did not mean to do so.

I have indeed already fulfilled my mission in coming, that being to introduce myself to you."

Jehan was dubious. "And that is all? You don't want anything from me?"

"That is all, unless you should wish something further of me."

"Such as what?" said Jehan with a leer.

"I might humbly mention that I am an extremely well-educated woman. I can read and write both Tnemghadi and Urhemmedhin, and a few other languages. I am well versed in history, geography, mathematics, the arts and sciences, and every other subject. As I've mentioned, I assisted my late husband in his public functions. I am therefore intimately familiar with the art of politics and government, and with the province which fortune has entrusted to your hands. For those reasons, you may possibly find my services and counsel of some usefulness."

Jehan Henghmani shifted in the stone chair and rubbed his chin. He was decidedly abashed at this proposition from a well-bred Tnemghadi woman, of exactly the class he was busily exterminating. But he was not going to be charmed into foolishness; he remained wary. After all, this woman might be aiming at sabotage or betrayal.

"Why do you come to me with such an offer?"

She smiled boldly. "I will not be disingenuous. My house has been wrecked, my wealth is gone, and I'm lucky to be alive. You know how dangerous it is in this city to be a Tnemghadi, not to mention the widow of the former Magistrate. But self-preservation is not my only motive. I have closely followed your exploits this past year—and, much as it may surprise you, I have a considerable admiration for you."

Against her disarming mixture of candor and flattery, Jehan put up a stony front. "How can a woman like you have any admiration for my cause?"

Golana's white teeth shone. "I did not say that I had admiration for your *cause*." She looked him straight on and lowered her voice. "No more than you yourself admire it."

Jehan Henghmani's head jerked up, taken aback by this audacious remark. Even a man wouldn't speak with such temerity. Jephos Kirdahi, seated nearby, leaned forward, and there was an agitated rustle among all those present. For a moment, the remark hung in the air, drawing no response.

"This lady has quite a tongue," said Jehan at last. He leaned back with studied laziness in the stone chair. Golana's face was fearless. Then Jehan snapped his fingers and ordered the hall cleared. Obediently, Kirdahi and all the others got up and shuffled out. They winked at Jehan, and at each other, surmising what would now happen to this brash, handsome Tnemghadi woman.

They faced each other alone.

He spoke softly, so that no eavesdropper might hear. "Don't fear me. I won't rape you."

When Madame Mutsukh replied by snorting with disdain, Jehan decided that she was a smart woman indeed. She could read his mangled face better than he could read her perfect one.

"Just what did you mean by what you said?"

"We may be from different worlds, but I think we understand each other, Jehan Henghmani. You are an opportunist, using the misery of the peasants to advance your own ambitions. You beat them into the ground during your old bandit days, and now you're giving them land and food only to get what you want from them in return."

"I thought you said you admired me."

"Yes, I do admire a man who knows what he wants, knows how to get it, and has the courage to do it."

"I think you are correct that we understand each other, Madame. You know why I have embraced the cause of the peasants. But what about you? Are you here to get what *you* want?"

"Certainly. I said so."

"But what, exactly, is it that you want?"

"The same thing you want."

Jehan smiled, then grinned, then shook with laughter. All the while Madame Mutsukh watched him soberly. Jehan stopped laughing and riveted his one eye on hers.

"I do believe," he said, "we understand each other."

"Cosmically."

BERGHARRA—Kingdom of Taroloweh, copper double falu of Jehan Henghmani, year 1182. *Obverse:* uncrowned portrait of Jehan, left, showing facial scars. *Reverse:* cornucopia with inscription, "Urhemmedhin Kingdom of Taroloweh," and Arbadakhar mint mark. Breitenbach 1987, 30 mm. Choice Very Fine with a rich dark green patina. Scarce. (*Hauchschild Collection Catalog*)

·5·

IT WAS SUNNY in the spacious garden of the Arbadakhar temple. The burnt plants and brush had been cleared away, and the garden had begun to sprout greenery again. The sun was warm, but there was a light breeze; a pleasant day to sit in the garden.

Sunny too, and light were Maiya's eyes as she relaxed on a bench. She was watching her son at play, and laughing with him. Everything seemed so happy and fine. And yet, to watch the boy's unburdened gaiety produced a gentle tug of melancholy. Maiya could not identify it, and shrugged if off. Perhaps it was because she had left her own childhood so prematurely, in another life.

Maiya never dwelt upon the past any more; its memories were at last becoming vague blurs, almost expunged. The past was not what mattered now. Ever since her arrival at Zidneppa, Maiya was swept up with a rapturous vision: that her father would become a king, and she herself a princess. And her son would be a king one day too. She would be the mother of a king, the founding mother of a glorious dynasty.

There was Maiya's vision of her certain destiny, shaped between two kings, father and son, her father and her son. To them, the mighty warlord and the little boy, Maiya would devote her life. She was mother to the boy, and to her father all but wife. And in thusly consecrating herself to father and son together, Maiya saw the perfect harmony, the three of them all linked together through her body, intermingled, spawned and spawning.

Such a pleasant little family it was, even in the midst of war and tumult. Jehan always found time for them to be together. He adored his daughter, returned to him as though from the dead. And he adored the boy who had his name, Jehan, Jehandai, *little Jehan*. He would spend

239

hours playing with Jehandai, carrying the boy on his massive shoulders, playing with balls and toy soldiers and many other games. He was the picture of a doting grandfather.

And no matter how often Maiya would insist the relationship was closer, Jehan ignored it. He gave up trying to reason with her and concluded that, at least regarding Jehandai, his darling little girl was mad. It was, if anything, fortunate that she had any sanity at all left; surely there was ample cause for her one mania. What she had been through! Who could come out of that dungeon with a mind all in one piece? Had Jehan himself?

So he forgave her touch of madness. It seemed little enough price to pay for having her alive and well.

Her eyes sunny and light, Maiya sat in the garden watching her son at play. It was a splendid day.

So quickly was her vision coming true! Hardly a year had passed since she'd trekked on foot, dirty and hungry, to Zidneppa. Now she was sitting in the pretty garden of the Arbadakhar temple, from which her father ruled the Province of Taroloweh.

He was, in everything but name, the king. He had carved out a new kingdom for himself, yet strangely, he'd abjured a crown. Even his newly minted Taroloweh coins portrayed Jehan bareheaded.

This Maiya found perplexing and irksome. One day, she fashioned a mock crown out of parchment with nuts, grapes, and berries for jewels.

"Won't you let me crown you, Paban?" she said, displaying her handicrafted work.

Jehan laughed with delight when he saw the charming toy crown. He knelt at Maiya's feet, bowing his head. Ceremoniously, with Jehandai watching, giggling, Maiya performed the coronation rite.

"In the name of Sainted Urhem, I crown thee Jehan the First, King of Taroloweh. And tomorrow, thou wilt be Emperor of all Bergharra."

Jehan solemnly rose to full height wearing the paper crown. "Emperor of Bergharra! Why, I am deeply honored, fair maiden. But don't you think we ought to wait until we get to Ksiritsa?"

Maiya cawed loudly. "Ha! Old Tnem Sarbat must be shaking in his boots. We'll be there soon enough."

Jehan took the crown down from his head and turned it slowly in his hands. "It's a very beautiful piece of work, you know? I'm impressed that you made such a lovely thing. I'm touched and grateful for it."

"My crown, Paban, is even better than a real one. When you grow tired of this crown, then you can eat the jewels!"

"Oh, Maiya, by the time I ever grow tired of such a pretty crown, these grapes and berries will be far too old to eat."

Maiya shook her head. "No, Paban, the paper crown is only temporary. You must soon exchange it for a real crown, a golden one with real jewels. You are the King now!"

Jehan nodded, sighing thoughtfully. "Yes, I suppose it's true, I really am the King of Taroloweh. It is what I dreamed, yet it seems such a miracle. Perhaps my dream was so audacious that the gods that be were tickled by it, and just for amusement's sake, they granted it. Sometimes I wonder, too, if the gods have raised me up only for the fun of knocking me down again."

"Oh, no! Don't let them!"

"No, Maiya, I won't let them. I will fight even the gods if I have to."

"And what about a crown, Paban? What about a crown?"

Jehan shook his head. "I have all the power of a king. That's what counts. But a crown—no, that would be a mistake. As long as I have the power, I don't need the crown; and if I take the crown, then I could lose the power."

"But why?"

"I did not get here on my own. It was the people who gave me this power. They shed their blood and died for me. They are the scum of the earth, and they fight for me because I am one of them. To put a gold crown on my head would change that. They've been ruled for centuries by men with crowns, and it was never good for them. In me, they see hope for something different. I can't afford to become just one more king to them."

Maiya reflected for a moment. "These words came from your lips, but not from your head."

"Perhaps."

"Then whose idea was it that you take no crown?"

"What difference does that make? It's a very prudent idea, and I agree with it."

"Then why are you ashamed to tell me whose idea it was? Was it Kirdahi, that Tnemghadi? No, he's too stupid; I know who it was." Maiya's voice became laced with scorn. "It was that *other* Tnemghadi. That *woman.*"

"That woman; that Tnemghadi woman."

These words were becoming annoyingly familiar, often whispered behind Jehan's back, sometimes even blurted to his face.

Madame Golana Resseh Mutsukh had manifested like a weird spirit from another world. Everything about this woman suggested that she ought bitterly to despise Jehan Henghmani. And indeed, had she not publicly insulted him? She had performed subtly, she had smiled, and her insult had the weight of truth. But it was nonetheless an act of gross impudence.

There was consternation among Jehan's entourage when there was no reprisal for the woman's insult. And that consternation was to deepen.

Jehan was as coarse as any of his underlings, yet he could appreciate the substance of Golana Mutsukh. He left their first encounter strangely moved; she stuck in his mind like a fishhook. She was more than merely intelligent. Never had Jehan met a woman who would dare speak out as Madame Mutsukh did, and her voice was not sheer nerve. This was a woman who knew what she was talking about. And what struck Jehan most powerfully was her candor. She had bared not only Jehan's motives, but her own as well.

Even so, Jehan was cautious at first. He invited her back to the temple, resolving to say little, but to get a firmer impression of her. On this second visit, she came prepared with a written agenda of items for discussion. One by one, she read them off, making detailed comments. For the most part, the points were routine: She advised repairing the decayed old aqueduct, permitting

Tnemghadi money to remain in circulation, reducing tolls on certain roads, and so forth.

"But these are minor things, Madame," he complained when she concluded her list.

The woman smiled indulgently. "Yes, they are all trivialities, albeit necessary ones. You see, you don't trust me yet—you couldn't—so I must start you off with trivia. Once I've gained your confidence, then we can proceed to more weighty matters."

"Leave your list with me," Jehan said.

And it was not long before he was discussing the most serious affairs with the Madame. He discovered that she hadn't exaggerated her depth of learning and political expertise. After a few weeks, Jehan could not imagine trying to govern Taroloweh without her.

Governing it was quite a task; the province was in a shambles. Its paramount problem was food. Not only was Taroloweh still suffering bad times, but all chains of supply had been disrupted. Indeed, the whole province was turned upside down, all local government had been swept away with nothing to replace it but chaos. Moreover, Jehan's triumphant march across the province had not meant the end of war. Taroloweh was still in the throes of bitter fighting, not just between the new order and remnants of the old, but among rival inheritors of the power struck out of Tnemghadi hands.

That was the state of the province Jehan had seized. It was easier to seize it than to tame it. But Jehan did not shrink from the challenge, and Golana joined him in meeting it with zest.

She moved in and was assigned private quarters in the temple, at the nerve center of the new regime. Jehan was unstinting in providing her with servants, secretaries, and whatever else she deemed needed. At her direction, the voluminous records stored in the old Vraddagoon were transferred over to the temple, and a library was started, with the remains of Mutsukh's books as its core.

Long were the hours that Golana spent alone in her offices, often far into the night, and often too closeted with Jehan, as they wrestled together to quell the seething cauldron of Taroloweh. Jehan kept her as close at hand as possible. When he held court in the great hall, she was stationed beside the stone chair, and she was among the guests at every meal. And it wasn't solely for her counsel that he kept her near: In this regime of former thugs and peasants, Madame Mutsukh was a dazzling ornament. Not only was she a handsome woman, but charming as well with a delightful wit and badinage.

But Madame Golana Mutsukh did not become the mistress of Jehan Henghmani.

Never did she offer herself, and never did he invite it. Not that he didn't want her—he had never seen a woman more desirable! But she was too indispensable to risk offending with a clumsy overture. Still, that was not the only reason for Jehan's reticence. Simply put, he was sure he couldn't have her. Golana did not need to use her body to get what she wanted. She knew her own worth, and could refuse him confidently. Even contemptuously— and that was what Jehan feared most.

There was no dearth of other women for him. He would bed them for a night, but never more than once. And pretty as they might be, he never paid attention to their faces. In the dark, no matter who was in his bed, he'd see only Madame Mutsukh. She was like a spirit that occupied and obliterated every woman Jehan had. It was always Madame Mutsukh, her pale face, her tall body, her blazing eyes, that held him fast.

He would send the harlots out before dawn, in the dark, so Madame Mutsukh wouldn't catch sight of them. In this secretive behavior, he was actuated by something new in him, something he had never felt before.

He felt guilty, an adulterer—betraying the one woman he could not have.

· 6 ·

THAT WOMAN: words muttered with venom throughout the Arbadakhar temple.

Jephos Kirdahi was one of those who muttered words like that. Kirdahi was still a general, the deputy commander of the army, Jehan's right-hand man. Now, after the conquest of the capital, he functioned too—ostensibly—as Grand Chamberlain of Taroloweh. He was still agog that a fugitive ex-dungeon turnkey could rise to such a station, but at the same time, he was soured by Madame Mutsukh's advent.

The Madame's presence made it all too plain that Kirdahi was just a flunky whose high titles were awarded only because Jehan wouldn't entrust them to anyone more dangerous. So Kirdahi was one of those who grumbled about "that woman."

Nattahnam Ubuvasakh was another. The Leopard, as at Zidneppa, was named Magistrate. He had no affinity for Kirdahi and resented the Tnemghadi's higher rank; but he and Kirdahi could agree on one thing, and that was Madame Mutsukh. The Leopard too could appreciate what little influence he had, with that woman hovering around Jehan. A woman! And even worse, a *Tnemghadi*.

As always, Kamil Kawaras cared nothing for himself. It did not bother the shaggy-haired zealot that a woman had more power. But that she was a Tnemghadi—that was another story! Even the ever-loyal Hnayim Yahu was openly heard to question Jehan's wisdom. The two people now closest to Jehan were Tnemghadi. Some fine Urhemmedhin movement this was turning out to be!

One night an officer approached Jehan, handed him a sealed message, and left quickly without speaking.

Since he had never learned to read, Jehan had Madame Mutsukh summoned at once to read this note, so mysteriously delivered.

"It is badly written," she commented, "from one named Gaffar Mussopo, battalion leader under Kawaras. Do you know him?"

"Yes, I think so. He's one of my youngest officers. What does he say?"

"He warns that there is a great deal of discontent among your officers and troops—concerning me."

Jehan nodded. "My men are upset because I take advice from a woman, and even worse, a Tnemghadi woman."

"Obviously. He does mention Kawaras as being particularly wroth about it."

"Yes, I'm sure crazy old Kamil must be wetting his kirtle over it."

"There's more. Mussopo says there's been talk that 'somebody should do something to get rid of this Tnemghadi whore.' "

"What do you think about this, Madame?"

"I'm not sure whether to worry or not. This message is not exactly startling news, but perhaps things are going too far. You know these men a good deal better than I do."

"All right. To be on the safe side, I'll assign some permanent guards to protect you. Men whom I trust fully."

"I would be grateful for that."

"And don't forget to send a note in my name to Mussopo, thanking him for his conscientious message."

Madame Mutsukh snickered. "Conscientious? The boy probably hates me as much as the rest of them. The word 'whore' is in quotes, but it's there. All he's doing is trying to curry your favor by betraying his own superior officer."

"In that case, he's a shrewd fellow." Jehan winked at Madame Mutsukh. "Send the note anyway."

She nodded. "I suppose so. Hypocrisy is a fitting response to hypocrisy," she said. Then she bit her lip thoughtfully. "Listen, besides assigning guards, I do believe more positive measures should be taken to deal with this problem. You can't have all your men so unhappy, and guards won't fix that."

"I will talk to them, bring it out in the open."

"Yes, that would be useful, it would clear the air. But

I also think you should make more of a show of consulting with the others from now on, to satisfy their egos. And less show of consulting with me. We could be more discreet in some ways, and less discreet in other ways. To put it bluntly, I had best appear nothing more than a glorified concubine."

Madame Mutsukh leaned back in her chair, in a slouching posture, and looked at Jehan through half-shut eyes. She knew full well what she had said.

"Yes," he answered, "it can be made to *appear* that way."

"Ksiritsa," said Maiya. "When, Paban, are we going to Ksiritsa?"

"Don't you like it here?" Jehan asked his daughter in return.

"That's not the point. We've been sitting here twiddling our thumbs for months now. I want to see you on the golden throne, at Ksiritsa!"

Jehan's answer was stolid. "When we are ready to go, we will go."

"And when will that be? When *Madame* says so?"

Jehan sighed and gave Maiya a gently reproving look.

"It's true, why don't you admit it? It's that woman who's persuaded you to stay here."

"Her advice is always very sound. We *will* march on Ksiritsa, just as soon as we've consolidated our stronghold here in Taroloweh."

"So you admit she's keeping us bottled up here. She is a sorceress," Maiya taunted; "she's bewitched you."

Jehan tried to brush this off with no more than an amiable chuckle. He hated arguing with Maiya. Patting her hair, he said, "Don't tell me that my little darling is jealous of Madame Mutsukh."

Maiya's face reddened. "I do not covet your . . . *favors*, Paban. I don't begrudge you a mistresss"

"I think then," Jehan said carefully, "you must be making more of Madame Mutsukh than she is."

"No, it is *you* making more of her than she is. Golana Mutsukh is simply a beautiful woman, a fine mistress I'm sure. Besides the fact that you're making a fool of yourself over her, I don't care if she is your mistress."

"You sound as though you do care."

"Not about that! Dally with her day and night, for all I care. But don't confuse her prowess in bed with wisdom at Court."

Jehan smiled sardonically. "Maiya, you don't know how wrong you are."

"Oh, I understand all too well, Paban. She has obviously seduced you and gained complete mastery over you. She's got you wound around her little finger. The real ruler of this province is not Jehan Henghmani; it's Golana Mutsukh, Queen Golana. You are nothing but her consort!"

"Hold your spiteful tongue!" Jehan bellowed, checking an ugly impulse to strike his daughter.

"It's true!"

"How dare you say such vile things? Now you listen to me. Every decision made here is my own. But I heed what Golana Mutsukh has to say, because I'd be a fool if I didn't. What do I know about running a province? She has forgotten more than I ever knew, and whatever success I've had in governing Taroloweh, I owe to her."

"You *owe* to her! Oh, Paban, don't you see what's happening to you? After all you've earned with your own blood and flesh, you're giving it all up to a Tnemghadi woman. She won't even let you put a crown on your head. Don't you realize what that means?"

With effort, Jehan controlled his voice. "Maiya, surely if you were the least bit objective—"

"Objective? Ha! It isn't *my* vision that's blurred by lust!"

"All right. That's enough out of you. I will hear no more of this."

"Very well, Paban, I can see it's hopeless. But I will tell you, you will yet rue the day that woman came here."

Jehan turned away. He wondered if there wasn't a grain of truth in Maiya's viewpoint. Golana Mutsukh was not his mistress, emphatically not, and yet that very fact was a merciless buzzing in his head. Perhaps his vision was indeed blurred by it. He could not deny the power of her hold over him, nor could he make any real sense of his jumbled feelings about it. The woman was an uncanny force that had turned him upside down in a way he couldn't fathom.

And as for Maiya, her own words echoed within her. She was ruing the day Golana Mutsukh had come to the Arbadakhar temple.

·7·

FROM BENEATH HER DARK Tnemghadi brows, Golana Mutsukh watched Jehan Henghmani.

Ugliness was the most striking thing about Jehan at first, stupendous ugliness, his mutilations magnified by his gargantuan dimensions: hairless, noseless, earless, one eye torn from its socket.

But Golana saw beyond Jehan's ugliness, just as she had come to see past the ugliness of Eshom Mutsukh. She had loved her husband, and had been his partner in life; his death had wracked her with grief.

Now there had come another misshapen man into her life. Jehan did not display the saintly virtues of the Magistrate Eshom Mutsukh, and Golana did not see him as filling the void left by Mutsukh's death. But no less powerfully, for different reasons she was drawn to Jehan, and her life would take a new course.

Indeed, Jehan's strong points could perhaps not be deemed virtues at all; it was their very strength that was compelling. That was why thousands had followed him across Taroloweh. While Golana's attraction to him was of the intellect, she could nonetheless feel the pulsing magnetism that had carried him so far.

It was not his physical strength that held people to him. It was his strength of purpose, strength of mind. Not by physical strength alone had he survived three years of torture. Other men of robust constitution might have done it too, but come out with pudding for brains. Jehan's faculties seemed sharpened by every ounce of agony that he'd endured, and all the vehemence expended on him was soaked up into his soul.

Even those who never saw him were drawn by Jehan's legend. Truly, his return from Ksiritsa was fit fabric for legend, and he did nothing to deter his own entry into mythdom. Never would he speak of what had happened at Ksiritsa; and with his silence, the myth could only grow.

Golana's husband, Eshom Mutsukh, had been a brilliant man, who perhaps should have achieved greatness. But Mutsukh had lacked ruthlessness; he was too scrupulous and timid to grab for the heights. Not so Jehan. Jehan would let nothing stand in the way of his ambition, and that was what Golana Mutsukh wanted now.

With glittering eyes beneath her dark Tnemghadi brows, Madame Golana Mutsukh looked across the table at Jehan Henghmani. It was past midnight, and the candles were burned to stumps. Piled high on the table were the documents of state business which they'd been discussing. They were alone, and it was very quiet.

They'd been hard at work for many hours. But now they were finally done for the night, and they leaned back in their chairs to relax briefly.

"You know," Golana said, "it's really about time you learned to read. At least Urhemmedhin, if not Tnemghadi. I would be most happy to teach you."

"Why should I learn to read, when I've got you to read everything for me?"

"That may be true—for now."

"What do you mean?"

"You may not have me always."

"What's the matter, Madame, aren't you happy about things? You know I've tried to accommodate you with everything you've asked for. If there's anything else you want, please speak up."

The woman shook her head with a little laugh. "That's not what I meant. I am very happy with the way things have turned out for me. It gives me great satisfaction to be working here like this, working with you. And yet. . . ."

"Yes?"

"May I have leave to ask a personal question?"

"Certainly, Madame. You are always free to say or ask whatever is on your mind. I value your candor."

Golana looked carefully at Jehan, and slowly wet her lips with her tongue. Jehan was leaning forward with his hands clasped tensely on the table. She could see how anxiously he was hanging on her every word.

"Why is it that you've never sought to have me in your bed?"

Jehan was startled, and his scarred features pinkened deeply. Never before had Golana seen him blush. He self-consciously averted his eyes, and tried to guess why she would ask such a shocking question. Was she testing him? Teasing him?

"Madame, why do you ask this question?"

"You have not been shy about these matters with other women."

"Don't compare yourself with those harlots! Surely you realize how different you are. Do you think it's shyness that lies behind my conduct toward you?"

"No, you're not a shy man about anything . . . except, it seems, my question."

"You have not answered my question either: Why do you raise this subject?"

Madame Mutsukh did not respond. She sat staring at Jehan with her eyes open strangely wide.

"It cannot be," he warily suggested, "because you wish my conduct toward you to change."

"You think it cannot? Why so?"

Jehan was suddenly convinced that she was teasing him, toying with him. Perhaps even baiting him. But he could not bring himself to chastise her for it. He bent his head to the table. What cause had he given her to be so cruel? Was it the whores he had at night, about which she evidently knew? Guilt pinched Jehan; his face was flushed deep red, and he wished he had been celibate. He felt so cheapened by what he'd done, behind her back. What contempt she must bear him!

"I will speak no more of this," he stammered abruptly, and stood away from the table.

"Please, don't go!" Golana seized his hand and held him back.

He turned his face to her, screwed up with anguish. "What do you want from me? I'm sorry, but I'm still a man not a god, and certainly no saint!"

"I want you to give me a straight answer."

"All right then, I will give it to you." Jehan pounded the table. "This is your answer: Yes, there are women who consent to lie with me. Do you know why? Of course you do. They come for money or favors. For that they grit their teeth and come to my bed. Behind their smiles and their kisses, they grit their teeth at the ugly monster they sleep with."

"Yes, you are ugly!" Golana emphatically avowed. "You are very ugly! But it isn't beauty that I seek."

"Then what *do* you seek?"

"I seek you, Jehan Henghmani," she answered instantly.

The man was dumbfounded, and took Golana by the shoulders across the table, shaking her. "What are you saying! You'd give yourself to me, even though you do not have to?"

"I would give myself to you because I want to. Because I want *you*. If you will have me."

"*If?* Surely you know it is respect for you that has governed my conduct. I feared to offend you. I can't even express how important you are to me."

Golana lowered her eyes. "Then you will have me?" she whispered.

"It is you who shall have me, if that is your wish."

She looked up with the demure, modest face of a little girl. "As what will I have you, Jehan Henghmani?"

"As whatever you desire."

"Then I will have you for my husband."

Tnem Sarbat Satanichadh twisted his porcine fingers in the perfumed curls of his latest favorite, lounging on the couch of his private chamber. He deliberately pulled on her hair until she winced, and then he slipped his hand under her garment and fondled her breast.

Sarbat was half-listening to the earnest words of his latest Grand Chamberlain. After a quarter-century reign, the words were beginning to seem like babbling, no matter what they were and no matter who spoke them. And the Emperor mused bitterly that he was changing Grand Chamberlains nowadays even oftener than his fickle favor shifted from one courtesan to another. For three decades, old Irajdhan had filled the post brilliantly. He was nearly eighty when he died, and what a loss his death had been! Then Hassim Baraka-Hatu had succeeded Irajdhan—but could not replace him. Nor could any of the three Grand Chamberlains who had, in quick succession, followed Baraka-Hatu. Were there no more great men like Yasiruwam Irajdhan?

But perhaps it was the times, not the men. For centuries, Bergharra's territory and influence had expanded; now, though, the great Empire was barely struggling to preserve itself. Perhaps Bergharra had overreached and grown too big to manage. Was the Empire like a bubble that grows and grows until the forces holding it together are unbalanced, and it bursts?

The latest Grand Chamberlain was Faihdon Royanis. His appointment had met with widespread disapproval, since he was a man of mean birth who had worked his way up slowly through a succession of lesser posts. Yet Sarbat knew this man was not weak and not stupid. Faihdon Royanis was in fact an able man who could ordinarily be expected to acquit himself well in high office.

But 1182 was a troubled year.

"It is my suggestion, Your Majesty," said Faihdon Royanis, "that for the time being, we make no further invasion of Taroloweh."

Sarbat scowled darkly. *Taroloweh.* How he had grown to hate the name of that vile place! Never before had such a humiliation been suffered by the mighty Empire of Bergharra. The Grand Chamberlain's proposal, to accept the status quo, certainly seemed unpalatable. But Sarbat held his tongue and kept fondling his concubine; he would give Royanis a chance to support his views.

"Jehan seems entrenched at Arbadakhar," the man explained. "As you know, it is a well-fortified, walled city. Jehan himself was able to take it only because he had the support of the civilian population inside. Their continued support would make it practically impossible for us to retake the city."

"Don't those Urhemmedhin fools know the monster is only exploiting them for his own ends?"

"I imagine that, in fact, they do. But regardless of Jehan's own ambitions, the people see him as offering a better deal than we."

The Emperor tugged on his beard. "Why must we consider only Arbadakhar? All right, let him have it, but can't we take back the rest of the province?"

"It's hardly worth the effort. Taroloweh is in sad

shape. Why fight over land like that? Besides, it would be a sign of weakness to invade the countryside while avoiding Arbadakhar."

"Isn't it an even worse sign of weakness to do nothing at all?"

"Perhaps the blunt answer is that we *are* weak, Your Majesty. The Taroloweh war has been very costly. Even so, if that were our only problem, it would be an easy one. But the trouble is that we're fighting the damned Akfakh too. It's as though they're wild beasts that can smell our faltering, and they're rising to take advantage of it. The time is not far off when we will have to deal seriously with them; perhaps even surrender a province or two to buy peace."

Sarbat stood up, leaving his courtesan alone on the couch. Ignoring her now, he paced in a circle, stroking his beard.

"No, Royanis, that's self-defeating. I won't give up an inch of territory, not to the Akfakh and not to Jehan. Somehow, we must scrape together enough soldiers to handle both of them."

Royanis shook his head. "I must be truthful, Your Majesty: It can't be done. It's getting tougher and tougher to recruit men and keep them in the army. Casualty rates are high and the pay is poor. The treasury is strained, and our desertion rate is becoming fantastic."

"Then debase the coinage and raise the pay. Or increase taxes again. The Empire must tighten its belt."

"We've discussed this before, Your Majesty." Royanis sighed, and spoke almost condescendingly. "Taxes are already far too high. You can't keep raising them without destroying the very economic activity that produces wealth in the first place. As for the coinage, it's already rather shoddy, and the people are noticing. That's part of the reason we're having such inflation of prices. They're leery of the new coins and hoarding the old. The troops want to be paid with good silver. And desertion's not our only problem. Our forces are being spread thinner and thinner. We've had to increase the garrison strengths throughout the South, to check the rising level of unrest. It's not only in Taroloweh that Jehan is causing trouble. The rising could easily spread to other provinces."

"Then isn't it obvious," said Sarbat, "that if we crush Jehan, we will kill the problem at its root?"

"But we must take care not to make a martyr of him. It's not Jehan's death we want, not his destruction, but his *failure*. The Urhemmedhins must become disillusioned with him and his land reform scheme. Only then will the unrest subside."

"You may be right," Sarbat said thoughtfully. "The problem is how to make sure Jehan fails."

"And we can't do it by invading. We must let him stew in his own juices. I wonder if Jehan himself understands the forces he's unleashed. Power may be going to his head; for example, taking a Tnemghadi woman was not very bright. More important, I doubt this ignorant ruffian will cure the miserable conditions in Taroloweh. Far from being a panacea, his land distribution program should even worsen things.

"And of course, we will wage economic warfare against this 'Kingdom of Taroloweh.' There'll be no food imports for them, not by land or sea, not from any province or any country. We'll see if Jehan can keep his people fed! When the people are starving, they'll turn against him fast enough. Then we'll move in. We will save them—save them from Jehan Henghmani!"

Tnem Sarbat Satanichadh turned suddenly and looked at this latest Grand Chamberlain with glittering eyes. Perhaps old Irajdhan had been replaced after all.

· 8 ·

No LONGER A CRUDE BANDIT of the hills, Jehan Henghmani was, to all intents, a king. And it was fitting for a king to have a queen.

Yet it was not just to gain a queen that Jehan was marrying Golana Mutsukh. Nor was it just to have her to bed. His desire was far greater. He wanted to penetrate her soul as well as her body. He would even mortify the flesh to exalt the soul. Bizarre visions of a union in celibacy would haunt him, a celibacy of witness to his consuming desire. But such peculiar fantasies he'd expel from his mind; he wanted her completely.

Jehan recognized how Golana paralleled his own life. By force of will and intellect and character, she had broken free of the bounds imposed on women; by similar force, he had sprung from the dungeon, and then gone on to smash the chains binding the people of Taroloweh. A liberator, like Golana he had made men give him power.

It seemed ironic that these two people, both of whom had seized freedom and power, each sought now to possess the other.

Jehan thought it significant that it was Golana who, six years before, had caused his being sent to Ksiritsa. It was as though some unseen hand was weaving together the threads of their lives into a single cord. Or perhaps there only was the single cord—and only in their pasts did it ravel into separate threads.

"There is a lot of opposition to the marriage," said Golana one morning in a matter-of-fact tone.

"It's to be expected," Jehan answered. "Ignore it."

"No. We must be sensitive to the feelings of your people. They mustn't be allowed to think we're thumbing our noses at them. So I've decided we had best not flaunt the wedding, and I've nipped in the bud most of the preparations. I want a small and private ceremony, no fanfare, everything downplayed."

Reluctantly, Jehan concurred.

"Even so," she continued, "the wedding will have to be neutralized. You can't afford to be dubbed a Tnemghadi-lover, even if you are marrying one. It must be made to seem that I have no influence over your policies.

"I have two ideas along this line—one for the short term, the other for the long term. The latter will be important beyond the immediate issue, but I haven't yet fully thought it through, so we'll defer its discussion. Meanwhile, for the short term, I think news of the wedding should be accompanied by some tough new anti-Tnemghadi decree. Perhaps a schedule of heavy new taxes . . . we can work out the details."

"Yes, or maybe a forfeiture of personal property, jewelry, and the like. To assure the people that my Golana is not making me go soft. And it will be the truth! Who would believe it was the Tnemghadi bride herself who counseled harshness against her own people?"

Golana shook her head forcefully. "No, Jehan, they are not 'my own people.' What does it mean for me to be a Tnemghadi? Does it all depend upon this eyebrow? Because of that accident of birth, am I to love all Tnemghadi and hate all Urhemmedhins? Should I kowtow before their emperor? No! I will not be constricted by my . . . my biology. Just as I refuse to limit my horizons because I am a woman, neither will I let my life be shaped by my Tnemghadi birth. If I did, I wouldn't be here now.

"I cannot deny that I am a Tnemghadi by virtue of this eyebrow, and my parentage—but that is all! That is but the smallest part of me. Far more important, I am a human being; and more important still, I am a *self*, a consciousness, an individual. That far transcends my being part of any group, and even my membership in humanity as a whole. More important to me than all other humanity is my own self.

"So I am no Tnemghadi, not a Tnemghadi of the heart. I will not peg my loyalties on the basis of what kind of eyebrows people have. My loyalties flow from my self, from what is in my own heart and mind.

"You see, I have no *people,* but I do have *persons.*
One of them is me. The other is you.

"I am not a Tnemghadi. I am a *Jehandi.*"

Jehan took her hand. "And I am a Golanadhin," he
said.

Maiya served her father dutifully and with ostensible
humility.

She cooked his meals, washed and mended his clothes,
tidied his quarters, and held her tongue. She acted to the
hilt the role of the perfect conventional wife who knew
her work and, above all, knew her place. And a woman's
place was definitely not in political affairs.

She was, of course, illiterate and ignorant of such matters, so that her quiet role was fitting by circumstance as
well as temperament. Not so Golana—and keenly did
Maiya feel herself outclassed and outshone by this strange
woman who refused to abide by all the feminine conventions. Bitterly she saw Golana as unfair, underhanded,
using her political know-how to steal Maiya's father away
from her.

It hurt all the more because Maiya blamed herself for
it. The girl still castigated herself that in the dungeon,
when she'd had Grebzreh at knife-point, she had unfor-
givably squandered that chance to free her father. Not
only did this guilt continue to gnaw at Maiya, but she was
now reaping its punishment. If only she had given her
father freedom! Then surely Golana couldn't steal him
away from her now!

Of course, Maiya was not being shorn of her chosen
role—Golana showed no interest in cooking and cleaning
for Jehan. No, the Tnemghadi aristocrat would hold such
work beneath her dignity—in effect, reducing Maiya to
the humiliating status of a maidservant.

The girl was not surprised when Jehan revealed the
betrothal. It was just one more insult heaped upon the
others. She looked at him with hostile eyes, and when he
spoke softly, begging her to accept Golana, she refused to
answer him at all. With her silence, Maiya would punish
her father.

He was still pleading with her when Maiya turned her
back and walked away. He even came after her, but still

she ignored his entreaties, and at her private rooms, she closed the door in his face.

She went to her little boy, picked him up and hugged him against her breast, and rocked him back and forth. To Jehandai she escaped from the insult of her father and Golana; the child was Maiya's great consolation. It was Jehandai who gave her the will to persist. It was Jehandai who would give her triumph in the end. It was still Jehandai who would be the heir.

Maiya would no longer speak to her father. But nor would she abandon him. *They would make me just a maidservant,* she resolved to herself, *so a maidservant I shall be.* And so she doggedly continued at her domestic chores, silent and sullen, behind a barrier that Jehan could not pierce. Gently he would speak to her, lavish presents on her, all to no avail. She would ignore the fine gowns that he bestowed on her, and in her meanest peasant smock, she would go about her chores. And not a single word would she vouchsafe to him.

Even Golana made a gallant attempt to penetrate Maiya's thickening shell.

"Look what I have brought you, Maiya dear," Golana said sweetly, holding out a birdcage delicately spun of silver thread. Inside was a bright yellow canary, capering on the perches, chirping.

"Isn't he pretty, Maiya? Just listen to him sing! I picked him out specially, as a present for you."

For the first time, the girl looked at Golana, a look of measured disdain. "I don't want any presents from you."

Undaunted, Golana sat down beside Maiya and tried to take her hand. But Maiya vehemently pulled away, turning her shoulder to Golana and walking to the far corner of her room.

"Why won't you accept my gift, Maiya dear? Why do you seem to hate me so? Do you feel that I'm taking your father away from you, is that it? But that's so silly! I love your father, just as you do, don't you understand that? I want to help him succeed, just like you do. I want to be his wife, and your mother too. I want us to be one family: your father and me and you and Jehandai."

"How dare you speak his name!" Maiya shrieked instantly. "Jehandai is mine, you'll never have him!"

"But of course he's yours, Maiya, I understand. He's your son."

"And the son of Jehan Henghmani, too!"

"Nobody's going to take him away from you."

Maiya turned suddenly to the birdcage, which Golana had placed on a table. She ran her fingers silkily over the iridescent silver strands that made its bars. Inside, the bird was merrily chirping.

"No, nobody will ever take him away from me," she said, more to herself than to Golana.

"Do you like the little canary I've brought you? Isn't he cute and pretty? Please tell me you like him, I want so much to make you happy. Can't we all be happy together? Being angry doesn't do any good; it only makes things ugly. Let me be your friend and your mother."

"My mother is dead!" Maiya's face twisted unrecognizably for a brief instant as she wrenched open the door of the cage, thrust her hand inside, and grabbed the canary. It gave a loud squeal of distress.

"Don't hurt it, Maiya!"

"Hurt him? No, he's a prisoner, and I'm going to set him free."

The girl took the screaming bird to the open window, and flung it out into the sky.

"Go away, poor bird," she said. "And you go away too, you Tnemghadi witch!"

· 9 ·

JEHAN HENGHMANI LOOKED with glittering eyes upon his bride, standing naked before him.

It was their wedding night.

Not until this night did they take each other. It had been an unspoken compact between them, that they would wait, like children being married shyly to each other. Their marriage was too solemn a thing to despoil with impatience.

Yet the wedding was as pretensionless as possible. An old Urhemmedhin holy man was summoned to the temple to officiate. He was a limping relic who had spent a life-time preaching underground, one step ahead of the Tnem-ghadi. It was Golana who personally selected this man to perform the ceremony. And so, upon his precious tat-tered copy of the Book of Urhem, Golana and Jehan swore their marriage vows; and the old priest blessed them, that they might attain the perfect state of love King Urhem bore for his Queen Osatsana, and thereby fully gain the glory of their lives.

The ceremony was followed by a wedding feast, but fewer than a dozen had the privilege of attending. Golana herself invited but a single guest: the holy man. As for the meal, it was hardly more elaborate than the usual dinner fare, and there was no dancing, no singing, no drunken revelry. The only concession to joyful spirit was the music of a zindala provided by a young soldier. Ev-erything was modesty and decorum; the wedding was marred only by Maiya's willful absence.

When the last course had been eaten, the last toast pronounced, Jehan rose from his chair and took his bride, Golana, by the arm. The others at the table all stood too in respectful silence as he slowly led her away through the huge temple halls.

It was a stately walk; they did not break its cadence with speech. As they passed, each soldier on guard saluted briskly.

At Jehan's chamber he lit a lamp and closed the door. And then they looked at each other.

She stood straight upright, her head thrown back a little to look him in the eye. It was a proud posture of self-satisfaction. Without a word, her hands rose to her throat and began untying the stays of her white wedding gown. She never took her eyes off Jehan. In a moment, the gown had fallen into a bundle at her feet.

Out of that white bundle she stood naked, as though freshly born out of it, like a goddess born whole from a cloth egg.

She reached up and undid the ties of her hairdo, letting her shimmering black hair cascade to her shoulders, and clasped her hands serenely behind her head.

Jehan closed his eyes and opened them again. The yellow candle light on her pale flesh made it look preternaturally soft and delicate, as inviting as her posture and her eyes. Her body did not evidence her nearly forty years: her calves and thighs and arms were smooth and lithe, her belly taut, her breasts thrust up like a young girl's.

"You are so beautiful," he said, and he came to her, to touch his hands hesitantly at her sides. She swayed forward and his hands slid around to her back, to her shoulder blades, to feel her cool smoothness and to draw her against his own body. She received him. Her hands pulled him into a kiss, gently at first; but they did not end it, and the kiss, and their embrace, tightened.

The marriage of Jehan Henghmani was not calculated to win the approval of his peasant followers. But in truth, the event created little stir; there were more important matters to concern Taroloweh.

The most obvious was the province's precarious situation. Never before had an Urhemmedhin revolt succeeded so fabulously, never had the Tnemghadi been driven out. But surely they would be back! That no further invasion had come so far seemed only to mean that the Tnemghadi were gearing toward a truly terrible attack. Jehan was shaping up his army too, but could he hold the northerners at bay indefinitely? Grave and widespread was the fear of invasion, and many believed that the Emperor would not be satisfied merely to regain Taroloweh. They believed the whole province would be punished as harshly as Zidneppa: destroyed, as a lesson to the entire south-land.

Meanwhile, by dint of prodigious exertions, Jehan and his regime were bringing under control the province's internal convulsions. The enlarging army managed to impose a degree of order upon the countryside. Most towns saw restoration of some sort of rough provisional government, administered by Jehan's army in concert with emerging peasant leaders. Likewise makeshift was the food rationing system promulgated to ward off starvation. The rationing was a colossal administrative quagmire, well beyond the ability of the fledgling regime to handle. It was widely undercut, abused, or ignored. But it did put food in the mouths of thousands who would otherwise have starved.

Preoccupied as he was with Taroloweh's problems, Jehan was thinking too beyond its borders. It was in the small hours of one dreary morning that Golana found him by himself, his huge pillar of a body hunched over a work-table. She entered soundlessly and stood in a corner, watching him.

He had to bend deeply to study the details of an enormous map that was spread out upon the table, with its edges flopping over the sides. Golana recognized it as a map of the Empire of Bergharra, one of the most complete and accurate available. She herself had procured this map for Jehan. Now his eyes and hands were riveted to it, his fingers tracing thoughtful lines upon it.

After some minutes, he sensed that he was not alone, and looked up. He smiled to see Golana, and she left her corner to join him behind the table.

"Your finger is upon Ksiritsa," she said.

"Yes." He jabbed at the oversized, decorated red blotch that marked the City of the Dragon, the capital of the Empire. "Ksiritsa. *Ksiritsa.*" He pronounced the name with an intense whisper of reverence.

"I have never been to Ksiritsa," Golana said.

Jehan's fist pounded down on the red blotch. "But you shall see it, Golana! I vow that you'll see it. More than half a year now, we've been at Arbadakhar. We have things coming along nicely here; Taroloweh's crisis is easing. Some of our men are growing restless here, others are growing complacent. Sarbat is weak; he hasn't dared attack us since we took this city. Perhaps he thinks we mean only to hold Taroloweh. But he is wrong."

Jehan's finger slashed a straight line across the map from Arbadakhar to the Dragon City. *"The time is coming for us to go to Ksiritsa."*

"No," Golana said quietly.

Jehan's head jerked around. "What? I don't understand. Maiya's always ranting that you want to keep us at Arbadakhar. Don't tell me she's right?"

"No, she is not right. My ambitions are no less than your own. But just look at what an attack upon Ksiritsa would involve: a northward march, through unfamiliar terrain, but worse than that, through the Tnemghadi provinces. You certainly won't be cheered along the way there, unlike your march across Taroloweh. Indeed, you would have to fight your way every lim from here to Ksiritsa, with no sympathetic local peasants to replenish your forces. Your lines of supply would be stretched out impossibly. I doubt you could even feed your troops; the Tnemghadi will probably burn their crops along your path.

"Then, if you do reach Ksiritsa: it's an impregnable walled city. The army inside will be huge, and you'll get no support from the civilian population. They'll resist to the bitter end.

"And finally, if you do take Ksiritsa, what have you accomplished? Sarbat would move his court to a new capital, he would retain the allegiance of the Tnemghadi people. You would have conquered a city—not an empire."

Jehan nodded at many of her points. "All you say is true, Golana. I never imagined it would be easy. It will take years."

"But it's not the North you should attack at all. That's what I'm getting at, Jehan. You want to conquer the Empire of Bergharra—but forget it. Do not be blinded by the brilliance of Ksiritsa. Turn your eyes away from it. Instead turn your eyes southward.

"This is what I've been mulling over for months. I saw it, in rough outlines, before you even came to Arbadakhar.

Jehan, you do not know your proper destiny, you do not know who you are. But I have always known."

Jehan smiled seriously. "All right, Golana. I will listen. Tell me who I am."

Golana breathed deeply and settled herself before speaking. When she began, she spoke with quiet firmness, and with a fluidity that almost suggested a carefully prepared speech.

"You started at Zidneppa as the champion of the downtrodden. That was a fine thing, perhaps a noble thing. You cleaned up the town, threw out the Tnemghadi, gave away food. You even proclaimed the land free.

"And, oh, how they flocked to your banner! For years this province was strangled by intractable famine, the people run off their land and starving by the thousands. You promised land and bread and they flocked to you. And, for a while at least, you actually fulfilled your promise.

"But now there is no more free food, and the land you've given them is proving to be a dubious gift. Is it bountiful in their hands? Can they get the seeds and tools and gaars they need? Will they fight over the land, neighbor against neighbor and brother against brother? And will the people wandering the roads prey upon the ones who have the land? But you know well enough what's happening out there. I don't have to tell you the ugly details.

"Perhaps we could overcome all that if we got help from other provinces. But the Tnemghadi have cut us off. They aim to starve Taroloweh.

"In short, what you are doing for the peasants, however noble, will soon stand revealed as a cruel illusion. They'll find out they're no better off under your regime than with the Tnemghadi—indeed, probably worse off. And the consequences of this should be obvious.

"But there is a solution.

"No matter how hungry they are, it may yet be possible for you to hold the loyalty of the Urhemmedhin peasantry. Yea, even to strengthen that loyalty. But your movement must undergo a drastic transformation.

"Heretofore, you have focused the people's attention on their empty bellies by harping on the promise of land and bread. Now, instead, you must divert them away from that hunger.

"The Urhemmedhin people are starving, but food is not

their only hunger. They have another hunger too, a more nagging hunger, a craving even more universal than that for food. Even those with food in their bellies possess this supervening hunger.

"It is the hunger for freedom: *yarushkadharra.*

"Freedom is what they hunger for, after eight centuries of slavery—freedom! They don't want their noses pressed to the mud. They hate being spat upon, made slaves, considered subhuman. They want freedom, and the dignity that goes with freedom: *yarushkadharra.*

"That, Jehan Henghmani, is what you must offer your people. Nothing more and nothing less.

"That is why you must not go north to Ksiritsa. Instead, your destiny lies south. It is Naddeghomra, the city of King Urhem himself. We will go south, to Naddeghomra." Now it was Golana's finger that jabbed exuberantly at the map.

"To Naddeghomra. King Urhem will be the guiding saint, and his creed will be our beacon light. Do you know the power of it, Jehan? For eight long centuries, that creed has been suppressed, the book forbidden. And yet, it survived. The southern people have not forgotten the creed of Urhem. It is the veneration of love and human dignity, it is the foundation of freedom, it is more powerful by far than mere bread and land. With the creed of Urhem, you will rally his people to your cause, and with the might of that belief you will mobilize great armies.

"So that is where your destiny lies: south, to Naddeghomra. And when you get there, it will be reborn. Naddeghomra will be the capital of a new nation, one that never existed before except in the hearts of its people.

"We will call it *Prasid Urhemma,* the Nation of Urhem.

"*Urhemma,* Jehan, *Prasid Urhemma.* The free Nation of Urhem. That is the dream for which the people will march."

Golana stopped to catch her breath. Her voice was carried musically aloft, her eyes were shining. "So now, my dear Jehan, do you know what you are?"

He looked at her, deep into her eyes, with transcendent gravity. "Yes," he whispered, "I do know what I am."

· 10 ·

ON THE SIXTH DAY of Dorotht in the year 1182, the criers and trumpeters fanned out through Arbadakhar, summoning the people one and all to the temple. And the people dropped what they were doing, to obey the summons, for it was an exciting one.

They were summoned to hear Jehan Henghmani. Never had he personally addressed Arbadakhar like this; it was obviously an occasion of great importance. No one knew what to expect, but they thronged the temple's courtyard by the thousands. So great was the crush of people that many fainted and were injured. It was a struggle for the guards to keep order.

At the appointed hour, Jehan Henghmani ascended to the temple's highest balcony. Flanked by his five generals, he towered over the crowd. There was no preliminary, no introduction; Jehan commenced to speak, in brief sentences and in a booming voice.

In broad outline he first recapitulated the history of the Urhemmedhin people. It began with their legendary spawning from the dragon Sexrexatra, together with their brethren, the Tnemghadi. Then Jehan traced through the rise and fall of King Urhem of Naddeghomra, to the conquest by Tnem Khatto Trevendhani and the ensuing centuries of subjugation. This reviled period he dwelt upon, telling his hearers how the Tnemghadi had taken the bread from their mouths, children from their mothers, and crushed their freedom underfoot.

That had been a nightmare, Jehan declared, but now the long dark night was ending for the Urhemmedhin people, and the sun was coming up to shine in their sky. Already in Taroloweh, the long-awaited dawn had broken, and it would break too in every other southern province.

Throughout the southern lands, Jehan Henghmani swore, the sun would shine.

And beneath that sun there would arise a new nation: *Prasid Urhemma*, the free Nation of Urhem.

It would be the greatest nation in the history of mankind. Prasid Urhemma would be founded on the credo of its namesake, that human life is sacred, and the highest triumph of human life is love. That would be the sun in whose warmth the new nation would bask and thrive.

No longer would they grovel in the dirt before tyrants.

No longer would they be herded into slavery.

No longer would they worship secretly and fearfully.

Freedom: this was the promised land into which Jehan Henghmani would lead his people. He would be their savior, the heir of King Urhem.

Jehan Henghmani was, at last, the *Ur-Rasvadhi*, at last the true *Ur-Rasvadhi*.

The forbidden book itself, strangely enough, was barren of any mention of the *Ur-Rasvadhi*. That was because its words had been set to paper only a century or two after the era of King Urhem. In those days the southern people had still been free; there was no need for any savior.

Then down from the north came the Tnemghadi, and the shackles of slavery.

Despite the conquerors' awesome power, sporadic outbreaks of rebellion always plagued their occupation of the South. One of those uprisings took place at Hsokhso, Prewtna Province, in the year 396.

Its instigator was a clandestine priest of Urhem, a mystical young firebrand who posed as a rickshawman and secretly recruited a cadre of Hsokhso peasants and tradesmen sympathetic to his cause. He was a wiry-framed fanatic with burning eyes, who bound his followers to him with a beautiful and eloquent voice.

His name was Nadghour Knidrach, but he called himself *Urhemma Raspadari Yevadhi*, which meant, roughly, *Sainted Savior of Urhem*. Somehow, the name became contracted to *Ur-Rasvadhi*.

Knidrach was reputed to be indeed saintly in his personal life. He had no wife, did no wenching, drank no wine, and slept little. His hours not spent organizing and proselytizing in his rickshawman guise were devoted to private prayer and meditation. Frequent fasts made his body cadaverous. He claimed to be the reincarnation of King Urhem, and swore that by the power of his own wisdom, love, and piety, he would deliver his people from bondage.

Finally, Knidrach dropped his disguise, and at his signal, his underground army rose up suddenly. Knidrach led them on a rampage through Hsokhso. Many Tnemghadi were killed, and the rest expelled. Briefly, Nadghour Knidrach reigned as the liberator of the city. But his asceticism was not a weapon that could daunt Tnemghadi horsemen. The army attacked and recaptured Hsokhso; Knidrach and a band of followers retreated into a mountain cave. For almost a month, they held out, but they had very little food. In the end, the soldiers overcame the hunger-weakened defenders. All except Knidrach were executed on the spot. The leader was instead taken to the catacombs of the Hsokhso temple, where he was tortured to make him renounce Urhem.

No matter what agonies they inflicted upon him, Nadghour Knidrach refused to give them satisfaction. They cut off his hands and feet, broke his body on the rack, and flayed the skin from him. When he still would not utter the words they demanded, his tongue was burned away down to its root with hot irons. When the rebel was barely half alive and delirious with agony, they dragged him out to the public square of Hsokhso, where he was nailed to a post and burned to death.

In the centuries that followed, the story reoccurred in many places; and while Nadghour Knidrach was forgotten, the name he had assumed—the *Ur-Rasvadhi*—became a talisman of hope for the Urhemmedhin people. This was the messiah for whose coming they prayed, the great holy man who would deliver them from bondage. Surely if enough holiness and purity could be concentrated in one man, they thought, his cause would be irresistible.

In the eight centuries since Nadghour Knidrach, countless people had proclaimed themselves *Ur-Rasvadhi*. Some of them even attracted large followings. The word of the new savior would go out across the southern lands, and the Urhemmedhins would pray—would this one prove to be the real *Ur-Rasvadhi*? But always, the end was the same: the Tnemghadi were too powerful and entrenched.

Or perhaps the would-be saviors were never saintly enough, and the true *Ur-Rasvadhi* was yet to come.

Now the word was going out once more, this time from Arbadakhar: a new messiah has arisen. But this time it was different, very different.

Jehan Henghmani was the antithesis of the classic *Ur-Rasvadhi* image. But Golana made the daring leap of insight and imagination, to seize upon the dream for a sainted holy man, and superimpose it upon a rough-hewn bandit warlord. It worked because Jehan possessed the one key thing that all the other claimants of the title *Ur-Rasvadhi* had lacked: the power to make it a reality. Jehan had already liberated one province, and that made him more the true messiah than any of his predecessors.

Golana was the first to understand this; and now the Urhemmedhin people understood it, once Jehan had proclaimed it from the balcony of the Arbadakhar temple. The notion of this monstrous brigand as *Ur-Rasvadhi* was breathtaking and electrifying, and the people embraced it enthusiastically.

Readily they cast aside the ancient vision of a savior so saintly that the Tnemghadi would melt away without his raising a finger. That had been a naive dream, born of despair. The Urhemmedhins had never imagined themselves capable of expelling the oppressors by force. But now they had a hero who could actually do that. No longer need they salve themselves with foolish dreams of bloodless triumph.

And so throughout the southern lands the people rattled against their chains of slavery. And they raised their eyes to the heavens, and their voices in united prayer:

Vahiy Jehan! Victory to Jehan!
Vahiy Prasid Urhemma!
Vahiy Yarushkadharra!

After the Great Proclamation of the Sixth of Dorotht, Jehan's first act was to vacate the Arbadakhar temple and move his headquarters to the less imposing Vraddagoon.

Then, the temple—the finest marble edifice in the province—was once more consecrated as a house of worship. The golden idol of the Emperor had been removed, and in its place there would be a new statue, hewn of plain stone quarried from southern earth. It would be a statue of Urhem.

Unlike the elaborately crowned Emperor, Urhem would be portrayed as a bare headed old man in coarse beggar garb. This was Urhem after he had abjured his throne and palace, in penance for his sin against the sanctity of life. Thus would the statue be more than a monument to Urhem; it would be a monument to all the lessons of his life and all he stood for.

This would be the first temple, but Jehan promised many more. In all the lands he'd liberate, temples would be raised to Urhem.

But no priests were consecrated to officiate. The reborn church of Urhem would be without hierarchy, without any formal structure. The temple itself would be maintained only by a corps of unobtrusive lay custodians, to keep it clean and open to anyone who cared to worship there. No offering was required. And although the shrine was dedicated to Urhem, the temple was open to all. The Tnemghadi era had seen enough suppression of free worship; there would be no more, no gods or creeds proscribed. Anyone might worship in this temple in any fashion he chose, so long as he did not disturb the others using it. So it would be in all of Jehan's temples.

On the day of its consecration, the first service in the new temple was conducted by the limping old priest who had performed the marriage of Golana and Jehan. They themselves headed the list of worshippers, bowing down before the still-unfinished statue of Urhem. Golana, who was responsible for all this, had the honor of placing the first votive offering upon the altar: many shokh baskets filled with plump fruits and vegetables. But the rich offering was neither consumed by the god nor appropriated by the priest. Instead, it was distributed among the hundreds of townsfolk who had gathered to observe the temple's dedication.

They lined up in an orderly queue, shuffling slowly toward the altar, where Jehan and Golana stood handing out the vegetables and pieces of fruit. Most would receive just one piece, but the very poor and dirty-looking would be given several. All of them bowed deeply and murmured thanks.

And as Jehan, the lord of Taroloweh, stood doling out gifts, already his thoughts were leaping far away.

Thirteen hundred and twenty-seven lim away: to Naddeghomra.

BERGHARRA—Nation of Urhemma, gold twenty tayels, circa 1182–83. *Obverse:* Ancient god-king Urhem, right, inscription "Urhem Nation." *Reverse:* large radiate sun, inscription "Jehan Henghmani, Sainted Savior," Arbadakhar mintmark. Breitenbach 1997, 27 mm.; according to legend, minted from gold taken from an idol of the Emperor Sarbat. Extremely rare, as most of Jehan's early coinage was copper or silver. Perhaps half a dozen known. Extremely fine and almost the equal of the Farouk specimen. (*Hauchschild Collection Catalog*)

BOOK FOUR

•

NADDEGHOMRA

· 1 ·

THERE WAS A TIME, perhaps a dozen thousand years ago, when there were no cities. Civilization was embryonic; people were nomads, shifting from camp to camp, living in hide tents or in the open, following the herds of goats and wild sheep and gaars. Man was just on the threshold of mastering these beasts. Nor had he yet mastered the secret of agriculture—he could do no more than search for grain and rice growing wild. He would stop and harvest the crops thus chanced upon; and then he would move on.

In time, it dawned upon Man that the crops which he could reap, so also could he sow. The discovery of this great miracle—that he could plant in the spring and harvest in the fall—enabled him to escape dependence upon the luck of finding what nature had left. He would shape the very processes of nature and tame them to his own use.

And once he had done that, no longer need he wander. He could stay in one place the year-round, planting and harvesting; and on this spot there would rise a village, and a civilization.

The land was vast, and the primitive towns were like tiny islets clinging bravely to the surface of a great sea. Buffeted by waves and storms, the little towns could endure only at favored locations. For example, there is a lazy river called the Amajap snaking westward through the heart of the Bergharran subcontinent; and there is a place where the Amajap twists into a half circle, inside which the banks rise steeply to a plateau, the result of some primordial convulsion of the earth. The land surrounding this uniquely formed plateau was rich and fertile, and it was here that a tribe of prehistoric nomads brought their journeys to an end. In the lowlands, irrigated

by the Amajap, they planted their crops; but for protection against raiders, it was upon the bluff that they
raised their crude homes.

In this ideal location they thrived, and so the name
they gave it was *Fruitful Table:*
Naddegh Omra.

It grew to be a great walled city, a major center of
commerce and culture, and the king who reigned there
was lord of all the lands around, the region called Khrasanna. In time, more and more power accrued to these
kings of Khrasanna, and at its height, the dominion
stretched across seven provinces: Khrasanna itself, and
Bhudabur, Nitupsar, Ohreem, Taroloweh, Diorromeh, and
Prewtna. Of this sprawling kingdom Naddeghomra was,
of course, the capital; and it reached its grandest flower
during the reign of Urhem and Osatsana.

Then, Queen Osatsana died, and in a sense, this was
the death knell too of the grandeur of Khrasanna. Not
one, but two wise rulers were lost, for Urhem threw down
his crown and fled into beggary.

All of their surviving children were girls. The eldest
princess ascended the throne as Queen Xalxe, and she
tried to emulate her parents' good rule. But the court
grumbled to be governed by a woman, and eventually
forced Xalxe to accept abridgement of her authority. Now
the palace was the scene of incessant squabbling, with
every minister intriguing for power, and one strong-man
following another. Unfortunately, none was strong enough,
and the kingdom fell apart. By the end of Queen Xalxe's
unhappy reign, it had broken into a dozen pieces.

For a few centuries, these remnants survived as independent fiefdoms. Then came the dreadful year 361, and
Tnem Khatto Trevendhani.

Through the streets of Naddeghomra the arrogant Tnem
Khatto rode on horseback, parading his warriors before
the sullen eyes of the people he had conquered. Already
the city had been looted, subjected to brutality and rape,
its houses of worship burned-out hulks with the charred
bones of their priests buried in the ashes. The stately palace where once Urhem and Osatsana had reigned was
stripped of all its finery, of all its art and historic relics.
Thus gutted, the beautiful building, together with Urhem's

famous library, was put to the torch. Finally, even its blackened stone shell was pulled down to the ground, into rubble. No trace of Urhem's palace was permitted to remain. On its site, the invaders built *The Maal*.

Maal was the Tnemghadi word for *temple*. However, when one spoke of *The Maal*, it was a reference to one temple in particular: the temple at Naddeghomra.

It was the greatest temple ever built. The only structure in the world larger was the Tnem-rab-Zhikh Palace, but not even Ksiritsa boasted a temple rivaling *The Maal*. And it was by design that the Tnemghadi chose to build their greatest temple not at Ksiritsa, but at Naddeghomra. Its calculated purpose was to grind humiliation into the conquered Urhemmedhins.

One hundred fifty thousand of them were harnessed into slavery to build *The Maal*. Whipped and driven like horses without mercy, they died by the thousand under the massive marble blocks. Their broken bodies were cast aside as offal, and more thousands were shackled to replace them. All of the people of Naddeghomra were pitched to the task. No one was exempt from dragging those marble blocks, not the sick or lame, not old women or young children. According to Khatto Trevendhani, the more Urhemmedhins that suffered and perished to build *The Maal*, the better. That was just why he was building it.

And there, they would be forced to worship him. Their backs were broken to erect a shrine to a detested god whose will was a savage caprice. For that god they were compelled to forsake Urhem. Surely the world had turned black.

The Maal was built of the largest blocks of stone ever quarried by human beings. It was built to last forever, so that the Urhemmedhins would never forget the tyrant Khatto Trevendhani. Indeed, lying like beached whales in the quarries outside Naddeghomra were cut blocks of marble so cyclopean that all efforts to move them had failed. There they remained, mute witnesses to Tnemghadi challenge against nature's limitations.

The Maal was actually a complex of buildings, all rising from a broad, square, white plaza. In a row along its west side were four pairs of towers—four soaring tapering white towers. Flush by each of them was a shorter, darker, squatter structure. On the eastern side of the plaza facing this phalanx like an officer with his troop, was the most gigantic building of all, of hellish gray and black stone. Standing as though at the head of the tower pairs, this massive sentinel pointed them in the direction of Ksiritsa, and it housed the grandest of *The Maal's* nine golden idols of the Emperor.

This was Naddeghomra. If there was one focal point for the agony of the Urhemmedhin people, it was Naddeghomra, where once their dreams had flourished, and where they now lay buried beneath the colossal, hateful towers of *The Maal*.

This was Naddeghomra, toward which Jehan the Savior would march in the month of Fekhor, late in the year 1182.

From the seven provinces of Urhemma, they came to join the march on Naddeghomra.

Some came driving wagons, a few came riding on the bare backs of horses and gaars and donkeys, but most came on foot. They were poor men, most of whom had lost everything, including their carts and their animals— and that was partly why they came. Impoverished, hungry, with nothing left, they had made a decision: that to risk death in a noble cause was better than starvation.

So they left their homes, left the soil of their ancestors, and on foot they trudged down the dusty dirt roads. Most of them left little behind. Some had a few belongings slung in sacks over their shoulders, but many carried nothing save the clothes they wore, and even those in tatters. A few had the great luxury of sandals, but the vast majority were barefoot. The soles of their feet were calloused, cracked, and broken, and they left bloody footprints in the dust, but still they walked to join the march on Naddeghomra.

This was the great crusade, the great adventure of the age. Led at last by the true *Ur-Rasvadhi*, they would take Naddeghomra or die trying. For some of them, it hardly mattered which. They were fathers who had lost their children, husbands who had lost their wives to starvation and disease. They were people with nothing left to live for, but now they had something to die for.

One way or another, they would gain the blessing of

yarushkadharra. Either the tyrants would be overthrown, or else the rebels would achieve the truest freedom of all: freedom, at last, from the agonies and struggles of their lives.

Down the roads they trekked toward Arbadakhar, coming there from every province, every town and village, heeding the *Ur-Rasvadhi's* call to arms. So many thousands came, there wasn't room enough for them within the walls of Arbadakhar, and so tents were pitched to house them outside the city, a sea of tents for the flocking pilgrims.

Absorbing all these thousands of new recruits, in preparation for the great march south, Jehan effected yet another reorganization of his army. Adding to the roster of veteran Generals Kawaras, Yahu, Ubuvasakh, and Ontondra, Jehan appointed two new ones, and created two new divisions under their command. Rodavlas Ilhad was a weaver from Zidneppa who had been Ontondra's chief aide; the other new general was Rimidal Vokoban, an old country peasant in his sixties who had nevertheless fought with great distinction and sagacity in the war against the land barons. Meanwhile, Jephos Kirdahi remained as the deputy commander of the whole army.

Four divisions would prosecute the march southward, and two remained stationed at Arbadakhar, those of Rodavlas Ilhad and Leopard Ubuvasakh. The Leopard was designated to act as Governor of Taroloweh.

It was decided that Golana would accompany Jehan on the invasion. They both recognized the dangers, but Jehan was reluctant to leave Golana behind without his personal protection. More important, he cherished her affection and counsel, and would not abide a separation from her. And Golana's personal choice was to go with the army whose fate would determine her own.

Both of them, however, begged Maiya to stay behind with her son, Jehandai. Her father strove powerfully to impress upon the girl what hardships the journey could entail, and that she would be much better off remaining at Arbadakhar.

"But your Tnemghadi is going with you," Maiya countered. "If she can make this journey, so can I."

The stubborn girl could not be dissuaded. Her resolve was strengthened by her belief that Golana's influence was responsible for the southern invasion. Maiya herself had argued for attacking Ksiritsa instead of Naddeghomra, and her defeat on the issue had deepened even further her hatred of Golana.

She would never permit her father to go off alone with his wife. Maiya would follow them all the way to Naddeghomra, doing her chores of cooking and washing. And she was strengthened, too, in her vigil by her certitude of ultimate victory. For Maiya knew that in all the years of marriage to Mutsukh, Golana had been barren.

Southward they marched, through the gates of Arbadakhar festooned gaily with flowers. The people waved flags and shouted slogans to cheer them on their way, many of them weeping with joy at the launching of this blessed army. Southward they marched, a gaudy caravan of men and horses and wagons, swaying along the rutted streets and roads to the music of tambourines and flutes and drums, their colored banners flouncing in the wind, their long spears scraping the blue sky. Southward they marched out of Arbadakhar, down through the Taroloweh hinterlands until they reached the River Qurwa.

Here they encamped, but only long enough to lash logs into rude barges, to ferry their horses and wagons across the river. And when Jehan's army reassembled on the south bank of the Qurwa, it had entered another province: Nitupsar.

Already, legend of Jehan Henghmani had spread throughout the South, and Nitupsar was not excluded. The people of Nitupsar had known that the coming of Jehan, the *Ur-Rasvadhi,* was imminent. Even before he'd crossed the Qurwa, the province was in ferment. Violence was rife in the towns against troops and priests, and peasant uprisings were toppling the land barons. Taroloweh's story was being repeated in Nitupsar.

It was evident that what the people needed was not a savior, but merely the spark that his coming provided.

And so Jehan Henghmani marched through Nitupsar, to cap the revolution already well in progress. Cadres of Tnemghadi troops, isolated in towns with their relief cut off, gave bitter-end resistance. Nowhere in the province did Jehan encounter an army of any consequence. Although the fighting was often bloody, the Urhemmedhins fought with passion, and the long-feared Tnemghadi power was broken like a dry twig.

And as his army cut its swath through Nitupsar, Jehan found it not diminished by the casualties sustained. In fact the army grew steadily, for wherever it marched, the farmers would drop their plowshares and would run to join it.

It was not just the Tnemghadi army that was trundled over by the southward march. As in Taroloweh, the Ksavra Land Decree was enforced against the barons, and their stranglehold upon agriculture was smashed. Some of them yielded without bloodshed, others barricaded themselves in their manor houses and fought to the death. But all of them were drowned in the surging peasant tide.

Through the towns and villages, too, Jehan carried the relentless war of liberation. Here it was the merchants, the officials, and of course the priests who were the targets of enflamed mobs. Temples would be set ablaze, the priests brutally slaughtered.

Red and black with fire and smoke was the sky above Nitupsar, evoking the tumult eight centuries before when Khatto Trevendhani marched here. Tnem Khatto had been reviled as the enslaver of the people, but Jehan was cheered as liberator. Through the towns he would ostentatiously parade, and the people would come out to hail him. They would throw flowers from the rooftops, while girls and children would strew bouquets in Jehan's path, and others would bang on tambourines and dance in the streets. Not even his ugliness could dampen their ardor; they had waited eight centuries for this. And so they clapped their hands and danced and sang and screamed and shouted.

"*Vahiy Jehan!*" they cried with tears in their eyes, screaming themselves hoarse. "*Victory to Jehan!*"

They screamed it endlessly: "*Vahiy Jehan! Vahiy Urhemma! Yarushkadharra, O Yarushkadharra!*"

And in three months it was done:

Nitupsar was free.

·2·

FIRST TAROLOWEH; then Nitupsar; and then Khrasanna. It was not prudent to display converging eyebrows in these provinces. The Tnemghadi were simply being extirpated, with no nice distinctions being made. Not the littlest shopkeeper, not the humblest scribe, not women nor children were spared. The Urhemmedhins had suffered long enough, and now the time had come for vengeance.

They were not squeamish in exacting it. Tnemghadi homes were ransacked and burned, their occupants put to death with hideous tortures, their women raped by ruffian gangs, dragged naked through the streets, their breasts cut off. They watched their babies torn apart by dogs and trampled under horses' hooves. The vengeance was merciless.

"Jehan," Golana pleaded one night in their tent. "You must do something to curb all this brutality. It is bestial, inhuman."

"Does it bother you because they are your people?"

"No! Because they *are* people. Oh, yes, some of them do deserve what they're getting, but most of the victims are innocent. What is happening to them is barbaric!"

"But it is necessary," Jehan answered coldly. "History demands it."

"No, Jehan, history does not demand torture, it does not demand rape, it does not demand the butchering of babies!"

"Then nor did history demand the enslavement of the Urhemmedhin people, the torture of *their* patriots, the rape of *their* women, the starvation of *their* babies. But it happened, and it can be neither changed nor forgotten. Perhaps we would not be here today if the Tnemghadi had been more humane. Don't you understand, Golana? Even a little dog will bite if you kick him enough."

286

"A dog is just a senseless animal. But maybe those who torture babies are animals too. Oh, Jehan, I do understand, I know that retribution is inevitable. But this barbaric savagery cannot be condoned. Some innocent people may have to die, but let it not be said that no finger was lifted to save them, let it not be said that more died than necessary. All I ask is that you speak out, and tell your followers that the creed of Urhem abhors barbarity."

"That won't stop them."

"Even if it saves the life of just one poor baby, don't you see that you must do it?"

Jehan shook his head. "A few might heed what I say. But most will revile me for it. I am not their leader because of the wisdom of my words, but because it is what they want to hear. If I start saying things they don't want to hear, I may not remain leader very long.

"Surely Golana, of all people, you're the one who understands this. You understand power. What we seek is a great prize. Nothing comes for free; and a great prize carries a great price."

Golana lowered her eyes, reluctantly nodded, and sighed.

"Aren't we fortunate," she sighed, "that the price is being paid in the currency of other people's children?"

As the Urhemmedhin army neared Naddeghomra, its commanders became embroiled in a crucial debate over strategy.

Thus far they had swept easily from victory to victory, taking estates and towns as one would pluck peaches from a tree. But Naddeghomra, the ripest fruit of all, would be a different story. Indeed, the rebels had fared so well in the countryside largely because the Tnemghadi were concentrating their forces for a showdown at Naddeghomra. According to reliable intelligence, the city was being transformed into a mighty fortress. Moreover, the Tnemghadi had learned the lesson of Arbadakhar, where they'd been defeated more by forces within the walls than without. That would not be countenanced again.

So why not simply bypass Naddeghomra? Jehan could continue mopping up the countryside, conserving his forces, and letting the Tnemghadi rot inside their Naddeghomra bastion. Occupying a lone enclave in the midst of hostile territory, they would be in a virtual state of siege even with Jehan nowhere near. Sooner or later, Naddeghomra would open to Jehan.

For a final resolution of the issue, he convened his generals in his tent. Jehan himself sat like a sphinx, listening carefully but revealing no hint of his own views.

The case for bypassing Naddeghomra had its most vocal advocate in Kamil Kawaras; for half an hour he held forth on its advantages. But Golana argued that Kawaras' plan would amount to a confession of weakness.

"And to fail at Naddeghomra," Kawaras answered, "would be a *demonstration* of weakness."

"That's right," added Kirdahi, "there's no assurance we can crack this nut. We could break ourselves trying."

"One must venture in order to gain," the woman replied. Then she looked straight at Jehan with a confident smile. "What we seek is a great prize. Nothing comes for free; and a great prize carries a great price."

"But this prize," said Kawaras doggedly, "*might* in time be ours for free. Why get bogged down and sap our strength in a siege, when our present strategy is succeeding so well?"

"We are succeeding, yes, but every mile we march is a mile farther from our home base. We are really just wandering in the wilderness. But capture Naddeghomra, and *that* will be our capital, and everything else will fall naturally into our hands, as the planets revolve around the sun."

Kawaras pulled his unkempt hair in exasperation, and began to frame a reply. But at that moment Jehan spoke up at last, to end the conference. "Your points are all well taken. We will go to bed and think on them."

He stood up; the others nodded, and departed wearily to their tents to await Jehan's decision.

"Are you really considering their plan?" Golana asked.

"No, I am merely humoring them. We came south for Naddeghomra, that is our destiny. And we cannot disappoint destiny."

Jehan Henghmani looked out upon the City of Naddeghomra.

There was a glitter in his eye.

The River Amajap was a muddy brown, surrounding Naddeghomra on three sides. Further protection was afforded by the steep bluffs rising from the river banks, the plateau upon which the city was built. As a continuation of the walls of the natural table was Naddeghomra's man-made wall, a muddy yellow color too.

Behind the wall one could glimpse the tips of the largest buildings, of yellow-white stucco, and here and there a dome, a taller tower or a narrow copper spire, all contained by the walls like fruit in a basket. And then, towering over everything else, looming godlike over the city, was *The Maal*.

The rest of Naddeghomra seemed to cling like humble moss at the feet of *The Maal*. Its immense size was staggering. And perfect in their clean, simple lines were the four pairs of towers, sweeping skyward, their white brilliance bouncing back the sunlight. The final tower, a shimmering crystal black, dominated with a serene and sinister arrogance.

This temple, thrusting up out of all the muddy colors, was what glittered in Jehan Henghmani's eye; he could not pull his gaze away from it. For all his life he had heard of this monument, and its renown was one of infamy. Now, standing before it at last, he was astounded by its beauty, unlike anything he'd ever seen or imagined. This was a work of art, a majestic sculpture astride the horizon. Built centuries before, it did not appear ancient at all, but rather like an apparition that had come down from a thousand years into the future.

Golana's eyes too were arrested by *The Maal*. "It's grand, isn't it?" she said.

Jehan agreed. "It accomplishes its purpose: to overwhelm us, to impress upon us the power and greatness of the Tnemghadi who built it."

"The Tnemghadi *are* a great people, Jehan. They are a people of vision and daring, to have conceived and built this temple. We must not begrudge them that."

"Yes. But nor must we be intimidated."

With her eyes still fixed on the brilliant white towers, Golana nodded her head.

"So take a good look at it while you can, dear wife. For we must destroy *The Maal*."

The siege of Naddeghomra began as did the one at Arbadakhar. The Urhemmedhin army was arrayed in a ring around the city, half of it on the lower bank of the Amajap, and the other half concentreatd to face the one wall unprotected by the river. There they pitched camp and set to waiting.

Naddeghomra waited too, for a sudden night attack. But unlike at Arbadakhar, this time the besiegers refused to attack at all. Days stretched into weeks, and still they sat doing nothing. This quiescent siege was quite unnerving to the Tnemghadi, for they realized the elegant simplicity of Jehan's strategy: starvation.

He had placed his lines too far away to be vulnerable to arrows. However, the Tnemghadi had the walls bristling with catapult towers, colossal wooden contraptions capable of hurling their deadly loads far across the sky. Day and night, Jehan's troops were pelted with fire bombs.

Yet this was a choice of weapons much to his liking. Gamely, he rigged up catapults of his own, knowing that the defenders confined within the city would sooner run out of ammunition than would the attackers. Moreover, a fire bomb could be far more devastating in a crowded city than on an open plain. Jehan's men might scatter as a projectile screamed toward them, but Naddeghomra's buildings could not be moved out of the line of fire. Every night would be illuminated by tongues of flame leaping above the city's walls.

Jehan spent the long daylight hours riding his horse around his circular encampment, from the line confronting the city's gates, across the Amajap by barge to the shadow of the bluffs, then across the river again at the other end of its twist, and around to where he'd started. Every day he made this circuit, sweltering beneath the pounding southern sun, to chat with the officers and troops, to bolster their morale as the siege dragged uneventfully on.

Each day, as he circled Naddeghomra, his eye moved irresistibly to the one landmark that remained always visible. And every time he looked at it, he swore *The Maal* would fall. The Tnemghadi had built it to symbolize their coming; and Jehan Henghmani would destroy it, to herald their fall.

At the end of each day's circuit, well after sunset, he would return, weary and sweat-grimed, to his tents. Maiya would have his supper ready, and often she would bathe his face and feet, and then take his soiled clothing to be scrubbed. But never would she speak with him.

"Why do you burden my heart so?" he'd beg her with palms outspread. "You are my only child, I love you and I crave your love. There were years I thought you lost to me, but it seems I have not really gotten you back."

Maiya's eyes bore the icy fire of crystal and she said, "I am not your only child."

Jehan would finally close the flaps of his tent, to be alone with Golana. But the day's labors were not over yet, for there still remained his lesson. Just as her first husband had taught language to Golana, now she was teaching her second husband.

Not until near midnight would they finally go to bed, naked in the baking southern heat. She would rub and knead his neck and arms and shoulders, massaging the pain that never left him—the enduring souvenir of Ksiritsa. They would make love. Then she would sleep with her arms encircling him, her head upon his chest and her thick hair bunched against his cheek. Jehan would often lie awake, thinking, and holding close her warm, soft body. Only now might the pain in his own huge body subside, to give him a measure of peace.

"I have news to tell you," she whispered one night, cradled in his arms.

"Yes?"

"I am with child."

Jehan sat up abruptly, and hugged her.

"Are you glad?"

"I am very glad. I am delighted. This is wonderful news."

In the dark, Golana could see the light of his smiling teeth. But then the light suddenly dimmed.

"What's the matter, Jehan?"

"Nothing."

"What are you thinking about?"

"Nothing."

But he was thinking about Maiya.

BERGHARRA—Naddeghomra, Obsidional or Siege Piece, the dies for a ten-tayel gold coin struck onto a crude, oversized copper planchet. Year 1184. *Obverse:* portrait of Emperor Sarbat Satanichadh. *Reverse:* Imperial dragon with Naddeghomra mintmark. Breitenbach 2008, 41 mm. As in the case of most necessity issues, these were used to pay the troops after silver had run out. Very fine or better for wear, but poorly struck and corroded. (*Hauchschild Collection Catalog*)

· 3 ·

IT WAS NEITHER Jehan's army nor the Tnemghadi who
were suffering most the horrors of the siege. The real
victims were the Urhemmedhin citizens of Naddeghomra.

Khrasanna's Viceroy, Hassim Alimansour, imposed a
desperately rigorous regime. He regarded every inhabit-
ant as a potential saboteur, and treated them accordingly.
Platoons patrolled through the streets day and night, ruthlessly enforcing order. Not the slightest crooked word or
look was tolerated. Offenders were hustled off without
trial. The punishment now for even minor crimes was
death, and there were daily public executions to instill
terror into the citizens, lest they entertain any notion of
aiding the besiegers.

Hassim Alimansour was determined to prevail, no matter what the cost. He would hold Naddeghomra for the
Emperor, even if he had to sacrifice all its people to do it.

In anticipation of the siege, Alimansour had long been
working to make Naddeghomra a self-contained world.
New wells had been dug, and tanks erected to catch and
store rainwater. Food supplies were hoarded up; many
in Khrasanna went hungry in order to provision Naddeghomra against the siege. To supplement the hoarding, roof-
top gardens were set up, and livestock was brought in to
be housed in cramped street-pens.

Of course, any Naddeghomran able to flee the city had
done so before Jehan's arrival. The only laggards were
those too poor to move, and the Tnemghadi, who had
no place else to go. Even with Jehan snarling at its gates,
Naddeghomra was the safest place for the Tnemghadi.
Outside, they would not escape the peasant mobs.

Despite the husbanding of food and trimming the population, Alimansour knew he could not hold out forever.
His only hope was to wear Jehan down and make the

rebel relent out of sheer frustration. But Jehan knew this too, and was determined to stick it out.

Patiently he waited, never attacking, only trading fire bombs. The war was one of nerves, a contest of wills. Both sides wondered how it could ever reach a conclusion.

But as the siege dragged into its second year, Viceroy Alimansour found himself staring at depleted larders. All supplies were dwindling. Prices had soared to outrageous heights, spurred not only by scarcity but also by the Viceroy's emergency coinage of larger denomination copper to pay his troops. This was to ensure that available provisions went to the soldiers and not to the civilians. Few could afford to buy food now, but there was very little left to buy in any case.

Meanwhile, Jehan's unremitting bombardment had taken its toll. Not only fire bombs, but heavy boulders had been thrown at the city, to smash down what could not be burned. Naddeghomra had become a shambles, every street bearing the scars of war, many whole blocks leveled. Little could be done to rebuild under such conditions. Thousands of people were left homeless, forced to wander in the open. These uprooted hordes posed a direct threat to order; and Alimansour commanded that they be rounded up and put to death.

And these poor homeless citizens were not the only victims of the Viceroy. Hassim Alimansour was indeed prepared to exterminate the entire population of Naddeghomra in order to sustain his soldiery. To this end, he promulgated a most incredible decree: It was declared a crime punishable by death for any Urhemmedhin to possess or to eat any food.

To enforce this monstrous decree, the soldiers were given free rein to enter any dwelling, confiscate all food discovered, and summarily execute the culprits on the spot. Since this was actually their own last resort before starvation, the troops did not quail from full enforcement of the decree.

The streets of Naddeghomra became a jungle of guerrilla combat between the troops and the people, fighting over the few scraps of food that remained. Alimansour's decree was an absurdity; in fact, all law had disintegrated by now, and naked force was the universal arbiter. Better armed and better fed, the soldiers had the upper hand.

Now they began the systematic murder of all civilians in the city.

The people ate the cats and dogs and rats; they bloated their bellies with water and clay; they chewed on hide and leather; ate their shoes and ate their belts; and many of them, half delirious with hunger, even sucked rocks and gnawed on wood. They prayed for the deaths of their neighbors and children, because the dead were unhesitatingly eaten. The corpses would be fought over; and frequently, a desperately hungry man would not wait for a friend to die.

Jehan looked out at Naddeghomra, its fires flickering in his eye. He could only guess at the horrors taking place behind the walls, but it was obvious the Urhemmedhins were suffering prodigiously.

He had come to liberate them; instead, he was their angel of death. But there was no turning back. He was as much the prisoner of the forces he'd unleashed as were the Naddeghomrans. He had locked the city in a hold that he was powerless to relax.

And he did not lament it. He wanted Naddeghomra, regardless of what suffering it caused. Had he not suffered too? Hadn't he been tortured? In the dungeon, he had dared to dream, and now he was so close, no remorse would hold him back.

Jehan armored himself too with the knowledge that he *was* liberating these people—even as they died like trapped rats, he was liberating them. They were dying so that their children could be free.

And then, in the fifteenth month of the siege— Endrashah, 1184—a breathless runner reached Jehan's encampment. He brought an urgent message from the North, from Arbadakhar:

A city besieged by the army of Bergharra.

Out over the ramparts of Arbadakhar, Nattahnam Ubuvasakh scanned the horizon with fretful eyes.

The Leopard's fine-hewn good looks and vicious cunning had brought him a long way in the world. Jehan's march across the Qurwa had left Ubuvasakh as Governor of Taroloweh, and he was exultant at this undreamed-of power. For a year he played at rulership, exploiting to the hilt his newly acquired station. The Vraddagoon was expanded, furnished in luxurious style. There he hosted lavish banquets entertained by lovely girls dancing nude. Around him, he cultivated a new, crude high society, but his true forte was debauchery. For his private use, he assembled a harem of concubines, all paid prostitutes, both male and female. Little real attention was paid to the affairs of the province which, outside the Vraddagoon, was starving.

Then Nattahnam Ubuvasakh's bubble burst.

Dug in around him was a Tnemghadi army six times larger than his own. It was true that the city's fortifications were sturdy, and the boiling pitch and arrows rained down on the attackers were holding them at bay. But the people of Arbadakhar had grown to despise their negligent and profligate governor. Moreover, the city was not really up to weathering another siege so soon after its last one. Thus Ubuvasakh's position was, to say the least, precarious.

Jehan Henghmani was in fact his only hope. Without massive aid from the outside, Arbadakhar was doomed. This was the desperate message entrusted to runners, sent out to try to breach the Tnemghadi cordon. Ubuvasakh assumed that at least one of his dozen messengers would reach Jehan. But he could by no means assume help would come.

After all, Jehan was himself mired in a bitter siege—of a city far more crucial than Arbadakhar. For Jehan to rush northward on a rescue mission would be nothing other than a supreme act of loyalty to Leopard Ubuvasakh.

And the Leopard wondered: What suspicions did Jehan harbor regarding his family's betrayal, eight years before?

That was why Nattahnam Ubuvasakh was looking out over the ramparts with worried eyes.

Jehan castigated himself. This disaster should have been foreseen!

The Tnemghadi were plagued by ever-increasing Akfakh depredations in the north and gripped in a deathlock at their southern underbelly. Sarbat had seen the chance to strike a blow in the middle. The attack upon Arbadakhar was an eminently sensible commitment of available resources. This way, even if Jehan took Naddeghomra, Sarbat would at least reclaim the northern Urhemmedhin lands, quarantining Jehan far to the south.

This placed Jehan on the horns of a cruel dilemma.

One alternative was simply to stay put at Naddeghomra. Under siege for more than fourteen months, its fall could only be a matter of time. Naturally Jehan was loath to let those fourteen months go in vain, to let this gem slip through his fingers. Naddeghomra was a far greater prize than Arbadakhar. He could burn his bridges, leave Taroloweh to the Tnemghadi, and establish himself in greater glory at the City of Urhem.

But on the other hand, what would his peasant followers think of him then? How could Jehan callously leave the province where he'd started, and the brave people defending it, to Tnemghadi vengeance? He reminded himself that the rebel army was still held together only by conviction and loyalty.

The sudden crisis provoked another debate among the leaders. All night long, they shouted and banged the table, while once more, Jehan kept his own counsel and merely listened.

Yahu, Kirdahi, Ontondra, and Ilhad all argued strongly for the relief of Arbadakhar. Ontondra, however, proposed a middle course, with half the army going to Arbadakhar while the other half kept up the siege. But Kawaras countered that such a strategy would likely result in defeat on both fronts, neither half of the army being strong enough to achieve its purpose. Of Jehan's generals, only Kamil Kawaras advocated remaining at Naddeghomra and letting Arbadakhar fall.

In this stance he had one key ally: Golana. She argued eloquently that at Naddeghomra, the realization of all their dreams was at hand. A man, she said, is given only one pass at the cup of such opportunity. Defy that opportunity and it will never come again.

Go to Arbadakhar, urged the generals. Go to Arbadakhar and regardless of the outcome, your place in history will be secure. If nothing else, you will be the man who gave up Naddeghomra to save his friends.

There was a lull in the debate. It was suddenly filled by a quiet voice whose presence in the tent had scarcely been noticed. "Stay at Naddeghomra," Maiya said. "Conquer this city and put a crown on your head. Conquer it, and make me a princess, and make your son, Jehandai, an emperor."

"Go to Arbadakhar," said Hnayim Yahu, "or the throne you take will become your grave, for your army will revile and desert you."

Stay at Naddeghomra, said Golana, glancing at Maiya; stay, for Arbadakhar may well be lost before you even get there, and you'll have given up everything for nothing.

Go to Arbadakhar, for its fall would open the way for the Tnemghadi to march south and relieve Naddeghomra.

Stay at Naddeghomra, *Paban,* and leave the Leopard to Sarbat's mercy.

Go to Arbadakhar, my lord, and save your loyal friends.

Jehan stood up, and saying not a word, quit his tent. The debate buzzed in his ears. If only he'd left fewer troops at Arbadakhar so that Sarbat could have swallowed it up in one quick gulp—obviating this horrible dilemma!

It was night. There was a faint breeze, refreshing after the stifling hours in the tent. Jehan stood leaning against a pole, and looked out at Naddeghomra. The city glowed, illuminated by fire, so that even through the dark of night, Jehan could see clearly the outlines of *The Maal.*

He felt a touch on his shoulder. It was Golana, and he wrapped his huge arm around her, folding her close. Pressed against him, he could feel the bulge of her body where their child was growing.

"This is an historic night," he said. "You and Maiya have agreed on something."

Golana laughed softly. "And do you agree with us?"

"I am very worried," Jehan said. "I fear what a forced march northward might do, considering your condition. We must not lose the child!"

"We must not lose Naddeghomra!" Golana snapped instantly.

Jehan shook his head thickly, like a shaggy bear. "Let us hope to save our child," he said.

· 4 ·

WHEN THE SUN CAME UP, a pink crust at the rim of the blue night, the white towers of *The Maal* burst into brilliance. Catching the light first, while the rest of the city was still in darkness, the great towers seemed to float in the sky, hanging down from the heavens like the fingers of a god.

With sleepless eyes, Jehan Henghmani looked at the beautiful temple one last time. Then he turned northward.

If he failed now, he knew that he would never see Naddeghomra and its *Maal* again.

His eyes fixed north, without looking back, he led his army away to Arbadakhar.

From behind the walls of Naddeghomra, the Tnemghadi watched the besieging army mysteriously strike its tents.

Not with the lethargy of defeat was the Urhemmedhin camp dismantled: They gathered their gear and loaded up their wagons hurriedly, as though fleeing. In their haste, they left Naddeghomra circled by debris, including the cumbersome catapults that had been so destructive.

The Tnemghadi watched this in relief mixed with consternation. They could not know the reason why the siege was abandoned, but despite their mystification, this was a miraculous eleventh-hour reprieve. Conditions inside the city had become a hellish nightmare. There was no food left, soldiers and civilians were killing each other, and even his own army was beginning to revile Viceroy Alimansour as a fiendish fanatic.

But the sudden lifting of the siege did not plunge the city into celebration. The few Urhemmedhins left were in fact embittered by this turn of events. They had endured monstrous deprivations on account of the siege, scores of thousands had been killed, and thousands more lost homes and kin. The survivors were hanging on by their teeth. Sustaining them through the horror had been the conviction that they were suffering to gain *yarushkadharra*. The savior was at hand. But now he had literally turned his back on them. They had gone through Hell for nothing.

Nor did the Tnemghadi rejoice. They were still in dire peril, stranded in a hostile land, still looking down the throat of starvation—and the lifting of the siege did not put food in their mouths.

As the last of Jehan's caravan disappeared over the horizon, the gates of Naddeghomra were thrown open, and hungry scavengers poured frantically out into the countryside. But it was barren, stripped clean by Jehan's army during the extended siege. There was nothing left to feed the city.

Quickly did this grim fact penetrate upon the Tnemghadi: The siege had succeeded after all. They were beaten.

But isolated in the government palaces, Hassim Alimansour didn't realize this. Flushed with triumph, he felt vindicated. He had broken Jehan's string of victories. This made him a hero, and surely his star was on the rise.

It was jarring to hear the officers insist there was no food. Alimansour refused to accept it, but his officers were adamant. According to them, the only possibility might be to transport provisions from many lim away, but that could not sustain starving Naddeghomra for very long. The upshot was plain: They must leave the city or perish there.

Alimansour exploded with rage. "We withstood a siege of fourteen months! We defeated the Man Eater! And now, on the very day of our victory, you dare suggest abandoning Naddeghomra? The greatest city in the South, simply thrown away after eight centuries? Are you mad? You must be raving mad!"

"We are not mad, Your Excellency. We are merely hungry, and there is no food."

"*Merely hungry,*" mimicked the Viceroy scornfully. "I thought I had brave, strong men. Look what rubbish you are speaking: For fourteen months we withstood Jehan

Henghmani's siege; now it is over; can we not persevere now?"

"*There is no food,*" an officer repeated flatly.

"I will not hear your sniveling treason! Tnem Sarbat Satanichadh still rules at Naddeghomra. We will save this city for him, or die here. Go back to your posts, all of you. That is a command."

For a tense moment, Hassim Alimansour stood glowering, brandishing his staff of office adorned with the Sexrexatra dragon. The officers avoided his eyes, unwilling to openly defy him.

Then one did speak up, in a strangely calm voice. "Your Excellency, we have given Jehan a defeat, and we must take our satisfaction in that. But Naddeghomra cannot be saved. There is nothing to be accomplished by staying except our deaths. That will avail the Emperor nothing. We can serve him better by saving ourselves. We are leaving; we ask you to join us."

"Traitor!" Alimansour screamed, lunging wildly at the man with his staff upraised.

The other officers converged upon the Viceroy, pinioned him, and wrested the staff from his hands.

"Traitors!" he fumed at them. "Damned traitors! I order you back to your posts. I command you!"

But all they did was to release him. They faced him now in a united line. "We are leaving. We beg you to come with us."

The Viceroy, his face contorted with contempt, answered by spitting at the floor where they stood. But they turned their backs to leave.

He shrieked curses after them as they made their exit, but he did not budge from his spot.

From throughout the scarred city, the surviving troops coalesced. Many of the wounded were left behind with the thousands of dead. Now, for the first time in weeks, the rubble-clogged streets fell eerily quiet as the fighting subsided.

One officer went to *The Maal,* and at his insistence the priests held a hurried conference. With profound reluctance they decided to give up their temple and throw in with the fleeing army, for they knew the standard fate of priests in cities overrun by Urhemmedhin mobs.

As the soldiers, joined by the priests, abandoned the street fighting and made for the gates, the Urhemmedhins grasped what was happening. They realized that the descending quiet was in fact their own silent dirge.

The precious riverboats were seized by the first Tnemghadi to reach the docks. Overloading the boats, and huddling into an armada for self-protection, they headed eastward down the Amajap. Once the boats were gone, the tardy were forced to take a land route—slower and more vulnerable to peasant retribution.

The first river-town reached was Tjabra, and the fleet of boats was beached. Without ado, the soldiers attacked. Caught unawares and unarmed, the Tjabrans were slaughtered like sheep, the town pillaged for every scrap of food. The Tnemghadi were ravaged by hunger and shed much blood among themselves fighting over the spoils of the raid. They gorged themselves on the spot, loaded up their boats, and pushed on.

Nothing at Tjabra was left for their comrades, straggling behind on foot.

Eastward across Khrasanna Province the Tnemghadi fought their way. Word of the Tjabra raid had swept ahead of them, and other towns prepared to defend themselves. Every lim of the way they battled the soldiers, who came like locusts, furiously stripping the land to feed themselves. To starve the raiders, the Urhemmedhins burned the fields on both sides of the river.

The refugees did manage to get through Khrasanna, but it was a bloody journey. The land was left littered with dead, Urhemmedhin and Tnemghadi alike. Then they pushed on toward the sea, through Ohreem Province, leaving their dead floating in the river behind them. Their goal was the port city of Mughdad, at the mouth of the Amajap, where they might finally escape by sea back to their homeland. It took them seven awful weeks to reach Mughdad.

By then, the land travelers had been wiped out entirely, and only a handful of the boats were left. It was a sorry remnant of the great army that had once lorded over Naddeghomra.

When they reached Mughdad, they found it had already

been liberated. And so, having gained their destination, the last Tnemghadi survivors of Naddeghomra lost their lives.

Hassim Alimansour dropped to his knees and pounded the floor with his fists. It was so unfair: On the very day of his magnificent victory, it turned to ashes in his mouth.

He called out for his servants, but no one answered him. He went running through the lofty corridors of the government palace, and found it utterly empty, deserted. He alone was the Emperor's last stand at Naddeghomra.

Alimansour's eyes stung with tears, not for the ending of his life—he could not even think about that—but for the ending of everything to which his life had been devoted. It all had come to nothing.

The only thing left to do was to die with dignity. He determined that he would not permit himself to starve or to fall into the hands of the mob. So he buckled on his jeweled ceremonial sword, and left the government palace, making his way to the nearby *Maal*. There he intended to play out the final act before the image of Tnem Sarbat Satanichadh, the god whom he had served now literally unto death.

But hardly had he reached the street, when he was set upon by a bedraggled throng. When he saw them coming at him with their hunger-crazed eyes, Alimansour unsheathed his sword, and slashed vehemently at them. Unarmed but numerous, they came at him undaunted by his blade. This was the devil who had tormented them, and now they would make him pay for it.

To the limit of his strength he fought back. He killed and maimed a dozen and more before they brought him down and got the bloody sword away from him. But they did not turn the sword on him; instead they broke it in two, and tore at him with their ragged fingernails and bare rotten teeth. Maddened with hunger and hatred, they tore the living flesh from Hassim Alimansour.

·5·

THE SUN WAS A BIG, broiling bubble on the horizon as Jehan Henghmani's army threw itself into the desperate northward march.

These men had not been trained to real exertion. Most of them were farmers and peasants, and what battles they had fought thus far, through Nitupsar and Khrasanna, had been easy. At Naddeghomra they had done nothing more than trade fire bombs with the enemy. But these men were now pushed without mercy by their commander.

It was 1,327 lim to Arbadakhar. From sun-up to sun-down they marched under the enervating sun; there was no time to stop along the way; there were none of the celebrations that had heralded the southward march. It was a straight, brutalizing, man-killing march—thousands of them dropped by the wayside—but Jehan knew he had to pay this price for speed.

At the Qurwa, he crossed back into Taroloweh on the same barges that he'd left on the south bank long before. There was not even time to mend the old lashings, and so some of the barges broke apart in midstream, with a loss of horses, wagons, and men. But Jehan pushed on.

On the twenty-second day he got within range of Arbadakhar, and arrayed his troops to do battle with the besieging Tnemghadi. Hnayim Yahu's horsemen were brought to the fore, while the wagons were unhitched and relegated to the rear. Jehan himself remained at the head of the column, but he insisted that the carriage holding Golana, Maiya, and Jehandai stay far at the back.

The Urhemmedhin army numbered approximately forty thousand men. The Bergharran troops were more than fifty thousand, and they were ready.

Their commander was General Tamar Ghouriyadh, a bluff man with roaring eyes and blazing moustaches, but

306

an extremely capable military tactician. He had come to Arbadakhar with the mission of recapturing the city and taking the head of the rebel governor, Ubuvasakh. He had not figured upon an attack by Jehan himself, yet Ghouriyadh saw this not as a threat, but as an opportunity. Now he could strike a really devastating blow. Now, crowed Tamar Ghouriyadh, he would have the heads of *all* the rebel leaders.

On the seventeenth of Jhevla, 1184, the two armies engaged on a plain a few lim from Arbadakhar. Unwilling to loosen his stranglehold upon the city, the Tnemghadi General left enough troops behind to maintain the siege; thus, the opposing armies were nearly equal in strength. Nevertheless, Ghouriyadh was confident of victory because his troops were fresh, whereas Jehan's had just finished an exhausting three-week march.

They met head-on in the open plain, in classic formations, the peasant army led by Jehan himself on horseback. Ghouriyadh had planned to charge first, but Jehan wouldn't stand for that; the insurgents charged forward even more ferociously.

Down they rushed with swords and war cries whishing the air. *Vahiy Jehan!* they screamed, *Vahiy Urhemma! Yarushkadharra!*

They collided in a thick yellow dust cloud.

As the dust suddenly engulfed him, Jehan hacked away with his sword, but he could hardly see anything. The noise was terrific; amid the screams of *Vahiy Urhemma!* were the screams of hundreds going down in agony.

Even in the haze of dust Jehan's huge figure was unmistakable. He was the one man every Tnemghadi wanted to kill. From every side they came at him, suddenly appearing out of the dust like phantasms, many at once, their swords and spears coming out of nowhere to slash at him. He struggled dizzily to parry, but they came at him so fast and thick he was sure he'd be killed. Being the Savior would not save him.

A slash wound opened up down the side of his head, cutting to the bone and spurting out hot blood. Then another on his shoulder; and another, on his thigh. Doggedly he fought on, but he was certain now that he was finished.

Death came to fifteen thousand of his soldiers, and several more thousand were wounded. In this close, savage combat, nearly half the Urhemmedhins were casualties.

Yarushkadharra! they had shouted as they fell, shouted with their last breath. For fifteen thousand of them, the freedom they had shouted for proved to be the freedom that death brings.

The Tnemghadi did not have *yarushkadharra* to die for; and because of that, they died in even greater numbers. Fully half and more were left dead on the plain, piled like debris on top of each other and among the moaning wounded. Five thousand were taken prisoner by the Urhemmedhins. A few more thousand beat a path back to their lines at Arbadakhar, and the rest scattered in flight.

Jehan was among the fortunate ones who had survived. He was numb with pain and loss of blood from three wounds, but he had survived.

As the dust settled and he reassembled his officers, he was informed that Kamil Kawaras was not among them. The selfless old Tnemghadi-hater—the one general who had argued against this expedition—had been killed, along with so many of his men. Kawaras' body was retrieved in a basket, for the enemy soldiers had hacked its limbs off.

Jehan directed that Kamil Kawaras' remains be given a duly ceremonious burial, befitting a hero of the movement and the first of its leaders to be killed. Then he awarded the vacant generalship to Kawaras' logical successor, the young battalion commander, Gaffar Mussopo.

To Jehan's tent Gaffar Mussopo came, to receive the sword of command. He almost staggered there, for he too had been wounded; his left hand hung in bloody ribbons. Later that night the surgeons would amputate the ruined hand, but Gaffar was grateful; he too was a survivor.

Jehan was similarly grateful: He had endured, and had won the battle. But he had foregone Naddeghomra for this. He had rejected the advice of his wife and daughter, and had risked everything in doing it. He had lost fifteen thousand men including one of his best generals, and had been thrice wounded himself.

So Jehan was not disposed toward magnanimity.

He had five thousand enemy prisoners to deal with. His own army being so depleted, Jehan decided he could not

afford the troops that would be needed to guard these cap-
tives. He ordered them killed.

Bound hand and foot, the Tnemghadi soldiers were laid
helplessly in neat rows on the flat plain. Urhemmedhins
went methodically down these rows with sharp knives,
slashing their throats, and they were left to bleed themselves out like pigs into the soil of the battlefield, a soil
already soaked with the blood of more than thirty thousand.

Of course, it still remained to break the siege of Arbadakhar.

Jehan was left with some twenty thousand men; so was
Tamar Ghouriyadh. But Ghouriyadh's troops were per-
force spread in a ring around the city, and the Urhemmedhins had a reservoir of further troops inside the walls.

They would have to count on these advantages; there
was no time to try to gather a larger army. Only two
days were begrudged to rest after the battle on the plain.

The rebels struck at midnight of the nineteenth of
Jhevla. The surprise was compounded by their swinging
around and attacking from the north, and the Tnemghadi
camp was thrown into complete disorder. They had no
chance to coalesce their thin lines into a force that could
meet the attack. Flames spread wildly as their tents
were torched.

This was seen by the sentries inside the city, and they
sounded the tocsin. The city came instantly awake, and
both soldiers and civilians rushed to the ramparts to look
out at the burning of the Tnemghadi camp. They knew
Jehan had come to save them.

Vahiy Jehan! they sang out in jubilation, *Vahiy Jehan!*

And their battalions poured out through the gates to
join Jehan's forces in wiping out the Tnemghadi. The
north camp was destroyed before those in the south knew
the battle was underway. Even among the Urhemmedhins,
confusion reigned, but their officers managed to direct
most of them back through the gates, so that they could
march quickly straight through the city and out the south
gate, to smash the besiegers on that side.

The army of Tamar Ghouriyadh was destroyed, and
Arbadakhar was saved.

But Jehan's own forces were left in a shambles, and

he was back to where he'd started. Naddeghomra seemed farther away than ever.

On the twenty-fourth of Jhevla, Golana Henghmani gave birth.

And like the siege of Naddeghomra, where it had been conceived, the child was stillborn.

·6·

To my honored stepmother,

May you know that I join you in mourning for the dear child that sainted Urhem has taken to his bosom. May he bless you with a bounty of children in days ahead.

This was Maiya's letter of condolence, when Golana miscarried. It was written in beautiful script, by a Vraddagoon scribe at Maiya's direction. She did not convey it personally, but delegated that to a servant as well. It was a perfectly composed formal note; it was perfectly meaningless.

Maiya did not grieve at the loss of her prematurely born half-sister, but nor did she take any satisfaction in it. The important thing to her was the fact that Golana was proven fertile. It put all Maiya's hopes in peril.

In view of Golana's long-standing childlessness, the revelation of a pregnancy had been quite a surprise. At first Maiya was distraught, but she had managed to pull her wits together and coolly assess the situation. She realized that she must not give up, she wasn't beaten yet: The child might be a girl, who would not take precedence over Jehandai in the line of inheritance.

So Maiya had gone about her chores at the Naddeghomra encampment, evincing equanimity at Golana's swelling belly. Even Jehan had been astonished at how well his daughter seemed to be accepting the fact of the pregnancy, and he prayed this signified a mellowing in her.

Maiya, meanwhile, prayed too: that the child would be a girl.

And there was another buttress underneath her seeming acquiescence. Even if Golana's child were a boy, Maiya decided that she still would not be beaten. Gradually, as she watched Golana's middle grow, Maiya nurtured inside her own mind the ultimate defense against this menace, boy or girl.

Jehan Henghmani knelt at his wife's bedside, holding her hand inside his own huge palms. The bloodied bedclothes had been removed, and she was draped in pure white now, clean and serene like her face. Normally very fair, Golana's features were whitened even further by her ordeal of birth; but they were no longer twisted by the pain of labor.

Jehan himself was convalescing. He had lost a great deal of blood in the Arbadakhar battle, and wore bandages on his head and thigh. His brush with death had been closer than he cared to think about. Of course, he was preoccupied now not with his own wounds, but with Golana.

"Are you feeling better?" he asked in a whisper.

The woman nodded without opening her eyes, and managed a small smile.

"How terrible it must have been for you! I wished it was happening to me instead. The doctors say the child came out the wrong way, that was why she died, and nearly killed you doing it."

"I am sorry, Jehan."

"I am sorry too. A pity this new daughter didn't live! Urhem knows that Maiya gives us little joy."

"That's not what I meant," said Golana, coming fully awake. "I too grieve to lose the child—and I am apologizing for it. I never gave Mutsukh a child, and now I've failed you too."

"Please don't speak this way!"

"Is it not a failure for a woman to miscarry, indeed, to live forty years without ever bringing a child into the world?"

"No, Golana. Your barrenness with Mutsukh was his fault, not yours; you know that well enough. As for this one, it was no one's fault, no one could have saved her. But regardless of that, you would not be a failure, even if you never bear a child.

"Any ignorant peasant can bear children. There's nothing exalted about it, it takes no magic or genius. But you're a woman who can accomplish things that even most men cannot do. You have helped govern a province, you have masterminded a revolution, bringing freedom to oppressed people.

"Leave the childbearing to the peasants, and commit yourself instead to a higher calling. All animals bear offspring; you must concentrate yourself on what distinguishes human beings from all other animals, not on what we have in common with them. It means nothing to give the world a brood of children, just a few more lost among the millions. But you can change the lives of all the millions."

The woman squeezed his hand. "'Of course you are right. You're perfectly right. But still, I want to give you a child. A fine son."

"A daughter will be just as fine, if she's anything like her marvelous mother."

"Yes, yes, enough of flattery. I have little strength right now to waste listening to that. You must tell me instead, what news is there since I've been confined?"

"Oh, there is much news! The intelligence from the North says that our poor friend Sarbat is certainly having his troubles. The Tnemghadi economy seems to be falling apart. They used to depend on milking the South for grain and rice, but of course now that that's dried up, they're getting hungry. There's little food to be had, and prices are soaring. His mints keep churning out more and more coins with less and less silver in them.

"And then we've learned there's a new chieftain among the Akfakh, a real terror by the name of Znarf. He's finally getting those tribesmen whipped into a disciplined force. The latest word had this Znarf taking over half of Jammir Province, and making major inroads into Gharr and Agabatur.

"Sarbat has his hands full keeping the Akfakh back; and losing Ghouriyadh's army didn't exactly improve matters for him."

Golana nodded gravely. "This is good news, Jehan. In the long run those barbarians may be a menace to all of us, but what counts right now is that they're distracting and weakening the Tnemghadi."

"There is news, too, from Naddeghomra."

"Yes?"

Jehan suddenly grinned. "I saved the best for last. *The Tnemghadi have abandoned Naddeghomra.*"

"What?"

"Right after we left, they fled, all the priests and troops. The latest dispatch says they're trying to fight their way back down the Amajap to the sea, and they're getting cut to pieces."

"I don't understand," said Golana, wrinkling her brow. "They withstood our siege—why give up the city? What can their strategy be?"

"It isn't strategy. There was simply no food. Our siege must have been on the verge of success. If we had stayed, we would have won Naddeghomra, possibly within days. So you were right, Golana, I should have heeded you. We should have stuck it out at Naddeghomra."

"No, no, no! Then we would have taken Naddeghomra and lost Arbadakhar. Now we get them both." Golana bolted up in her bed, throwing back the covers. "Yes, both! And now we can return south and walk into Naddeghomra, just walk right in!"

"Yes, we shall," Jehan affirmed.

"Naddeghomra is ours. It's all ours, Jehan, all ours, the whole South! We've done it, we've won—Urhemma is free!—*Prasid Urhemma has been born!*"

"And you," said Jehan, "are its mother."

·7·

His southern invasion had been aborted, his army greatly reduced, and Jehan was back at Arbadakhar licking his wounds. But the setback was illusory; the fact was, his strength and power were greater than ever. The whole South was his for the taking.

Preparations for a consolidating expedition were commenced at once. The call went out to fill the army's depleted ranks, and once again, the peasants answered it in droves. Eagerly they came, for news of the Tnemghadi abandonment of Naddeghomra had galvanized the southlands. For the first time, it was clear that the oppressors' power was on the wane, and that they would indeed be uprooted from southern soil.

The new army that converged upon Arbadakhar was a young one. Many were boys who had reached their teens since the last recruitment, sent out by parents who could feed them no longer, or by mothers to avenge husbands already killed, or by fathers too old to go themselves. They were young, because many of their elders had already died for the cause, fighting in Jehan's army, and countless more of them fighting the Tnemghadi in the towns and villages and through the farmlands.

Camps were set up to accommodate the new recruits, to train them in soldiery and inculcate them with the pious spirit of Urhem, with *yarushkadharra,* the dignity of freedom. These were soldiers who would know why they marched; these were soldiers who understood that they were part of a great historic drama.

Meanwhile, everything was meticulously planned by Jehan and Golana. The invading force, they decided, need not be large; a strong rear-guard would be left at Arbadakhar, which would be an armed fortress-city. It would be the impregnable first line of defense this time instead of a weak limb.

It was clear that something would have to be done about Ubuvasakh. As Governor of Taroloweh, the Leopard had been a disaster: a callous autocrat as bad as any Tnemghadi satrap, who had allowed conditions in the province to deteriorate alarmingly.

"We obviously can't leave him in charge again," said Jehan. "Nor can we keep a firm hand on Taroloweh from a thousand lim away. We've got to delegate someone."

Golana nodded with lips pursed in thought. "Who?" she said.

"Well, how about this new fellow—Mussopo? He seems quite serious and dedicated."

"Too young. It might go to his head, and he'd be resented by the older men who were passed over. I'd prefer someone more seasoned: Ontondra? Vokoban?"

"Vokoban's a real son of the soil; that would count in his favor."

"He's also an old grayhead. Stalwart, respected."

"Good. Shall it be Rimidal Vokoban then?"

"Yes."

"Can you brief him thoroughly? He's sensible enough that he'll mind what you say. And he'll know better than to follow in the Leopard's tracks."

"We'll also make him responsible to a council of officers. I'll leave him some detailed written guidelines too."

Then Jehan raised the more difficult point: What about the Leopard?

"Jehan, I truly think the time has come to get rid of him. I never liked that man, I never trusted him. He's got some grudge against you from the old days, and now that he's being shorn of the governorship, he'll have another grudge. It's not wise to keep a man like that around."

"Are you suggesting that Ubuvasakh be . . . done away with?"

Golana ruminated briefly, and said, "It's worth considering. He could well be put on trial for the mess he's made here."

Jehan shook his head. "It's been said that a revolution devours its children, like Sexrexatra. Perhaps so; perhaps we'll all be devoured, but I don't want to be the one to start it. A trial like that won't boost morale, and besides, that man still has one of the most cunning brains of any of us. He might still be an asset."

Golana sighed. "All right. Put him back in the army with a fancy rank to mollify his ego. And take him south so we can keep an eye on him."

"So it shall be."

"I hope we don't regret it. Now then, when do we leave?"

"Everything is ready. We leave as soon as possible."

Golana emphatically assented. "Our moment is now," she said, "let's snatch it!"

The moment was now; eight centuries had labored to produce this moment.

That was how long the Urhemmedhins had waited, but they would wait no longer. They smelled Tnemghadi blood, and they all rose up. The entire South from end to end was pitched into a state of violent rebellion.

City after city was falling into the hands of insurgent mobs: Touhbul in Bhudabur Province; Khedda and Hsokhso in Prewtna; Mughdad in Ohreem; Anda Lusis and Ganda Saingam in Diorromeh; and in Khrasanna, Bebjella, Ourkesh, and Pamliyah. There was even agitation in the client states of Valpassu and Laham Jat.

Everywhere the story was repeated: The imperial governments were being swept away; their palaces and temples sacked; the troops, the officials and the priests all massacred or hunted down through the countryside; the manor houses were under attack, and the lands not seized by the peasants were burned.

There were more Urhemmedhin victims than Tnemghadi—Urhemmedhins left impoverished, homeless, starving, mourning their loved ones or joining them in death.

Into this convulsed, tormented southern land, Jehan Henghmani once more marched: the Savior, the *Ur-Rasvadhi*.

This time he did not cross the Qurwa. Since Nitupsar had already been traversed, the Urhemmedhin army took a westward route into Diorromeh.

It was not an army of liberation, because liberty had already been won by the people. The revolt was sanguinary but quick, the Tnemghadi presence had weakened to the point where it could offer only puny resistance, once the peasants had risen up with the full power of their numbers. All that remained was to mop up the last stragglers of the Imperium, to bludgeon the last recalcitrant land barons into submission. There was little real fighting, and triumphant stops were made at every town along the way.

At Ganda Saingam the battle had been extremely vicious. This was a major city where there had been a well-fortified garrison. Assaulted by rudely armed insurgents, that garrison's walls were demolished and in a bloody battle its soldiers were slaughtered to the last man. It took more than a week, and the cost was grievous. Many, many rebels died for every soldier in that accursed garrison. Ganda Saingam's lifeblood had been sacrificed to shake off the Tnemghadi yoke; almost every family in the city lost someone. Now, handicapped by the heavy casualties, the Saingamese were struggling to climb out of the rubble, patch their city back together, and to simply feed themselves.

Despite the bitter travail into which Ganda Saingam had been thrust, a spirit of uplift prevailed among its people. They were free, and the terrible price they had paid for their liberty made them cherish it all the more. Importantly, unlike many towns racked by rebellion, Ganda Saingam was not afflicted with disorder. A council of respected elders had been established to afford civil government; committees were recruited to oversee the enforcement of law and justice, the rebuilding of the ruins, and the procurement of food and other trade. Cooperation reigned, as the people were caught up in the intoxication and responsibility of forming their own destiny.

All symbols of the deposed regime were effaced from Ganda Saingam. The temple was razed to the ground, and the fancy curling Sexrexatra dragons were chiseled off the gates—the Saingamese denied their heritage as children of the dragon. Meanwhile, the old Tnemghadi coins were gathered up and restruck with the word *yarushkadharra* and with Jehan's shining sun device, to symbolize the passing of the eight hundred years' darkness.

And when Jehan the Savior himself neared, Ganda

Saingam prepared to greet him with the greatest celebration it had ever witnessed.

Colorful banners festooned its walls and gates, and the main road to the city was bordered with flowers. Flowers were in abundance everywhere. The Saingamese had little food, but they grew flowers to welcome the *Ur-Rasvadhi*.

The Urhemmedhin army neared the city and camped for the night just three lim away. The next day dawned clear, and when the sun was well up, Jehan Henghmani mounted his white stallion. Following him rode his generals all abreast: Jephos Kirdahi, Nattahnam Ubuvasakh, Hnayim Yahu, Revi Ontondra, Rodavlas Ilhad, and Gaffar Mussopo. Then, in an open horse-drawn carriage were Golana, Maiya, and Jehandai.

In stately cadenced dignity, Jehan led them and his whole army up the flowered path through the open gates of Ganda Saingam. Flanking the gates stood lines of men at attention, members of the Saingamese citizen constabulary. Inside, on a platform a band was playing, a band of drums and horns and tambourines and cymbals, playing repeated pulsing martial beats, setting a rhythm for the prancing of the army's horses.

Jehan and his generals upraised their right hands in salute. His expression was rigid, his mutilated face showing only cool acknowledgment of all this homage. His huge body was held stiffly, except that he would nod his head and dip his hand to the people thronging him.

With almost dour sobriety, the city's council of elders stood in white robes on an elevated reviewing stand, their arms also lifted in solemn salute. But the commonfolk of the city were unrestrained in giving vent to their enthusiasm. They had all come out this fine morning, from the smallest tots to the oldest graybeards; even the sick and the lame had left their beds to come out and see the legendary Savior and to scream their adulation.

Barely parting to let the horses by, the people clogged the streets, climbing on wagons and chairs and tables, fathers holding up their children to see over the heads of the crowd. They hung on balconies and out of windows, they stood looking down from rooftops. On every side the scene was a tumult of motion, of people waving arms and banners and jumping up and down; the air was full of flowers and the bits of cloth and paper that were tossed like snow; and the cacophony of cheers almost drowned out the steady beat of the band.

"*Vahiy Jehan!*" they screamed their lungs out in a transport of rapture and with tears flowing down their flushed cheeks. "*Ur-Rasvadhi! Vahiy Jehan! Yarush Saingam! Vahiy Urhemma! Yarushkadharra, O Yarush-kadharra!*"

Their exultation knew no bounds. Even Golana, to her pleased surprise, found herself the object of adulation. Either they overlooked her Tnemghadi brows or forgave them since she'd come with great Jehan; but they cheered Golana as they cheered her husband. And from her open carriage she laughed and smiled at the people, waved her hand enthusiastically and blew them kisses. Finally, she reached down with both hands out of the carriage, touching them and letting them touch her, thousands of them straining to pull at her hands and sleeves. Her cheeks too ran wet with joyful tears.

Through this wild demonstration Jehan continued his stately ride, the people mobbing him at every step along the way to kiss or just to touch him, like a talisman. They kissed his feet and his horse, prostrating themselves in worship before him. Jehan Henghmani was the Sainted Savior of Urhem; he came to Ganda Saingam as a god.

And he wondered what still grander reception would await him at Naddeghomra.

BERGHARRA—Local issue, City of Ganda Saingam, copper ten falu, overstruck on a worn imperial copper of the same denomination. Year 1184. *Obverse:* Radiate Sun, Urhemmedhin legend "G. Saingam." *Reverse:* "Yarushkadharra" (Roughly, "liberty"). Breitenbach 2021, 32 mm.; sloppily struck, so that the original designs show through clearly. Fine or better, light green verdegris. Quite a scarce issue of the Urhemmedhin rising. (*Hauchschild Collection Catalog*)

· 8 ·

IN THE MONTH OF Okhudzhava in the year 1185, Jehan
Henghmani looked once again upon the City of Naddeghomra.

It was morning when he saw it first: the tips of the
great towers thrusting over the horizon to catch the sunlight, glowing like torches. Jehan had vowed destruction
to those towers once. This time, his hand would not be
stayed.

With his eye fixed on those beautiful, hateful towers,
Jehan Henghmani led his army toward them in an undeviating course. Once more they had assumed parade
order, decked out elaborately with the generals prancing
in a row followed by Jehan's family in an open carriage.
They were buoyed with excitement. For months they'd
been looking forward to the heroes' welcome they would
surely receive at Naddeghomra.

As the city perched upon the bluffs came fully into
view, its skyline was quite familiar to these men. But a
peculiar detail was noticed: the main gates were not
open, nor were they shut; in fact, the colossal wooden
doors were half ajar.

And there was more strangeness. No flowers adorned
the road to Naddeghomra. There was no honor guard to
greet the liberation army. There were no gaudy banners
to be seen, no strains of music to be heard except the
wind.

Jehan and his followers could not help being struck by
all this, but none would make any comment. Silent, they
trekked the last mile to the silent city.

Naddeghomra was a derelict.
It was the empty shell of a city, like the rotted hull of

323

a sunken boat washed up on the shore. The life that had flourished here since the dawn of history was gone.

Hardly a building stood intact, and whole rows of them had fallen down, blocking the streets with rubble. Many of those houses still standing had been gutted by fire; the yellow-white stucco and gray stone was everywhere scorched black with ash and soot. There was no living greenery, only drab brownish weeds, and pasty vines creeping everywhere like fungus.

But the city was not entirely dead. Making their homes among these dismal ruins were a few scattered stragglers. The only ones still here were those lacking enough sense to crawl away. Most of them were old and crippled, and most of them were mad, driven out of their minds by the horrors they had witnessed. Of course, most of those left behind after the siege soon perished in the wasteland of Naddeghomra, but somehow, a few managed to eke out a grim existence here, scratching food from the weeds and vines, killing rats and even gnawing on the dried flesh of the dead who littered the city. They lived mutely, secretively; they were terrified even of one another.

But these poor human survivors were few. The true heirs of Naddeghomra were the rats and flies.

Once Tnem Khatto Trevendhani had marched through these same streets. He was met with silence, the eyes of the inhabitants stared coldly at him, hating him.

It was silence of a different kind that met Jehan. Tnem Khatto had enslaved Naddeghomra, but it had endured. Jehan had liberated the city, and he had destroyed it.

Through the eerie silent streets, Jehan led his column. The only sounds were the clopping footfalls of their own horses like stones dropped down a well, the wind blowing debris against broken walls, and the scampering of rats and of the wretched survivors, cowering in their madness. None even stood to watch the spectacle; they cringed in the shadows or fled, wondering wildly what new horror might be coming.

The ones who did not run away were dead. Almost a year after the siege had ended, thousands of its victims still lay in the streets where they had fallen. Some were

Tnemghadi soldiers, mauled and blood-browned bodies
that had been clawed or stoned to death by mobs. But
most were Urhemmedhins, wrapped in stiff rags or naked,
their clothes picked off by scavengers. Many were mutilated, but many were simply victims of starvation and
disease. The corpses of children were most numerous.
The remains of mothers lay propped against walls, holding their dead infants to their breasts.

There was no stench of death. The bodies hadn't
putrefied, but were cured like smoked meats in the hot
dry climate. They were yellow, dusty, leathery mummies,
with the skin shriveled back and molded tight upon their
skeletons. But many of the bodies had been pulled apart
and gnawed, leaving only the powdery white bones strewn
about.

These were the people who welcomed the Savior to
Naddeghomra.

Everything was nothing.

They marched through all this, returning the city's
silence. Not until reaching *The Maal* did Jehan rein his
horse and stop. But even here, he still said nothing.

He sat in the saddle of his white stallion, in the middle
of the broad white marble plaza, in the shadow of the
great white towers, staring up at them. Their incredible
size could be grasped fully now. They bulked in the sky
like cliffs and seemed to press down upon the men as
though they were insects.

Behind them, dominating even these huge towers as a
father looking down over his children, was the final
black one. It reached up magnificently into the clouds.
Surely here was a place that touched the powers of the
heavens.

The Maal alone was unstained by the death that choked
Naddeghomra. On the vast white plaza there was no rubble, no corpses, no weeds growing. There was silence,
but it was a majestic soundlessness, as though this place
had been consecrated to silence and a noise would mar
its sanctity. And whereas the rest of the city was clogged
with filth and crumbling, the tall towers and the broad
plaza floor gleamed as brilliantly as ever, their milk white
and crystal black surfaces retaining their polished mirror-
smoothness.

One could detect the jointure lines between the marble blocks, but barely, for the honing of these blocks approached perfection, the measurements exact and the lines plumb-straight. And the building blocks were gigantic. Jehan was astounded. He could scarcely believe such blocks of stone could be moved by human beings, let alone fitted together so perfectly. *The Maal* was a stunning triumph of architecture and engineering.

It had been built as a hateful symbol of conquest and enslavement, but it had to mean more than that. There was something more that its builders were saying, to all the generations who would look upon their work:

The Maal was a monument to their refusal to limit their dreams, to their will to realize the full breadth of their imagination, a human will that could triumph over any obstacle. *The Maal* was a monument to the greatness of the human race.

Jehan cantered his horse around to face the troops. With the towers at his back, he let them look at him, so that the significance of this moment in history would penetrate upon every one of them.

And then, in a firm voice ringing like a bell through the silence, he spoke to them.

"This is the most hallowed spot on earth. On this spot, King Urhem and Queen Osatsana reigned. Their palace was here, at the peak of the ancient civilization of our Urhemmedhin forebears. Its center was at this very spot.

"We came here to give rebirth to that civilization—and we have arrived to find a dead city.

"Yes, Naddeghomra is dead, but verily, death must come before rebirth. It cost countless lives to give rebirth to the Nation of Urhem; and now that *Prasid Urhemma* has come into being, Naddeghomra will be reborn as well. Here we will stay, to resuscitate this city, rebuild it, re-populate it, make its streets teem with people and the fields around it lush again with crops.

"Naddeghomra will be our capital, once more to take its place as the center of the Urhem Nation. Naddeghomra will be the glorious sun that will shine over our *Prasid Urhemma.*

"And here, on this spot, the towers of *The Maal* will stand. It will remain, this awful symbol of oppression, so that our people may never forget the suffering out of which their nation was forged, and how precious is the liberty they've won.

"And *The Maal*, built of tyranny and hatred, will instead become a monument to love and freedom. We shall consecrate here within these towers a new temple, and here our people will pilgrimage, to worship sainted Urhem and to celebrate *yarushkadharra*."

· 9 ·

From the summit of the high tower, Jehan looked out over all Naddeghomra.

Everything was his. He could see the whole city and far beyond spread out before him. The city was alive with activity.

So much work confronted them that Jehan and Golana were occupied from dawn until after dark overseeing all the various projects. Of course the chief one was the conversion of *The Maal*.

The nine golden idols of the Emperor were removed and smelted, their gold to finance the reconstruction. In their place, new statues were commissioned. The first would be a monument of King Urhem, modeled upon the one at Arbadakhar, only much larger. This statue would preside within the great black tower.

Then, in the head white tower would be a statue of Osatsana, and this would become her temple. The next tower would hold a statue of an Urhemmedhin peasant, and this would be a memorial to all who had died in the eight centuries' struggle for freedom. The third tower pair would house the second-rank offices of the developing Urhemma government; and finally, the last pair would become the palace of Jehan and his leading officials.

He had come to destroy *The Maal;* instead, he would live there!

Meanwhile, not just the temple complex, but the entire city was being rebuilt. The first order of business was, of course, to clean it up—to clear the streets of debris, to demolish those buildings beyond rehabilitation, and to rid the city of its dead.

Although they were, in a sense, honored casualties of the war of liberation, it was not feasible to identify the bodies or even to give them a ceremonious burial. With

so many heavy demands upon resources, time and sweat
could not be wasted on the dead now; they were stacked
on wooden biers and burned in the open air. The dried
corpses burned quickly and cleanly; and the ashes were
used to fertilize the fields, where crops were planted
anew. Thus the dead would help to feed the living.

Restoration of the surrounding lands to cultivation was
a key point in Jehan's program for returning Naddeghomra to its ancient status as the hub of a prosperous
land. The other key point was, naturally, repopulation.
From throughout the province families were exhorted
to come and make new homes at Naddeghomra. Young
people were wanted, women were wanted, patroits were
wanted, people of strength, people of drive, people of
vision, tradesmen, farmers, craftsmen, laborers, artisans.

Naddeghomra was to be not just a great city, but a city
of great people. Those who would come to Naddeghomra
now would not be ordinary men and women. Its earlier
population had been destroyed so that something finer
could take root in its place. It would be a city of great
people, of diverse people, of strong, bright, self-reliant
people, with the courage to pick up stakes and emigrate
to a new place, to help build a new idea.

Inspired by Jehan the *Ur-Rasvadhi* and his vision, sharing that vision, the new people came to Naddeghomra.

The new start was an exuberant one, but there were
still tremendous problems to cope with. Throughout most
of the Urhemmedhin provinces, the war of revolution was
still very much in progress. There were still Tnemghadi
troops about, and plenty of skirmishes and battles. The
war to free the land from the barony was still underway
too. The upheaval left many areas floundering in anarchy,
and millions of people dislocated.

In a similar class were the new emigrés to Naddeghomra. There were urgent problems of assimiliating all
these people, of integrating them into the new structure,
of finding homes for them and work to occupy them, and
even of feeding them. The revivified farmlands had barely
been started, and tremendous exertions were required to
ensure that Naddeghomra would not starve a second time.

And in the midst of all these pressing challenges, only
now did Jehan and Golana finally come to grips with the

need to establish a permanent government. They decided to build it from the top down, first sketching its broad outlines and then later filling in the details.

Jephos Kirdahi was invested as the Grand Chamberlain of Urhemma, despite many counseling against it. Leopard Ubuvasakh assailed the former dungeon guard as a stupid dolt, incompetent for such a high position. Revi Ontondra and Gaffar Mussopo were loudly critical too, begging Jehan to consider the public reaction to bestowing so great an honor upon a Tnemghadi. It was certainly incongruous that the first prime minister of the Urhem Nation should be of the other race.

The arguments of these men and others were heard respectfully by Jehan, but he rejected them. The Leopard, Ontondra, perhaps even Yahu, fancied the honor for themselves. Only by appointing Kirdahi, who had been his deputy throughout, could Jehan dampen the jealousy that would inevitably attend his choice.

It was obvious, though, that Kirdahi would be a figurehead chief minister, merely carrying out Jehan's bidding. In this, his Tnemghadi eyebrows were a plus: they shackled him to Jehan. Kirdahi's life itself still depended on Jehan's protection.

The other key assignments followed more or less naturally. Ubuvasakh's keen intelligence was put to use in his investiture as Minister of Foreign Affairs and War, which gave the handsome ex-bandit responsibility for the deployment of the army. Rodavlas Ilhad and Gaffar Mussopo were made his deputies, Ilhad to oversee recruitment and strategy, Mussopo as Quartermaster General in charge of provisioning the army. Hnayim Yahu, crude and unimaginative but solid, was given command over agriculture and land reform, a program which Jehan actually expected to run personally. Similarly, while Revi Ontondra took the Treasury portfolio, financial matters were really under Golana's supervision.

Governors were also commissioned for each of Urhemma's seven provinces, but these were bereft of real importance in the emerging political schema. The old Bergharran system of administration had been three-tiered: the throne, the provincial viceroys, and the local officials. Now the middle tier was to be phased out. Power would be shared between the Palace at Naddeghomra and the local city halls, with the provincial capitals reduced to little more than communications links.

And, as *Prasid Urhemma* began to take form, the innovation was more fundamental than merely increasing the authority of local government.

Under the Tnemghadi, the mayors of every town and village throughout Bergharra had been appointed by the throne. Almost never were they chosen from among the local citizenry. Even Tnemghadi cities were run by outsiders, usually career bureaucrats, military officers, or palace politicians from Ksiritsa.

This, Jehan would change radically. He would appoint no mayors at all!

He and Golana had been deeply impressed by the example they had seen at Ganda Saingam, with its council of elders and citizen committees. Since the council had arisen from the people, its edicts had remarkable moral force. The townsfolk cooperated fully, with a sense of their own personal stake in the city and its future. Save for this, Ganda Saingam might have remained a broken city. Instead, it was pulling itself up by its bootstraps.

Such was the model that would be adopted for all Urhemma. From Naddeghomra down to the tiniest hamlets, they would set up their own autonomous councils.

The idea that ordinary people might thusly govern themselves was revolutionary, but it fit perfectly with the new nation's guiding creed, the creed of Urhem. It was yet another thing for which the people would be moved to fight, but not for the sake of any ideology alone did Jehan and Golana embrace it. What concerned them equally was success, and if the success of Ganda Saingam could be duplicated throughout Urhemma, that would justify any political expedient.

Such was the framework of the government of *Prasid Urhemma*, as Jehan and Golana began to rough out the structure. And holding that structure together, as its nails and mortar, was Jehan Henghmani himself:

The Emperor Jehan.

Long had he shied away from a royal title, but it could not be gainsaid any longer. Jehan Henghmani, having taken for himself the name *Ur-Rasvadhi*, was soon being called by everyone the Emperor of Urhemma. There was no fanfare to it, no coronation ceremony, nothing formal at all, but his rulership was by now such a settled fact that it was simply natural for his underlings to regard him as Emperor. And he accepted it. There was no point to coyness, for the nation needed an emperor now. Likewise did Golana become the Empress, so they would rule jointly, in the tradition of Urhem and Osatsana. And so too, at last, to her unbounded delight, Jehan's daughter had become the Princess Maiya.

In six years Jehan had made himself from a dungeon prisoner into an emperor. Indeed, he was more than that; he was virtually a god, not merely obeyed by his subjects but loved and worshipped by them too. He had achieved more than he'd dared to dream in that dungeon. His dreams had been of power, but not of veneration and certainly not of love. Yet now he found love the greatest prize of all: Golana, his love.

He was certain that his love for her was greater than any man's love for someone merely as a woman—it transcended the sexual. He respected her profoundly. On a deeper level she was part of him, of his very flesh and blood and bone. Inarticulate though it was, there was in him a sense that his relationship with Golana was a perfect symbiosis, with each giving to the other what the other needed, with both enriched and completed by the exchange. Individually they were nothing; together they were everything.

Golana as well was flushed with an abiding sense of how far they had come. "We sought power and got it," she said to him, "but we deserved it. No name is more to be honored than *liberator,* and we have freed millions, amply earning it.

"Yarushkadharra. It is such a big word for such a simple thing, really. People living their own lives, the way they want to, without being ordered about, without their self-respect being trampled.

"In a way, isn't it just what Urhem taught? The sanctity of human life. You know, in Kuloun they have sacred goats that are allowed to wander free wherever they please, and it is sacrilege for anyone to interfere with them. Well, here in Urhemma, we are making *people* the sacred goats.

"That's what our Ganda Saingam system is all about, Jehan. The people of every town and village will for the first time have their lives in their own hands. They will be their own masters, free to steer their own course. They may choose wisely or they may choose badly; freedom carries with it the responsibility for one's choices.

"The only certainty is that none of our people will do things exactly the same way. We have planted the seeds so that diversity can bloom throughout Urhemma, with different people thinking different thoughts and choosing different paths. Not drab conformity but diversity—the exhilarating vigor of diversity! Diversity is the child of freedom; and it is the mother of progress, too, for out of all those different people thinking differently and seeking different solutions will bubble up the best thoughts and the best solutions.

"You see, Jehan, we have fought our way to power, but the real struggle is only beginning. We have earned the privilege of ruling; what we must strive for now is the wisdom to rule well."

Jehan could not help nodding in agreement to Golana's flights of eloquence; he was almost mesmerized by her lofty concepts. But he himself found it difficult to emulate her in this. The hardness of the world always tugged at him.

Now he pulled his eyes away from Golana's and went to the window. Spread out below was the bustle of activity —carts clattering through the streets, gutted buildings being torn down, the rubble dragged away, and everywhere the scaffoldings of new construction. But Jehan's eyes drifted northward.

"I fear that you are right," he said, "I fear that you are right."

· 10 ·

GAFFAR MUSSOPO yawned and rubbed his eyes. For long
hours he had been at work, by candle light, at his chamber
in *The Maal*.

Gaffar had just turned twenty-five; he was the youngest
of Urhemma's leaders. Yet he no longer thought of himself as young, and felt instead quite aged, as though he'd
been through a full lifetime already. His life on the farm
with his parents seemed in the remote past; it was a
strain even to remember what they'd looked like. His
memories of them were static pictures, stiff, frozen bits
of time. His father was pictured gazing across the fields;
or riding on the gaar; or handing shokh baskets over to
the Tvahoud. But it was difficult to recall an animate,
living Samud.

Gaffar had come a very long way since those days.
There had been hardship and starvation, and the heady
excitement of triumph. He had lost his left hand, a permanent badge of heroism on the field of battle, fighting for
freedom. Now, finally, he had come to Naddeghomra, and
here he hung up his sword and shield. The implement of
warfare that he wielded now was the pen.

He had realized his most swashbuckling boyhood
dreams, and had grown beyond that. Instead of the clandestine vendetta he'd envisioned as a youth, now he was a
high official of a new nation, helping to build it. The
freedom once thought impossible had gained a foothold.
The sun had managed to pull itself up into the sky; it was
struggling to survive there, and Gaffar Mussopo was
in the very forefront of that struggle.

He had left the field of battle for a desk, but the headstrong youth who'd once assassinated a Ram-Tvahoud
was not restless. He knew the importance of his work;

he regarded himself still as a warrior for the freedom of millions, and took fierce pride in this.

Gaffar pushed himself, working to exhaustion. He was responsible for provisioning the far-flung Urhemmedhin army, keeping it armed and clothed and fed. This was a staggering burden in such times of poverty and scarcity. Only by ruthlessly putting the army's needs above all else was Gaffar able to function at all; a weak or compromising man would have failed. While Gaffar Mussopo was Quartermaster, many were the peasants who starved so that the army could eat.

It grieved him to cause his own people want, hunger, even death, but he never wavered in his single-minded dedication to the priority of the army. When all else failed, he would order food stores seized by force. Nothing would stand in his way. It was clear to him that only a stern and strong Urhemma might survive. The freedom that was purchased at such prodigious cost still stood threatened, and it was worth tremendous sacrifices to preserve.

The war of independence was far from over. While the enemy was temporarily disarmed by Jehan's victories and distracted by economic woes and Akfakh aggressions, no one at *The Maal* was making light of the Tnemghadi threat. The Sexrexatra dragon was still very much alive.

So vigilance was the watchword. Diorromeh and Taroloweh had to be bolstered to fend off an eventual Tnemghadi invasion. Likewise, the ports were guarded against a sea attack. Meanwhile, although the Tnemghadi were holding back from any major assault, this didn't mean the front was quiet. Incessant skirmishes plagued the northern frontiers of Urhemma, with the enemy constantly probing for weakness.

Also occupying Jehan's forces was the job of spreading the revolution into every corner of Urhemma. When its capital was first established at Naddeghomra, *Prasid Urhemma* existed more as a grand conception than as a political reality. Proclaiming a nation is only the first step down a very long road. Jehan had really pressed his stamp only upon Taroloweh, and to a lesser degree, Khrasanna. He had cut a swath through Nitupsar, Diorromeh, Prewtna, and Bhudabur during his marches, but only a small fraction of that territory had been affected. In one province, Ohreem, his armies had never even set foot.

The exciting part was done; now it was time to roll up sleeves for the real work. Most of the towns and cities were being governed on some makeshift basis as independent little states. Some were being run by rebel warlords who had sprung into the power vacuum left by the Tnemghadi fall; some were being fought over between rival gangs; in some places complete anarchy reigned.

Into this maelstrom of confusion and disorder, the Urhemmedhin army fanned out to forge stability. The undertaking was multifaceted: to extirpate the last Tnemghadi vestiges, to unhorse the warlord usurpers, and to put civil government into the hands of locally elected councils modeled upon the Ganda Saingam plan.

It was quite a task. Not only were those toughs who had grabbed power unwilling to relinquish it, but self-government was not an idea readily embraced by the peasants. Autocracy had prevailed for thousands of years, and many people did not grasp what it meant to run their own affairs. It was bewildering for them to choose their officials and make their own decisions—and to be responsible for them. Whatever its drawbacks, tyranny had at least made life simple. Now, in many places, democracy had to be imposed by force upon recalcitrant citizens!

While all this was going on, land reform was also far from a *fait accompli*. The landlords proved to be a hardy species. Entrenched for centuries, they were not to be uprooted overnight. Many had ostensibly yielded their lands peaceably, but then they sat back and waited, hiding the gold they'd hoarded—and as soon as the peasants ran into trouble, the old landlord was ready to move in again and even to repurchase his land. As long as there were men with enough money to buy up large tracts, the ancient estate system kept recurring.

So the army of Urhemma had to guard the borders and the ports; pacify the provinces; root out the petty warlords; install self-government; and continue battling the landlords. All of this required a huge army spread out across the seven provinces.

To provision such an army, to keep track of all its movements and ensure that supplies arrived when needed, was an enormous undertaking. Gaffar Mussopo was in charge of a considerable bureaucracy doing that job, but his personal burden was nonetheless heavy. That was why he burned his candle into the small hours of the morning, reading dispatches from all over the country, writing replies, inquiries, memoranda, and instructions to his subordinates. It was a bone-wearying job. Gaffar's writing hand would often cramp, his shoulders ache from bending over his desk, his eyes blur. To add to these strains, the stump of his left hand had never healed properly, and often shot lances of pain through his arm.

But Gaffar bore up. He never lost sight of the fact that his work was of paramount importance—unglamorous yet indispensable—and he felt an exhilaration in performing it.

He blinked and rubbed his eyes. It was very late at night, it was a strain to go on reading under the yellow light of a candle. The chair felt hard against his bottom, as though his tail bones had broken through the skin, and his stump was starting to hurt again. He decided that he would examine just one more dispatch and then go to bed.

Gaffar sometimes wondered whether he would be able to keep this up indefinitely. And the answer, it soon developed, was no.

It was the month of Elgheber in the year 1187. This happened to be the month in which a certain Tnemghadi sailing ship was blown off course by a tempest, as a result of which it happened to beach on the Urhemmedhin coast, near the ruins of Zidneppa. This ship happened to be transporting a pouch full of official correspondence, which consequently happened to fall into Urhemmedhin hands. Ordinarily the local commander receiving such an intelligence windfall might have forwarded it to Minister Ubuvasakh, but on this occasion, the officer in question thought it best to transmit the documents directly to the Emperor Jehan.

Among these documents there happened to be a certain letter from one very high Tnemghadi official to another, alluding obliquely to a certain plot being arranged by the Lahamese ambassador to the Court of Urhemma. The discovery of this letter prompted the surreptitious surveillance of the said ambassador. It developed that the ambassador was meeting at unusual times and places with Nattahnam Ubuvasakh, the Urhemmedhin Minister of Foreign Affairs and War.

The scheme under discussion was apparently a grotesque one in which Jehan would be delivered to the Tnemghadi and Ubuvasakh would seize power in The Maal. Its full details were never actually brought to light.

There was considerable discussion as to whether the Leopard ought to be placed on trial for his treason. However, it was finally agreed that this would ill-serve their regime, which was still new and feeling its way along. Instead, the culprit was presented with the evidence of his crime, and given the opportunity to take his own life. This was an opportunity of which he availed himself with no small degree of outward gallantry. The alternative would have been torture.

Minister Nattahnam Ubuvasakh was accorded the lavish funeral due to one of the great heroes of the Urhemmedhin revolution. His body lay in state for three days on The Maal's plaza, while a queue of citizens filed solemnly past. The cause of his death was not announced.

On the day following the funeral, it was decreed that Ubuvasakh's post as Minister of Foreign Affairs and War would be filled by Gaffar Mussopo.

· 11 ·

Scarcely had he donned the minister's robes when Gaffar Mussopo decided that the Urhemmedhin army—whose many thousands of soldiers he had had to work so feverishly to provision—was not, in fact, large enough at all. There had been no mass recruitment since the march on Naddeghomra, and in the interval the attrition of casualties and desertions had taken its toll. Meanwhile, the country was far from pacified.

Accordingly, to replenish the forces now under his command, Gaffar ordered recruiting proclamations drafted up and sent out among the seven provinces. But the response was distinctly lackluster. In truth, the country had been drained by the widespread strife extending over so many years, in which probably millions were killed. Urhemma was simply becoming sick of the continual fighting.

Kirdahi, Yahu, and Ontondra all joined Mussopo in urging that, as volunteers were insufficient, conscription be inaugurated. The proposal received intensive discussion, only to be rejected by Jehan. "Conscription," he said, "is tantamount to slavery," and he insisted that they would have to make do with whatever troops they could raise by noncoercive means.

This would probably suffice if the army's functions were limited to defending the frontier and imposing order on the countryside. But Gaffar Mussopo had more ambitious plans.

The Tnemghadi, he argued earnestly, remained a potent threat to the fledgling Urhemmedhin Nation. The northerners were temporarily distracted by the Akfakh war, but the day would surely come when they would try to recapture their southern empire. Thus, Prasid Urhemma could not hope to bask in the sunshine of freedom and

339

peace as long as there remained a Tnemghadi cloud on the horizon.

Accordingly, in Mussopo's view, the Tnemghadi Dynasty would have to be annihilated. The southern nation could not coexist with a Tnemghadi Empire of Bergharra.

It was obvious and simple: The way to keep the North from ever again ruling the South was for the South to rule the North. The enemy was weak, pressed harder than ever by Znarf the Akfakh, and its economy was coming apart at the seams. Ksiritsa itself seemed ripe for attack. Gaffar Mussopo proposed that such an invasionary expedition be launched as soon as possible.

Jehan firmly resisted the idea. "There has been enough war," he said. "What our nation longs for now is peace. We must lick our wounds and repair the devastation which years of conflict have brought upon us. Let there be an end to war and killing. We are so weary of it!"

"But this," Gaffar persisted, "is our great chance to deal the Tnemghadi a conclusive blow. It is in our power now to conquer all of Bergharra! And we must do it if we are to secure a genuine, lasting peace."

Jehan shook his head. " 'Conquer all of Bergharra!' Such fire-eating words. Are we to turn around and enslave the Tnemghadi, just as they enslaved us?

"No, Gaffar; we will have no invasion. For too long we have fought against the hateful idea of oppression. I will not see us become the new conquerors, the new oppressors. Let the North alone; there remains more than enough to occupy us yet in the South."

Mussopo reluctantly agreed to shelve his grandiose scheme for an invasion of the North. But many in The Maal had supported the plan, and were chagrined at Jehan's newfound pacifism. The issue would arise again and again, every time there was a report of further Tnemghadi deterioration. But Jehan remained adamant: He refused to invade.

Few among his councilors were capable of understanding, but conquest and military glory were the furthest things from Jehan's mind now. Always in his thoughts were Golana's words: power had been won, and what was wanted now was wisdom. It was not an invasion that he and his Empress were planning, but something far more daring.

Not Mussopo, not Kirdahi or Ontondra nor any of the others could even guess at it. Quietly and alone the two rulers worked on their peculiar project, nurturing it in secret, as though like a delicate flower it might wither in the glare of attention.

The flower took root in their minds and grew. It was to be a major new decree. Many nights they spent ruminating on its every facet, laboriously composing their thoughts into sentences, only to cross them out and try another set of words. Save for the kernel of a visionary idea, there was nothing to guide them. But gradually, as they worked at it, the concepts and the language took shape.

When it was finally proclaimed on the twenty-fourth of Okhudzhava, 1188, the decree was a lengthy, detailed one. But its language was simple, and the official copy was executed in the Emperor's own plain penmanship.

This decree, to be carried into every corner of the nation, established the twentieth of Elalbatar as the date for a great assembly to convene at Naddeghomra. The entire population was to be represented, with each province called upon to send a certain specified number of delegates. Estimates of population provided the basis for this apportionment, and the respective governors were directed to likewise use population as a guide for allocating the call for delegates among their localities. The largest province, Khrasanna, would send sixty-five delegates; the smallest, Bhudabur, would sent thirty. In all, the assembly would number exactly 350.

It would sit for six months. During that time, the delegates would receive a stipend, paid out of the national treasury, to provide for their room and board and a reasonable compensation as well. An allowance would also be made for their traveling expenses to and from Naddeghomra.

Also specified in the decree was the manner by which the delegates were to be chosen. With at least one month's notice spread by broadside, each town would call a mass public meeting, similar to those at which they were electing their local councils. Attendance at these meetings was to be open to all, and there were no restrictions either on who might be chosen delegate. This was not to be an assembly of noblemen and notables, but an assembly of the common people of Urhemma.

Nevertheless, its assigned task was a weighty one. Jehan's decree set forth boldly the agenda for the assembly: to write a new code of laws to govern Prasid Urhemma.

Bergharran law had ruled the conduct of her people for eight centuries, but the law of Bergharra was more a concept, a way of looking at relationships, than a specific set of regulations. The Bergharran code concerned itself primarily with the investiture of power to execute law, and only secondarily with the substance of the law to be executed. Absolute power resided in the throne; there were no legal rights in the face of the Emperor. Nearly as unbridled in their fiat were the local magistrates, mayors, and viceroys. And aside from these assignments of hierarchical authority, there was little Bergharran law, almost none of it formally codified.

Of course, even that negligible law had been abrogated by the revolution. Justice in Urhemma had become an extremely unsettled and haphazard proposition, wholly up to the local officials. In this respect the people had, if anything, fewer concrete rights than under the Tnemghadi.

This breach Jehan was proposing to fill with a completely new code of laws, promulgated not by the Throne as might have been expected, but instead thrashed out in open meetings of a representative popular assembly. It was something that had never been done before, something that boggled the minds of many who read this novel decree.

But Jehan and Golana had applied a prodigious amount of thought to his plan before unveiling it, and in a few terse sentences, the Okhudzhava Decree explained its foundation:

Government, wise people acknowledge, is most admirable and worthy when it best serves its citizens, enhancing their liberty and well-being. Thus, not as a master unto his slaves should a government rule its people, but instead the people should be master, and government the slave, doing their bidding. And if the good of the people is to be paramount, then the laws under which they live should be such laws as they desire, as being needful to

their welfare. It should be the people who make
the laws.

Recognizing the impossibility of having the millions
participate directly in lawmaking, Golana had hit upon
the idea of an assembly of commonfolk to accomplish, as
closely as possible, the same thing.

In fact, the purpose of the assembly went even beyond
that of bringing ordinary people into lawmaking. He and
Golana perceived how the incompleteness of the Bergharran law was tailored to autocracy and tyranny. The law
was what the magistrates willed it to be, and that was
as good as no law at all. But Urhemma's new code
drawn up by the assembly was going to be very different.
The rights of the people would be specified, committed
to paper and published far and wide. No criminal would
be punished, except as the law provided; no person
would lose property except as the law prescribed.

For the first time ever, the people would be making
their own laws; and for the first time ever the law,
and the rights of the people, would be clear, real, vital.

· 12 ·

ON THE TWENTIETH OF ELALBATAR, the National Assembly of Prasid Urhemma convened at Naddeghomra.

The meeting place was the broad white marble plaza of The Maal, where row upon row of wooden benches had been installed, in the fashion of an amphitheater. They were actually well-made chairs with armrests, backs, and cushions, to ensure the comfort of the delegates as much as possible under the hot southern sun.

To this open-air meeting hall, the 350 had been arriving for weeks. Naddeghomra was abuzz with anticipation over this remarkable Assembly, and yet the delegates themselves seemed unremarkable. At least half of them were mere peasant farmers. Most of the others were laborers, petty merchants, and artisans such as carpenters, wheelwrights, candle-makers and smiths. Most of them were illiterate, but a few towns had purposefully sent lowly professional scribes with the thought that their skills would be useful. A few of the delegates were really ragged sorts—servants, peddlers, possibly even a cut-purse or two. Some were priests of Urhem, adventurers and rabble-rousers. Three of them were women, and there was even one—a baker from Vdarheddin in Ohreem—who was half Tnemghadi.

At the appointed hour on the twentieth of Elalbatar, all of these delegates were in their seats on the plaza. On all sides were Naddeghomrans by the thousand, and sitting on special benches to one side were the ministers of the government. They were not voting members of this Assembly.

Then, heralded by a blast of trumpets, loud but brief, the Emperor Jehan Henghmani emerged from inside the palace. He walked alone, unaccompanied even by servants.

Thus in solitary splendor he made his way the short distance to the platform at the well of the Assembly.

And of course, the delegates were all on their feet, applauding furiously, and roaring their cheers together with the crowd of onlookers. Many waved bandannas in the air, and shouts of *"Vahiy Jehan!"* and *"Gavashat Jehan!"*—*Long Live Jehan!*—threw up an ear-splitting din.

Jehan ignored all this commotion; it was old hat to him. He stood behind the lectern at the platform, and while he waited for the demonstration to subside, he looked carefully into the faces of these delegates who would shape the future of Urhemma.

And, when quiet was restored, that was how he welcomed them. "You three hundred and fifty," he said, "have been sent here by the people to build the destiny of Prasid Urhemma."

He read to them excerpts from the Okhudzhava Decree, and exhorted them to keep well in mind the principles there expressed. It would be those principles, he said, and not the hand of an autocrat, that would henceforward guide Urhemma. He would attend the Assembly's deliberations with a keen interest, and might suggest subjects for their consideration; but never would he dictate to them, never would he bully them into any action. This would be an Assembly of free men and women, acting freely and for the public good, consistent with the creed of Urhem and with *yarushkadharra.*

Accordingly, Jehan announced that he would refuse even to chair the meetings of the Assembly. They must select their own presiding officer, responsible to them and not to the Throne. He urged the delegates to ponder carefully over this choice, and to find a man of strength, wisdom, and tact. To that end, the Assembly would be adjourned overnight.

That evening was one of great festivity in Naddeghomra, celebrating this historic event. The streets were alive with people and music, and with many earnest discussions of what the new institution of the Assembly might mean. There was much outdoor feasting and revelry, and the sky was lit with fireworks.

The next day, with a fanfare almost equal to its opening session, the Assembly reconvened at noon. Once more, the Emperor Jehan was at the podium, this time carrying a tall bronze staff emblazoned at its crown with Urhemma's polished sun symbol.

Thumping the staff upon the floor, Jehan brought the Assembly to order, and directly to its first business, the election of its president. He called for names to be nominated by the delegates, and at first, none of the timid commoners would rise. But upon Jehan's third coaxing, an unknown man rose trepidatiously from his seat and named one Muhamar Chouris.

"Very good," Jehan said, and he called upon this Chouris to ascend the podium and introduce himself to the other delegates, so that they might judge his fitness for the presidency. The man turned out to be a middle-aged salt dealer from Mughdad. He spoke very briefly, nervously, and received a few cheers.

Despite this uncertain beginning, the ice was broken and eleven more candidates were proposed. Each nominee took his turn and addressed the delegates, but it was clear that only a few made much of an impression. Several soon spoke up to withdraw their names.

Jehan solicited opinion on the remainder by means of a voice vote. Two of the nominees received easily the loudest response, and finally, the Assembly was asked to choose between them. Their favor fell upon a man named Razhak Taddhai, from Ganda Saingam, a tall white-bearded man who was a wine merchant and a veteran member of his city's council. Jehan was much pleased. This Razhak Taddhai gave promise of being a fitting first president of the Urhemmedhin National Assembly.

Taddhai returned to the podium amid the enthusiastic cheers of all the delegates and onlookers. With a ceremonious gesture, the Emperor handed him the bronze staff, to be his symbol of authority. Banging it forcefully upon the floor, Taddhai called the Assembly back to order, while Jehan retired to a special bench reserved for him, off to one side.

Taddhai thanked the Assembly for its vote, and then proceeded to the next order of business, selection of someone charged with keeping a record of the proceedings. It took little time to settle upon a scribe from Prewtna named Mawurisay, who took up duties at a table beside Taddhai.

And with these preliminaries accomplished, the Assembly of Prasid Urhemma got underway to make the laws.

Every day they met, with only one day a week reserved for rest. The deliberations began in the morning and would last until dusk.

These 350 were largely simple people, and they were starting virtually from scratch upon an undertaking entirely novel to their ken. But they did not shrink from tackling it. Perhaps it was the enthusiasm of innocence that gave them confidence in a project that would have intimidated more experienced hands.

The Okhudzhava Decree had set forth their agenda in broad scope. The questions they had to consider were clear enough: "What should be the law of crop rent?" or "What should be the law of marriage contracts?" There was a wide range of questions, and they wrangled long and hard to arrive at answers.

The Assembly quickly developed into a truly deliberative body. Each new topic brought forth a plethora of diverse ideas; some would be sheepishly withdrawn under criticism, others would be debated for days. Many of the delegates lacked the boldness to address the body, but they would listen attentively, express themselves in the taverns at night, and vote when the time came. Many, on the other hand, were unafraid to speak before the full Assembly, and so the debates were lively ones, punctuated by rough-and-tumble questioning and heckling. President Taddhai had his hands full keeping order.

As they made the new laws, the clerk Mawurisay would write them down. Each law adopted by the Assembly would be transcribed in a clean copy, signed by Mawurisay and Razhak Taddhai, then by the Emperor Jehan himself, and then passed along to a corps of scribes Jehan had caused to be employed. These men would recopy the laws many times over for dispatch to all the provinces of Urhemma, while the original signed copies would remain for safekeeping as national treasures in The Maal.

The Assembly, at Jehan's suggestion, had early made a decision to address first in broad outline the most fun-

damental issues, concerning the most crucial rights of the
Urhemmedhin people. Later, they could retrace their steps
to fill in greater detail and tackle secondary matters.

Many weeks were consumed in hammering out the
rights regarding land and property—its ownership, trans-
fer and rental, rights to water, the inheritance of property
and its just taxation. An even more complex realm was
that of crimes and punishment. But here too, the idea
that people should have rights was not forgotten, and
even criminals were given rights. Indeed, overlying the
whole criminal code adopted by the Assembly was the elemental precept that no person should receive punishment
except strictly according to the procedures of the law.

No longer was the law limited to the question of which
officials should have authority to determine and punish
crime. The Urhemmedhin Assembly would give no such
unbridled power to any official, not even the Emperor.
Instead, those charged with responsibility for law and
order would have to discharge it lawfully, in conformance
with the code. Thus, a thief in Arbadakhar had a right
to be treated the same as a thief in Jamarra. It was a
completely new idea.

Thus too, it was not only laws governing the people
that the Assembly was enacting; they went far beyond
that, and took upon themselves the power to establish
laws for the conduct of government itself.

This was truly a breakthrough, for the Assembly's
only authority sprang from the Okhudzhava Decree, which
was a very generalized mandate. They were making a
great leap of assumption, which although never actually
articulated, was clear in their deeds; and the Emperor
Jehan did not contradict it. These 350 farmers and tradesmen assumed to establish themselves as the ultimate political authority of Prasid Urhemma. This was where power
would henceforward reside.

The relationship of the Assembly's authority to that
of the Emperor was a question no one raised; probably
they took for granted that the Emperor, who had created
the Assembly, superseded it. But as long as Jehan kept
to his resolve of respecting the Assembly's every act, the
question fortunately seemed academic.

Thus the government which Jehan Henghmani and the
National Assembly gave to Prasid Urhemma was of

uncertain outlines. Its underlying principles had not been fully thought through, much less stated clearly. It was all rudimentary and rough; but Prasid Urhemma had established the beginnings of a republic.

·13·

JEHAN HENGHMANI had won more success and fulfillment than he'd ever imagined possible. Everything was his. And then Golana once more swelled with child.

This tore him apart with anxiety, inasmuch as her first pregnancy had ended in tragedy—very nearly a double tragedy, in fact. Shaking him more than the loss of the child had been those horrible hours in which Golana's life hung in the balance. The fear of losing her was worse than the tortures of Ksiritsa.

Thus he was opposed to another pregnancy, and he begged Golana to take measures against it. But she would not hear of it; she insisted that she wanted a child. With great misgivings, Jehan acceded to her wish.

His worry proved wasted; this time, the birth went smoothly. Golana brought forth a healthy, squalling, nine-pound boy. Jehan was overjoyed, as much that his wife was well as that she had given him a son.

The baby exhibited Golana's fairness of complexion, but only a wisp of her straight Tnemghadi eyebrow. He had Jehan's pug nose, but nevertheless was a pretty child who gave every promise of growing into a handsome boy.

The naming of the baby occasioned much weighty deliberation; but they settled upon Golan.

It was the name Golana's father had originally picked out when he had hoped his child would be a boy; he had given her the feminine form of the name. Golan meant "wise ruler" in Urhemmedhin as well as Tnemghadi —and so Jehan named his son in honor of the wife who had borne him, as well as giving him a name to live up to, as heir to the Throne of Urhemma.

Crown Prince Golan Henghmani was born on the

twenty-fourth of Elgheber, 1188; it was a night of celebration and rejoicing.

From the summit of Jehan's palace tower, its big new bell was rung for the first time. Accompanying it were fireworks shot into the air, sunbursts in the night that lit up the white towers in flashes. The people of Naddeghomra knew instantly what the fireworks and bellringing meant. They poured out of their homes to watch the grand display in the sky, and to cheer the safe delivery of the child of the *Ur-Rasvadhi*.

Jehan watched the fireworks too. Satisfied that Golana was resting comfortably and safe, he had come out to the tower's roof to look up at the skyrockets bursting over his head. This was not the first time he had been to this high parapet, but tonight, Jehan Henghmani felt that he stood higher than ever before.

In the flashing light of the fireworks, the people caught sight of him atop the tower, and by the thousands, they flocked there. The white marble plaza at the foot of the palace was black with the people as they gathered to look up at their Savior and cheer him.

"*Gavashat Jehan!*" they cried in unison. "*Long live Jehan!*"

"*Gavashat Jehan! Gavashat Golan!*"

He raised his arms high into the sky, and they amplified their cheers. Again and again, he thrust his arms up vigorously.

"*Gavashat Urhemma!*" he bellowed down at them at the top of his lungs. And even at the base of the tower, they could hear him, and they cheered.

At the high parapet, in the midst of the cheering adulation of the crowd, the Princess Maiya came out to join her father. She was wearing her finest white gown, one of Jehan's gifts, and in the intermittent light of the fireworks her face seemed flushed with excitement.

"I come to congratulate you, Paban," she said. "Congratulations on the birth of your second son."

Jehan turned to her in surprise. Despite Maiya's heavy-handed reference to Jehandai's provenance, her words of congratulation actually did not sound sarcastic. This seemed a generous gesture; perhaps she would accept

Golan's birth after all. "Thank you, daughter," Jehan said. "Thank you dearly."

Maiya's eyes lit up like the skyrockets above their heads: "So you do acknowledge that this new baby is your *second* son!"

On this joyous night Jehan was in no mood to rehash the familiar argument with Maiya, especially when he'd been so pleased by her congratulatory gesture. He answered jocularly: "In fact, I suppose I've sired many sons in my lifetime."

"Yes, including my Jehandai."

"Let us not discuss this. Look instead at the fireworks; aren't they beautiful?"

"What could be a more appropriate occasion to discuss Jehandai? I will not be silent—especially not now, when you have a second son. I won't let you cheat Jehandai out of his inheritance. You know that Jehandai is your true heir; you know it in your heart. Paban, tonight I ask you once and for all to do what is right: acknowledge the truth and give your first son his rightful place."

Jehan looked at Maiya and was suddenly struck by a surpassing irony. His eldest living child was neither Golan nor Jehandai, *but Maiya herself.* Inheritance only by sons was the custom, but it was not an absolute, and certainly Golana's capabilities convinced him that women could be men's equals. There was no real reason why he could not have designated Maiya herself to succeed him on the throne—and he would presumably have done so, had the girl not been disqualified by madness. But she had proven her own madness by venting her obsession with Jehandai's claims to the throne! Never had she thought of *herself* as ruler!

So Jehan shook his head wearily to her. "What you ask is impossible," he said.

"Then you would suppress the truth? Has truth no value in your empire? Is that the teaching of Urhem? Paban, can't you see what a dreadful thing you are doing: You would let the crown of Urhemma, which millions died to gain, pass to your successor on the strength of a lie. You will tarnish that crown forever. The crown is sanctified with the blood of our people, and you would wash it away with a cowardly lie."

"But I deny your truth."

"No, Paban, the truth is simply what is true, and a thousand emperor's edicts cannot change it. You can hide from it because you are ashamed of it, because you are a coward, but you cannot change it. The truth is, you are the father of Jehandai." Her finger jabbed straight at him. "Face the truth at last, Paban, it was you who did it, you who stuck your—"

"Stop! If you want truth, I'll give you truth: It was not I who did it, it was you, Maiya. I refused, but you seduced me to save your own neck. So don't tell me I did that unspeakable thing, when it was you yourself who did it."

"There! So you acknowledge the truth after all. It is my child who is your first son, not the child of your Tnemghadi witch!"

"Bite your tongue, to call her a witch! She loves me. But perhaps that is beyond your understanding, since you seem not to join her in loving me."

"Oh, you are wrong, Paban, so very wrong. I pity you, truly. You said that I once used my body to get what I wanted. Well, maybe I did, but don't you see that Golana has done the same thing? Oh, she is a far greater seductress than I was; she's used much more than just her body. She has ensorcelled you completely; she has you believing what she wants you to believe. She has so bewitched you that you don't even know who it is who really loves you. It is certainly not Golana!"

Jehan snorted. "I suppose you'd have me believe it's you who loves me?"

"You seem to forget that I walked on foot from Anayatnas to Zidneppa, with not a falu in my pocket. I left my own daughters, just to come to you, Paban."

"Yes, but not because you loved me. You wanted to make yourself a princess."

"Isn't it strange that you will believe this about your own daughter, your own flesh and blood—but you refuse to believe it about this scheming Tnemghadi stranger? How could you be such a fool as to imagine she really loves you? She's only using you. She made you marry her so she could have power and become empress. That's what she loves: power, not Jehan Henghmani. How could she love you? You are the ugliest man in the world; no one can even stand to look at you. No one could love you but your own flesh." Her tirade was punctuated by the crack of a skyrocket.

Jehan had not stopped her bitter words. "All right, daughter," he finally said coldly. "We have no more to say to each other."

"And I will say to you only this: that your son Jehandai is your rightful heir."

"We will just see about that."

Maiya suddenly flashed an eerie smile, with her lips drawn back from her teeth, lit up by a burst of fireworks.

"Yes, my dear Paban, we will see about that in the morning."

In the morning, both Golana and her newborn son were found dead, stabbed through their hearts.

Jehan Henghmani looked upon his wife and son with an eye that poured out tears.

Everything was nothing.

He beat his fists upon his face. It was so unfair, so absurd, it made no sense that they could be dead. Golana had survived the birthing; how could she be dead now? It was impossible, it was grotesque!

So absurd it was that they could be dead. Only the night before, so much alive they'd been. What was different now? Nothing but a small wound in the breast of each, such minor imperfections. Surely the wounds could be smoothed over and they would be restored to life. Such small repairs to make—a doublet, a wagon, a table could be torn in half and still somehow be put back together. Why not a person too? *Oh Why not a person?*

He beat his fists upon his face because it could not happen, because people are such poor fragile creatures. He had the power of an empire, but it could not repair his wife and child. Absurd! They would soon be buried in the ground to rot away. So absurd, so outlandish!

How could such beauty of body and spirit be destroyed so easily? How could Golana be mortal? How could her flesh, that had given him such joy, be buried beneath the ground? How could her mind, so full of inspiration, fall forever silent?

Jehan Henghmani beat his fists against the terrible, terrible absurdity.

* * *

He had been awakened early on the twenty-fifth by
Revi Ontondra and Hnayim Yahu, who took upon them-
selves the duty of conveying the horrendous news to
Jehan.

The Emperor fell back upon the bed, stricken, as
though by a spear through his heart.

And he knew at once who was responsible.

Maiya had planned this all along, as her ultimate resort
to defeat Golana. She had acquiesced in Golana's presence only because she had reserved to herself the dagger,
should all else fail. It seemed so obvious now; why had
Jehan never seen it?

The night before, the girl had come to him, asking
one last time for recognition of Jehandai as heir to the
throne. When Jehan refused, the course that Maiya
had long before set down had to be played out to its
dreadful end. Jehan could have averted it by giving in
to her; but once he'd refused, the tragedy was ineluctable.
Compelled by all the past years, Maiya had to act, as
much a victim as the ones she'd killed.

All of the protection Jehan had arranged for his wife
could not save her. She had been guarded around the
clock, but guarded not at all against the one true menace.
Maiya had come late at night, carrying a blanket, which
she told the guards was for Golana. Naturally they did
not stop or search her; they did not imagine that the
blanket would conceal a dagger.

The murders were carried out swiftly and silently.
Golana and her child were murdered in their sleep. Maiya
left the weapon in her stepmother's breast and covered it
with the blanket she had brought. Then she bade the
guards good night. Not until morning was the deed discovered.

Maiya, of course, did not flee.

When he recovered some measure of coherence,
Jehan gave orders to fetch her from her chamber. They
found her there with her son; she kissed the boy, and
then willingly went before her father.

"It is my place now, Paban, to offer condolences upon
the tragedy that has befallen you."

Jehan stared at her wordlessly.

"Yes, I do offer condolences, even though I killed them.

It was regrettable. It had to be done, of course, but that doesn't make it any less regrettable."

Maiya smiled queerly; her head was thrown back as though with pride. Jehan neither spoke nor changed his expression. He was still shocked numb.

"It did have to be done; surely you can see that now, Paban. I tried to make you see, but you would never listen. Don't you understand that the most powerful thing in the world is Truth? Truth must be served; it cannot be suppressed.

"It's a pity that a poor innocent baby had to die, but don't you see now that it was *you* who killed him, Paban? You killed him by trying to fight Truth. I wielded the dagger, yes, but it was Truth that guided my hand, and it was you who forced the hand of Truth.

"You wouldn't heed Truth, and so a poor little baby had to die, to save the throne for the rightful heir of Urhemma. And as for that Tnemghadi, of course she had to die too, she deserved to die, that sorceress, that witch—"

Jehan lunged viciously at Maiya, a sudden explosion of insensate fury. He threw himself upon her and grabbed her thin throat in his huge, broken hands.

Ontondra and Yahu jumped on him and managed to pull his hands from Maiya. They piled on top of him, down on the floor, to hold him back, thrashing in their grip, while tears sputtered out of his one good eye and flooded down his face.

Slowly, he quietened, and they let him stand up.

He was shaking and glowering at her while Maiya resumed speaking, undaunted by his attack. "Yes, she was a sorceress who bewitched you; she should have been burned at the stake. Surely now that she is dead, her spell is broken, and you can see it for what it was. She never loved you, Paban, all she loved was power.

"Well, it's been taken away from her now. You are finally the Emperor in truth as well as name. And after you, Jehandai will be Emperor, and his son after him, and his grandson after that, forever onward, the greatest dynasty in the history of the world. And all Urhemma will have me to thank for it, who sired the dynasty and who performed the glorious deed that made it possible!"

Maiya was radiant with the flood of her words. Jehan

watched her bitterly, not opening his mouth, struggling to control himself.

Then she thrust forward her hands, as though delivering them to be bound. "You will have me put to death now, Paban. But I am not afraid. My life's purpose has been accomplished, and I am ready to die. I am a martyr, Paban—a martyr to you, a martyr to our son, a martyr to our country, and a martyr to Truth."

Jehan shook his head sadly. "You are not a martyr. You are a madwoman. You will not be put to death.

"Lock her up," he said to Ontondra. "Lock her away somewhere in the palace. She is hopelessly mad. She will do no more harm."

In his hands, Jehan Henghmani held a paper crown. The paper was brown and fragile now, the berries and raisins that had been its jewels were moldy and withered. It was not a real crown, but Jehan had kept it with him.

He touched his fingertips to the berries, touching them lightly, almost caressing this toy crown.

And then he crushed it in his hands.

BERGHARRA—Urhemmedhin Nation, funerary medal upon the death of the Empress, Year 1188. *Obverse:* portrait of the Empress, left, surrounded by inscription, "Golana Henghmani, Mother of Urhemmedhin Freedom." *Reverse:* large Radiate Sun above a view of the temple and palace complex of Naddeghomra; inscription, "Born 1143 Arbadakhar/ Died 1188 Naddeghomra/Nation of Urhemma." Breitenbach 2051, Bronze, 46 mm. A very beautiful medal; extremely fine, chocolate toning. Fine medals of this era are not frequently encountered. (*Hauchschild Collection Catalog*)

·14·

ONLY SLOWLY did Jehan begin to grasp that Golana was gone.

Life itself seemed what he'd lost. He no longer considered Maiya's old insidious question: Did Golana truly love him? At the beginning he had been lashed by self-doubt, but that passed. Golana was his love, there could be no other. Of his own love for her, he was certain, and he was certain too of the ecstasy she brought him. That, he would not depreciate by doubting.

"I am a Jehandi," she once had said to him—didn't that mean she shared his faith in their love?

"And I am a Golanadhin," he'd answered her.

A Golanadhin he would remain for the rest of his life. On the day of Golana's funeral, Jehan Henghmani swore on her white body an oath of celibacy.

And thus did Maiya gain her ends: It was her father's very devotion to Golana, which the girl had so detested and fought, that gave her victory. For Jehan's devotion to Golana's memory would keep him celibate—and there would never be another son to bar Jehandai's way.

The misery that prostrated Jehan was more than simple loss. He saw himself as a tragic figure. Misfortune alone is not tragedy; tragedy is misfortune that one brings upon oneself. And that was what he'd done.

Maiya had had the effrontery to place blame for the murders upon Jehan. He had not contradicted her—for compounding his anguish was his guilt.

He himself had indeed killed Golana, when he'd refused to acknowledge Jehandai as his heir. Mercilessly Jehan castigated himself, and swore he should have realized what bitter fruit that refusal would bear. For years he had lived with Maiya's derangement, plagued by her obsession with

361

Jehandai. He should have realized what extreme measures she'd be driven to by the birth of a rival heir.

For that tragic blindness, Jehan wanted to burn out his one good eye in penance. His sin was great, and his sin was more than just blindness.

Maiya had accused him of suppressing truth. It was indeed a fact that Jehan wished to forget what had happened with his daughter in the dungeon. It was true that he had defiled her, but he refused to face that truth. He would close his ears to it, and when Golana asked about it, he denied Maiya's story and called it a perverse lie.

For his own lie Jehan was paying dearly.

He paid with his wife and son, and he had lost his daughter too. Even now this was part of his grief. Through all the bitterness and estrangement between them, she had remained his own daughter and he cherished her. No matter how obnoxious she waxed, Jehan did not put her out of his heart. But now it was finished. Maiya had at last compelled her father to despise her. The embers were stamped black and cold, they would never sparkle again. Never again would Jehan even see the girl.

He had lost everything: wife, baby, daughter. And he'd even lost Jehandai.

The boy was eleven years old, and his life had been an odyssey of following Jehan's army back and forth across Urhemma. Now he had come to live in the palace at Naddeghomra. He was the Crown Prince, heir to the throne, and he understood fully what that meant.

He was also, today, a virtual orphan.

It was not until after his mother had been locked away in a tower of The Maal, and not until after Golana's state funeral, that the boy was summoned into the Emperor's chamber for a private talk. He had known that this talk would have to come sooner or later, and that it would be a very difficult one. He went with shaking knees, feeling very much a helpless child in confrontation with a powerful emperor, instead of a boy meeting his grandfather.

Of course, up to now, his grandfather had been abundantly fond of Jehandai, had loved to play games with him and give him presents. But both the man and the boy realized that such playful intimacy could never be resumed. Jehan knew he could never again look at this child without seeing him as the root of the tragedy, the person responsible for Golana's death. Certainly Jehandai was innocent; but all the same, he was the reason Golana had died.

"Hello, Jehandai."

"Hello, Garpaban."

There was an acute silence, which Jehan finally broke clumsily. "Do you understand what happened?"

"Maban told me, but . . . I don't know what to think!"

"What exactly did she tell you? No, don't say it. Jehandai, your mother killed our dear Golana and her baby. Do you understand that? Your mother went mad and put a knife in the heart of her own newborn half-brother, and in the heart of our Golana." Jehan winced to be bluntly reciting such horrors to a mere child of eleven; but it was not to be glossed over. The boy would have to understand why his mother was being taken from him.

"Do you see, Jehandai? Your mother is not right in the head, she isn't responsible for what she did. That's why she must be locked away."

"Maban said to me—" The boy didn't finish, but bit his lip and screwed up his face with a look of intense distress.

"What did she say to you? You can tell me now, Jehandai, it's all right."

"She told me that . . . that the one who really murdered them was . . . was *you*."

"No, Jehandai, it was your mother alone, she admitted it openly. Revi Ontondra will tell you that she admitted it, right here, the next morning. She was off her head when she did the thing. She went into their room and stabbed them while they slept."

"Yes, she told me all that. But she said it was all your fault. I don't understand. . . . What did she mean, Garpaban?"

"I do not know what she meant," Jehan said. He could not finally bring himself to lay it all bare for the boy, it would be cruel to place the guilt on his shoulders. Someday perhaps he would come to understand the whole strange story. "Your mother just went mad," Jehan said, "that's all, she just went mad."

Reluctantly, Jehandai nodded in acceptance. "She said something else to me, that morning afterward. She said again that you are really my father, not my grandfather.

She'd been saying that for years, but I never knew what she meant. Why did she say that?"

"Your mother is mad," the Emperor said softly. "Jehandai, your mother has been mad for a long time. She believed what she told you; but it was not true."

"Then who *was* my father? No one has ever told me, except Maban's saying it was you. Who was it then, really? Was it that farmer we lived with when I was little?"

"No. It was not Gadour Pasny."

The boy felt at a loss. Why was this such a mystery? "Garpaban, do you know who my father was?"

"Yes, I do know."

"Then please tell me. Whatever the truth is, *please* tell me, I'm old enough now to know, aren't I?"

"Are you so sure you want to know? Once I tell you, Jehandai, the words can never be erased. You will have to live with them for the rest of your life."

"I want the truth."

"All right. I know who your father was. I've always known. I can never forget your father, and his face. His face I can see clearly stamped on yours, Jehandai.

"Your father was the man who tortured me in the dungeons of Ksiritsa. Your father was Nimajneb Grebzreh."

Jehandai ran back to his own room, threw himself on his bed and gave himself over to uncontrollable tears. He was not even clear why he was crying, there was so much to cry about. How could everything have turned so bad so very suddenly? What would become of him now? His mother was gone, Golana was gone, and even his grandfather was cut off from him as surely as if he were dead. They were both so very much alone now. Jehandai cried for his grandfather, and cried for himself.

And Jehan began to know that Golana was dead and gone forever.

· 15 ·

ON THE DAY that the news of the tragedy struck them, the stunned members of the Assembly had convened only to pass a resolution of mourning, and then hastily adjourned. Golana, a Tnemghadi after all, had never been a beloved figure to them. Scarcely did any of them realize that the Assembly itself had been born in that woman's fertile mind. Nevertheless, the murder of the Empress and new-born heir shocked them near to bewilderment; and their compassion for Jehan was quite heartfelt.

That awful morning the Assemblymen had neglected to set the time when they would reconvene. Indeed, now they were in a quandary whether to resume their sessions at all. They still possessed a powerful sense that they had no authority save what Jehan vouchsafed, and with the Emperor so crushed by tragedy, who knew what his attitude might be? Certainly President Taddhai was reluctant to call the Assembly back together on his own, lest it infuriate Jehan. Many of the members were considering quietly departing for their homes, and not disturbing the poor ruler in his time of misery.

For five days following Golana's funeral, the Assembly members bided their time in Naddeghomra, wondering what, if anything, they ought to do. And then, on the sixth day, proclamations were to be seen posted throughout the city: Upon the order of Jehan himself, the Assembly was to reconvene at once.

Trepidatiously they obeyed; and when they returned to their benches on The Maal's plaza, there was the Emperor Jehan, occupying his usual seat to observe the deliberations.

He sat as always, his hand pensively upon his chin, saying nothing, only watching and listening closely. To all appearances, nothing had changed; it was impossible to

365

ever guess what thoughts were concealed behind his mutilated mask of a face.

The debate resumed just where it had left off, albeit
without its previous jaunty verve. Decorum reigned as
never before. Those who did open their mouths spoke in
somber tones, careful to introduce not the slightest note of
levity. No one dared mention the Emperor's name, nor
dared to look openly in his direction. But more than ever,
he was the brooding omnipresence shadowing every word
of the debate. Out of the corners of their eyes, all of the
delegates watched him anxiously. They watched him as
though he were a capricious god upon whose sufferance
they existed shakily, as though he would sweep them away
at any moment.

Little did these peasants and shopmen imagine that at
this moment, there was nothing in the world more precious
to Jehan than their Assembly. Indeed, but for this Assembly, there was little in the world giving him cause to
remain in it.

What he had held most dear was demolished; yet the
Assembly was a living piece of Golana that had escaped
the bloody knife. Their son, Golan, was destroyed, but
their child, the Assembly, survived.

Quietly, from his shaded chair, Jehan Henghmani
watched the delegates debate. More faithfully now than
ever, he attended the sessions. Nothing, not the most pressing matters, could draw him away. In order to attend the
Assembly from morning to dusk, it was necessary to devote
half the night and more to all the other tasks required of
him, and Jehan slept little. The regimen suited him well.
By day he allowed the Assembly to absorb him, and by
night, the work of rulership. Never did he permit himself
a free moment, never did he allow his mind to wander;
and when he staggered to his bed in a stupor of exhaustion, he would sleep as though drugged, and would endure
no nightmares. Only in this way could he manage to live
outside of his own tragedy; only in this way could he
manage to live at all.

Sitting quietly, Jehan watched the delegates debate with
an unstinting dedication that amazed them. This was his
vigil of mourning: a vigil to honor the memory of great
Golana, whose loss he could not dare allow his mind to
dwell upon, and yet whose loss consumed his every waking

moment—and it was a vigil too of honor for the great child she had left behind.

It soon became evident that the six months which Jehan had originally allotted to the Assembly's session was quite inadequate. As the half year neared a close, the delegates had only begun to hammer out the laws, but they were becoming increasingly exhausted and homesick. President Taddhai proposed that the Assembly adjourn, so that its members could return home and report back to the people. Then, in another half year, they would reassemble to continue their work.

Taddhai's proposal met with immediate approval; but one of the members rose to suggest that the people be given an opportunity to elect new delegates if they wished. After some debate, this motion was carried overwhelmingly. The delegates also voted that the elections be made permanently annual, and that henceforward, the Assembly would meet every year at Naddeghomra on the twentieth of Elalbatar.

On the final day of the session, President Taddhai turned the podium over to the Emperor. As promised, Jehan had scrupulously refrained from injecting himself into the Assembly's debates throughout the six months. He had attended the meetings only as an observer, and had worked closely with Taddhai in making useful suggestions. Now at the Assembly's close he allowed himself to take the platform a second time to address the delegates. His speech was brief and to the point:

"I thank you, and the people who sent you here thank you for your mighty labors over these last six months. The hopes and expectations embodied in the Decree of the Twenty-fourth of Okhudzhava have been more than fulfilled. And the hopes of the people who sent you have been more than fulfilled.

"Your work here was done for the everlasting good of the people of Urhemma, and for people everywhere throughout the world, now and for as long as people may inhabit this earth. What you have done will stand as one of the great milestones in Mankind's history—as one of the most triumphant steps forward in Mankind's never-ending struggle for freedom and for dignity—*yarushka-dharra.*

"You can be justly proud of these six months. All our people can take pride in them, and Sainted Urhem would take pride in this Assembly as his true legacy. The code of laws that you have written, guaranteeing the rights of the people against tyranny and oppression, is a monument to the sanctity of human life.

"You have labored long and well; but your decision to reconvene this Assembly is a wise one. For there are more laws to be written, more rights to be secured, more injustices to be corrected. The liberty of our people remains threatened by forces both within and without, and it will require ever-tenacious vigilance to safeguard that precious liberty.

"You have made a great, bold start; may the challenge that you have taken up be never again laid down!"

The second Urhemmedhin National Assembly convened at Naddeghomra on the twentieth of Elalbatar, 1189. But in contrast to the jubilation that attended the commencement of the first Assembly, the newly elected delegates gathered here under a dark cloud of agitation and apprehension.

As Jehan had obliquely noted in his last address, and as many of his ministers had argued all along, the Tnemghadi threat had never been neutralized. The Emperor Sarbat was still intent upon someday reconquering the South, and the past few years had been marked by a continual sniping at Urhemma's frontiers. Battles continued to be fought, and Urhemmedhin soldiers continued to lose their lives.

In the month of Dorotht, 1189, a sizable Tnemghadi force entered Diorromeh Province and soon chalked up a victory, killing or capturing most of a two-thousand–man Urhemmedhin division. Those taken prisoner were bound hand and foot, and thrown into a river to drown. Then the invaders headed straight for Anda Lusis.

This, despite being traditionally the provincial capital, was not a great city. It had no wall and was not particularly well defended. The Tnemghadi army struck Anda Lusis like a brigand gang pillaging a country town.

And yet, they were ruthlessly methodical about it. Once the town was under their control, they systematically rounded up all the adult males they could find, and massed them in the public square. Finally, these unarmed civilians were set upon by the Tnemghadi troops and butchered, almost as though for sport. The death toll from this single atrocity alone was more than three thousand.

And thousands more lost their lives in the sacking and burning of the town.

Intending only a quick raid, the Tnemghadi headed swiftly back to their northern sanctuary; on their way, they stopped long enough, however, to destroy two small villages. By the time the Urhemmedhin army was able to mobilize against the threat, the raiders had fallen back across the border.

Anda Lusis was still in flames as the second Assembly met on the twentieth of Elalbatar. It was with a somber unanimity that the delegates reelected Razhak Taddhai to the presidency; Taddhai was a native of the afflicted province.

As one dispatch from the North followed another, each detailing more vividly the horrible extent of the raid, it became the Assembly's sole topic of discussion. That the invaders had quickly retreated was scant comfort; nor was the incident viewed as an isolated one. It seemed clear that the Bergharran Empire would never permit Urhemma to exist in peace.

Gaffar Mussopo, the Minister of War and Foreign Affairs, was renewing his agitation for a northern invasion. Only by subjugating the Tnemghadi, he argued, could Urhemma be safe, and the other ministers in The Maal were virtually unanimous in supporting him. Jehan found himself besieged with advocates of war; scarcely could he confer with any official without being implored to take up arms against the Tnemghadi.

The Assembly too was a hotbed of sword-rattling. Razhak Taddhai preached calm and moderation, and tried to return the delegates to their legislative agenda. But it was no use. Speaker after speaker rose to excoriate the Tnemghadi and call for a bloodbath of reprisal. A small minority followed Taddhai in holding out against the warhawks, and the debate entered a bitterly divisive phase.

These developments were anathema to Jehan. More opposed to invasion than ever, he violently said so whenever the subject was raised. He believed that full-scale war would be a tragic mistake, and he had no stomach for it.

Instead, what he wanted dearly was to see the Assembly one day complete the law code.

But the Assembly itself was no longer interested in making laws, and was moving swiftly toward making war. And Jehan pondered: should he stop it?

Day and night he wrestled with his conscience, agonizing over this decision. Deeply as he loathed the prospect of war, he had sworn an oath to uphold the integrity of the Assembly. Never had he interfered with its acts, and he had deliberately allowed the Assembly to take ultimate political authority into its hands. It was Golana's memorial: an assembly of the people, freely chosen and governing free of autocracy's specter.

But now it was screaming for blood, for the subjugation of another people. Jehan wept at the perversion that was gripping his child, the Assembly.

But should he intervene? He realized the war-hawks were not completely without sense. The rape of Anda Lusis was a ghastly outrage, and it would not be the last. Moreover, the Tnemghadi were overripe for conquest. So deeply had their fortunes plummeted that unless the Urhemmedhins took over, quite possibly the Akfakh would instead. Weighing too in the balance was the possibility that the Assembly's hysteria could not be quenched even by Jehan. To intercede and fail would be a humiliating repudiation.

Yet he knew in his heart they were wrong! Jehan, who had unleashed so much war and violence, felt powerfully compelled to make up for it now by holding tight the rein on peace.

Endlessly he paced through the hallways of The Maal, assailed with indecision. What would Golana have counseled? If only she were here! Jehan went on his knees before the statue of humble Urhem in the great tower, but received no sign here either. Then Jephos Kirdahi burst in upon him with the news:

The Assembly had just voted war.

By an overwhelming majority the resolution had passed, mandating an army of two hundred thousand to conquer the North, with conscription to be used if volunteers were insufficient. In addition, the Assembly was specifically calling upon the Emperor Jehan Henghmani to lead the march.

All Naddeghomra was churning with exultation at the Assembly's act. Spontaneous public meetings gathered to applaud it, and young men were already stepping forward by the hundreds to join the army. Inside The Maal, Mussopo and the other ministers were jubilant.

Only one man, it seemed, was plunged into gloom: Jehan Henghmani.

His face ashen, his shoulders slumped, he walked with a labored shuffle up the winding stairway into his tower sanctuary, there to meditate upon the grave situation and upon his own course. With him he brought only a tattered copy of the Book of Urhem. Locking the door behind him, he would see no one and refused even food. Not a word would pass that locked door for a night and a day, while at the foot of the stairs the leaders of the nation waited.

For a night and a day, Jehan Henghmani remained locked in the tower, alone with his thoughts.

Then, finally, the door opened, and the Emperor advanced down the steps. He was wearing his armor, his helmet, and his sword.

Several months were necessarily consumed in recruiting the army and making preparations. Raising the two hundred thousand troops prescribed by the Assembly proved to be no stumbling block. People who had been unwilling to volunteer to guard their borders and keep the peace rushed to join the army of invasion. It was more than liberty that danced in their eyes now. After centuries of knuckling under to the Tnemghadi, they burned to turn the tables and make those same Tnemghadi taste the bitterness of subjugation.

All of the ministers of the government insisted upon accompanying the invasionary army. In addition, more than fifty of the Assembly delegates left their seats to take up the sword. Even Prince Jehandai begged for permission to go along, but this the Emperor refused.

Jehandai went then to Gaffar Mussopo, asking to join the army as a water-boy if necessary. Gaffar was reluctant to cross the Emperor, but decided it might be wise to gain the favor of the heir to the throne. "You may come along," he said, "but on one condition. If—or rather, when—your grandfather finds out, you must tell him that I had no knowledge of it." Jehandai readily agreed to this stipulation and joined Mussopo's entourage, disguising his identity.

In the month of Sutarappa, 1190, the march began.

Like a weary but dutiful old soldier, Jehan Henghmani climbed painfully into the saddle once again. Only the Assembly's express command had persuaded him grudgingly to do this. He hoped fervently that this campaign would be a short one—and his last.

Northward through Khrasanna they marched, stopping at prearranged points to assimilate more and more thousands of new recruits. They marched in a steady northward path, bypassing the cities of Ourkesh and Bebjella; then up through Nitupsar, with a brief respite for resupply at Jamarra; then by barges across the River Qurwa into Taroloweh, with a final provisioning at Arbadakhar; and then on northward, farther north than Jehan's armies had ever penetrated.

On the seventeenth of Okhudzhava, Jehan Henghmani crossed through the Usrefif Mountains and entered the Province of Kholandra.

Its terrain was not much different from Taroloweh's. The softly sloping Jaraghari hills were very like the hills where he had been a bandit once. Jehan had to remind himself that this was Tnemghadi territory.

He kept away from the populated areas, avoiding all contact with the enemy. The plan was not to mutilate the Tnemghadi lands, not to flail away at the limbs of the dragon. Instead, Jehan would strike a dagger at its heart.

BOOK FIVE

•

KSIRITSA

· 1 ·

TNEM SARBAT SATANICHADH looked out upon his world with bleak eyes.

Everything was nothing.

The religion of the Tnemghadi avowed no afterlife, only the life on earth, controlled in its last detail by the Emperor. His was the power of life and death. And yet, in whose power was the Emperor's own life? This god with boundless power over millions could not save his own life, and in this religion without a heaven, death was complete, even for its god.

For thirty-four years, Sarbat had sat upon the Tnemenghouri Throne, but only in the last years had he come to realize that its golden carving was of a setting sun after all, not a rising sun. And now an Urhemmedhin army was at the very gates of Ksiritsa. Perhaps it had been inevitable since the year 361, when the Tnemghadi had conquered the South. Now the southerners were conquering the North. Sarbat wondered whether the Urhemmedhin primacy would last eight centuries too. And would the cycle then repeat?

Or would everything fall to the Akfakh? Would a dark age descend upon the human race—and would it ever lift? Sarbat looked out of his window, and a shiver ran through him. The sky was growing dark already.

The Grand Chamberlain, Faihdon Royanis, barged unannounced into the Emperor's chamber. But Sarbat chose not to scold him for this breach of protocol. It really didn't matter any more.

"Your Majesty." said Royanis with a dramatic flourish, "there is only one hope!"

Sarbat continued to look out of the window, and shook his head.

375

"You must listen, Your Majesty, we're not through yet. We still have an army up north. We must send orders for those troops to leave the northern front temporarily, and to attack Jehan and free Ksiritsa from the siege."

The ruler slowly turned from the window to face Royanis. "And how long would it take before Ksiritsa is once more besieged—by Znarf?"

"Yes, it's true that we would be giving ground to the Akfakh. But what is our alternative? The immediate threat to the capital is Jehan Henghmani. We'll worry about Znarf later."

Sarbat gave a very hollow laugh. "Royanis, stop dreaming. Nothing could be more clear: We have strength to fight only one enemy, and unfortunately we have two. Juggling our forces can't save us any longer. It's over."

"Perhaps so. But I submit that we have a sacred obligation to spare no effort in trying to defeat this Urhemmedhin pig Jehan. You must fight to save the honor of the Satanichadh and to keep gloried Ksiritsa out of the hands of those Urhemmedhin brutes. You owe it to the honor of the Empire of Bergharra."

Sarbat sighed, almost as though he were bored. "I have the honor of Bergharra well in mind, Royanis. Nothing remains but that. *Bergharra:* a great empire, but more than that, a great civilization, a great people.

"Yes, a great people, Tnemghadi and Urhemmedhins both."

Sarbat walked over to a cabinet, and extracted from it one of his clear glass cubes. Inside this container was a small lump of hard gray clay, roughly exhibiting the outlines of a human face. The Emperor peered at it for a moment.

"Royanis, this little sculpture was unearthed at Mashrathghazi. Its age can only be guessed at. Probably it is more than five thousand years old; it could date from prehistoric times, ten thousand, twenty thousand years ago, who knows? Its crudeness is pathetic, and yet it excites the mind. This poorly executed little face shows us how far our civilization has come. Indeed, the man who made this object was undoubtedly quite advanced compared with his forebears, even more thousands of years earlier. No one can study artifacts like this without gaining an under-

standing that civilization is not static. We have arrived
where we are now by rising out of the muck.

"Once we were making crude little faces in clay. Now
we are a great people, a great civilization: the Tnemghadi
and the Urhemmedhin.

"Our myth of the dragon Sexrexatra is not meaningless,
Royanis. The children who escaped the dragon's jaws and
defeated Sexrexatra were our ancestors, but they were
neither Tnemghadi nor Urhemmedhin. They were the
first Bergharrans, and the people of the South are their
descendants, just as we northerners are.

"The history of the Tnemghadi and the Urhemmedhins
has not been one of brotherhood, yet we are brothers
nonetheless. Even through all the hatred and bitterness
between us, our differences are overshadowed by what we
have in common. Our great civilization was built by Tnemghadi and Urhemmedhin alike. For eight centuries, the
Tnemghadi played the role of ruler, but that was only a
quirk of history, it could just as well have been the Urhemmedhins. Bergharra would not have been very different for it. And if the scepter passes now, from North to
South, Bergharra will not change radically. Our civilization will go on. At least I so hope and pray.

"This is my legacy. I cannot pass the Sexrexatra scepter
to my son, nor can I even pass it to another Tnemghadi.
But I will pass it to a Bergharran.

"To Jehan Henghmani, a Bergharran brother.

"It is not Jehan, but Znarf the Akfakh who must be
kept from the gates of Ksiritsa. For if Znarf prevails, then
the great civilization of Bergharra ends, and a dark curtain
will fall. It took us untold millennia to rise out of the
muck, but if the barbarians win, we could very quickly
slide back into it. Mankind will be reduced once more
to the level of this pathetic artifact from Mashrathghazi.

"And so, Royanis, we shall not call our armies down to
battle Jehan. We will give him Ksiritsa. And as for our
troops in the north, let them fight as fiercely for Jehan as
they have fought for me. Let Tnemghadi and Urhemmedhin join forces to drive back the curtain of darkness."

Royanis nodded gravely. "Very well, Your Majesty, I
can see that your mind is made up. There's no use arguing
with you. I understand."

"Do you? There is much I understand now too. I believe that I am doing right, at last. So much of what I've done has been so wrong, so stupid, even depraved and evil. Whatever happens to me now will be deserved.

"Do you remember the parable in the sacred parchments concerning an emperor named Sahyid Sarvadakhush?

"When Jehan Henghmani was a prisoner in my dungeon, I wished to see the man who had killed his own executioner! But mindful of the parable, I took care that he was not in chains at my feet when I first set eyes on him. I was a fool, Royanis.

"I was taking the prophecy at its literal words. But the chains themselves meant nothing, they were only symbolic. The real point of the prophecy was that a man whom I could have destroyed at whim, but spared, would destroy me.

"And that is the irony, too. Instead of trying to evade the prophecy by looking at Jehan standing up and unchained, I could have simply had him killed. It was like holding an insect in my hand. I could have simply closed my fist and crushed him.

"*But I didn't.*

"Now I understand what stopped my hand from killing him. While I was acting superciliously, Bergharra was acting to save herself. By some mysterious force, it was Bergharra that stayed my hand.

"That was the essence of the prophecy: that when Bergharra would need a strong man, it would find him in a man with the power to rise up out of chains. What greater test of a man's strength? He would rise up, he would destroy the weak ruler who had once enchained him, and then he would save Bergharra.

"That was the prophecy.

"All my life, I hoped that prophecy was false.

"Now I pray that it is true."

· 2 ·

WITH COLD EYES, the people of Ksiritsa looked upon the conqueror.

They were stunned; this moment in history had crept up on them with very little warning. Likewise astonished was Jehan Henghmani. He had been prepared for a protracted struggle, but hardly had he reached the gates of Ksiritsa, when an offer of surrender was received.

He thought it was a trick at first. They offered to give him the city—indeed, the Empire—with the sole proviso that the Tnemghadi troops and Palace functionaries be permitted to evacuate the capital unharmed and that there be no reprisals levied upon the citizenry either. Cautiously, Jehan responded that he could not guarantee the good behavior of his men once inside the city; that the defending soldiers would have to relinquish to him all their armaments; and that the Emperor Sarbat would have to be delivered into his hands.

To Jehan's amazement, these conditions too were accepted by Sarbat's emissary. A protocol of surrender was drawn up and signed on the spot.

There had been no real hostilities; the conquest of Bergharra was accomplished with hardly a single casualty. True to the surrender terms, a caravan of wagons soon arrived at the Urhemmedhin encampment, delivering the armor and weapons of the Tnemghadi army. Meanwhile the disarmed soldiers themselves left the capital, pouring out of all its gates and permitted to pass through the Urhemmedhin lines. Joined by a great host of priests, Palace officials, courtiers, merchants and other people of the old order, they dispersed into the countryside, looking fearfully over their shoulders. They could not understand what was happening.

Now the gates of gloried Ksiritsa were open to Jehan

379

Henghmani; and on the twenty-sixth of Jhevla in the year 1190, he marched into the city.

With frosty eyes, the people of Ksiritsa looked upon the conqueror, marching through their streets.

To be sure, there was no demonstration, no cheering, no celebration. Few people at all were out; most were barricaded in their homes with shuttered windows and bolted doors. They were hiding, cowering in fear, with their money buried in the ground and their women locked away. Only a handful, the bold and curious, were out in the streets to watch the Urhemmedhin procession.

The sky was overcast, a chalky white color, and the wind was blustery, blowing clouds of dust and dirt through the streets. For these men accustomed to the burning southern sun, Ksiritsa was a cold city.

Through these cold, tense, somber streets, Jehan Henghmani led his conquering army, a great column on horse and on foot, marching with a stiff, flawless rhythm, bristling with pikes and spears. Jehan's own horse was surrounded for protection by a squad of tough cavalry, but he stood out in their midst; he had aged, but he was still a very big man. He rode with a majestic posture, both of his hands clasped tightly on the reins. He gave no salute, and his face was cold and hard.

So were the faces of the few who stared at the conqueror with gritted teeth, neck muscles standing out as taut cords, and their lips drawn into thin bloodless lines. Their faces were red with anger or with shame. Some of them, though, watched with quivering lips, fighting back tears or quietly weeping.

Some of the most brazen dared to scream curses at the conqueror and his troops. *"Monster!"* they would shout, shaking their fists, *"Damned ugly monster!"* Never had they seen a man so big and hideous, mutilated and disfigured by the torture he had once endured in this very city.

There were even a few with the temerity to throw vegetables or stones.

"Bloody tyrant!" a boy yelled out, picking a rock off the ground and hurling it vehemently at Jehan.

"Don't!" cried the boy's father, pulling him back from the street. "Are you crazy? They'll beat you to death!"

But the stone had missed its mark, and none of the marching soldiers paid any attention to the boy. Forcefully held back by his father's hands, he watched them march past, staring at them with sullen, burning eyes. The boy's name was Tifsim Jarba.

Jehan had marched through many towns and cities. Here, he rode through the hostile streets with a stern face, trying to ignore the curses thrown at him. Yet they made him uneasy in what should have been a great moment of triumph. He had conquered gloried Ksiritsa, the legendary Dragon City, and was now the most powerful man on earth; and yet he felt stifled with a disturbing melancholy.

He wondered if this was the way Tnem Khatto Trevendhani felt, eight centuries before, when he'd marched through Naddeghomra.

In the Tnem-rab-Zhikh Palace, the Palace of the Heavens, Tnemghadi kings had ruled for as long as there had been kings in the world.

Now Jehan Henghmani sat at the head of its cavernous great hall, upon the golden Tnemenghouri Throne; lying across his knees was the heavy scepter, perch of the dragon Sexrexatra.

And at the foot of the throne, kneeling in chains upon the red carpet, was Sarbat Satanichadh.

Sarbat was not much older than Jehan, but age had ravaged him deeply. He was wrinkled with gnarled limbs and whitened hair; his teeth were gone and his spindly legs seemed scarcely able to support his fat torso. The former Emperor was clothed in a rough sacklike smock. His hands were chained together and his feet bore heavy shackles.

Only one servant remained at Sarbat's side: Halaf the clown, still wearing his outlandish featherhat. All the rest were gone.

"Do you know who I am?" Jehan asked the deposed Emperor. "Do you remember who I really am?

"Yes, I know who you are, Jehan Henghmani, *Man Eater*. It was fourteen years ago that we met in the dungeon."

"You said that I would suffer so horribly that I would beg for death. And I did suffer, but never begged to die.

Instead I thanked you, for you had given me the gift of life."

"I gave you life, Jehan Henghmani, and so now you will give me death."

"Yes, but it is not for my sake that you must die, Sarbat Satanichadh. Your crimes are as numerous as there are pebbles on the shore."

"Indeed," Sarbat said tartly, "I know my crimes. I acknowledge them. And I am ready to die for them."

"That is scant comfort to your victims."

"Nor is it any comfort to me. I do not relish dying—*especially* because my death is deserved. I am no martyr, no hero; no one will mourn my death."

"You have no one but yourself to blame."

"Are you sure? Do you remember the prophecy of which I spoke, fourteen years ago, in the dungeon?"

"Yes, I remember it well. And the prophecy has now come true."

"Let us both pray that that is so."

"You speak in riddles."

"Then let me speak straight now," said Sarbat earnestly, "and I beg you to mark my words carefully before I die.

"At this very moment, Znarf the Akfakh is gazing in our direction. His barbarian horde has already overrun much of Agabatur, Gharr, and Jammir provinces; every day they plunge their knives more deeply into the heart of our country. You have never fought these Akfakh. They are wild animals, dirty and crude and ignorant, but they know no fear and fight with savage cunning. This Znarf is a beast, and he's chewing us to shreds.

"You must fight him, Jehan Henghmani, you must fight him. His victory would trample all our culture into mud, and the nightmare might not end before Mankind is back in the caves."

Sarbat paused, wheezed, and shook his head. "But I don't have to tell you this," he said in a lower voice. "You will surely fight them. You will fight them because that is why you have been made Emperor of Bergharra. For what it is worth, I wish you well, Jehan Henghmani."

Sarbat fell silent, closed his eyes and bowed his head.

"And now what about you?" said Jehan to Halaf. "What shall we do with you, clown?"

"Tnem Sarbat Satanichadh is my lord and master; he always has been and he always will be. I will not leave him now."

"But he is going to die."

"Then I will die too," said Halaf.

"Very well," Jehan answered. "I now direct that you both be removed down into the dungeons, and there, beheaded."

Jehan Henghmani looked out upon the world with impenetrable eye.

Everything was nothing.

That was because it all was his. The world was Jehan Henghmani's to exalt or curse, to fondle or lay waste.

For Jehan Henghmani himself was god.

He was the Emperor of Bergharra.

BERGHARRA—Urhemmedhin Empire, silver two tayel of Emperor Jehan I, circa 1192. *Obverse:* Crowned portrait of ruler, facing, with Urhemmedhin inscription in exergue. *Reverse:* Radiate Sun, crown mint-mark (Ksiritsa). Breitenbach 2132, 21 mm.; fine with a greenish cast typical of low-grade silver issues. *(Hauchschild Collection Catalog)*

·3·

THERE WERE MANY PEOPLE to come before Jehan Henghmani in those first days at Ksiritsa.

One of them was a wretched aged woman. Her white hair was an unruly bush; her body was emaciated, a parchmenty yellow; she was crabbed and stooped, toothless, dressed in tatters, so filthy that she stank. And yet, out of this human wreck shone eyes peculiarly vital.

"We found her locked in one of the Palace chambers," a soldier explained. "What should we do with her? She is quite mad, and even insists that she's of royal blood!"

Jehan peered down at this miserable old crone. Her claim to high station seemed ludicrous, indeed mad. And yet he noticed that her faded, dirty garment might once have been a very fine one.

He asked the woman who she was.

"My name is Denoi Vinga Gondwa Devodhrisha. I am Princess of Laham Jat and the Empress of Bergharra. And you are called Jehan Henghmani, the Man Eater." The old woman smiled with barren gums. "Yes, I remember you. I was with Tnem Sarbat in his litter when he went down into the dungeon, and I remember that day very clearly. You were so marvelously defiant! When Tnem Sarbat condemned you to a diet of human flesh, you vowed one day to eat *his* flesh."

Jehan gaped at the old woman, flabbergasted. "It's true," he said. "But still, how can you possibly be the Empress? It's well known that she went back to Laham Jat years ago and never returned to Ksiritsa."

The woman shook her head. "Tnem Sarbat ostensibly agreed to my journey home. All the arrangements were made, and I said my farewells. But then I was locked away in a chamber of the Palace, where I have remained ever since. No one knew about it, but I have been there from the year 1176—the same year that you yourself were imprisoned here. What year is it now?"

"Eleven ninety, Empress. You have been imprisoned fourteen years. Why did Sarbat do such a treacherous thing?"

The woman raised her bony shoulders. "It's so far in the past, it seems meaningless now. He promised some concubine to have me killed, he promised me a return home; perhaps it amused him to break both promises. It was all absurd, all mad."

"And how is it that, locked up so long, you didn't go mad yourself?"

She shrugged again and smiled. "Perhaps because this Palace was already saturated with madness, filled to the brim and couldn't hold another drop. I don't know. Perhaps it was because my life didn't change so very much, when that door was shut upon me. I had really been alone long before that. In a sense, I've been imprisoned since the day I came here, and that was almost forty years ago."

"But now you are free," Jehan said.

"Am I? The world must have changed greatly in these fourteen years."

"Yes, it truly has. The Tnemghadi primacy is over. Sarbat Satanichadh is no more."

"And what about my friend Irajdhan? He must be dead too."

"Irajdhan passed away years ago."

The old woman sighed.

"I understand how lost you must feel now, Empress. But I want to do whatever I can for you. If you wish, you may remain in Ksiritsa under my protection; or, if you choose to return to Laham Jat, you will be safely taken there."

"I have not been there since I was a girl; I hardly know what Laham Jat is like. Tell me, what has become of my country?"

"The regime subservient to the Tnemghadi has been deposed. The House of Devodhrisha is restored; your people are free."

"Then I will go home," said Denoi Devodhrisha. "I will finally go home."

Jehan bowed his head to her, and she reciprocated. Then she turned her shrunken body and walked slowly

down the center of the throne-room. She hobbled haltingly, stooped over, yet unaided and with dignity.

The Emperor watched her, thinking of Golana.

Once a peasant thug, a vicious bandit, a prisoner tortured in the dungeon, Jehan Henghmani walked pensively
through the high-ceilinged halls of the Palace of the Heavens. Even the ceilings were splendorously embellished with
frescoes, gold leaf and fixtures, silk and velvet hangings,
intricate chandeliers. Jehan looked up at them in awe.

Gaffar Mussopo was with him. "Just look at all this,
Gaffar!" he said. "Compared to this, our Palace at Naddeghomra was a pig-sty. Look at all this, the tapestries, the
luxurious carpets, the carved wooden paneling, the paint-
ings and marble sculptures, gold and silver and jade and
crystal and pearls and precious stones everywhere. I feel
as though we do not belong here."

"But we do belong here!" Gaffar said emphatically.
"This Palace is more rightfully ours than it ever was
Sarbat's. He was merely born into it, but we earned it with
our sweat and blood and with the sufferings of our people.
It was Urhemmedhin slaves who built this Palace. We
rightfully own every stone, every tapestry and jewel. They
even left two hundred concubines!"

"Did they?" Jehan said. "The poor women were probably too frightened to flee with the rest. What is being done with them?"

"I have made sure they are guarded, and untouched—
not an easy thing to ensure, obviously."

"Yes. But I trust there are plenty of brothels in Ksiritsa
for our men."

"Frankly, sire, a lot of them are taking matters into their
own hands."

Jehan's face pinched with distaste. "Say what you mean:
rape."

"Yes, rape, sire. Rape. And looting. Tnemghadi getting
what they deserve, sound beatings and smashed homes."

"But I gave orders!" Jehan said harshly. "There was to
be decorum!"

"Decorum, indeed! Did you seriously expect two hundred thousand men to march all the way up here, conquer
at last the people who've been oppressing them for centuries, and then treat them daintily? It's not just women and

plunder that our men hunger for. They want revenge, and frankly so do I. We're entitled to it. I personally can never forget what they did to my family. What is happening out there now is justice."

"Is it? Was it the women of Ksiritsa who destroyed your family?"

Gaffar spoke intensely through clenched teeth. "Thousands of our people were butchered like cattle at Anda Lusis. Someone has to pay for that crime! It can't be wiped away, ever. The same is true of all the countless abominations of the last eight centuries. The Tnemghadi cannot ever be forgiven!"

Jehan slumped into a chair, closed his eyes and rubbed his forehead. "I understand what you are saying, Gaffar. I understand what is happening now. But for the sake of Urhem, let us not visit as much evil upon the Tnemghadi as they did upon us."

"Yes, Your Majesty."

"See to it that the concubines are moved safely out of the city. Will you do that, Gaffar?"

"Yes, Your Majesty."

"Now, we do have some important things to discuss."

"Yes, indeed. Have you given thought to changing our government?"

"I don't believe major alterations are warranted, Gaffar. Kirdahi, of course, will be the Grand Chamberlain of Bergharra. I want you to remain in your present post, and as always I will rely heavily upon you."

"But what about the Assembly?"

"The third Assembly will meet as scheduled, eight weeks from now, at Naddeghomra. It will continue the work of making laws."

"That is all well and good, sire, as far as Urhemma is concerned. But will you have the Assembly's laws apply in the North as well? I strongly advise against that. First we must consolidate our rule here, and we can't allow laws to get in the way. Perhaps when things get settled down, we can have laws for the whole Empire."

Jehan nodded. "I recognize the problem. Our first step will have to be military rule of the North, I suppose. We'll have to send troops out everywhere, establish garrisons to rule in every town. In time, one hopes we can allow the

Tnemghadi towns to choose their own councils, as in the South."

"Your plan is well conceived," said Gaffar. "But it will take a great many soldiers, and we have the Akfakh to worry about too."

"I haven't forgotten them. Sarbat was quite right: They pose a grave threat, and I don't know if we'll be any more successful than he was in holding them back. How ironic it would be if we've come to Ksiritsa only to replace Sarbat on Znarf's dinner plate."

"Your Majesty, as long as I'm in charge of the army, I swear to give those barbarians a tough fight. But it will take a lot more troops than we have mobilized now. We'll have to try to keep the Tnemghadi army fighting the Akfakh."

"Yes, we must use the Tnemghadi. They'd be fighting for their homeland, even though it's ruled by us now. We must impress on them that they're fighting for Bergharra, not for Jehan Henghmani. And we'll have to continue paying their wages."

"I agree," said Gaffar, "but I also think it will be necessary to draft them, with severe punishment for shirkers and deserters."

Jehan mulled this briefly and then nodded. "Very well; you can draw up the necessary decree."

"We'll need an awful lot of Urhemmedhin troops too, to staff the garrisons and keep the Tnemghadi in line."

"Are you suggesting conscription for Urhemmedhins as well?"

"Positively, sire. We can't possibly get enough soldiers any other way. The time has come to face this reality."

Jehan bit his lip, chewed on it. "What an abhorrent idea; it's little more than slavery! But I suppose you're probably right, we haven't much choice. All right, do this: Put a quota on each province. If the number of recruits falls short, then draft enough to make up the difference. But we must try to get most of them as volunteers. Perhaps we should even raise the pay, as a means of avoiding conscription."

"Good. But are you sure we can afford it? I think it would be unwise to debase the coinage the way Sarbat did."

"We can get away with some modest debasement, at

least for the nonce. I really don't know where we stand yet financially. We still haven't got an accurate account of what was left in the Tnemghadi treasury. They may have left the concubines, but presumably they took all the gold they could carry. At any rate, we'll simply have to impose whatever taxes are necessary."

"Upon the Tnemghadi, I trust."

"Mostly. Taxation will continue in the South, but obviously we will put a major burden on the Tnemghadi. They took plenty enough from us over eight hundred years!"

"I have one more important question, sire."

"Yes?"

"Will you remain here at Ksiritsa? I strongly urge you to do so."

"Naddeghomra is still our capital," said Jehan with a trace of admonishment. "But I suppose practicality does require us to remain at Ksiritsa, at least for a while. Obviously, our domination of the North would be imperiled if we were to vacate this city."

"The North cannot be ruled from Naddeghomra. I'm glad you see that, sire. As for me, though, I will not remain with you at Ksiritsa."

"What?"

"I will be out bringing all the towns under Urhemmedhin rule and directing the fight against the Akfakh."

Startled, Jehan looked at Gaffar. "You're a high minister of state; you don't have to take the field personally."

"But I choose to. What happens up there will cast the fate of all of us."

"Then I will miss your counsel," said Jehan.

"I will be back," Gaffar answered. "I will return when I've defeated the Akfakh.

"If I defeat them."

· 4 ·

ELEVEN NINETY was a bad year in northern Bergharra.

As a numbing wave the news of the fall of Ksiritsa spread and the Tnemghadi people saw the world turned upside down.

For eight centuries they had grown accustomed to worshipping rulers of their own race. No other people were as proud and mighty as the Tnemghadi. Their power grew and grew, shining ever more brilliantly, until the entire globe revolved around the emperors at gloried Ksiritsa.

Truly did these emperors seem gods, and dearly did the northern people worship them. The emperors were omnipotent; even the Akfakh incursions were seen as a minor nuisance that must ultimately dissolve in the face of Tnemghadi power.

Now, quite abruptly, the end had been rung with a resounding finality. Their Emperor-god was vanquished, destroyed, and an alien horde occupied their capital. Their whole comfortable world was shattered at a stroke. Where could the Tnemghadi people find even a glimmer of hope? Between the dual Akfakh and Urhemmedhin depredations, with no emperor to fight them, suddenly the Tnemghadi saw doom writ large and clear.

With incoherent apprehension they awaited the horrors to come. There were the tales of Akfakh savagery from the north: laughing as they pillaged, burning whole villages, chopping people in half. The Akfakh were feral beasts. And what of the Urhemmedhins? How much mercy could be expected from these people, enflamed by eight centuries of pent-up hatred? From Ksiritsa too there came atrocity stories, growing with each telling.

The Tnemghadi people pitched themselves into fervent prayer, and their ceremonies before the old idols of Sarbat Satanichadh took on a very grim aura. The priests would

stand in their robes before the fiery altars, their arms up-
stretched, sacrificing their offerings now to an unnamed
god—for their own god had already been swallowed up by
the holocaust engulfing them all.

They prayed for deliverance with desperate urgency,
crying themselves hoarse with prayer as their ritual
flames licked the sky. For deliverance they were praying
to any god who might listen.

Fanning out from Ksiritsa, the Urhemmedhin armies
began to permeate the northern countryside, carrying their
new regime to all the provinces, all the towns and cities,
all the landed baronies. The Tnemghadi military had long
been divided between battling the Akfakh and the southern towns. Their need elsewhere had never been imagined
—no one had ever dreamed this day might come.

As a result, the population in the North was almost
completely at the mercy of the conquerors. One swiftly
following another, like shoveling potatoes into a sack, the
towns and villages were brought under the Urhemmedhin
heel.

The occupation of every town would begin with executions. The mayor and other officials, the priests, together
with the wealthy leading citizens—those foolish enough
not to flee—were put to death. There were no trials and
the executions would take place in full public view. More
than anything else, their object was to instill fear—fear of
the Urhemmedhin race, of whom for centuries the northerners had only had contempt.

The next step was to raze the temples. Worship in the
old Tnemghadi manner was forbidden; and teams of able-
bodied men would be pressed into service quarrying the
stone for new temples, temples to Urhem.

Gaffar Mussopo led a section of his army northward
from Ksiritsa toward the front where he would eventually
command the war against Znarf the Akfakh. But he was
in no hurry to get there. And so along the route it was
Gaffar who directed the transition to Urhemmedhin rule in
town after town.

By word of mouth, his name marched ahead of him—
and the Tnemghadi dreaded the coming of Gaffar Mussopo.

It was in the month of Nrava, 1191, that he came to a town in the Province of Rashid, a good-sized town of some three or four thousand inhabitants; it was called Rayibab.

Here, the usual massacre was executed: the old mayor, the officials, a few merchants, all were lined up in the public square and beheaded one by one. Then, bound to stakes, a half dozen priests were roasted to death, so that their screams and stench and smoke would penetrate to every corner of the town. Meanwhile, their temple was being desecrated, and many houses were ransacked, the women and children driven through the streets and raped and beaten. A few were killed by the Urhemmedhin soldiers.

When this rampage was over, Gaffar Mussopo left a garrison to occupy the town, and moved on.

Unbeknown to Mussopo, however, one priest of Rayibab had escaped—a popular young fellow named Arbez Ohadi, who had hidden himself in the forest. Once the tumult subsided, Ohadi sneaked back, and visited surreptitiously many of the stalwart men of Rayibab. He exhorted them to join him in rebellion against the hateful occupiers; and one night within a week of the Urhemmedhin arrival, Arbez Ohadi surprised the garrison with a bold revolt.

The battle was brief but violent. Although most of the rebels, including Ohadi himself, were killed, the Urhemmedhins were wiped out. Rayibab was freed of them.

But word quickly reached Gaffar Mussopo, who had progressed a few towns northward. He purpled with rage when he heard how his men had been massacred by brazen Tnemghadi peasants. This could not be tolerated. Rayibab's revolt, he swore, would be crushed and punished, the town made an example for any other Tnemghadi of rebellious mind.

Mussopo turned his army around and headed back toward Rayibab.

At noon they hit the town at a gallop and with naked swords.

A few of the townspeople fought back, defending themselves with rocks or sticks, but they could hardly stand against armed horsemen. Most of the people ran, and covered their heads with their hands as the swords came down

at them. But nothing availed against the furious Urhemmedhins.

Back and forth through the dirt streets they cantered
their horses, smashing down the booths of the marketplace,
killing everyone they could slash at. The carnage went on
until hundreds lay bloody and dead in the streets, and the
remaining townspeople were cowering in their dwellings.

Then Gaffar Mussopo rode through the town calling out
new orders: There was to be a cessation of the slaughter.
Now Rayibab was to be burned, with its people thereby
rousted out of their homes and herded into a ravine near
the outskirts of the town.

Mussopo's order was carried out, and Rayibab went up
in flames. As smoke and ashes choked the town, the cowering people were pushed out into the open. They fully expected death, and indeed, many refused to leave their
homes, preferring to perish in the flames than beneath
Urhemmedhin swords. But no one was killed now; instead,
they were whipped along and herded through the smoke
into the ravine.

It was deep but narrow, a gouge in the earth, and it was
filled up with people. It soon fell dark, but the refugees
huddling there were given light by the conflagration of
their town. Although they were not being molested, they
were kept in the ravine by a ring of Urhemmedhin troops
at its rim, holding their swords poised.

All night long the people crouched there, sleepless,
frightened, in shock. They wept for their own who lay
dead, and they wondered what the morning would bring.

As the sun rose, the soldiers remained standing guard,
but nothing else was happening. The refugees were
let alone, and they began crawling among their neighbors,
looking to reunite families and friends. Some were praying,
and mourning for the dead; some tried to cadge food from
the few who'd brought some; mothers nursed their babies.

The shock was wearing off. Some began to speculate
that they would be relocated in some other town. The sun
was well up in the sky now, and the afternoon of horror
was many hours behind them. Surely, they said, the Urhemmedhins would not harm these surviving refugees.
After all, had it been their intent, the soldiers could have
killed them in the night.

Then, at midmorning, a gaar-drawn wagon drove up

near the ravine. It was laden with heavy wooden kegs, which were methodically unloaded by the soldiers and rolled up to the rim of the ravine.

"It's food!" a few of the refugees cried out. "Thank goodness. They're going to give us breakfast!"

An excited, relieved hum spread through the ravine; many saw the arrival of these kegs as proof that they were safe now.

The kegs were stationed all along the rim. When that was finished, the lids were prised off, and the soldiers dipped big iron ladles into the kegs. Then the soldiers began ladling the liquid from the kegs clumsily out over the crowd of people in the ravine, spraying them with it.

The people could not understand this. One woman put her finger to a big droplet of the stuff that had fallen on her forehead, and she put the finger to her nose to sniff it.

Her face turned white.

"Naphtha!"

The terrible truth hissed through the ravine, as the soldiers worked to ladle it out quickly, two men at each keg, dipping and flinging, sloshing down the people with the naphtha.

A few tried to scramble up out of the ravine, a hopeless try for escape, but the soldiers merely kicked them back. A few were slashed with swords, killed and thrown back. But most of the people made no attempt to get out. They sat in the dirt, keening with fright and terror. Pale and trembling, they covered their faces with their hands and wailed. Some affected dignity: Mothers embraced their children trying to comfort them; husbands comforted their wives; daughters comforted their aged mothers, stroking their white hair.

And a few people screamed out loud, screaming curses at the Urhemmedhins or at their own ghastly fate.

It did not take long for the entire shipment of naphtha to be dispersed. The people were drenched with it, many of them with their clothes plastered wet against their bodies, and the floor of the ravine was a big muddy puddle. Many of the people were vomiting from the noxious naphtha odor, and from their own shock.

The kegs were up-ended to spill out the last drops, and then the soldiers brought forward firebrands of dried grass sheaves and lit them. At a signal from Gaffar Mussopo, all of the brands were tossed simultaneously into the ravine.

Instantly the crowd was overswept with flame. So quick was the flash of the fire that the soldiers leaped back to avoid being singed.

The screams of agony were an ear-splitting crescendo.

A few, on fire, tried to struggle up out of the oven; flaming like torches, their flesh crackling, they shrieked and tried to clamber out of the ravine. But the soldiers shoved them back.

With the dirt baked hard by the heat, the ravine became a crucible in which the people of Rayibab were destroyed.

Within minutes, there were no more trying to escape. There were no more screams to be heard, only the sizzling, roaring of the fire.

While it burned, Gaffar Mussopo gathered his soldiers and moved on.

· 5 ·

ELEVEN NINETY-TWO was a bad year in southern Bergharra.

Its food-producing regions had never fully recovered from the drought of 1176. Even in ordinary times, famine cannot be turned to bounty overnight, and hardship persists for years before the country swings back. But these were times fraught with unrest and upheaval. The system that was first unbalanced by the drought of 1176 was never given a decent chance to right itself.

The Land Decree of Ksavra, promulgated in 1181, was Jehan Henghmani's nostrum to deal with the South's recurring agricultural woes. Had it been implemented in fruitful times, the land reform might well have been successful. But the attempt to radically alter the whole tenure system during a time of want could only exacerbate the problems already present.

Even where they do succeed, land redistributions always involve an initial period of impaired productivity, a natural consequence when the land is being fought over. Farms cannot be tilled, sown, tended, irrigated, and reaped through a season when they are being trodden by conflicting claimants. Not only were the peasants struggling against the barons, but once the barons were dislodged the struggle became even more disruptive, with the tenants fighting among themselves for the biggest, choicest plots. Indeed, these newly landed peasants often tried to make themselves petty landlords in their own right, and the process had to be started all over again.

The complications were many. Under the old sharecropper system, the landlords had often provided the farm implements, draft animals, and seeds. Exit the landlords and these vital resources became unavailable. Few tenants could afford them, and moreover, much was destroyed in the upset. It was hard to protect goods like that. The countryside was swamped with roving bands of the dispossessed. Robbing what they could, trampling fields, ruining half-grown crops, these gypsy bands created havoc.

While outlawry was on the rise, the ranks of the honest farmers dwindled. Continual warfare, constant recruitments, and civil strife meant a steady attrition of able hands to work the land. Particularly acute too was the shortage of livestock. Few peasants had been able to afford to keep and feed their animals, and millions of these were slaughtered for food. During past famines, the landlords had always acted with an eye to the future in protecting livestock, but the starving peasants could think only of today's hunger. They did not consider what animals they might need next year. As lean times continued, the goats and chickens, the gaars and oxen to pull the plows all became fewer and fewer.

Perhaps the most pernicious effect of the turmoil was the haphazard, heedless cultivation of the land. Most of the southern soil had never been very rich. Only by judicious crop rotation and the development of sophisticated agricultural techniques had the barons been able to make this land profitable. But such niceties went by the boards now. Without the landlords insisting on crop rotation and instructing them on all details, the peasants gave these matters no thought. They were starving, and were desperate to grow as much as they could. The result, inevitably, was the ruination of the soil. Year after year, the harder the peasants beat their land to squeeze more crops out of it, the poorer did the soil become, and the smaller the crops.

Not just the landlords, but all social and political stability was gone. The old Tnemghadi regime had relied heavily upon the barons as the bulwark of the order; the whole political infrastructure had rested upon them. Now their power had collapsed, but Jehan Henghmani's presence could replace them only gradually. In the meantime there was a gaping power vacuum that was filled by an assortment of brigands, warlords, and adventurers. With small armed bands, opportunists of this stripe carved out little spheres of power, reigning by terrorism and extorting tribute from the peasants. These gangs left the populace completely impoverished, without the means to continue working their land.

Jehan's attempt to replace the Tnemghadi political structure—and the warlords—with locally elected councils was plagued by problems. The councils concentrated on administering the towns and cities, leaving the unruly peasant farmers largely to themselves. Attempts to tax the farmers or mandate crop rotation always met with violent resistance. Besides, the councils were elected by the peasants themselves, and responsible to them; hence taxation of the rich became the undeviating principle. But the rich were quickly taxed out of existence. Whence then would needed revenues be garnered? The councils naturally quailed from taxing their own constituency—and thus became bankrupt and impotent.

It proved impossible to establish local councils that could stand against the armies of adventurers. While Jehan's own armies had spread throughout Urhemma in the late 1180s setting up the councils, after them came the bandits and warlords, undoing the work.

It was a ceaseless tug of war. For a number of years, the Urhemmedhin army did manage to keep the brigands under some degree of control, returning to town after town, ousting them again and again. This could be done as long as a large southern army was maintained. But once the Urhemmedhin military force became concentrated instead upon the North, the power vacuum in the South was larger than ever. One by one, the villages succumbed to more or less permanent warlord rule.

The disease even afflicted the larger towns and cities now. Sometimes bloody battles would be fought between the citizen militia and the outlaw forces, but sooner or later, the attackers would prevail. One after another, the important cities fell: Ravdasbur, Jamarra, Hsokhso, Rabiznaz, Bebjella, Mughdad, Pamliyah.

It had all started with the drought of 1176. Since then, despite the elements' benignity, a vicious cycle had set in, and each bad year made the next one more difficult from the outset. Each year brought smaller crops and more hunger. Plainly, it would only take one year of bad weather to produce an epic disaster.

That cruel year came in 1192.

In 1192, the skies were unstinting with broiling sunshine and were niggardly with rain. The gray soil was beaten by the sun, baked like clay in a kiln, scarred across with the cracks and fissures of dehydration. Clods of this soil were hard dry chunks that would crumble into powder.

This was hardly soil at all. Seeds refused to germinate, and where shoots did dare poke through the crust, even the hardiest were quickly stamped down by the merciless sun.

The people were seized by a starvation more brutal than any plague or any warlord. Even a warlord might relent, but not this famine. The suffering was titanic. Millions died. Few even hoped to survive—for surely this was Sexrexatra, returning at last to fulfill his vow, and to devour all his children.

Affected most severely were the infants. Births were times of weeping, not of joy. It seemed perverse to bring babes into a world where they had no chance. So ill-fed were the mothers that there was rarely milk in their breasts to feed their infants.

The children could not withstand the dual ravages of malnourishment and the diseases to which it made them vulnerable. For such weak children, any slight infection would be fatal. Those who did not perish of disease wasted away slowly. With not even water to bloat their bellies, grown children shriveled to baby weight, their muscles lost the power to move their sticklike limbs. Even if food came, they were too sick to take it.

Adults too suffered the same slow death. Discolored bags of bones, they would crawl in hopeless search for food, until they could no longer move. Then they would remain lying in the open streets and roadways, unable to come out of the blistering sun, their mouths filled with their black, parched tongues. Blind from hunger and the sun, they would not fend off the scavengers who would feast on their few remaining shreds of flesh.

At Ksiritsa, Jehan Henghmani sat upon the Tnemenghouri Throne.

As though mirroring the travail of the lands he ruled, his health was suffering. The strains and exertions of the last sixteen years had taken a heavy toll. An ordinary man might not have survived them, but not even one of Jehan's robust constitution could endure such a life without effect. Now he felt himself weakening and aging rapidly. The old aches from the dungeons assailed his body with unrelent-

ing acuteness; he was beset too by powerful headaches,
fever, dizzy spells, nausea. Some days he would have to
struggle to pull himself up out of bed, and often his hands
would tremble like leaves in a breeze. But through it all,
he kept going, he refused to be mastered by the frailties of
his body.

He pushed himself like a master whips a slave. Ever
more deeply he immersed himself in governmental business, spending endless hours conferring with his underlings, poring over documents, penning state papers. Little
time was begrudged to sleep. Ignoring his abused body, he
worked harder than ever before, since what afflicted him
most now was not physical. More than ever, Jehan Henghmani was gnawed by apprehension and uncertainty.

Every day the problems seemed to multiply. In the
north, the Tnemghadi were stubbornly resisting his rule,
and the Akfakh were pressing ever harder; but it was the
South that made Jehan's heart ache. The starvation was
massive and he felt impotent to deal with it. He could not
draw food out of the air. Moreover, the political structure
which he had so lovingly nurtured was collapsing. Starvation made the people ever more vulnerable prey to bandits
and warlords, and the map of Prasid Urhemma was becoming meaningless. The real map would have shown not
one great country, but a thousand little fiefdoms. Bit by
bit, Jehan felt his people slipping away from him.

Even the City of Ganda Saingam fell, in 1192, to the
warlord Nekatsim Nosnibor. This was a particularly bitter
piece of news for Jehan to swallow, for Ganda Saingam's
council had survived through nine years, having been the
model for the system he had tried to establish throughout
the South. Well in memory too was the ecstatic welcome
he'd received at Ganda Saingam.

Dearly Jehan wished that he could mass an army and
redeem this beloved city from the warlord Nosnibor. But it
was out of the question: every Urhemmedhin soldier that
could be put under arms was desperately needed in the
North. By now, in fact, all but token forces had been withdrawn from the South.

Jehan wept for Ganda Saingam, and he wept too for
his child, the Assembly. The divisiveness that had marked
its vote for war had only worsened. In the third Assembly
wise old Taddhai was deposed as President, and the body's

deliberations degenerated into nothing but partisan bicker-
ing. The fourth Assembly had been ill attended and had
adjourned itself after only two months.

Once, all too briefly, the heart of the nation and the
fount of all political authority, the Assembly's work now
seemed pointless. Its members had little will to go on making laws, and what laws they did make were simply ignored by the usurpers who ruled most of the country.
Unwilling to see this once-bright hope become a travesty,
Jehan issued a decree indefinitely postponing the fifth Assembly.

There was nowhere he could turn for solace. Even
within his own Court the disease of disintegration seemed
rampant. Jehan was repelled by the decadence of his entourage. Coming into luxury after years in the wilderness,
the Urhemmedhin leaders supped deeply. All around were
fine foppish clothes, pretty giggling women, and feasts of
rich delicacies.

These affectations Jehan might have tolerated had he
not felt so keenly a basic dearth of competent and honest
men. The regime was worse than merely decadent; everyone to whom the Emperor turned seemed unscrupulous
and worthless, ridden with cupidity.

One exception seemed to be the Treasury. The Minister, Revi Ontondra, was an old fish dealer who knew nothing of finance, and did not pretend to know anything.
After Golana's death, however, Jehan had recruited a
crafty merchant named Chardar Kozhbob to serve as Ontondra's deputy. In reality, of course, the affairs of the department were placed almost entirely in Kozhbob's able
hands.

But then Jehan happened to notice that some of the
shipments of silver coins from the mint had more of a
greenish tinge than others. An assay revealed their fineness
fell short of the prescribed level, and this was not happenstance. A discreet investigation proved that Kozhbob was
responsible, embezzling the silver and replacing it with tin.
It turned out to be only the crudest of several schemes by
which he was milking the Treasury.

Reluctantly, Jehan ordered Kozhbob put on trial and
executed as a deterrent against further such misdeeds.
Hapless Ontondra was sent away to fill the conveniently

vacant governorship of Prewtna. But deprived of an adroit hand at the till, the Treasury Department floundered, and with it, the Empire's finances. Meanwhile too, corruption went on unabated. The more Palace bureaus and officials Jehan investigated, the more thievery and graft he uncovered. It was a virulent cancer permeating his regime.

One of the most troubled bureaus had long been that of Agriculture, having the impossible task of managing the land tenure tangle in both North and South, while the country was in the grip of its worst famine ever. This grave responsibility belonged to Hnayim Yahu, as it had for eight years now; and despite being an unlearned former thug, Yahu was bearing up well.

Then, Jehan was made aware by informers of a massive scandal infecting the Agriculture Ministry. Instead of uniformly pushing forward the land redistribution, its officials were extracting systematic bribes from landlords in return for leaving them alone. Literally dozens of men were implicated, up to the highest level. This included the Minister, Hnayim Yahu.

Jehan could not bring himself to act until the evidence had mounted so powerfully that Yahu could not be exonerated. Loath as he was to lose such a loyal old comrade, the Emperor finally called him in for a private audience, and showed him the affidavits detailing his corruption.

Hnayim Yahu sat in a chair and silently examined the documents. He had never been very good at reading and writing. But slowly, his face turned red, and beads of sweat popped out on his forehead.

"Well," Jehan whispered, "what have you got to say?"

"There is no point in denying anything." Yahu's voice was so choked as to be almost inaudible. "I guess it's all over for me."

"Hnayim, I thought you were the most loyal of my friends. We have been together for a quarter of a century. How could you do this? How could you do this to me?"

Yahu turned his beet-red face away, and begged Jehan to spare his life.

But the Emperor said no.

·6·

ELEVEN NINETY-TWO was over, but the new year brought no joy, no deliverance.

Jehan felt suffocated, sinking in quicksand. He too remembered the old Sexrexatra myth, and it did seem as though some cataclysmic force was at work to wreck everything. A glimmer of comfort might be taken from the Bergharran army's tenacious defense against the Akfakh—but even here, the war's cost was staggering, and the Bergharrans were being slowly ground down. The Akfakh shadowed Jehan like a huge boulder poised on a ledge, on the verge of crashing down on him.

Conferences with his ministers were ever more frequent, and ever more depressing. Repeatedly he would broach dramatic proposals for dealing with the crisis.

"Let us try to make peace," Jehan might say. "At least let us open up negotiations with Znarf. We can offer him a few Tnemghadi provinces. What is that to us?"

"No," the answer always came, "we can't give up a single inch of ground. The Tnemghadi lands are the only ones right now producing any food. And they're part of Bergharra. It's our sacred trust to defend it, to prevent those jackals from gaining a toehold."

And someone else might say: "Besides, Znarf won't be appeased with a few meager provinces. That would only whet his appetite for more. We must be strong in resisting."

Jehan would wrangle for hours, only to leave these meetings in exhaustion and exasperation. His ministers preached strength, but they themselves were weak. All the good men—Kawaras, Yahu, Ontondra—all the strong men were gone. Yahu had been succeeded by his deputy, Avdoul Ktahrassa, but Ktahrassa himself was complaining that the regime was now comprised of second-raters. Ex-

cept for Jehan, there was not a strong man at the Palace
on whom responsibility could rest. And not even Jehan,
with his health ebbing and his stamina broken, could cope
with the ever-deepening morass.

An infusion of new vigor was needed; even the weakest
reeds of the regime could see this now. Some tough, fresh
blood was needed, to replace the useless Kirdahi as Grand
Chamberlain and impart a forceful new direction. It
was, indeed, a new Jehan they wanted—but where could
he be found?

Before long, all fingers were pointing in the same direction. Ktahrassa and the other ministers were clamoring
with one voice for an obvious candidate. He was a man
who had known suffering and want, they said, who had
risen from the peasantry, proved himself in combat, ascended through the ranks and had ably acquitted himself
in high responsibility. Through all that, he was still a
young and vigorous man.

"Too young, perhaps," Jehan objected.

"He is past thirty."

"At any rate, he's too headstrong and bloodthirsty. He
hates the Tnemghadi almost beyond reason."

"But that's precisely what we need now," Ktahrassa answered. "A tough, no-nonsense man, untainted by corruption. And who among us loves the Tnemghadi?"

Jehan resisted. But in his own mind, he was unsure. It
was clear enough that a strong man was needed; was
Jehan afraid that that man would be stronger than he? His
own accelerating weakness was an infuriating thing for
him to bear. And, in his weakness, he knew that he would
ultimately yield. His ministers were right. There was no
alternative.

For more than two years, Gaffar Mussopo had been at
the northern front, fighting the Akfakh.

The war's fortunes went back and forth, but the barbarians' gains always kept ahead of their reverses. At one
point, the ferocious tribesmen even succeeded in pushing
the Bergharrans back to the border of Rashid Province.
They were advancing upon the town of Kirithmedda, and
there, Gaffar Mussopo vowed to stop them. Many of his
troops were Tnemghadi, who were difficult to keep in line,

but this time Gaffar devised a plan for surmounting that problem.

Just outside of Kirithmedda, he built a sturdy wall of wooden posts. His officers derided this, believing that no wooden barrier would hold the wild tribesmen back. But Gaffar persisted in his strategy.

Then, as the enemy neared, he ordered his men to dig in their defense-works—*outside the wall.* They protested and cursed their General, convinced he had gone mad, but Gaffar was unrelenting and he whipped them into line.

He had thereby put his own army up against a wall. When the Akfakh struck, the trapped Bergharrans could not flee. Gaffar had built a barrier against cowardice, and with their backs against it, his troops fought for their lives.

This time, the Akfakh were turned back; Kirithmedda was saved, and the barbarian advance was checked.

It was through ingenious schemes like this that Gaffar Mussopo was able to stave off a rout. In another major battle, he had his own men chained together to prevent their running away. He armed them with peculiar long hooks of his own design, to hold the enemy warriors at bay while swatting them. He even created exploding bombs principled on fireworks, and armored wagons with archers concealed inside them.

These innovations were often brilliant successes, but they could not effect miracles, and the Akfakh pushed slowly forward.

And mightily as Gaffar Mussopo labored to defeat them, his mind was not exclusively fixed upon the battlefield. He received a constant stream of letters from his allies in the Palace at Ksiritsa, keeping him abreast of developments throughout the Empire. Gaffar was well aware of the corruption of Kozhbob, Yahu, and so many others, of the miring incompetence that was suffocating the capital, of the ravaging warlords in the South. He was acutely aware of the mass starvation that was becoming murderous even in the North.

Now, suddenly, in the year 1193, all these problems were dumped into Gaffar Mussopo's lap. He received a summons from the Emperor Jehan and the entire council of ministers, asking that he return to the capital—to become Grand Chamberlain of Bergharra.

Leaving the further prosecution of the war in the hands

of junior officers, Gaffar Mussopo hastily selected a group of his most trusted aides, and together with them, left at once for Ksiritsa.

Immediately upon his arrival, still dusty from the road, he was ushered straight up to the Emperor's private chambers in the Heaven Palace.

"His Excellency, the Grand Chamberlain Gaffar Mussopo," announced a costumed squire, stepping smartly aside to open the way into Jehan's presence.

Gaffar was stunned, the breath whipped out of him by what he saw.

The Emperor was lying abed, propped up by a mound of pillows. Although swathed in robes and blankets, it was plain that Jehan's body had shriveled into a shadow of its erstwhile burliness. It was a stringy neck that jutted out of the bedclothes, and the bones of Jehan's face stood out, further altering his already mutilated features. His complexion was lifeless, and the whole image was one of debility.

The young man bowed, keeping his face down to conceal his astonishment at Jehan's condition.

"I've had a little seizure or something," the Emperor explained with a crooked smile. His voice, coming from one side of his mouth, was slightly slurred, and to compensate for that he was speaking with careful slowness. "My left side isn't much good to me right now, but the doctors assure me it will improve. I should be back on my feet before long."

"I dearly hope so. I will pray for your health, and I'm sure that millions are praying for you too."

"Well, I didn't call you back here to prattle about my old bones. Sit down, Gaffar." Jehan pointed to a chair with his right hand, while the left remained motionless on the bed.

"Yes, Your Majesty."

"As you know, it was the consensus of the ministers that you become Grand Chamberlain. Frankly, there's no one else left who's worth a falu."

Gaffar nodded. "I am honored by your trust and will do my best to be worthy of it."

"I am sure you will."

"Tell me, though, what about Kirdahi?"

Jehan coughed and shook his head. "I offered to give him some other post, but I suppose he couldn't stand the humiliation of being replaced. He's gone. He was always a scared chicken, and must have decided to scat while he still had his head."

"Not surprising. Weakling."

"Unfortunately, Kirdahi took more than just his head with him. He made off with a goodly bit of gold. I'm afraid that raiding the Treasury has become a very popular sport."

"And we've got to crack down on it!"

"Crack down? I've executed Kozhbob, Yahu, and scores of others. What more could be done?"

"You were lenient. They should have been tortured."

"You toss that off so casually. But I suppose it's to be expected from the *Hero of Rayibab*."

Gaffar's face reddened. "Rayibab! Let me tell you something about Rayibab! What I did there strengthened your crown more than anything else in the last two years. Should I have let those rebels defy us with impunity? Our country is in desperate trouble, and desperate action is needed to save it."

"What 'desperate actions' do you propose, besides massacring women and children?"

"Have I been called here to be Grand Chamberlain, or the butt of insults?"

Jehan wiped his face with his one good hand. He seemed to shrink down into the pillows. "All right, Gaffar," he said hoarsely, "let us not quarrel. The country can't afford it. Rayibab won't be mentioned again. So let's get on with it; we have more pressing subjects to discuss."

"I agree completely, Your Majesty," said Gaffar, as though subserviently. "I have given much thought to our predicament, too.

"Number one: We need still more troops, and I propose a greatly expanded conscription. The penalty for refusing to serve will be death. Southerners will have to be drafted to fight the warlords down there and to strengthen our garrisons in the North; food has been getting scarcer there, and unrest has been on the upswing. Then, to bear the brunt of the war against Znarf we must draft more Tnemghadi soldiers, just go rounding them up from village to village and ship them to the front. The Akfakh will chew them up as fast as we can send them, but Tnemghadi are expendable."

"How many Urhemmedhins do you propose to draft?"

"One million."

Jehan gagged. "One million? They won't like that, dragging so many husbands and sons off into the army."

"I don't care whether they like it or not. It's got to be done. And another thing they may not like: The village council scheme must be abolished. It was perhaps a well-intentioned experiment, but the councils have proven themselves impotent."

"But Gaffar, they must be given a fair chance."

"We can't take chances in times like these. At any rate, the truth is that the councils exist more on paper than in reality now. Even Ganda Saingam has succumbed. We must have strong local officials; and they must be appointed from Ksiritsa. Perhaps in better times we can give your scheme another try."

Jehan looked long and sadly at Gaffar. Then he said, "All right, what else?"

"Then, of course, we have a terrific food shortage. I have a twofold plan. For the short run, it must be our firm policy that the Tnemghadi starve before our own people. Every shokh of produce raised in the North must be shipped south.

"For the long run, it's obvious that land redistribution is a failure. The old Decree of Ksavra must be rescinded. We must reverse our policy of giving land to the peasants, and promote once more the development of large estates—take the land away from the peasants if necessary. Only then can the land be worked sensibly, and our agriculture put back on its feet."

"You offer me some very bitter fare."

"Good medicine is often bitter."

"But Gaffar, think what you're proposing! To steal land from the peasants! After so many of them have fought and died for that land!"

"It must be done," Gaffar said drily.

Jehan's eye closed, and his head sank deeper into the pillows. The muscles twitched around his neck and mouth. Finally, he spoke.

"I will not do this thing," he said.

"Very well," Gaffar answered, "then I will."

Jehan's eyes jolted open in astonishment.

"You heard what I said. If you won't cooperate, I will get it done somehow myself. But it's got to be done. It's crucial to our future. Unless I can take the necessary steps to improve crops, it is pointless for me to be Grand Chamberlain."

Jehan shook his head slowly, but it was not a gesture of negation. It signified his weary resignation to the inevitable.

"Do what you must," he whispered.

· 7 ·

ONCE ENSCONCED in the Heaven Palace, Gaffar Mussopo quickly took control of the government into his one hand.

He began with a housecleaning among its top officials. Many of them were summarily dismissed, replaced by the young officers whom Mussopo had brought back with him from the front. They in turn ousted dozens more subordinates. Meanwhile, the war upon corruption was prosecuted with ruthless vigor, and torture was reintroduced both for extracting information and for punishment. There were no complacent faces at the Palace now.

Aiding Mussopo's assumption of power was the Emperor's condition. Jehan was not improving; he remained bedridden, partially paralyzed, and thus isolated. He was unable to attend the meetings of the council of ministers; and while he tried to keep abreast of things through frequent briefings by Mussopo, the new Grand Chamberlain had a relatively free hand. This was true not only of the day-to-day minutiae of government, but of the major policy reversals that Mussopo sponsored.

Expanded conscription swelled the Urhemmedhin armies to enforce the new decrees, many of them unpalatable to Urhemmedhins as well as to Tnemghadi. Unrelenting, Gaffar Mussopo ignored the protests. Throughout the South, the land Jehan had given to the peasants was taken away from them by Mussopo. In many places it was the army officers who seized the land and became the new barons, building old-style sharecropper estates. Meanwhile the same army men displaced the village councils and took up arms against the warlords.

This new ascendancy of the army was resisted widely by the peasants, many of them waving copies of the laws passed by the National Assembly, laws which supposedly guaranteed their rights. But the new Grand Chamberlain would not let laws stand in the way of his reshaping Urhemma. Where the laws conflicted with his program, Gaffar browbeat Jehan to abrogate them; and whenever the Emperor summoned up the energy to refuse, Gaffar responded by simply ignoring the inconvenient laws.

His rule over the Tnemghadi tightened too, bolstered by the reinforcements he brought up from the South, and every month saw the promulgation of new strictures. A dozen different taxes were imposed. The Tnemghadi were even taxed to pay for the temples to Urhem. Most obnoxious to them, though, was the food policy: In every northern village, food stores were expropriated by force to feed the army or to be shipped south.

Thus, the agony of starvation that had tormented the South now fell with all its fury on the North as well.

Despite all of the dramatic changes wrought by the new regime, despite its bold vigor, this demon of starvation laughed in its face. Little or no progress was made in restoring prosperity, and a similar tale was told of the Akfakh war. Despite the ever-mounting numbers of troops thrown at them, the barbarians could not be stopped. By the end of Mussopo's first year in office, the Akfakh had completed their conquest of Jammir and Agabatur provinces, most of Gharr, and the major part of Rashid. Kirithmedda, where Gaffar had once blocked their advance, was finally overrun.

From the afflicted regions, a flood of refugees poured southward, crowding into Muraven, Kholandra, and Tnemurabad, the provinces thus far untouched by Akfakh depredations. By now, the people of the outlying regions had scant confidence in the regime's ability to hold the Akfakh back; and as the tribesmen neared, the people would abandon their homes and flee. This constant stream of bedraggled refugees aggravated the severity of the food shortage, and many of those who escaped the Akfakh could not escape starvation.

Then, in the month of Jhevla, 1194, at Sajnithaddhani, the provincial capital of Muraven, the Tnemghadi rose up in rebellion against Urhemmedhin rule.

This was not the first such rising; there had in fact been many flare-ups of unrest throughout the North. All of them, like Rayibab's, had been quickly and brutally suppressed. But the Sajnithaddhani revolt was different. This one was carefully planned, organized with military precision, and well financed. The rebels were primed with a sophisticated array of armaments. And, unready for such an astutely managed insurrection, the large Urhemmedhin garrison fell.

Not only was Sajnithaddhani liberated, but the Tnemghadi citizen militia that sprang into being then routed a second Urhemmedhin force sent to recapture the city. The Urhemmedhins were expelled from the whole western half of Muraven.

Sajnithaddhani was proclaimed the capital of a new Tnemghadi nation, that swore to reclaim all the lands overrun by the Urhemmedhin usurpers and restore freedom to the northern people. The guiding hand behind this rebellion was a man well versed in the ways of revolution, for he had spent more than a decade at it.

His name was Jephos Kirdahi.

"So now we are mired in three wars," Jehan Henghmani said with a surpassing weariness. "We are fighting the Akfakh; we are fighting the bandit warlords in the South; and now a war against the Tnemghadi rebels and our old friend Kirdahi."

"A fine old friend!" snapped Gaffar. "I never understood your keeping him around. He was one of your own torturers, murderer of your child. Now he's stolen your gold and uses it to fight you. You should have gotten rid of him long ago."

Jehan shook his head against the pillows. "As long as we were in the South, I could have found no one more loyal; he was bound to me by fear."

"And well he should fear you now," Gaffar said crisply, smacking his one hand on the chair arm. "We shall crush him."

"No, my friend."

There was a moment of silence.

"What do you mean?"

"Just what I said." Jehan coughed from deep in his lungs and then resumed in a scratchy, low voice. "We shall not oppose Kirdahi."

"But for the sake of—"

"Please hear me out, Gaffar. Lying helpless here in bed, all alone, I've had plenty of time to think. And I have reached a decision.

"Sarbat Satanichadh tried to save this country. But he lacked the means as he was a weak, decadent ruler, beset by rebellion within as well as by invasion from without. No matter what he did, the Akfakh gained ground.

"When Sarbat's failure was clear, Bergharra turned to us, asked us to save her. We seemed stronger. But we too have been hounded by internal strife: the warlords in the South, Tnemghadi resistance in the North. Perhaps more important, we are doomed to failure simply because it's not our land that we're fighting for. It's Tnemghadi land, and we are Urhemmedhins. So the Akfakh continue to gain.

"Now, Gaffar, it is Jephos Kirdahi's turn. He may not be a brilliant man, nor even a strong man. But the important thing is that he is a Tnemghadi, he is of this land. He's neither decadent nor a despot, and so, the Tnemghadi will fight for him—certainly with more enthusiasm than they fight for us.

"And then, what of the South? I consecrated myself to the crusade to make Urhemma free. But we have drifted away from that noble struggle. We originally came north only to secure the permanent freedom of the South. Yet now we are a thousand lim removed from our homeland, fighting an enemy our people never knew, over land they don't need. Instead of lifting tyranny from our people's shoulders, we are pressing it upon another people. And in doing it we are draining ourselves, bleeding ourselves white. To prosecute this insane war, we have even sunk to enslaving and starving our own people.

"Yes, it is insane." Jehan shook his head sadly. "How could it have happened? We have reached too far away from our true goals. Too far away from home.

"But the time has come for sanity to be restored: for us to go home.

"We shall go home now, home to our own city. Naddeghomra, in the bosom of our people. We shall breathe the pure air of Naddeghomra, and there we'll be regenerated. Home at Naddeghomra we shall bind our wounds, and go forth to fight the true enemies, lawlessness, tyranny, and hunger. Nevermore need we fear the Tnemghadi. Prasid Urhemma can thrive in freedom now, *yarushkadharra* will reign; as we envisioned so long ago,

we shall come to the nation of peace and love and bliss.
"We shall come home."

Jehan's hoarse voice finally became silent. This speech
had greatly taxed his weakened body, and with difficulty
he caught his breath in gulps. But despite the strain, his
face was almost beaming in a calm, as though his words
had carried him home already.

"Your Majesty," Gaffar Mussopo said firmly, "it cannot be done. Kirdahi would never succeed in holding the
Akfakh back. They'd overrun the whole North in months
and then they'd come right after us in the South."

"Then let them! I would far rather fight them on our
own territory, fight them for our own homeland. Then we
can beat them."

Gaffar shook his head. "What you propose is out of the
question. Perhaps your mind has become muddled by
your illness. Not only do you ignore the obvious military
consequences that would ensue from abandoning the
North, but you seem to be caught up by some ethereal
vision of the South. 'Breath the pure air of Naddeghomra,'
you say. *The South today is a snakepit, the air is the air of
death!* The bandits and warlords are running riot, people
are starving to death by the millions, so fast they're not
even being buried. It's a jungle, a nightmare. All right,
abandon the North you say, and fight the hunger. But
right now the only food with which to fight it happens to
come from the North.

"After what the damned Tnemghadi did to us for centuries, I will hang before I see them get back an inch of
their land. We will stand and fight if we all must perish
doing it."

Jehan coughed and struggled for breath. "Gaffar, Gaffar, my dear friend," he said, in a voice that begged indulgence. "I have given you a free hand up to now.
Admittedly I've been in no condition to interfere much.
But I must tell you that on this decision, my mind is set,
and I must insist upon it."

"You may insist all you like. It won't be done."

"Gaffar, if you will not cooperate I'll have to find myself another Grand Chamberlain, and that would be most
regrettable."

"No, sire, I will not cooperate with your mad scheme,
and I will not relinquish my position either."

Jehan's face had been growing increasingly red with consternation; now he was seized by another violent fit of coughing, and when it was over, he spoke with a barely audible croak. "You seem to forget that I am still the Emperor. I shall call the ministers together."

"They will not come. They won't obey you any longer; they are my men now. The fact is, everyone in the Palace believes by now that you've gone off your head. It's become a lamented but accepted fact. This scheme of yours to return to Naddeghomra will only be seen as evidence of your madness.

"Bergharra needs a strong ruler now," the Grand Chamberlain said, rising from his chair. "And that is why you are no longer ruling."

·8·

WITH A CLOUDED EYE, Jehan Henghmani looked upon his grandson.

The vision of his one eye had been impaired by his illness, but Jehan knew that standing before him was the living reminder of his most hideous memories. The boy bore the face of Nimajneb Grebzreh, who had begotten him that night of horror in the dungeon. And it was for the sake of this boy that Maiya had murdered beloved Golana and her newborn son.

Pained by the very thought of this grandson who grotesquely bore his own name, Jehan had seen little of him in the past seven years. Despite his being the Crown Prince, Jehandai was barred from the Court at Naddeghomra. There were no friends for him as he grew up, his position was too exalted, and at the same time, too accursed. So Jehandai grew up alone.

He kept to himself, playing endlessly with his toy soldiers, and later, reading to pass empty hours. He was quiet, secretive, almost furtive. Rarely did he even show his face outside his room.

Jehandai had come to Ksiritsa only through Gaffar Mussopo's acquiescence. But he hadn't stayed there long, and followed Mussopo to the northern front. It was only in the life of a common soldier that the boy found any satisfaction. That's what he was, a soldier in the ranks. But Mussopo kept him close at hand, as a part-time aide-de-camp, and when he became Grand Chamberlain, Jehandai was among those who returned with him to Ksiritsa. Mussopo made sure the boy did not revert, however, to a sullen confinement. With the Emperor bedridden, Jehandai was free to roam the Palace under Mussopo's aegis, and even to consort with the other ministers.

419

Now he was almost eighteen years old, grown to manhood. He stood erect before the Emperor wearing a military tunic.

"Hello, Jehandai," the old invalid said, trying to smile.

"Hello, Garpaban."

"I am deeply pleased that you agreed to come to me." Jehandai nodded, but did not otherwise respond.

"I summoned you, frankly, because I am dying. The doctors keep talking optimistically, but I am not fooled. There isn't much time left to me."

Jehan paused, and coughed, intentionally giving Jehandai an opportunity to make a profession of sympathy and concern. But the youth said nothing.

"So very soon now, Jehandai, you will become the Emperor of Bergharra."

This time, Jehan thought he could detect a smirk of satisfaction in the boy's face, but he ignored it. "I want us to be on good terms before I die. I want us to forget the past. I am willing to admit that my conduct toward you has been cold and bad. It was unfair to you. But perhaps too, you can understand what made me act that way. So let us be reconciled before I die. Please say so, grandson."

"All right," the youth said, revealing nothing of his attitude.

Jehan blinked his one eye firmly in acceptance, and said, "I am glad. I am very glad. I bear you only good will now, and I earnestly wish you the utmost success in your reign."

"I will try to achieve it."

"I am sure you will. But would you permit this old man to unburden himself of some advice, upon which he has thought much?"

"I will listen to what you have to say."

"Once I am gone, once you've become Emperor, there is only one possible course to be followed, only one plan that can save you. This thing you must do, or else reap a whirlwind of disaster.

"As soon as you take the crown, Jehandai, you must quit Ksiritsa. You must leave the North, leave off fighting the Akfakh, leave off fighting Kirdahi, leave all of that morass behind you, and repair homeward to the South. It is a troubled land, but it is our homeland. You must take us to Naddeghomra."

Jehan repeated all the arguments he had given Gaffar Mussopo for abandoning the North. And then, he had one further piece of advice: Gaffar Mussopo must be un-horsed. This man, Jehan said, had gotten too much power into his one hand; he was a cruel fanatic and a despot. The old Emperor warned that unless Jehandai destroyed Gaffar, Gaffar would destroy Jehandai, and the whole nation with him.

"Please Jehandai, I beseech you to heed my words, for the good of our people and for your own good too. Tell me that you will do it. Then I can die in peace."

Jehandai stuck his chin out. "No, old man. I will not get rid of Gaffar. He and I are of one mind. He warned me to expect this last-minute plea from you. But I agree with him, not you. You are wrong, indeed, you are mad."

"How can you speak to me this way?" Jehan stammered in confusion, his face turning livid.

"What do you expect, old man? For years you treated me like a cursed creature, a criminal, all on account of other people's crimes. For seven years you wouldn't even see me. Only now that you're dying, and everyone else refuses to listen to you, have you come to me in desperation.

"You say you want our reconciliation, but what you really want is to use me, to reach beyond the grave and accomplish through me what you're too weak to do yourself."

"Jehandai—"

"But I won't let you. I will not go back to Naddeghomra—the wretched place where your curse was branded upon me. Naddeghomra was your city, but it won't be mine. This is my city, Ksiritsa, the city where my seed was planted. Here I shall rule, I shall be the Emperor of all Bergharra.

"After all, who is better apt than I to rule the whole of Bergharra? The Empire is half Tnemghadi, half Urhemmedhin, and the two have always been at each other's throats. But I myself am half Tnemghadi and half Urhemmedhin! That is why it always was my destiny to rule Bergharra. I will not give up half the Empire, I will not give up half my birthright—not when my mother sacrificed herself to save it for me!

"So may Naddeghomra burn, as far as I'm concerned.

And the same goes for you, old man. I won't forgive you. To hell with your reconciliation!"

Jehandai spat at his grandfather and stalked out.

Jehan Henghmani looked out upon the world with a dying eye.

All had come to nothing.

The last embers of his life were dimming and sputtering out at last, but he was not aggrieved, not at that. If anything, his grief was coming to an end.

His life had been an odyssey of pain. It had known high moments, but more persistent was the pain—in the dungeons and now in his lingering death. And physical agony was the least of it. Love, it seemed, had been vouchsafed him only to inflict pain when it was taken away. All the people he had loved were lost to him; some had even betrayed him. Perhaps, he thought, he had not loved them well enough. But that provided no solace. He was dying all alone.

Not only for his personal tragedies was Jehan full of grief. His own travail would soon be buried with his ashes. Not so the tragedy of his people.

On his deathbed, Jehan Henghmani wept not for himself, but for his people—the Urhemmedhins and the Tnemghadi too. The distinction seemed immaterial. They were all people, regardless of their eyebrows. The wrongness of suffering did not depend upon the race of people who endured it. And Jehan, who had labored to relieve suffering, had actually brought more misery to the world than perhaps any other man in history. He had struggled to end starvation, but more people were starving now than ever. He had worked himself into an early grave trying to give men freedom, but more than ever they were tyrannized. He was like Sexrexatra, chewing up his own children. Indeed, was Jehan Henghmani the *Ur-Rasvadhi* —or the prophesied return of Sexrexatra?

How could this nightmare have descended? How could all Jehan's works have turned out so perversely?

His thoughts turned to the Book of Urhem, the creed that was the guiding light of his whole movement. Jehan had put an end to the Tnemghadi emperor-worship and had given the religion of Urhem its day at last. So noble a thing this had seemed! So good and right and rational the Urhem creed had seemed!

Only now did Jehan suddenly see the ironic truth. He had been wrong, the whole religion was wrong. When he thought about the Book of Urhem now, he could only laugh bitterly at it.

King Urhem had not been a saint, but a fool. When he had prayed for Osatsana's life, his only mistake had been to imagine that any god might hear his prayer at all. Neither Urhem nor any god could have saved her, any more than it was a god that took her life.

Stupidly though, Urhem blamed himself for her death. Supposedly he had sinned against the sanctity of life. But what sin was it to pray for life against death? And how could it have upheld the sanctity of life to extinguish one person's life for the sin of another?

Yet, in penance for his wholly imagined sin, King Urhem renounced his throne and died a beggar. Jehan now saw this as ridiculous and contemptible. What did Urhem's act accomplish? This asinine renunciation left his kingdom leaderless and directly paved the way for the Tnemghadi conquest. That was what sainted Urhem had done for his people.

The Book of Urhem vaunted the sanctity of human life. And at this, too, Jehan could only laugh bitterly.

His own life now was passing from the world. And even he, who had molded that world in his hands, was dying in humiliation, labeled mad and abjured by everyone. Not even great Jehan Henghmani's life was held priceless now, it would not fetch a copper falu any more.

And if an emperor's life was devoid of value, what about the life of a peasant? What could it mean, when millions of them had died for a man who himself proved worthless? When millions starved to death because of what that worthless emperor had done?

It was in a very different light now that Jehan could reassess the old Tnemghadi religion. They had accounted life valueless, existing for no purpose save the pleasure of the emperor. To him they prayed, and yet were told they couldn't know the pleasure of such a being. His whim was always a mystery, and his reasons for taking or sparing lives were always locked behind his mask of inscrutability. It was as though there were no reasons at all.

For worshipping such a seemingly absurd god, the Tnemghadi were mocked by the Urhemmedhins. But the Tnemghadi religion had never been properly understood. They had not believed in the existence of any god at all. That was the heart of it: *Their enigmatic emperor was merely the symbol of the fact that there is no god.*

There is no god at all, no god to reward the good and punish the wicked, no god to bestow order, justice, or rightness on the world.

There is no god. There is no justice. There is no salvation.

That was the Tnemghadi creed.

And it was true.

Moreover, this truth underscored the basic valuelessness of life. How could the playthings of such an unfathomable fate be considered at all sanctified? With no god having put them on earth, human beings had arisen out of the muck by sheer happenstance and for no particular purpose. It defied logic to hold something priceless when the earth was teeming with it, when it had no purpose, when it was so despised and wantonly destroyed. That was human life: the cheapest commodity in the world.

People had not been put on earth for any reason at all, and the human race was not pursuing any goal, save perhaps that of survival—and the ultimate purpose to be gained by their surviving was an open question. And yet, Jehan could see that this was *not* a negation of all purpose to a man's existence.

The fact that people are not ruled by any god frees them to rule themselves. The fact that fate is blind frees people to take their fate into their own hands. The fact that the race has no purpose frees its individual members to pursue their own purposes. And so the fact that bare human life is without intrinsic value does not mean human endeavor is pointless.

Just as a worthless chunk of stone can be sculpted into a precious work of art, so too can a raw, common life become great by what its owner makes of it. And that endeavor is the key to life—with no god, no other value to existence—a man's own endeavor is everything.

Having gained, at last, this vantage point, Jehan Henghmani could now look back and assess his own life. It was neither wholly bad nor wholly good; filled with accomplishment and failure, it was not wholly wasted. To grasp the truth of life was itself a great achievement, perhaps the greatest of all. But Jehan could only lament that he had reached it on his deathbed.

BERGHARRA—Urhemmedhin Empire, billon tayel of Emperor Jehan II, 1195. *Obverse:* Crowned portrait of ruler, facing, with inscription in exergue. *Reverse:* portrait of the Regent Mussopo, facing, and showing his missing hand; crown mintmark (Ksiritsa). Breitenbach 2087, and the plate coin in the Breitenbach reference. A most unusual double portrait issue, and excessively rare. Very fine. (*Hauchschild Collection Catalog*)

· 9 ·

At the Tnem-rab-Zhikh Palace at Ksiritsa, Jehan Henghmani, the Emperor of Bergharra, died quietly in his bed on the seventh day of Nrava in the year 1195.

Except for servants and guards, there was no one with him when he died. It happened that Urhemma was in the midst of preparations to celebrate the fourteenth anniversary of the start of its revolution; and now, as the news of Jehan's passing filtered through the country, it was accompanied by a proclamation from the council of ministers that declared the Empire to be in mourning for a full year.

Jehan Henghmani's final instructions stipulated that his funeral would take place at Naddeghomra. Nevertheless, there was a full-scale, day-long memorial service at Ksiritsa to send him on his way. This ceremony took place in the Heaven Palace, and was closed to the Tnemghadi population of the city. When it was over, with a blast of drums and bugles, the oakwood sarcophagus containing his body was borne away from Ksiritsa. His remains, upon a bier drawn by eight white stallions and followed by a procession numbering nearly one hundred, were borne southward under the protection of an Urhemmedhin army division. Through the gates of Ksiritsa they carried him, through Tnemurabad and Kholandra, through the Jaraghari Hills and the Usrefif Mountains, through Taroloweh past Arbadakhar, across the River Qurwa, down through Nitupsar and Khrasanna, and finally, to Naddeghomra.

Along the way, millions came out to watch the black-beribboned processional, marching miles with it as a second protective army, or bowing and prostrating themselves on the ground as it passed, kissing the dirt along its route. They were ignorant, poor, illiterate peasants, and while their understanding was dim, they grasped that the man whose body lay in that casket had profoundly changed their lives. They did not even look upon Jehan Henghmani as a man; he was more than that: He was a god, a force of nature. This colossus transcended good or evil and, unable to take his measure, the people fell down in awe before him.

"*Vahiy Jehan*," they would whisper as they bowed before the passing bier. They would whisper again the war-cry of old: *Victory to Jehan.*

"*Vahiy ley Ur-Rasvadhi*," Victory to the Savior.

It was a journey of months before the processional finally reached Naddeghomra. By this time, more than a thousand peasant pilgrims, from all across Urhemma, were walking with it. Many of them were old veterans of the rebel armies, survivors of the battles of Zidneppa and Arbadakhar and the siege of Naddeghomra. Some of them were white-haired now and crippled from their wounds, but some of them had traveled a thousand lim on this final march with their old leader.

Naddeghomra was ready to receive Jehan one last time. On the broad white marble plaza of The Maal, a great funeral pyre had been built, and many thousands flocked to personally add to it their own bits of wood. Here Jehan's remains were burned, a fire that lit up the city. Here at Naddeghomra, the city he had raised from the ashes, Jehan Henghmani's own remains were rendered into ashes.

When it was over, the ashes were spread upon the fields, and the fields were tilled and sown with a new rice crop.

On the same day that the Emperor's remains were sent forth from Ksiritsa, his grandson took the crown as the Emperor Jehan II. And on the same day, the council of ministers met and decided to designate a regent to act with full imperial powers until the youth should reach the age of twenty-one. The regent named was Gaffar Mussopo.

Historians have speculated upon rumors that Jehan Henghmani left a written political testament. But if such a document ever existed, it was presumably suppressed by his successors, and its contents can only be guessed at.

Meanwhile, Gaffar Mussopo had already decided that the country could not be defended against the Akfakh invaders so long as it was torn within by insurgency. With the concurrence of the young Emperor Jehan II, Regent Mussopo thus gave first priority to dealing with the Tnemghadi uprising. The rebellious western province of Muraven was attacked in force. In a series of bloody battles, the rebels were driven back to their stronghold of Sajnithaddhani, and there, the Urhemmedhins laid siege.

Although Mussopo's army suffered terrible losses in repeated assaults upon the stubborn city, the victory was eventually gained. Sajnithaddhani, the gem of western Bergharra, was returned to Urhemmedhin rule, and the Tnemghadi rebellion was crushed.

All of the captured rebel soldiers, along with more than two thousand citizens accused of collaborating with them, were executed in a mass burning. Their leader, Jephos Kirdahi, was hustled away to Ksiritsa, chained in a cart; and in the dungeons where he had started his career as a guard, Kirdahi was tortured for weeks before being put to death.

However, Mussopo's success at Sajnithaddhani had been gained at a heavy price.

While the Urhemmedhin forces were locked in battle with the Tnemghadi, the Akfakh had been taking advantage. In fact, their chieftain Znarf was absorbing territory now almost as fast as he could push his hordes forward. Ahead of him, terrorized by the wild tribesmen, the peasants were fleeing. But by this time there were few safe havens to which they could go. There were only two bastions that might still be held: Sajnithaddhani and Ksiritsa. And each day brought thousands more refugees into these two cities.

The dislocation and disruption made these cities bubbling cauldrons of humanity, milling homeless and hungry through the streets, living in open alleyways, scrounging desperately for food. Lawlessness was rampant, as people tried to board up their homes and bury their valuables, and others formed into unruly gangs and mobs. Sajnithaddhani and Ksiritsa seethed on the verge of explosion.

Then down into Muraven the Akfakh swept from two directions, and soon even Sajnithaddhani was threatened, with the invaders bearing down from both the north and west. But Sajnithaddhani was defended by a huge Urhem-medhin force, still occupying it in the wake of the Kirdahi revolt; and, vowing to hold the city at all costs, Mussopo hurried more troops there.

A titanic battle loomed, and as it grew more imminent, panic took hold of Sajnithaddhani. The atmosphere was charged with terror, as the refugees swelling the city re-newed their lurid tales of Akfakh atrocities. Few had any real confidence that the Urhemmedhins could save the city from Znarf. Those who had fled into Sajnithaddhani began to flee away from it. In desperate haste to save themselves, the people struck out eastward toward Ksiritsa, grabbing up their belongings and launching boats and rafts down the River Gnanad, in wagons along the road, or even on foot. The exodus out of the beleaguered city quickly became a rushing flood.

The Regent Mussopo swore that he would stop the Akfakh at Sajnithaddhani, but not even his own soldiers believed it any more. Along with everyone else, the army panicked too. Indeed, it was the officers who bolted first, taking what they could and getting out, leaving their troops to fend for themselves. Almost overnight, the gar-rison collapsed, the soldiers broke ranks and madly scrab-bled for escape.

It was too late now to go on foot, and most of them lacked horses. Few boats and wagons were left. So the troops attacked the fleeing peasants, seizing their horses, gaars, carts, and boats, shoving the hapless peasants aside, stabbing them, cutting them down, running them over, trampling them, enraged with their desperation to get out of the doomed city. Fences, buildings, and tables were torn up to make crude rafts. Boats were attacked as they left the docks, the peasants thrown out of them and into the river. The boats filled up with soldiers, more than they could carry. Men would hang onto the gunwales, trailing in the water; others swimming behind would grab their legs and try to pull them off; while those in the boats would beat and slash at their hands and heads to get them off, as the overloaded boats listed deeply in the water, and many of them capsized, drowning their human cargoes.

Thousands got out, but thousands did not. Sajnithad-dhani fell to the Akfakh.

And then the barbarian horde converged upon Ksiritsa.

The brutal, tragic scramble for escape was repeated at Ksiritsa. But there was no escape any longer. Most of Tnemurabad was gone, as was Kholandra to the south. All roads from Ksiritsa were cut off, the city was surrounded and its gates were locked up tightly, holding the people in as well as holding the Akfakh out. The horror of the situation was aggravated by the city's having swollen with refugees to almost double its normal population —and there was no food.

It was pointless, but Mussopo insisted on holding out to the last. The city was burning down all around him, bombarded savagely with fireballs. The Akfakh even turned against Gaffar Mussopo his own invention, the exploding projectiles. The city was plunged into such a state of disorganization that the attackers met no resistance when they started tearing down the gates.

As the Akfakh finally broke through and surged into Ksiritsa, the Regent Gaffar Mussopo threw himself from one of the high parapets of the Heaven Palace and was dashed to pieces on the stone floor below. The Emperor Jehan II tried to escape in disguise, but was apprehended, and he died torn apart between galloping horses.

In the South, the Nation of Urhemma had already fallen apart. Just as once Tnem Khatto Trevendhani had found the South broken up into tiny kingdoms, and hence easy prey, now too the Akfakh came down upon a land fought over by a hundred petty warlords. By the end of the year 1198, the entire South was conquered.

Only Naddeghomra put up resistance worthy of the name. Many thousands died to defend it. But eventually, Naddeghomra too was taken by the Akfakh.

When the conquering warriors searched through The Maal, they came upon a chamber in one of the high towers in which a disheveled woman had been locked. Her hair was an unruly bramble patch, her fingernails grown long. She was filthy and her flesh was wasted away, but her eyes were wild and burning.

"I am Maiya Henghmani," she proudly shrieked, "I am the Mother of Urhemma!"

They quietly closed the door on her, and locked it again.

Znarf, the Emperor of Bergharra, looked out upon his world with glittering eyes.

Everything was nothing.

BERGHARRA—Akfakh Empire, copper drehm of Emperor Znarf I, circa 1200. *Obverse:* Crowned portrait of ruler, facing, holding sword. *Reverse:* crude image of a bull or some other animal. Breitenbach 2140. Very poor style, typical of Akfakh coinage. Fine to very fine or so, but struck as usual on an irregular planchet with a large defect. (*Hauchschild Collection Catalog*)

· 10 ·

TIFSIM JARBA looked back over his shoulder, across the tall grasses, at the City of Ksiritsa.

Its walls seemed to fill up half the sky. Beyond them, Tifsim could glimpse the majestic towers and spires stretching up to grasp at the clouds. These were the towers of the Palace of the Heavens, where Znarf reigned. The sun was setting, making the copper tower roofs glow like beacons.

In all his nineteen years, Tifsim Jarba had never actually seen the city like this. He had always lived inside it, but he had never ventured beyond its walls. His people were poor and had no occasion to go far from their home. So never before had he stood at this vantage point, looking at Ksiritsa from the outside, seeing the whole city at once. Seeing the city's glory, he felt a curious exhilaration.

Tifsim Jarba stopped and stood at the top of a little hill. He looked long and hard at Ksiritsa this fading afternoon, as though to store up its image. He knew it would be a long time before he'd ever set eyes on it again, or upon the people he was leaving behind, inside it. Quite likely he'd never see them again at all.

The city held tenaciously on Tifsim's gaze; it wouldn't let him turn to go. Feeling this pull, he smiled sardonically. Even now, Ksiritsa was holding him as though he were its slave.

But Tifsim Jarba knew it was not Ksiritsa that enslaved him and countless million others. It had been people who enslaved other people, for as long as history had been recorded, and even before.

Tifsim was old enough to remember the reign of Tnem Sarbat Satanichadh, the last ruler who had been of the boy's own Tnemghadi race. It was finally the Urhemmedhins who had rebelled against Sarbat; but in truth, all

437

of Bergharra had been enslaved and oppressed by the Tnemghadi dynasties. And nothing changed under their successors: Jehan Henghmani the monster, and the tyrant Mussopo. Now, the latest slave-master sat upon the golden throne at Ksiritsa: Znarf the Akfakh.

It was with a righteous fire and a deep sadness that Tifsim thought about this history. He was saddened that the ambition of despots seemed so powerful, and that a people could not long enjoy freedom before someone would come along to make them his slaves. What burned in Tifsim was the fire of another universal:

The will to resist tyranny, the passion to be free.

That was what impelled him forth from Ksiritsa now. He would leave that capital of oppression and make himself a free man. He would dedicate his life to making others free too. And perhaps some day he might return to Ksiritsa, to free the millions.

It seemed a wild dream, yet not a hopeless one. The human will to freedom, Tifsim told himself, persisted as ever. It cannot be destroyed, no matter how the despots might try. While tyranny might now prevail, it would not reign forever. The world moves in great cycles. Just as the night must yield to the morning sun, just as the Tnemghadi had given way to the Urhemmedhins, and then to the Akfakh, so too would the era of tyranny give way to the era of liberty.

Ksiritsa tried to hold his eyes, but Tifsim pulled himself free. He turned his head and started on his journey.

Behind him, the glow of the towers faded with the dying of the light.

Tifsim Jarba would walk until the morning sun.

REPUBLIC OF URHEMMA, silver five pastars, commemorating the tenth anniversary of independence, 1976. *Obverse:* conjoined busts of medieval Emperor Jehan Henghmani and President Ragadan K. Devrahal. *Reverse:* modernistic depiction of the ancient temple of Naddeghomra superimposed on the flag of the Republic. Yeoman 17. Uncirculated. (*Hauchschild Collection Catalog*)

AVON ⬢ MEANS THE BEST IN FANTASY AND SCIENCE FICTION

URSULA K. LE GUIN

The Lathe of Heaven	25338	1.25
The Dispossessed	24885	1.75

ISAAC ASIMOV

Foundation	29579	1.50
Foundation and Empire	30627	1.50
Second Foundation	29280	1.50
The Foundation Trilogy (Large Format)	26930	4.95

ROGER ZELAZNY

Doorways in the Sand	32086	1.50
Creatures of Light and Darkness	35956	1.50
Lord of Light	33985	1.75
The Doors of His Face, The Lamps of His Mouth	18846	1.25
The Guns of Avalon	31112	1.50
Nine Princes in Amber	36756	1.50
Sign of the Unicorn	30973	1.50
The Hand of Oberon	33324	1.50